'A white-hot pacy thriller w
reluctant fugitive Buster as
he never knew he had to outwit The Most Dangerous Man
in Brighton. Martin Webb is a refreshing and welcome new
voice in Crime Fiction.'

Graham Bartlett, best-selling crime writer

'Brighton is a city that exists under a veneer of glamour and
sophistication, but in Martin Webb's novel the naive Buster
Brett scratches that surface and finds himself dragged into a
dangerous criminal underworld. An intriguing journey into
the dark side of the city by the sea.'

Andrew Kay, Latest Brighton

'This is a fast-paced British gangster ride that wouldn't look
out of place as a Guy Ritchie film. Plot twists and action
galore, thoroughly enjoyable villains, and a big old robbery.
What more could you want?'

Sam Harrington-Low, Silver Magazine

'A dazzling roller-coaster ride through Brighton's murky
underworld'

Absolute Magazine

Martin Webb is a former clubland boss, entrepreneur and columnist for *The Telegraph*. He also presented Channel 4's *Risking It All* and is the author of *Make Your First Million: Ditch the 9-5* and *Start the Business of Your Dreams*. He is currently a Special Sergeant with Sussex Police and lives near Brighton with his partner and kids.

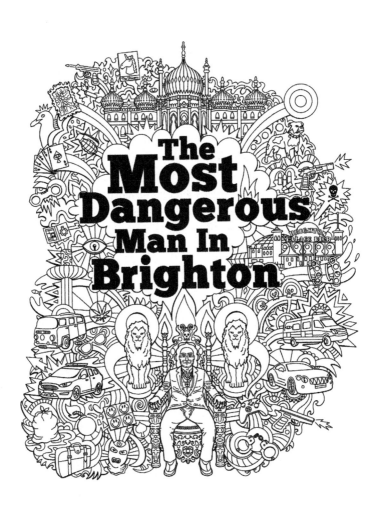

The Most Dangerous Man In Brighton

Martin Webb

First paperback edition 2023

Cover design by MANIC MINOTAUR
manicminotaur.com

978-1-80541-153-6 (paperback)
978-1-80541-154-3 (ebook)

www.dangerousman.co.uk

Five Years Earlier

"Oi! You at the back! Wake up!"

The voice that boomed around the room was dripping with irritation and demanded immediate attention.

"Do you realise how rude it is to sleep when someone's talking to you? Well, do you? Can someone *please* give sleeping beauty a nudge?"

The person next to Buster Brett poked their elbow into his shoulder and he woke with a start, lifting his head from the cradle he'd formed with his folded arms. His face flushed red as he registered the staring, amused faces of his university classmates.

"Sorry, sorry, sir."

His tired brain raced to find words that would make the situation better.

"I was up until 4 am revising for the exam we had this morning," he started to explain, before getting cut off.

"Excuse me, young man, but unless I'm very much mistaken, everyone else in this lecture hall also did exactly the same exam. But they, by some miracle that you failed to get the memo about, have managed to stay awake!"

There were lame smiles all around.

He wanted to stand up and shout out that the others probably didn't have pushy parents whose unrealistic expectations were weighing them down. They weren't getting pressured into finding a fast-track route to the top or being constantly reminded about the cost of their private education. They'd still be welcome at home if they failed to get a first. But reading the energy in his tutor's voice, he kept his mouth shut and resigned himself to sucking up the lecture within a lecture that was coming his way.

"Just because today's topic isn't your favourite subject, doesn't mean you don't need to know about it. You'll all be out in the big bad world soon and, I hate to break this to you, ladies and gentlemen, it isn't always the kind and pleasant place that you think it is right now. Quite the opposite, I'm afraid!

Things happen that you, as the nation's next generation of accountants, need to be fully aware of and prepared for! And one of those has been the subject of my lecture this afternoon, as those of you who have been awake, will already know.

Yes! Money laundering! An insidious criminal activity that goes on right under our noses every single day of the week. It's probably happening right now in a pub you drink in or a restaurant you eat at. And I guarantee that none of you will have even realised. And you won't *ever* realise if you nod off during my lecture, will you, my young fellow?"

The lecturer paused to acknowledge the rash of sycophantic grins that his weak humour had generated across the room. He looked distinctly pleased with himself and self-satisfied.

As soon as the lesson was over, Buster left as quickly as he could. He couldn't wait to get away, knowing that he'd be the butt of further jokes if he were to hang around. He didn't have the energy to fend them off. He felt tired, embarrassed and overwhelmed with the effort of the week's exam schedule. There was no one there who'd offer support or make him feel any better, so he just slipped away. He'd write today off and hope that tomorrow would be better. He didn't need to know about money laundering anyway. He was aiming for the top. He wanted a seat in the board room and that was what he was going to get. What sordid little criminals got up to in back street pubs was none of his business.

As he walked home from the University of Brighton campus on Lewes Road, he stopped to buy sweets and a drink to cheer himself up. This particular BP forecourt shop was the place he always went to when he needed something sugary to lift his mood. The other reason for the visit was to see the girl who worked behind the till. She was pretty and there was a hint of mischief in her smile that had caught his eye weeks ago. He'd been building up the courage to ask her out.

After checking out the confectionery selection for longer than was strictly necessary, he settled on a Twix and a cold can of Coke from the fridge. He did his best to catch her eye, but she barely acknowledged his presence. Despite his good intentions, he bottled the fleeting opportunity to strike up a conversation. It was a simple exchange of words, thanks and goodbye, before he was back out in the cold.

Buster's mood slumped even further. He'd let himself down. She hadn't even looked up as she'd passed him the change. He was too drained to sparkle today, he tried to console himself. He tried to stifle the depressing notion that she still hadn't noticed him after all his previous visits to her place of work.

As he walked, cursing his insecurities and lack of confidence, he was too mired in dark thoughts to notice a black Bentley as it came roaring towards him across the garage forecourt. In a blur of tinted windows, alloy wheels and shining chrome, it missed him by just inches. It had pulled away from the pumps with such haste and screeching of tyres that it was apparent the driver had very little regard for inconsequential pedestrians, especially depressed-looking ones who appeared to have the weight of the world on their weary shoulders.

Buster was sent reeling backwards, his can clattering across the ground. His elbow smashed sharply onto the tarmac and he gasped in pain as the Twix flew out of his hand. Winded and dazed, he lay shocked on the ground, trying to assess how badly he'd been hurt.

The girl from the shop dashed out to help. She was suddenly animated and alive, free from the confines of the till and security screen he'd always seen her behind. Despite his shock and the growing pain, Buster's first thought was that she looked great in her uniform. His surprise at seeing her rush towards him momentarily numbed the agony in his arm.

"You OK, mate? Do you need me to call you an ambulance?"

There was sincerity and warmth in her voice. She sounded genuinely concerned.

"I saw exactly what happened, if you want me to call the police? I can't believe the way that bloody lunatic just drove at you."

She reached out her hand and he took it. It felt soft, warm and reassuring. For a second, despite having been knocked over, he felt as if the day was finally looking up.

"I'm fine, I'm fine, I really am," he said, unconvincingly, as she helped him to his knees. He didn't want to let go of her hand. She pulled it briskly away as soon as he was on his feet.

"I don't think you're fine at all, mate, just look at the state of you," said the girl, looking him up and down, as he nursed his injured elbow.

"No, I'm alright, seriously. Probably wasn't looking where I was going, was I," lied Buster, not wanting to whinge or appear weak in front of her. This was the only conversation they'd ever had and he didn't want it to go wrong or end.

"Well, Okay, if you say so."

She glanced back into the shop. A line of customers were getting restless as they waited to pay.

"Look, I've got to dash. Get that arm checked out, will you? Looks nasty."

She touched his hand, squeezed his fingers and was gone. Buster was alone again, cold and in shock. As he gazed at the sticky blood oozing from his freshly grazed skin, the pain in his arm suddenly began to feel much worse.

Not sure what to do next, feeling deflated and angry, he went to retrieve his drink. It was dirty from where it had rolled against an unleaded pump, but appeared to be otherwise intact. Wincing as he reached to get it, he caught sight of a large brown envelope lying next to it on the oily concrete surface. Since it looked incongruous, lost and out of place, he instinctively picked it up.

It was A3 in size and stapled shut across the opening end. It appeared to be stuffed with items, which he could feel through the paper, were round and ribbed. As it was clean, dry and unmarked by tyres, he deduced that it had somehow fallen from the Bentley shortly before it had tried to run him over. Intrigued and distracted by what he'd just found, he slipped the package into his college bag and continued home as swiftly as his injuries would allow.

When he got back half an hour later, he was relieved to find that his flatmates were all out. Curiosity naturally got the better of him. Using a sharp pair of scissors, he opened the envelope by carefully undoing the eight staples that secured the flap. Peering cautiously inside first, he then tipped the contents onto his kitchen table. Out tumbled seven tightly rolled bundles of £20 notes, each held in place with a single red elastic band. He counted the money and then quickly counted it again. He rolled up the notes and slid everything neatly back into the envelope. Eight sharp compressions of his stapler safely re-secured the package.

The cash amounted to precisely £3,500, which to a twenty-one year-old with a huge student loan, felt like a wildly exotic sum. The sight of the money was exciting and helped him to forget about his injury. It smelled of wealth and reminded him of where he wanted to be in life. The crisp coolness of the notes had felt good as he counted them out. That night he slept with the package under his pillow, dreaming of dancing aboard a yacht with the girl with the soft hands and kind words from the garage.

When he came to his senses the following morning, he knew exactly what had to be done. It was a significant sum which needed to be returned to its rightful owner. Even if that person was a lunatic who'd tried to run him over, it was the correct and proper course of action. That was the way he'd been brought up. It's what his parents would expect of him. It didn't even matter that the owner was riding in a Bentley and clearly had lots of cash to burn. Returning the package was the upstanding and

citizenly thing to do. Before he did anything else that day, he needed to figure out who the mystery money belonged to.

When he revisited the garage on his way into college, Buster was deflated to discover that it was his potential new girlfriend's day off.

"Oh! I know you! You're that kid who got run over yesterday, aren't you?" said the manager, greeting him as if he were some sort of minor celebrity who lost his way and wandered, by mistake, into his shop.

"Yeah, Polly told me all about what happened. She was really worried about you, mate. Didn't you bang your arm really badly or something?"

That was reassuring to know. Maybe she did care about him a little, after all. And her name was Polly. He now liked that name very much indeed.

"So, listen, I've got some really good CCTV footage of what happened. If you want to hang around for a minute, I could show you?"

'Of course, I bloody want to see it,' thought Buster. 'Hurry up, will you?'

"Oh, yes please, if it's not too much trouble," he said, politely.

In a back room, full of cartons of fizzy drinks, crisps and cleaning products, they set about watching the recording. Backwards and forwards and from every different camera, it was clear to see that he'd only narrowly avoided serious injury. The best part of all was when his saviour, Polly, rushed out to help. She looked good from all angles the system had to offer.

"So, the thing is, I know the bloke in the car. Not the driver, but the one in the back. He's Billy Murphy. I don't know him personally, but I've heard a lot about him. Everyone's heard a lot about him."

The manager lowered his voice and beckoned Buster towards him.

"He's a proper villain, I'm afraid. When you've been knocking around this town for as long as I have, you get to know all the local characters. And he's one of the worst. In fact, I'd say he is the *actual* worst, hands down.

Now, normally I'd say to you, call the police and tell them what's happened. I'm no expert, but it looks to me like a clear case of hit and run or failure to stop, or whatever it's called nowadays. They'd be all over it, I'd say, and you could probably get a nice little claim going on their insurance too.

But I'm not saying that in this case. In fact, I'm saying the complete opposite. Don't get involved whatever you do, even if you are in the right. The thing is, this Billy Murphy's proper bad news. You'll end up in trouble if you cross him. No ifs, no buts. You'll get hurt, simple as that. I absolutely guarantee it.

He's literally the most dangerous man in Brighton, and that's saying something, in a town like this. A mate of mine used to cut his grass up on Dyke Road Avenue. He's got a big flashy place up there with stone lions on either side of the door, massive railings, a pool and about twenty bedrooms. All fur coat and no knickers, like most of the houses up there.

Well, they had a falling out when Mr Murphy thought the lines on the lawn weren't straight enough. He's got a thing about stripes, apparently. He ended up strimming my mates ankles with his own Black and Decker and he couldn't walk for a month, poor sod."

As the manager talked, Buster ummed and ahhed in all the right places as he studied every screen of the CCTV footage. He could see the Bentley arrive and he could see it leave. The package wasn't there and then it was. It must have dropped from the big black car when the driver went to pay.

Primed with this information, he spent the day at college with his head aching at the uncomfortable realisation that he'd got himself into very hot water. He cursed his decision to pick up the envelope, but knew for certain that he needed to return it as quickly as possible. Not only was it the right thing to do; it was now the only safe thing to do, ideally before the notorious Bentley owner retraced his steps, spoke to the obliging garage guy, and found out that a skinny student, whose fresh face could be seen very clearly on the CCTV, had hold of his valuable package of cash.

That evening, Buster spent a cold hour walking up and down Dyke Road Avenue looking for a house with stone lions and railings. He had a rucksack on his back containing the envelope and his best running shoes on his feet, in case a situation arose in which he needed to leg it.

It was known as the smartest street in the city and without exception the houses were huge and flashy. In his opinion, they were also vulgar and showed that being rich didn't often go hand in hand with having good taste. They all had sweeping drives, ornate gates and expensive cars parked conspicuously outside.

It seemed to Buster that these houses were statements as well as homes, with all the additions and adornments that their owners thought would reflect their wealth and status. He imagined a residents' welcoming committee popping around with a tick list of approved add-ons whenever a new estate agency boss, drug lord or lottery winner moved in. Featuring porticos, columns, porches, vestibules, topiary and animal-based statuary, as well as a comprehensive range of expensive drive-laying materials, the more options they ticked, the poorer was their sense of style.

But rather than finding one house with door-guarding lions, he found three. He also found one with Great Danes in the place of lions and another with huge bronze eagles on top of the gateposts. However, none of these had a big black Bentley on the drive. Undeterred, Buster decided to try knocking on the doors that most closely fitted his tip-off. He'd try them one by one, until he found the one he was looking for.

As he approached the tall gates of the first house, he felt nervous. All was dark and there were no cars parked outside. It definitely looked like the sort of place a criminal would live. Huge, showy and unwelcoming, he counted eight security cameras on the front elevation. He noticed that the tips of the tall railings along the garden edge looked as if they'd been deliberately sharpened. Probably to prevent any poor soul from climbing over without incurring a terrible injury, he thought, feeling less confident by the second.

He'd pressed the buzzer and waited. He began to shake with fear and cold, but nothing happened. The silence was intimidating. He pressed again, but still there was no response. No floodlights snapped on and no heavies came rushing out to apprehend him. Deflated, he wondered if he was being watched from some lair deep within. Maybe a bunch of gangsters were huddled around a screen trying to figure out who their skinny caller was. Or, more likely, he just had the wrong address altogether.

Before he had a chance to wonder what to do next, Buster's senses were overwhelmed by the roar of a powerful engine directly behind him. Pivoting around to face the noise, he was blinded by the full-beam glare of a huge car's headlights. It had turned from the road and onto the pavement, stopping with its front bumper just inches away from his trembling knees.

Simultaneously, the gates began to open and a fearful voice rang from the driver's open window.

"What the actual fuck are you playing at, you wanker? Get the fuck out of the way before I fucking flatten you, you little twat!"

Not wanting to cause offence or irritate the source of the voice any further, Buster took two paces to the side. He watched, terrified, as the vehicle, which was clearly the black Bentley, purred past him and continued on down the drive.

As the gates began to close, he mustered all his courage and stepped gingerly between them and followed the taillights towards the house. Hearing them lock with a secure clank behind him, he wished he'd just kept the money and spent it on having a good time. The resulting hangover and guilty conscience would have been far preferable to the stress and anxiety that he was experiencing right now.

"You've got a fucking cheek coming in here, I tell you," said the man who'd been driving, shaking his head. He was now in the process of lifting heavy suitcases from the boot.

"If you're delivering pizza menus, you can fuck right off. Does this look like the sort of gaff that wants two for one on fucking pizzas? Tell your fucking boss that we don't do pizzas, burgers or fucking curry. Now do one, you little shithead, and don't come back."

Buster was momentarily stumped by the man's attitude, body language and colourful language. He wasn't used to such rudeness. He was a polite boy who, up to this point, had only met people who'd been fair and reasonable with him. He wasn't sure how to respond or why he was being spoken to in this manner.

"Why you still standing there? You a fucking retard, or what? Watch my lips, son. Turn the fuck around and clear off, before I fucking sling you out.

What do you think this is, anyway? Bob a fucking job week? Whatever you've got mate, we don't want it. So, stop being a cunt, will you, and be a good little boy scout and fuck off."

Buster watched the veins on the man's forehead swell and glisten in the glare of the security lights, as he worked himself into a frenzy at his on-going presence on the drive. Although he could sense that at any second his encounter might culminate in a painful physical confrontation, he managed to force out a few timid words.

"I'm not delivering anything, sir. I've actually come to see the owner of this car, if that's OK."

The man's demeanour changed instantly. He hardened up and stepped forward. His menacing red face and sweaty thick neck were now only inches from Buster's.

"Tell me why you're here, which cunt sent you and what the fuck they want. And if I think you're lying to me, I'm going to knock you into fucking tomorrow."

"I'm sorry sir, I really didn't mean to cause any offence," stammered Buster, hardly able to get his words out, anticipating a blow at any moment.

"It's just that I've found something that I think belongs to him and I want to return it. No one has sent me. I'm here all by myself. Honestly."

The man softened a shade and stepped back.

"So, what exactly do you have that you think belongs to Mr Murphy then?"

He took the rucksack off his back and opened it up as best he could, with hands that were shaking from the unpleasantness of the situation. He pulled out the envelope and the man snatched it briskly away before marching into the house, barking over his shoulder as he went.

"Wait there! Don't you dare move a fucking inch!"

Buster duly obliged. Not that he'd had an alternative since he was stuck on the wrong side of the locked gates and the razor-sharp fence. He stood on the drive for around twenty minutes, slowly getting colder and more dejected until the front door of the house opened and out walked a man that he instantly realised was the notorious owner of the black car.

He feared the worst as the most frightening person he'd ever encountered strode purposefully towards him. An old but powerful man, with a baldhead, barrel chest and an angry, pitted face, he was wearing a three-piece suit and had huge rough hands, adorned with tattoos and gold rings. He wasn't wearing a tie and there was further jewellery hanging around his thick neck. He stopped directly in front of Buster and stared at him with eyes that could melt concrete.

"Let's get a few things straight, son. You found me money wherever me fucking dip shit driver lost it and now you want to return it? Got that right, have I?"

"Yes, sir, that's correct. That's why I'm here."

"And why exactly, young man, are you doing this? What's in it for you? You think you're going to get a fucking reward or something?"

"No, sir, of course not. I just thought it was the right thing to do. It's a lot of money after all. And I'm not expecting anything in return. Honestly."

The man continued to stare at Buster, clearly unable to fully fathom the situation that had presented itself.

"Well, in that case, my boy, I'm very grateful to you," he said, his hard face cracking into an uneasy grin.

"I'm impressed with your honesty, son. Very few honest fuckers around these days, I tell you. Very few indeed.

Anyway, I'm forgetting me manners. Let me introduce meself. I'm Billy Murphy. Maybe you've already heard of me?"

The man paused for a second and Buster realised that he was anticipating a flicker of recognition on his guest's face.

"Right, would you like a little drink, young fella? Least I can do for yer. You look fucking freezing."

Before he could muster an answer, Billy Murphy grabbed Buster's arm and led him firmly towards the house. He wondered at that moment if he'd ever leave again. He wished he'd told someone where he was going. The police might then have had a head start on where to start looking for his body. He imagined how painful it would feel to have his ankles strimmed as he was ushered in through the dark front door.

Once inside, a neat malt whisky was pushed into his hand. It was a drink he'd never tried, but he was too petrified to refuse it or ask for an alternative. Billy led him into an oak-panelled office and they sat down together in leather armchairs on either side of an open gas fire. The room was silent apart from the hiss of the flames and the ominous tick of a clock on the mantlepiece. As it counted out the seconds, Buster calculated how long he might have to live.

But as he slowly warmed up and calmed down, the conversation began to flow, his tongue loosened by alcohol. As Buster recounted the events of the previous day, his host nursed his glass and stared, hanging on every word. As they emptied the decanter, the conversation turned to his studies, ambitions and future career prospects. The old man nodded, asked a few questions and smiled in the right places, all the while trying to comprehend the skinny student who was drinking his malt at an alarming rate.

After an hour it appeared as if he'd heard enough.

"Young man, it's been a proper pleasure meeting you this evening, it really has," he said, holding up his hand, cutting Buster off in mid-flow.

"But I'm afraid I've got work to attend to now, so we'll have to leave our little chinwag there for the time being. I don't know how much you already know about me, but I run a little business down here. A few bars and clubs, that sort of thing. Plus a number of properties I rent out at the lower end of the market, if you get my drift.

Most of my work is up in London, but I keep this little place for the weekends. The Mrs loves it down here for some reason. All queers and students if you ask me, but each to their own. No offence, of course. I also dabble with importing, security and some community-based finance. All legit mind, obviously."

He'd paused again, shifted his position in the chair and smiled uncomfortably.

Buster judged that he was trying to work out how much he already knew.

"So, how's about you doing a little bit of work for me then?" said Billy, leaning in towards Buster.

"Doing me accounts, keeping on top of the invoices, all that sort of thing? I'd see it as a real favour if you said yes."

Billy Murphy stared at him, his hard dark eyes making it quite clear that a negative response would be unacceptable.

"You see, I think I'm a pretty good judge of character and everything I've heard tonight makes me think that you're the sort of straight-up geezer I'd like to have on the firm. Honesty is a rare thing these days. Extremely rare," he smirked.

"You didn't have to return that cash, but you did. Even got yourself hurt, for your troubles. And then you went out of your way to find me, walking up here in the freezing cold, when you could have just spent the cash on drugs or cider or whatever you students get up to these days. And I'd have been none the wiser, would I? I appreciate that. Says a lot about you. Marks you out as a man of principle".

"Much like meself," he added, with a thin grin.

"Plus, you've got all the skills I'm looking for. I like a bloke who's got a proper education and done some book learning. We've got a good little firm here, but I'd be the first to admit it needs a bit of modernising. So, what do you say, son? You up for it? And of course, I'll make it worth your while. Goes without saying. I'll pay you double what you could get anywhere else. What do you think, son? Start with Saturdays and see how it goes. You fancy a bit of that, do you, Buster?"

By this point, Buster could hardly stand up, never mind decide whether he wanted to start working for his new best mate, Billy Murphy, the well-known notorious criminal. But not wanting to cause any offence, he took the easy option and agreed to everything that had been suggested. He'd start at the weekend and a car would be sent to collect him on Saturday morning at 11am sharp. He'd work from the big house and get £200 a day in cash for his trouble.

Ten minutes later, he was in the rear of the Bentley and heading back down Dyke Road Avenue. He felt drunk, sick and hugely relieved to be on the way home. He was happy to be alive and completely in awe of the man he'd just met. He'd never met anyone remotely like him before. Although he'd spoken calmly and politely, Billy exuded brutality. He was a charismatic creature from a world far removed from his own and that made him instantly fascinating. Billy was the opposite of everything Buster had ever encountered. Raw, rough, exciting and dangerous, he was everything that his parents weren't.

He woke the next day, terribly hungover and with his arm still aching and stiff, wondering if recent events had all been a terrible dream. But on Saturday, half to his surprise and half to his horror, Billy's car turned up as arranged.

His new employer greeted him enthusiastically at the front door of the big house and took him straight through to an office at the back, over-looking a perfectly manicured lawn.

"Welcome to the firm Buster, my boy, welcome," he said, gripping his hand like a vice and shaking it forcefully up and down.

"You're going to remember this day as the one your career properly took off, son. You mark my words. I've got a very good feeling about our little arrangement, a very good feeling indeed. You're just the person I need to bring things bang up to date. Honesty and brains don't often go together, son, but you're the real deal."

Buster then got straight to work and for a long time he didn't look back.

In the months that followed, Billy watched in quite admiration as his newest employee digitised the operation, implemented efficiencies and helped the organisation grow. And while he quietly devised new ways to launder the takings and hide the profits, Buster also got hooked on the money, cars and praise that were lavished on him by his appreciative new boss.

The perks soon overwhelmed his young mind. Free rein at Billy's clubs and bars made him irresistible to the girls he'd previously considered to be out of his league. The pretty ones who wouldn't have given him a second glance at university, now flirted and jostled for attention. Being part of the gang felt like a good and exciting place to be. He was dazzled by the luxury, status and thrill of being on the inside of a crew that was respected and feared. They jumped the queues, sat at the best tables and parted the crowds wherever they went. Blinded by his new lifestyle, the money, status and bad-boy chic quickly became addictive.

Somewhere, deep in his heart, he knew it was all wrong, but for a long time he didn't care. He was only doing the numbers. He wasn't hurting anyone. It was just business and that's what he'd been trained to do. Where was the harm in spreadsheets, financial reports and getting the books to balance?

But over time, almost imperceptibly, it became harder to enjoy the lifestyle he'd become accustomed to. A feeling in the pit of his stomach began to pinch and nag. The banter with the boys became more strained. The money seemed less important. Even charismatic Billy began to lose his magnetism. As time passed by, a growing sense of emptiness began to take hold. A sensation deep inside was fermenting, spoiling the fun, waiting for an opportunity to undertake a different path.

Chapter 1

Razor was aware that the man trapped behind the glass door of the burning restaurant couldn't hear a single word being said to him. As the smoke got thicker and his screams became louder and more frenzied, the boss continued to talk to him calmly and slowly.

The man gasped frantically for air through the letter box at the bottom of the frame, as the crackling of burning woodwork became overwhelming. Razor wondered if he should intervene and say something, but he knew better than to interrupt the boss when he was giving one of his talks, so he kept his mouth shut and foot pressed firmly against the door. He applied just enough pressure to resist the increasingly feeble efforts of the man on the other side to free himself from the inferno.

"You do understand why you're in this predicament, don't you, son? And you do realise it's nothing personal? It's not as if I actually enjoy burning people's restaurants down now, is it?"

The boss smirked to himself at the irony of his words. He was clearly enjoying himself very much indeed.

"It's a simple matter of business management, you see. I'm just making sure that what makes me money, keeps on making me money. Basic economics if you like. The problem is, if I let a cunt like you get away with not paying me, then all the other cunts will think I've lost my touch, and that wouldn't do at all, would it? Game over for poor old Billy Murphy if we go down that road, my friend. I'd be out of work in no time and I'm sure you wouldn't want to see that happen to a straight-up old fella like me, now would you?"

Above the man's muffled wailings, the first hint of a distant siren could be made out in the distance. Razor knew that time was slipping away.

"For fuck's sake! Concentrate on what I'm trying to say to you, fella!" shouted the boss abruptly, rapping on the glass with his huge knuckles, trying to get the semiconscious man's attention in the swirling smoke below.

"At least do me the courtesy of listening, will you, for fuck's sake. I've made a special trip to come and see you this evening. You'd better fucking appreciate that. You've actually caused me a great deal of inconvenience, if I'm honest. Mrs Murphy was incandescent when I said I had to go out to speak to you, son. You don't want to go upsetting Mrs Murphy again now, do you, you little shit?

So, listen up, will you, and stop taking the fucking piss. All I'm asking for is a little respect. That's not too much to ask, is it? No, I don't think it is. The sooner you appreciate the gravity of what you've gone and done, the sooner I can think about letting you out. You got that?"

The man behind the door clawed at the glass, desperate to escape. The only sound to come from his mouth was a smoke-choked wail, as he fought for his next breath.

"I know, I know, I appreciate it's hot in there and all that, but what do you fucking expect when the building's on fire? Just stop being a noisy cunt and shut the fuck up moaning for a minute and we can try moving things on a bit quicker. Do you get my drift, son? Can you do that for me, can you?"

Razor could see that the man's cries were starting to irritate the boss. There was a heightened agitation in his voice that could easily erupt into an even worse situation for the man behind the glass door. He'd seen it all before. Making out the blue lights of a fire engine weaving its way along Essex Road, he realised that he needed to act.

"He can't hear you, boss. The fire's too noisy. We need to go right now," he blurted out, anticipating an immediate rebuttal.

"Sorry for interrupting, Billy."

The boss glared at him.

"Alright, alright, stop making excuses for the cunt and you get down on your fucking knees then. Tell him through the letter flap thing what I've been trying to say. And be quick about it. They'll be here in a second. I'll hold the door while you do it.

And don't forget to tell him he's brought it all on himself. And all that bollocks about respect I like to tell 'em. And make sure he knows I said he's a cunt - don't forget that bit. In fact, tell him twice, so he doesn't forget."

Razor resisted the temptation to point out how much time the boss had already wasted as he dropped down. He put his hands on the ground and lowered his mouth to the letterbox, before shouting to the terrified man on the other side.

"Mr Murphy says you're a cunt and this is what happens when you don't pay what you owe. Don't say a word to the fucking police or fire brigade or your brother's place will be next. Can you hear me? Nod if you understand. You're not getting out of there until you fucking nod, mate, so you might as well just nod."

The desperate man on the other side of the glass nodded, tears cutting channels in the soot on his blackened face. Razor ignored the pain and hurt in his terrified eyes.

"Not quite as eloquent as I'd have put it meself, but close enough," said the boss with a grin as Razor stood up and they swapped feet holding the door closed.

"Right. Open it up, will you? I've got one more thing to say to this little shit."

Razor released his boot from the door and pulled it open. The man inside crawled forward and slumped on the pavement, gasping at the cold evening air as plumes of black acrid smoke billowed from the opening behind him.

Without warning, Billy took a brisk step back and aimed a sharp kick at the man's stomach. The speed and viciousness of the attack shocked Razor, who was caught off guard. Another kick followed and then a third. Billy then crouched and shouted in the man's face as he lay groaning, trying to protect himself from further blows with burnt arms and blistered hands.

"Nobody gets away with fucking over Billy Murphy. Especially not a little Chinky cunt like you. You made me do this. You brought this on yourself. You got your own shitty restaurant burnt down. You've only got yourself to blame, son. And now you've gone and got yourself an extra little kicking, just because I felt like giving you one. Do you understand me? Do you?

You knew what the rules were, didn't you? You had them explained to you nice and simple. We even translated them into Chinese for you, didn't we, Razor? All neatly printed out on a little piece of paper for you.

And now you know what happens when you don't stick to them rules, don't you? Remember that, you little cunt, next time you think about not paying me. You got all of that into your thick head, have you?"

Billy straightened up and composed himself before appearing to have a change of heart. He aimed two more savage kicks at the man's head, as if for good measure.

"Right, Razor, let's leave this gentleman to reflect on the error of his ways. Hopefully, this can be a useful learning exercise for all of us, but particularly for this disrespectful little git."

#####

Across the road, Buster observed the action from the rear seat of a black Bentley. The curious expression on his face morphed into one of horror as he watched events unfold through the car's open window. As Razor and the boss walked over, two fire engines pulled up outside the burning building.

"Budge over Buster, mate. Let me get in. Chop, chop," said Billy impatiently, as he levered his frame in through the door.

"Forgotten your fucking manners, have you? And for fuck's sake take that dopey look off your face, will you? What the fuck did you think happens to people who don't cough up? Cream cakes and a polite chat?" he chuckled.

"Get over it boy and toughen up. It's about time you got to see how things really work around here. I'll make a man of you yet," he said, grinning, high on the night's adrenaline, as the car pulled away into the darkness.

"And that includes taking you to that strip club I told you about for your birthday next week. Proper naughty place it is, son. Proper naughty. Take it from me Buster boy, that cunt's lucky he's not dead. He got off lightly, I tell you. He was fortunate enough to catch me in one of me better moods tonight. You don't want to see what I'm capable of when I'm pissed off, son, you really don't. You know what I'm like though, don't you Razor, me old mate? We've been in a few scrapes together over the years, haven't we?"

The boss smirked, punched the back of the driver's seat and launched into a monologue outlining the violent highlights of the past. Razor didn't respond or react as he drove the car carefully through the city's busy streets.

"You see, Buster, the biggest difference between you and me is that I love a scrap. Always have and always will. I don't think it's something you'll ever be able to understand.

You're a clever fucker, but you're soft as shit. No offence. It's just the way you was brought up. Have you ever actually had a fight, son?"

"No, Billy. It's not my thing, is it? Anyway, you know that already, don't you?" Buster added apologetically, trying to nudge the conversation in a different direction.

"See, most people shy away from a fist fight, but I never have. You can't beat a proper good ruck, if you ask me. It makes you feel proper alive, son. The smell of other people's blood and that sweet crack a fist makes when it breaks a nose. For me, they're life's little pleasures, son.

When I was your age, donkeys' years ago, I'd already learned that hurting people got me what I wanted. I'm not saying it was right or nothing, but it's just the way it was back then. I got paid good money to punch people and I enjoyed me work. And I was fucking good at it. Simple as that. And that's what tonight was all about.

When you're the boss, like I am, the opportunities to get out and enjoy a bit of old-fashioned quality violence are few and far between. It's the boys who get all the action and I don't think that's very fair. Do you, son? So, when I heard about old Mr Wan not coughing up, I jumped at the chance to meet him in person and have a bit of fun for meself. And I must say, it was every bit as satisfying as I hoped it would be."

By the time they arrived at the office, ten minutes later, Buster was left in no doubt as to the homicidal tendencies of the man he worked for. He listened intently as his employer rambled away to himself, buoyed and enlivened by the pain he'd just inflicted and the sweet recollections of his hurtful earlier years.

He'd always known that his boss was an angry man with a fearful reputation, but tonight was the first time he'd seen the violence properly for himself. As he absorbed what he'd just witnessed and the words being said, he'd started to dwell on the career choices that had led him to being where he was right now.

As they got out of the car, Billy put his arm around Buster's shoulder and drew him close.

"Listen, son, let's forget all about that nasty physical stuff for now. I was only playing with you. I know you don't like it when I talk like that. The only fight you've got to worry about is the one next week in court. That's the one we've got to win big. And that's where you come in, my boy. You and that great big clever brain of yours.

You'll be there for me in me corner. You'll be me coach and trainer for the day. You're the one that's good with words and you're the one who knows the law. Let's just get stuck in and show that fucking jury what a nasty bastard I really am.

And if it all goes well, and I'm sure it will after all the work we've put in, then that's when we'll properly start raking it in. And that, my boy, as I've told you a hundred times before, is because fear is the biggest fucking money-maker of them all. Fear is our best friend, Buster, and don't you ever fucking forget that."

Chapter 2

Billy Murphy's day had started remarkably well. Listening to the radio in bed, as he always did from 6.30 am, once the phone-in and farming slots had given way to real news, he'd been heartened by the ample and largely accurate coverage of his preceding day in court.

An earthquake in New Zealand and the death of a retired politician had relegated him to the bulletin's number three slot, but that was good enough. Things were going to plan and he couldn't be happier with what he was hearing. He punched the air and beamed as he heard his name broadcast across the nation's airways.

He listened as several contributors, all proclaiming to be experts, gave their opinions on the previous day's court proceedings. They were of the view that Billy Murphy had set a new low in the provision of sub-standard and potentially lethal housing.

Something needed to be done, and quickly. They couldn't agree on what that ought to be, but were unanimous in their opinion that he was a despicable and morally bankrupt modern-day slum landlord who deserved to be locked up and had been lucky to get away with merely a fine.

Billy couldn't disagree with any of this. He was particularly interested to hear the newly appointed and enthusiastic Minster for Housing talk about the radical new legislation he wanted to introduce to prevent and curtail these odious types of activities. This had made him laugh out loud as the minister was a regular and energetic member of his adult-themed nightclub in Hove.

He was sure that his government department would be less keen to make changes once they'd had a proper chance to become acquainted over a nice cup of tea and a quick flick through the album of stills he'd had lifted from the club's CCTV system.

He decided to grant himself a rare lie-in, hoping the segments would be repeated again. He wanted to savour his achievement and imagine what other people would be thinking on hearing the news. To his immense delight, he was treated to the details of his crimes a further five times before 8.30 am. Each time he heard his name read out, he shouted down to his wife, who was clattering about in the kitchen below:

"I'm on, Fliss! Are you listening to this? Turn that fucking music off and put Radio 4 on, will you?"

Every time she didn't respond he shouted louder and hardened his tone.

"I'm on the fucking BBC. Did you hear me Fliss? You do realise who listens to this, don't you? I'll tell you who; the fucking King, that's who. And the Prime Minister. I bet you his majesty's just choked on his fucking crumpets!

Are you listening down there? That Prime Minister geezer's going to be proper fucked off I didn't get sent down. I bet you he fucking is, Fliss.

Fliss! Are you fucking listening? Felicity Murphy, stop pissing around and answer me before I come down there and teach you a fucking lesson."

#####

In the room below, Felicity Murphy wasn't listening. She could hear her husband shouting away, swearing and getting himself worked up. She knew the routine and anticipated that he'd haul himself downstairs in a few minutes for a row. But she was already angry with him this morning and ready for the fight. She turned up the volume on her radio to drown him out and carried on with what she was doing.

She knew exactly what he was shouting about. She'd watched the television news at 6 am, but turned it off as soon as she'd seen his grinning face on the courtroom steps, surrounded by a throng of microphones, all trying to bait him into saying something that would get him into even more trouble.

Why did he always have to have the last word with these people? Couldn't he just slip away with a simple 'no comment' like any regular villain? No, not her Billy, the loudmouth who had to dominate every conversation. Not replying would wind him up and that was the very least he deserved. She filled the kettle, flicked on the switch and went to open a new packet of teabags.

The radio DJ was playing a Motown classic, but despite the familiarity of the melody, she couldn't recall the artiste. Listening to the lyrics, she struggled to work out why he was so uncharacteristically enthusiastic about what was being said on the news.

The court appearance hadn't made him any money, which was the usual source of his happiness and the motivation for almost everything he did. On the contrary, she calculated that he was likely to be thousands out of pocket once all the fawning lawyers had submitted their bills. She couldn't figure out how he'd let himself get caught out like this. It seemed odd that the slippery Billy she'd shared her life with for decades could be held to account over something as mundane as housing code violations.

It was out of character for a man whose serpentine abilities to wriggle off the hook were legendary. In the past he'd literally got away with murder more times than he'd been caught. Perhaps the old man was finally losing his touch. She'd been waiting for that day to come, as had most of London's underworld. She poured the boiling water from the kettle into a mug for herself and the special Wedgwood cup that Billy insisted on drinking his Earl Grey from.

Of course, she'd be the one who'd have to face the neighbours and put on a brave face. She'd have to pretend that everything was all right, when it clearly wasn't. It was her world that was going to be turned upside down by his selfish little performance. And he wouldn't be the one explaining to the kids either, trying to soften the blow and make excuses for their dad's behaviour. Her most bitter regret was that they'd chosen to cut their ties and only rarely called nowadays.

After fifty years of marriage she'd learned that it wasn't wise to know too much about her husband's dealings. What she didn't know wouldn't hurt her, Billy had always said. What he got up to had to stay firmly in the back streets and clubs of London and Brighton. He could never bring it home, especially when the kids were small. It was their unspoken agreement and, by and large, he'd stuck to it.

And that's why they'd moved further away from the office with every move, to greener suburbs and houses with bigger gardens, longer drives and wealthier neighbours. She'd be the homemaker and raise the kids. She'd look after him, iron his shirts and put food on the table. Billy could do what he needed to do at the weekends to pay the bills and keep a roof over their heads.

But today, having their business broadcast into the kitchens, living rooms and bedrooms of everyone they knew felt like a violation and a betrayal. The thin veneer of a conventional lifestyle had been ripped away, exposing the ugly underbelly and the reality of how they really made their living. Billy had let his side of their agreement slip.

The half-truths and rumours that had always swirled around their lives together would all now seem plausible. People's worst fears would all be confirmed and the little respectability she'd sown together would be ripped away. She'd make out it was all a fuss over nothing, but she could already sense curtains twitching, gossip being spread and decades of fragile middle-class living tumbling into the gutter.

But why was he being so loud and pleased with himself? Why did he suddenly want the whole world to know what he was really like? They'd worked so hard at hiding it for all these years, so what had prompted him to throw the towel in now? He'd barely said a word to the neighbours in the time they'd lived in the current house but there he was, beaming away like a fool, plastered all over their television screens, proud of what he'd been accused of doing.

Things would be different now. She could no longer pretend that she was just another well-off suburban lady with a big house and a husband who was rarely in the picture, like the wives of the bankers and accountants she counted as her friends. People would stare and talk behind her back. Worse still, she'd be asked to explain and invited to talk. They'd want to give her their pity, all apparently well-meaning and supportive, but at the same time humiliating and impossible to answer without admitting that her husband was a crook. And not just a regular crook but a nasty violent criminal. One who'd smack you in the face just for giving him a sideways look, if the fancy took him.

And what use would he be when she confronted him about it? He'd fly off the handle for a start. 'What do you expect?' he'd say. 'You're quite happy to live in the big flash house when it suits you,' he'd shout. 'Don't pretend you don't know what's what. You've always known the score. You're no better than me, Fliss Murphy. We both started off from the same place, you and me. So, don't think you're one of them now, because you're not and you never fucking will be.' She knew every single line he'd use because she'd heard them all a thousand times before.

Maybe he was right. They'd met fifty-three years earlier when they were both just kids. Change was in the air and London was an optimistic place where anything was possible. The East End was still scarred by bombing, but there was opportunity at every turn. Billy had been collecting rents for the Delaney Brothers and quietly running his own loan book on the side. Even then he was mean and feared, but he had a twinkle in his eye that she'd mistaken for a warm heart within. He was a looker too, stocky and dapper in his crepe-soled shoes and dead grandad's Edwardian suits.

The first time they'd met, she'd been working the market at Poplar, selling oranges and bananas and any other exotic fruit her dad could knock off the boats down at the Canning Town docks.

He'd turned up one day with a quiff in his hair and his chest puffed out, offering to protect her stall from the 'the wrong sorts' as he'd put it, with a smirk. She'd refused his advances and told him where to stick it, but rather than get his lads to return the next day to tip the stall and send her stock rolling into the gutter, he'd taken a shine to her and asked her to come and have a coffee. She'd said yes and the rest, she thought sadly, was history

They'd weathered a few scrapes together, with a bit of prison time for him, but nothing they hadn't been able to shake off, explain away or ignore. She'd stuck with him when the south London gangs, and then the Albanians, had come looking for a fight. But now, they were getting old and the times were different.

She'd slowly changed but he'd stayed exactly the same, stuck in his rut. He was the same old Billy, the bull in the china shop, thick-skinned, crafty and constantly on the lookout.

But now she knew something he didn't; information she'd kept from him because there was nothing he could do about it. It was a secret that might break him when he found out. Or maybe he wouldn't care. She didn't know anymore. What she did know is that she'd soon be dead. Probably not next week or even next month, but certainly within a year the doctors had said, unwilling to commit themselves to anything more specific.

And as she soft-shoe-shuffled across the kitchen floor to the final bars of the Motown classic, still unable to recall the artiste, she wondered if, by some miracle she'd be granted enough time to make her peace with the world.

Worrying about who would make the arrangements for her funeral and whether the kids would even turn up, she turned on the grill and poured some milk into her tea. She slid Billy's favourite smoked bacon rashers under the heat and buttered two slices of white bread. She might be dying and she might be angry, but if Billy didn't get his breakfast the moment he came downstairs, there would be merry hell to pay.

Chapter 3

Buster's dad pushed away his untouched plate of food. His wife glared at him as he tried his best to ignore her. She'd spent the afternoon carefully preparing the meal and now the vegetables she'd grown in their garden would go to waste, not to mention the neighbour's gift of a freshly dispatched poussin. He was a fussy eater at the best of times, but for him to lose his appetite completely was unusual. She put it down to the shock of what they'd both seen on last night's evening news.

"So, have you heard from the little sod yet?" he asked, already knowing the answer.

"I guess not or you'd have said something. This bloody suspense is killing me. I didn't sleep a single wink last night worrying about that stupid boy.

The least he could do is answer the sodding phone or reply to the email you sent him. I can just picture him reading it and deciding to ignore us, the little shit. He treats us with utter contempt darling, he really does. He's been like that for years now. He's got a pathological disregard for our feelings."

Buster's dad continued talking, not waiting for a reaction or response.

"I still can't believe it was him on the ruddy news last night. What the hell does he think he's playing at, working for an awful man like that? Carrying all the court papers and trotting along behind him like a little lap dog. It made my stomach turn.

It's not right, dear. We didn't pay for a first-class education just for him to end up working for the likes of this Murphy character. It's an absolute joke. He's taken us for fools darling, he really has.

I blame that bloody idiot, Dexter Ward. That marijuana incident at school was the start of the rot, you know. If it wasn't for my golf club connections, Buster would have been expelled too. And to be fair, he'd have bloody deserved it! Might have actually been the making of him, darling. Not to mention the small fortune I'd have saved on fees.

I can't believe the web of lies he's told us, dear, I really can't. One minute he's working for a property company, the next a major landlord. We've never had the truth. Not once. And for good bloody reason, it would now appear. The man he really works for is a total crook and scoundrel. No wonder he didn't want us to know.

And it's all so embarrassing. What will people think? It's alright over here, because we don't know anyone, but I shudder to think what it will be like when we get home. Curtains will be twitching the second we pull up. We're going to be absolute laughing stocks!

Oh, look, there go the gullible Bretts; the ones with the criminal son who's probably going to end up dead or in prison. They must be so proud of what he's achieved! They must be so pleased that they wasted all their money on his education! By the way, darling, did you read all that stuff I found on the internet this morning?"

Buster's mum nodded. He'd already made her look at the printouts twice and she had no intention of reading them again. She was biding her time and waiting for him to run out of steam, before saying her piece.

"I've filled three bloody ring binders with the stuff. Two murder convictions. Extortion. Prostitution. Witness intimidation. Arson. Pyramid schemes. Drugs. Even seedy sex clubs where anything goes, so I've heard. It reads like an A-Z of criminality. And our darling little boy is right at the bloody heart of it. I hate to even say the words, but our dear little son is a mobster. He's a top man in an organised crime group. A modern day Al Capone. Do I need to go on?"

Buster's mum had finally heard enough.

"Darling, I'd rather you didn't go on, actually. In fact, I'd quite like it if you could just shut up for a moment and listen to me. I've cooked a lovely meal that you've not touched, I've got a splitting headache, and to be honest, I'm not feeling too good about Buster myself."

Buster's dad went to continue, only to be silenced by his wife putting her finger to her lips.

"Shush, darling. Let me speak, please. I emailed him at just after 7am, as I couldn't sleep either. You were snoring your head off by the way, so you did manage to get some rest, whatever you think.

I told him that we love him very much, but how deeply disappointed we are. I said that we know exactly who he works for now and how horrified we feel. I described our shock and sadness at the choices he's made. But the main message I wanted to get across was that it's not too late for him to get away and put things right. I told him that he can come home and talk to us whenever he wants. And I said we'd do whatever we can to help him get back on track.

It wasn't an angry email. Just an honest one from a concerned mother to her little boy. And in my head, he still is my little Buster. It was hard to write, especially as it's his birthday today."

Buster's dad looked unimpressed.

"Well, I'm sure the sentiment was heartfelt but I'm not convinced we can do anything to actually help him. We're not exactly well-versed in the ways of the criminal underworld, are we darling? And I hope you didn't say we'd give him any money, for Christ's sake. There's no point in wasting any more cash. Good money after bad and all that. The thousands we spent on that bloody school haven't exactly done him much good, have they?"

He continued talking, ignoring the irritation on his wife's face.

"Anyway, I don't know how you actually go about leaving the mob. I assume you can't just resign and walk out. I don't imagine that's how the Cosa Nostra works. In all the movies I've ever seen, the person who wants to go straight always ends up dead in a hail of gunfire in some dark alleyway."

Buster's mum was close to tears now.

"Will you just shut up, you stupid, insensitive man!" she shouted, stunning him into silence.

"That's the last thing I want to think about right now. I can't believe you've actually just said that out loud about our son. Talk about tempting fate. Listen, I just want to go home. Right now, please. This holiday is ruined. I love France and I love this cottage, but we need to go. Let's just pack up and leave as soon as possible. We can drive up to the tunnel and sort all of this out from home. It'll be much quicker than that confounded ferry."

Buster's dad looked at his wife and considered his options.

"But darling, we've already paid for the boat and I don't think we can change the ticket. We'd probably lose our money if we take the tunnel."

His wife glared at him so he decided to change tack.

"Okay, okay. But what about your brother? Isn't he house-sitting until the end of the week? I appreciate he's family and all that, but you know I can find him, you know, rather hard going. Couldn't you just ask him to leave slightly earlier than planned, so we've got the place to ourselves when we get back?"

Buster's dad realised immediately that he'd hit another raw nerve and visibly flinched as his wife bit back.

"How dare you suggest that I ask him to leave! He's my brother, for heaven's sake. And he's actually been doing us a huge favour by watering the garden all week and feeding Garfield. How can you be so mean when you know what he's been through? The things he saw in Afghanistan are beyond anything you and I could ever comprehend."

"I'm more worried about the things he *did* in Afghanistan, rather than what he saw," replied Buster's dad, wishing again that he'd kept his mouth shut.

He'd learned through bitter experience that the subject of his wife's ex-military brother was one that was best avoided. He sat in silence and resigned himself to the barrage that was inevitably coming his way.

"Woah...that was low, even from you. How dare you sit there and say that! Yes, he was wrong to do what he did. And yes, they were unarmed villagers. But how was he supposed to know that in the middle of a fire-fight? He simply got carried away. Can you honestly say that you wouldn't have done the same thing, darling, if you'd been there?"

Buster's dad was pretty confident that he wouldn't have murdered five civilians who were reportedly holding their hands up, but he kept this thought to himself as he listened to what else his wife had to say on the matter.

"He's served his time and admitted his guilt. What else can he do? I know he can be a bit strange, but that's just the way he is, I'm afraid. Who wouldn't be affected by what he went through? And you've just got to deal with it. If you want me, then you get him as a brother-in-law. We come as a package."

Buster's dad wanted to say that he hadn't been aware he was marrying into a package on his wedding day, but he tried not to let this show on his face. Before she had a chance to say anything else, he saw a way out of this awkward conversation sitting conveniently on the table in front of him.

"Darling, I think I may have just got my appetite back. Do you think you could pop this in the microwave for a minute? There's a good girl."

He reached over, picked up the plate of cold food and handed it to his incredulous wife.

As she tutted and waited for the ping of the oven, he searched on his phone for the Eurotunnel timetable and the small print of the ferry company's cancellation policy.

Next time he saw Buster, he'd make quite sure the stupid boy knew exactly how much money his latest round of idiotic behaviour had just cost them.

Chapter 4

Detecting the aroma of his favourite bacon grilling in the kitchen below, Billy swung his legs out of the bed, visited the bathroom and started to get dressed.

It was 9 am and he'd grown bored of his lie-in. He'd heard his name on the radio a further six times, and although he'd beamed with delight on each occasion, he was now restless and wanted to get on with the day. He was anxious to see if the seeds he'd so carefully sown the day before were beginning to take root.

Realising that his wife was ignoring him downstairs, he decided that he wasn't going to let her little game ruin his rare good mood. The silly old cow could play her ridiculous music just as loud as she fucking liked. He knew why she was upset, but this was a day to savour and nothing was going to stop him from wringing every last little drop of enjoyment from it. He was a celebrity now, splashed across the nation's media and she'd just have to get used to it, whatever the stuck-up neighbours might think.

He didn't understand why she had to spoil things for him. She was happy living the life they'd created together when it suited her, with the cars, the holidays and the donations to her fucking do-good charities. He didn't even mind all the cash she sent to the kids and the bloody grandkids, whatever their fucking names were, behind his back, thinking he wouldn't notice.

He selected his favourite brown brogues and took one of his expensive hand-stitched shirts from the wardrobe. His wife was the only person her trusted to iron them just the way he liked. He was irritated to see that only his second-favourite tailored suit was hanging on the rail. His best one was still at the dry cleaners, having been splattered by the blood of a client who'd failed to pay his dues two days before.

It was unusual for Billy to visit clients personally nowadays, but this particular person had become problematic. An Eastern European with a nasty attitude, he'd defaulted only the month before, resulting in a quick slap and words of advice from one of the lads. Billy had decided to nip things in the bud when he'd failed to pay a second time. He'd joined his boys to add a little gravitas when they made a further unannounced home enforcement visit.

Things had got a little rough when the man, not appreciating the ramifications of missing another payment, failed to pay him the respect demanded in these delicate situations. Billy was a firm believer in the unwritten bond between himself and his customers.

This particular person, despite his noisy protestations, had to be reminded of those responsibilities by way of a further butt to his recently healed nose. A mirror had been broken and he'd ended up sprawled on his hallway floor. Blood had been spilled and some of it, very inconveniently, had found its way onto his favourite suit. Billy had not been best pleased and vowed to keep a keen personal eye on this troublesome individual from now on.

Noses always bled a lot, but even he'd been surprised by the copious flow on this occasion. He'd tried to step back from the outpouring as quickly as possible, but hadn't been quite nimble enough. His favourite jacket and trousers had become splattered by the floored debtor's blood and saliva. He made a mental note to send the client the dry-cleaning bill, just as he'd had to do the month before, following the boys' first visit. It was incidentals such as this that could really dent the bottom line and it was only right that the customer should have to cover them. It was only by keeping his costs down that he could offer such competitive rates of interest, he thought, with a grin.

Unsurprisingly, considering Billy's line of work, this was not the first time that his clothes had become soiled. But after years of trial and error, he'd found the perfect dry cleaners to rectify such outcomes. Eastwoods on the Essex Road had cleaned up for the firm for over twenty years now. They did a first-rate job of removing the obvious signs of a rough and tumble by making expert repairs and cleaning away all traces of a wide range of bodily fluids. They were respectful, loyal and thorough. But most importantly, they guaranteed complete discretion, helped along by a fear of

Billy's detailed knowledge of the proprietor's many past indiscretions.

He made a further mental note to collect the suit himself on the way into the office. This was a special day that warranted wearing his best suit.

Sitting down at the kitchen table and biting into the bacon sandwich that Fliss had just placed in front of him, he felt a little better. He'd been drained by the previous day's exertions, but it had been worth it. As his wife passed him his tea, he started to talk with his mouth full, crumbs tumbling on to the floor.

"You know what, Fliss, I'm having the fucking day off today and I don't care what you say. I'm going to go and play golf and enjoy meself for once. After the show I put on yesterday, it's the least I fucking deserve."

His wife's blank expression momentarily angered him. How could she be so unappreciative after everything he'd done for her?

"I don't think you quite grasp the importance of what I did yesterday, do you love?"

He waited for her face to register some semblance of understanding, but when it didn't, he continued regardless.

"Fucking hell, Fliss, what don't you understand? I've set us up for life, that's what I've gone and fucking done. We're not in the shadows anymore. All that fucking around in court and me on me best behaviour all day has made us famous. Everyone who's anyone knows who I am now. And they all think I'm a fucking nutter. I'm a celebrity now, love. A living legend. I'm up there with Ronnie and Reggie and the Richardsons. No one, absolutely no one, will want to mess with us now. And I intend to milk it for all it's fucking worth."

He stuffed the rest of the sandwich into his mouth and drained the tea, the delicate china looking incongruous in his rough hand.

"Anyway, where have you put my golfing stuff, you dozy cow?" he snapped, as she kept her eyes down and started to clear away the mess.

She'd heard his bluster a hundred times before and the words washed over her.

"Oh, and I forgot to say, I want to invite Buster up for Sunday lunch when he's back from his trip. He played a blinder yesterday. I don't know what I'd do without that boy sometimes, I really don't. Worth his weight in gold, he is.

Best decision I ever made was to take him on. Knew it from the moment I clapped me eyes on him. Not may like him around, I tell you. Why can't our fucking kids be more like him, Fliss? Ungrateful bastards, they are, each and every one of 'em. And make sure you put on a proper spread, will you, and get some bubbles in too. Not the cheap stuff neither. We've got a lot to celebrate, Fliss, we really fucking have."

Chapter 5

How many T-shirts was the right number to take on holiday? Buster folded ten into his case along with a couple of shirts, some jeans and a new pair of trainers. He couldn't focus on what else he needed for his trip. He was still shaken from yesterday's visit to court. He felt distracted and alarmed by the exposure he'd had thrust upon him.

Up until that point, all his work had been private. Not even his parents knew how he earned his living, but now that cat was well and truly out of the bag. The email he'd read earlier from his mother had brought him to the brink of tears. Her words cut through any delusions he was still carrying about the worth of his current position.

He had the television on in the background, with his back to the screen, as he arranged his toothbrush, deodorant and other holiday essentials in the case. They were talking about Billy now. He didn't want to listen, but he couldn't bring himself to turn it off. The workings of their dirty little world had been laid bare and now the presenters that he looked up to and admired were picking over the bones.

"Billy Murphy was yesterday accused of renting overcrowded, damp and windowless spaces with no escape routes or sanitation to vulnerable people who didn't understand what they were signing up for, but, as he explained to the judge, he was simply providing an affordable place to live in central London to people who'd be otherwise shunned by the private rental sector.

Murphy, responded to the allegations by asking the jury how else the people, who clean the city's offices and serve the workers' fast food could afford to live in this expensive city, if he wasn't there to offer his services. He'd conceded that the premises weren't strictly the safest or most pleasant places to inhabit, but argued that it wasn't possible to have every amenity at the budget end of the market.

Murphy, who has a long string of previous convictions, controversially mounted his own defence and certainly put on a performance. He shocked and persuaded the jury in equal measure.

But after they found him guilty of seventeen breaches of the Housing Act 1988, Judge Tabitha Richards QC fined Murphy £20,000 and ordered him to pay the costs of Islington Council, estimated to be in excess of £100,000. In her summing-up, she described Murphy as 'a contemptible and loathsome rogue who, without conscience or regret, had preyed on the most vulnerable members of society'. She concluded that he was guilty of 'Dickensian breaches of the most basic standards of human habitation'. Murphy was approached for a comment, but declined to make a statement."

Buster spun around as he heard the next bit of coverage. There he was on the screen. They were broadcasting Billy's departure from court. He'd been right behind the boss as they'd been chased down the steps by a throng of reporters.

"Mr Murphy, would you like to comment on your alleged links to organised crime?" one shouted.

"Sir, what do you say about the rumours of people trafficking?" yelled another.

"Billy, is it true you're the most dangerous man in London?"

Buster was transfixed by the images of himself. He winced at his depiction as the cowering servant. The little self-respect that he still had left drained away as he saw himself as others would this morning - the white-collar criminal... the simpering subordinate in awe of the alpha male, who'd bought him off.

As he slumped on his bed and held his head in his hands, the news stream turned to an earthquake somewhere far away. But before he could think any more, Buster's phone rang on his bedside table. It was Billy.

"Buster! Buster! Buster! What a morning to be alive! Have you been tuned into the radio, son?"

It was clear from the background noise, that Billy was in the car. These were always the worst calls from the boss. He'd be bored and in need of someone to talk to other than his monosyllabic driver. These conversations were notoriously difficult to end.

"We nailed it, Buster! All that planning, all that stress, but what a fucking pay-off! I'm famous for being the nastiest cunt in the country now - brand Billy, here we come! We're going to turn this into the biggest money-making opportunity we've ever had, son. This is going to be the making of us, you mark my words!"

Buster had never heard his boss sounding so happy. He felt guilty for not sharing his delight. Billy had been planning this court case, which he'd arranged, choreographed and walked into with his eyes wide open, for months. He'd tipped off the council inspectors, told the witnesses what to say and even laid a trail of evidence to his own front door. His new found notoriety was something he wanted to 'monetise' in due course. It was a word he'd just learned and it peppered all their conversations.

"That's fantastic Billy, it really is. This is something we can really capitalise on to expand the operation. Your reputation's nationwide now."

Buster knew that his voice was conveying little of the enthusiasm his boss would be expecting of him, so it was a relief when he didn't pick up on it.

"Listen, son, I'm having the day off today, so you're not going to see me 'til tonight. I'm off to play golf, if you want to know. I'll meet you at Upper Street at eight and we can have a proper catch-up before you go off on your little trip. I want you and the boys to count the safe before I get there, but keep a close eye on those lazy fat fuckers for me, will you?"

"No problem, Billy. That's all fine. Just leave it to me. You just try to relax a bit."

Buster knew that his words sounded hollow, but yet again the boss didn't react. Holding the phone between his shoulder and his ear, he closed the case and zipped it up.

"You deserve it, boss. I'll make sure everything's in order by the time you get in."

"Good boy, good boy - just don't fuck anything up, will you?!" said Billy laughing, as he put the phone down.

Chapter 6

Zaid Kodro lifted the dressing from the cut above his left eye. It still hurt, but less intensely than it had the day before. Squinting at his reflection in the bathroom mirror, he could see where it was starting to heal, the clean sides of the wound held together by six tight stitches. His black eye was also on the mend. The bruising had started to yellow and, as he raised his eyebrow, he could feel the soreness subsiding.

The nurse at the emergency room had said that his split lip would also heal if he kept it clean and didn't pick at the scab. She couldn't help with the two broken teeth though. For that he'd have to find a dentist. She didn't think the NHS would be able to offer replacements, she'd explained, letting him down as gently as she could. She'd given him a leaflet, some fresh dressings and a few kind words as she'd sent him on his way.

The attack had been three days ago and now, as he stared at his battered face, a profound anger began to rise within him. He tried to control it, but as he opened his mouth to test the soreness in his cheeks and ran his finger along the broken stumps of his teeth, he realised he might not be able to control the rage.

The men had come on a Sunday afternoon. They'd knocked at the door and when he'd not opened it, fearful and quiet in the back room, they'd kicked it down. The two regular guys had let themselves in first, with an older man following behind. Bulging out of their cheap suits, a mixture of fat and steroid-grown muscle, Zaid could recall the smell of their cheap aftershave flooding his hallway.

"You know, it's very rude to keep callers standing on the doorstep," said the older man, with a face as hard as granite.

"I might even suspect that you were trying to avoid us! Would I be right in thinking that, Mr Kodro, would I? I assume you know why we've had to disturb you, don't you? See, you didn't pay us last month and now you've gone and done the same thing again. Seems to me that a little pattern is establishing itself here, which I find very disturbing indeed.

My boys here tell me that they had a very frank exchange with you last time and despite that, here we all are, with no apparent improvement in your behaviour. So, either you've not learnt your lesson or you just think I'm a cunt."

The old man looked at his reflection in the hall mirror as he spoke. He rubbed his hand on his chin as he gazed into the glass.

"I don't think I look like a cunt," he continued, "What do you boys think? Do I look like a cunt to you two?"

"No, boss, not at all; you don't look like a cunt at all," one of them chimed back obediently.

"Thing is, I don't like being treated like a cunt and neither do my boys, and that's exactly what you've gone and done, son. You've taken my money and not stuck to the terms that were very clearly explained to you at the outset."

The old man paused and looked in the mirror again.

"So basically, you think I'm a cunt, don't you?"

Zaid knew what was coming. The dialogue from the older man sounded staged and scripted. They'd played out this routine many times before. They were waiting for the boss's cue.

And there it was.

He felt a violent blow and a searing pain to the side of his head. The man who'd punched him last month hit him again, harder than last time and more violently. More blows landed and he fell to the ground. The rest he couldn't remember.

Staring into the mirror at his own dark eyes, Zaid could feel the pressure rising at his temples. He counted his pulse and wondered how much more stress the arteries in his brain could take before they burst and left him crippled. He knew that something had to be done if this rage was to be conquered.

But what exactly could he do? His options were limited, but there had to be something that would hurt, embarrass, or at the very least, inconvenience them. He just needed to think what it could be. And once that was done he could leave, join his daughter on the coast and keep his head down. She'd told him a lot about Brighton and it was a place where he thought he could thrive. A fresh start by the ocean felt like the right thing to do. After years in the dirty city, the prospect of a fresh sea breeze on his face was something to relish.

Despite paying the men every week for three years he still owed around half of the original £2000 loan. It wasn't a lot to them. They'd look for him for a bit, but they'd soon give up. They'd given him two good kickings already, so they wouldn't lose too much face. It wouldn't be economical to spend very much time chasing such a small sum. They'd have factored the occasional runner into their nasty little business plan. They could keep his passport too. He'd leave it a few months and then tell the embassy he'd lost it. It wasn't as if he was planning on taking a holiday anytime soon.

But what were his options? He didn't have much to go on. He'd met the boss now, the infamous Billy Murphy, who'd been just as unpleasant as he'd imagined. And the faces of the collection men who'd beaten him twice were scorched onto his memory.

He also had the paper receipts they'd handed him after every visit. They were roughly scribbled with the amount of interest charged that week along with the outstanding balance and the date of the next collection. They were torn from a printed pad with an address on Upper Street and the mobile number they always called him from to make their threats. He kept them neatly stacked in his bedside draw, next to the regular bills for his phone, electricity and rent.

Flicking through the pile, his heart sank as he totalled the amount they'd extracted from him. How had he allowed himself to get caught in their trap? He'd managed to escape death, war and cold-blooded murderers in Bosnia, only to get snared by these lumbering British thugs. What a fool he'd been.

Something on one of the receipts caught his thumb. It was a staple that had been used to attach a rectangular scrap of paper. It was an invoice from a dry-cleaning business on Essex Road called Eastwoods. It was for £39.50 and the same amount had been added as a 'Sundry' item to the outstanding balance for that week.

He could remember one of the big guys telling him that it was for getting his suit cleaned after the first beating they'd given him, when Zaid's blood had stained his jacket. The boss always insisted that 'incidentals' were covered by the client in cases like these, he'd explained, almost apologetically, giving the distinct impression that it was a frequent occurrence.

He wondered if they'd charge him again this time. There had been a lot of his blood spilled and there was a good chance that some of it would have ended up on one of the big guy's clothes. A concerned neighbour had done a good job of mopping the floor, but there were stains all over the walls when he'd got home and his living room rug would need to be replaced. Not that it mattered now. He'd leave most of his stuff when he did his flit to the coast. The next tenant could wonder what mysterious horror story had led to its current condition.

If their clothes had got messed up again, then the odds were that they'd have got them cleaned immediately. No one, not even those thugs, would want to hang around in a blood-soaked suit for any longer than they needed to. And as most dry cleaners would want a suit for a couple of days in order to do a thorough job, there was a slim possibility that it could still be there.

Zaid wondered if Billy Murphy's office address was the one printed on the receipts they gave him. It could just be a decoy to keep irate punters and the authorities at bay. He'd have to check. A germ of an idea was beginning to form in his mind. He'd have to be quick if he was going to pull it off. If their clothing had been dirtied, then an opportunity existed. A sliver of one perhaps, but it was just about worth pursuing. There was little certainty in the tentative plan that was forming in his mind, but it was low risk and worth an hour of his time before he fled.

He packed his bag and changed into the cheap black suit he'd last worn to his brother's funeral. Leaving his bag by the front door, he walked ten minutes to the Upper

Street address printed on the receipts. It turned out to be a large pub called the Medicine Bar. Painted bright red, with an intricate leaded glass window spanning the ground floor, it was an old coaching inn that had been reinvented for the Islington hipster crowd.

Sitting in a café opposite, he bought a coffee and watched. As the business ebbed and flowed with mums with buggies and guys with beards using the free internet, he observed the punters entering the pub.

Small groups of office workers having a pint after work came and went but there was nothing to indicate that the place had any connection to the men who'd put him in hospital and broken his teeth. There were two floors above the ground-level bar. The first was clearly a function room of sorts. Even with the poor view the café afforded, he could see two chandeliers hanging from the ceiling and a large speaker fixed high up on a wall. It wasn't an office or a den of organised crime; just a place for people to get drunk, flirt and dance.

The top floor was more interesting. The windows had mismatched blinds pulled down, giving the impression of a tatty live-in manager's flat. Maybe this is where the operation was based. It would make sense. High up, with a good view of the street below, it would be difficult for anyone to get up to it quickly. There was sure to be a handy rear exit or escape route across the roofs, in case the occupants ever needed to get away in a hurry.

He couldn't be sure, but the six modern cameras he'd counted fixed to the front of the building made him suspect that this was more than just a regular pub. They were expensive and sophisticated. They were positioned to look up and down the street, as well as covering the customer entrance... overkill for a regular bar.

A mint tea and a bottle of water later, he noticed a familiar figure walking along the opposite side of the road. It was the less aggressive of the two men Billy Murphy had sent to visit him. The one who almost sounded human when he explained about the suit-cleaning charge. With him was a younger man. He was different. Mid-twenties, slim build and wheeling a suitcase. He didn't look tough like the others. The two men entered the pub and disappeared from Zaid's view. It wasn't conclusive, but instinct told him that this had to be the dragon's lair.

Hidden upstairs, protected by locked doors, cameras and alarms, was the place that the tentacles of Billy Murphy's operation led back to. This was the den where he plotted his misery and counted out his cash.

Zaid pondered for a while about what to do next. His plan was a long shot. It wouldn't achieve much and probably wouldn't work, but it was marginally better than doing nothing. If it only alleviated a little of the powerlessness he felt in the current predicament, then it was worth a try. It would make a statement if nothing else. Something that would tell them that he, Zaid Kodro, had finally had enough.

Draining the last drops of his water, he made a mental note of the Victorian lamppost standing outside the pub and the exact orientation of the watchful surveillance cameras. With his heart pounding, he got up, left the café and walked briskly in the direction of Essex Road. As he went, he practised in his head what he was going to say when he arrived at Billy Murphy's preferred dry-cleaning shop.

When he got there, the business was less impressive than he'd been expecting. It was positioned in the middle of a terrace of tired-looking shops. A convenience store with Day-Glo stickers in the window advertising deals on six-packs of lager and a greasy workers café were to one side. A bookies and a bathroom showroom in the final days of a shutting down sale stood at the other. Amongst the pavement clutter of refuse bins, bike racks and café tables was an A-frame for the dry cleaners proclaiming attention to detail, invisible mending and the other prompt professional services offered within.

Standing on the other side of the street, Zaid could see that there were two customers at the counter. He couldn't tell if they were there pointing out stains, making payments or collecting their favourite frocks, but he was certain that he needed them to leave before he could try out what he'd been rehearsing. Three long minutes later the shop was empty, except for a young employee who appeared to be tapping away on his mobile phone.

Dodging the slow-moving traffic, he crossed the road, puffed out his chest, got into character and entered. The boy behind the counter continued to look at his phone for a few seconds longer than he ought to, which annoyed him.

"Mr Murphy's sent me. I'm here to collect the suit," he said with as much authority and menace as he could manage, channelling his anger. He hoped that his battered face would add to the illusion he was trying to convey.

This first line was crucial. He didn't know for sure that there was a suit here at all and he certainly didn't know who it would belong to. The young man looked a little startled and then responded politely;

"No problem at all, sir. Do you have the ticket for the garments, please?"

Zaid reached into his pocket and gave the boy the rectangular invoice he'd found stapled to his weekly receipt. He glared at the youth, making it quite clear that he was pushing his luck by demanding such inconvenient formalities.

"Please hurry! Mr Murphy is waiting and he's not in a good mood."

"One moment sir, won't keep you long. I'll be as quick as I can."

So far so good, he thought, as the boy turned and disappeared to the rear of the shop, vanishing between rows of cellophane-covered clothes.

After a minute of waiting, the initial euphoria of Zaid's confident entrance began to wane. It was taking too long. Perhaps he'd been rumbled. Maybe calls were being made behind the scenes to check and verify the situation. He edged towards the door in case he needed to make a quick escape. Thirty seconds later, an older man emerged from the back holding the piece of paper.

"I'm terribly sorry to keep you waiting, sir, but my young colleague has only been working with us for a couple of weeks, so I'll take over from here. I'm the manager and I like to serve all our preferred customers, such as Mr Murphy."

The man's thin smile and false politeness put him on edge, but for the moment he had no option other than to continue with the plan that was beginning to feel frailer and less plausible with every passing second.

"So, sir, this is actually an invoice for a suit that was collected five weeks ago I'm afraid. Do you have the ticket for the suit that Mr Murphy has with us at the moment? I wouldn't normally bother with such formalities, but I don't think I've had the pleasure of serving you before, have I sir?"

So good and bad news. A suit was definitely here, but he didn't have the correct paperwork to collect it. The man was clearly suspicious. Zaid knew that he only had one more shot at retrieving the situation.

"This is what Mr Murphy gave me this morning. He needs the suit for a meeting tonight. I think maybe he gave me the wrong piece of paper. Do you want me to call him and explain?"

He realised immediately that his reply was weak and hadn't impressed his suspicious opponent on the other side of the counter. The man smiled again and cocked his head to one side.

"I'm really sorry sir, but yes, if you could, that would be great. Will you be collecting the dry cleaning on a regular basis from now on? I'm very familiar with Mr Murphy's other associates, but obviously we've never met before, so I'd just like to be on the safe side if that's OK with you. It's just company policy sir, no offence."

Zaid saw that his chances of pulling this off were draining away. Pulling himself together, he gave it his last shot. He leant across the counter and whispered quietly in the man's ear.

"Listen to me, you wanker, do you really want me to call my boss and tell him that he's not going to get his suit because *he* gave me the wrong piece of paper and *you're* making a big fucking fuss over it?

Do you want to explain to him that you fucked up his whole day because of your ridiculous rules? Do you want him to come down here and talk to you personally, because I know he fucking will if I have to disturb him?

He's sent me to get his suit because he knows he can rely on me. So, we can do this one of two ways, but either of them will result in me walking out of that door with my boss's fucking suit.

Look at my face, will you? All you need to know is that Mr Murphy pays me to sort his problems out. Not cause him anymore. Do you know what that fucking means? Think about it. If you want to be a problem, then I'm happy to sort you out too. Do you get it, Mr Dry Cleaner, do you?"

The man's smile evaporated as he reviewed the situation, whilst staring closely at the condition of Zaid's battered face.

"I'm sure there's no need for any unpleasantness, sir. And I'm sure we don't want to inconvenience Mr Murphy in any way at all. If you could remember the right ticket next time, that would be smashing."

And with that he vanished for thirty seconds before returning with the freshly cleaned suit, neatly bagged up and ready to go.

"Here you go, sir! Please send our best wishes to Mr Murphy. I'll add it to the monthly account, so there's nothing to pay for now."

Zaid left the shop, stifling a grin and scarcely able to believe that he'd pulled off the first part of his plan. High on adrenaline, he broke into a jog and was soon back at his flat, panting and ready to examine the suit.

Ripping off the plastic, he could see that it was expensive, hand-stitched and made of a heavy woollen tweed. Something of such quality could only belong to the infamous Billy Murphy himself. This was a bonus and would make what he was about to do all the more satisfying.

Using some parcel tape, a plastic broom and a selection of his bedding, he fashioned a passable scarecrow from the suit. Grabbing some string, a lighter and a bottle of white spirit that had been under his sink for the last three years, he threw his bag over his shoulder and departed with the freshly crafted effigy. He knew exactly what had to be done next before he fled the city and went to find his daughter on the coast.

Chapter 7

Buster stood quietly and stared at the boss's open safe. It was chock-a-block with cash and a small gun was taped to the back of the door. This situation had never arisen before. It was unthinkable and forbidden. A golden rule had been broken. He was alone in the office for the first time ever. He'd never before seen the inside of this treasure trove without Billy or the boys crowding around.

A commotion had just happened downstairs. Something involving fire and smashed glass. The boys had disappeared in an instant to investigate. In their testosterone-fuelled rush they'd forgotten all the basics that Billy had spent years drilling into them.

The jarring silence in the room felt completely alien. In that moment Buster appreciated the unique nature of the opportunity. A chance to change his life had presented itself when he'd been least expecting it. He felt overwhelmed by the weight of the decision he was about to make.

Two seconds later, acting on instinct and for reasons that he would later struggle to articulate, he started to steal from his employer. He didn't hesitate or think too deeply. He just did what his conscience led him to do.

He'd never been brave before or known for his bold behaviour. He was a modest accountant, a man of numbers and reason, so what he did in those fleeting moments came as a great surprise to everyone involved.

Stepping forward, he rushed to scoop out the things he wanted to take. His heart was pounding and his hands were trembling as adrenaline took hold. What he snatched were the substantial cash contents of his employer's private safe and other items considered to be sufficiently valuable to be kept under lock and key by their prudent, but famously homicidal, owner.

These included a memory stick holding the digitised ledgers of his boss's operation, an Italian handgun and two boxes of cheaply made Russian ammunition. This was the gun that Billy had placed there to deter anyone from ripping him off. This irony was not lost on a panicking Buster as he frantically placed the items into his brand-new suitcase under the watchful eye of the office CCTV. The system did not judge, condone or intervene, but simply recorded the insane events that had commenced at precisely eight minutes past seven in the evening.

Under the digital gaze of two cameras that he knew about and a further three that were hidden and known only to Billy, Buster crossed a line that could not be uncrossed. Not only had he bitten the hand that fed him, but he'd also ripped it off, chewed it up, spat it on the floor and stamped on the bloody remnants of what was left.

The second he saw the boys disappearing through the doorway, a stark choice had presented itself. He could either stay and live with a growing loathing of the person he'd become, or take advantage of the opportunity, betray his employer and flee. He knew that he'd run the risk of severe retribution but at least, for a while, he'd be free to undo some of the damage he'd helped orchestrate, as his boss's most trusted and beloved lieutenant.

He could start to make amends and do the right thing for a change. Right up, that was, until the moment that Billy and his band of happy thugs caught up with him. And he was sure they would catch up, probably sooner rather than later. It wouldn't take them long.

Buster's decision-making in those seconds was coloured by the fact that he was due to fly away on a Caribbean vacation paid for by his generous and grateful boss. Recognition of all the hard work, diligence and, up to that point, absolute loyalty, shown by his favourite employee and golden boy, Buster Brett.

In practical terms, the destination wasn't as significant as the actual suitcase he'd carefully packed that morning. He'd hauled it into the office so that he'd be ready to leave for the airport as soon as the day's work was done.

New clothes nestled next to the snorkel and fins he'd ordered online a couple of days before. He'd even picked up a couple of novels to read by the pool, keen to reacquaint himself with a pastime he'd enjoyed when life was simpler.

Perhaps if he hadn't had a physical means of carrying away the contents of the safe conveniently to hand, he might have stayed, subdued his conscience and let a different future take its course. But the smart designer luggage was the proverbial straw that finally shifted his corroded moral compass.

Pushing the valuables from the safe into the case and the items that it had just contained into a black bin liner, snatched from an office drawer, he made his exit. And with that bold act, the itch that had been bothering him for weeks was well and truly scratched. The relief in those first few moments was intoxicating. It had been so more much than just an itch. The feverish cancerous sore that had given him no peace for weeks had been finally appeased. For the first time in years he felt free. A dead man walking perhaps, but at liberty for the time being.

With his suitcase clattering along the pavement on its tiny plastic wheels and the bin bag containing his clothes sitting uncomfortably on his shoulder, Buster ran along Upper Street towards the tube station as fast as he could manage.

His haste, the wildness in his eyes and the noise generated by the escape made sure that he was noticed by all. Greengrocers, baristas, hairdressers and traffic wardens all looked up from what they were doing. Perplexed by the panic on his face, people stood aside, held their children tight and recoiled into doorways as he rushed by.

Even for a street accustomed to eccentric behaviour, noise and disruption, his flight stood out. His departure was recorded by the CCTV systems of three shops, two cafés and a popular bookmaker owned by his boss. People stared, wondered and got out of the way. Even as Buster ran, he knew that he wasn't being clever, but in his panic, he didn't have the time to care. He was intoxicated by his own determination to flee. The thrill of his snap decision to leave blinded him to the folly of what he'd just done.

Leaping down the stairs at Highbury and Islington underground station, as quickly as he could manage with his unwieldy baggage, he was lucky that his arrival on the southbound platform coincided with that of a Brixton train.

In the seventeen minutes that followed, he could have changed his mind, returned the cash, shoved his holiday clothes back into the suitcase and continued with the life he'd lived for the last five years. It wouldn't have mattered about the office CCTV because no one would watch it if there wasn't a problem. He could have stayed, controlled his doubts and carried on as if everything was fine.

Alighting the tube at the next station would have given him ample time to double back, return the things he'd taken, regain his composure and be thankful to the Gods of Preventing Pain and Misery that his reckless ten minutes would go unnoticed.

However, riding the Victoria Line south, the usually sharp mind of Buster Brett was blank. Like an accountant who's drunkenly punched his neighbour at a family barbecue, he sat shocked and appalled by his own behaviour. One moment he was proud of what he'd just done, the next in terror of the repercussions. As the adrenaline drained away, he was left to dwell on the inevitable consequences of his actions. They could only be substantial, real and painful. He began to feel sick as he weighed the potential outcomes of his awkward new reality.

Catching his pale reflection in the carriage window, he pulled down his tie and used his jacket sleeve to wipe the sweat from his forehead. Gripping his suitcase between his knees and hugging the bin bag on his lap, he fought to control his breath. He'd made either the best or the most stupid decision of his life. Only time would tell. He'd done what he thought was right in the heat of the moment, but now he felt exposed and hopelessly alone.

When, at exactly twenty-three minutes after his reckless act, he emerged onto the busy bright concours of Victoria Station, his last chance to reverse events had gone. Deep underground, somewhere between Green Park and the secret war bunkers of Buckingham Palace, the train had passed the point of no return. The die was cast and the tracks to his future lay fixed and rigid in front of him. In a second of clarity, he realised that death, redemption or freedom could all lie ahead.

As he stood and stared at the departures board, the fog in his mind began to clear. Whilst he appreciated the appalling gravity of his actions, he felt deep down that he'd made the right decision. A weight had been lifted. An unusual lightness washed across his mind like a cool breeze. Euphoria and dread jostled for prominence in his mind.

He was free for the first time since the day he'd met his boss. The spell had been broken. He now had a slim chance to put things right. But first he had to deal with the not inconsiderable problem of trying to stay alive, with his body parts still connected as God intended, rather than having been roughly butchered and posted first-class to unsuspecting family members. There would soon be a team of the hardest men after him, led by a vicious and enraged madman. Buster's legs began to feel weak and unreliable at this prospect and cold sweat washed over him.

To steal from Billy Murphy was madness, but to do it on a whim, with no strategy or plan honed over months of secretive preparation was suicidal.

He knew that his boss would be shocked by his amateurish approach and disappointed that he'd learned so little from his valuable apprenticeship. He'd wonder why he'd not covered his tracks or taken any measures to deflect his inevitable pursuers. He knew that his employer would be saddened and enraged in equal measure; an anger that would burn unchecked until he'd been caught and held to account. He'd want to know why his protégé had turned on him. He'd need to understand. And then he'd want his pound of retribution with plenty of interest on top, for good measure. Buster couldn't bear to think about the bloody reality of what this could mean. It was too brutal to contemplate.

Forcing his thoughts back into the present, he made himself concentrate on the practicalities of his escape. He stared at the orange pixelated departures board for just long enough to extract the details of the next south bound train. Platform 6 in two minutes time was the best that it had to offer. His shaking hands made the ticket machine difficult to operate. Despite this, he managed to feed a note into the slot and grab the ticket.

With a pounding heart, he grabbed the handle of his case, threw the bin bag over his shoulder and ran towards the barriers as fast as his legs would carry him. It felt good to be running again, the physical exertion confining the dread to the back of his mind.

It seemed as if every other passenger he passed had a copy of the Evening Standard in their hands. The words on the news stand shrieked at him as he raced along the platform. The headline was unavoidable and a chilling reminder of what he already knew to be the truth.

"BILLY MURPHY:
THE MOST DANGEROUS MAN IN LONDON?"

Chapter 8

All Billy's boys knew that you didn't contact him on the golf course. He'd spent his life working in a world where the money was made at the weekend, so the middle of the week was his own private downtime. He wasn't to be phoned, contacted or in any way interrupted while he was trying to unwind. A special kind of fury was reserved for anyone foolish enough to break this rule.

And fifty years of working every Friday, Saturday and Sunday had made Billy a very rich man. As a consequence, he loved his weekends. He'd learned that people were predictable then and easy to manage. They were always at home, in their poky little living rooms, glued to their televisions like pathetic sitting ducks, getting fat on nasty fast-food and drinking cheap alcohol to numb their senses. They'd be wearing slippers, with their bratty little kids hiding behind the sofa, when the boys arrived, tooled-up on their doorsteps, eager to collect whatever was owed. They wouldn't want any fuss or trouble, but they'd get it anyway if they didn't cough up.

His clubs were also busy, full of people wanting to buy drugs and sex and too drunk to realise that they were being fleeced and filmed. They'd have a great time and empty their wallets straight into Billy's deep tills, while he watched, grinning from the office above.

The same went for the protection clients who always had plenty of cash to hand after a busy Saturday night selling the Chinese food, or whatever other foreign rubbish they served to their customers. No point trying to collect on a Monday when they'd pretend to have spent it, paid it into the bank, or sent it back to their poor sick families in Thailand, or whatever shit-hole country they claimed to come from.

But best of all, working the weekends got Billy out of the house, away from Fliss and the noisy kids who wanted to play, talk, make a mess and do all the other things that he detested about normal family life.

He phoned his driver from the clubhouse at 5pm. When there was no answer, he left an expletive-ridden voicemail articulating his intense displeasure. He knew that Razor was a lazy bastard who'd probably be sleeping somewhere nearby, waiting for his call. Most likely, he'd have made himself a little too comfortable on the pristine soft leather seats of the Bentley, with a sausage roll and a copy of the Racing Post, before dozing off. He'd check for crumbs and greasy fingerprints later and there would be hell to pay if he found any. He decided to wait five more minutes before calling again. If he didn't answer a second time, he'd punch the cheeky fucker the moment he saw him.

The other boys grumbled that Razor wasn't the full ticket, but he was a man of few words and that's exactly why Billy had chosen him to be his driver. He didn't encourage conversation when he was being driven. Car time was for thinking and he didn't want chitchat or any other distractions. Just so long as Razor could get from one place to another and turn up on time, Billy was happy to keep him. But today he was seriously pushing his luck.

He felt uneasy. Things had gone well on the golf course and he was still buzzing from his day in court. But something he couldn't put his finger on was starting to play on his mind. Nagging doubts began to spoil his mood. Had he overplayed his hand in the dock? Would his newfound notoriety be just a flash in the pan? Something, somewhere, didn't feel right.

He'd teed off earlier with the remaining handful of club regulars who could still be bribed into playing a round on the promise of drinks in the bar afterwards. He was tolerated at the club, a colourful enigma who contrasted with the dreary bank managers and estate agents who normally clogged up the fairways.

The flow of the game had been interrupted by a barrage of calls from associates, rivals and hangers-on, each keen to congratulate him on his performance in court. Some were genuine but others, he suspected, had only called to see if they could sense any hint of weakness in his voice. They'd seen him on the news or read about him in the papers and wanted to pay their respects, so they said.

Billy liked to believe that he could detect a new deference in the way most people were speaking to him today and that pleased him very much. Money well spent, he thought. He puffed out his chest and took their calls, bragging and boasting, making a note of who had phoned and more importantly, who had not.

By the final hole, he found himself playing with just one other member. The others had made their excuses and drifted away to the clubhouse, having grown bored of the constant interruptions and bravado. There was only so much nonsense they could tolerate on the promise of a free round of drinks.

Sinking the last ball, Billy had a quick whiskey with the last man standing and asked his driver to collect him at 5.30pm, once he eventually got hold of him. He told Razor to clean the car inside and out and turn up promptly with an unread copy of each of the national newspapers, as well as the Evening Standard and Brighton's Argus.

The drive into the office, which normally took about an hour, would give him ample time to read the coverage in full and revel in his notoriety, while it was still hot off the press. He asked the club manager to lend him a pair of scissors and a folder so he could keep the cuttings safe, clean and organised for his future perusal.

Sitting in the back of the car, he carefully read the papers, neatly cutting out the articles that pleased him. One in *The Times* displeased him very much by taking the wrong tone entirely and it now lay screwed up and discarded on the Bentley's deep pile carpet. He made a note of the journalist's name. He'd get his own back when an opportunity presented itself, which he'd make sure it would very soon.

There was another cutting that made his old heart melt. This was the one he was going to get framed. It was perfect in every detail and the editor had written it exactly as he'd asked, once they'd had a little conversation on the telephone the previous evening. It was amazing what a simple threat to call an innocent spouse could achieve. The big, bold, beautiful front-page headline of the Evening Standard sang in Billy's ears.

It would look magnificent on the office wall. He pictured an elaborate gilt frame that would make it stand out and do justice to the poetic words. Perhaps he'd get it enlarged too. The bigger the better, he decided. He was just wondering about how many further copies to have made to hang in his various clubs, bars and bookmakers when the car came to a sudden and unwelcome halt.

They were stuck in heavy traffic. Looking out of the window, Billy could see they were on Essex Road. Overcoming his initial annoyance, he decided that the timing was actually fortuitous. He could use the delay to pick up his best suit from Eastwoods. Distracted by the newspapers, he'd completely forgotten about it. With any luck, it would be ready by now, clean, fresh and looking as sharp as the day he'd stolen it.

Pulling up outside, he told Razor to go into the shop, and to be sharp about it. He watched impatiently from the car as the man behind the counter shook his head, gesticulated and failed to produce the garments. What the fuck was going on here, he fumed, his already short temper beginning to fray. He just wanted his favourite suit back.

A minute later, Razor knocked on the rear window of the car.

"The geezer in there says he hasn't got your suit, boss. One of the boys picked it up an hour ago, he says."

Billy thought for a second. He couldn't be too mad at them for trying to do him a favour. But, on the other hand, he'd not asked them to stick their noses in and now his precious time had been wasted as a consequence.

"Right, call the office and find out which one of those clever cunts picked it up. Tell them that if it's not on me desk by the time I arrive, I'm going to shove this fucking phone straight up one of their fat backsides. You got that?"

"Yes, boss," said Razor as he got back into the driver's seat and tried to pull out into the congestion, the traffic unwilling to yield to the Bentley.

As Billy listened to the conversation that followed on the hands-free, his blood began to boil. It was simply unbelievable. Incomprehensible. As he tried to understand the sounds coming out of the phone, he felt old, exposed and alone.

The more he heard, the angrier he became, gripping the borrowed scissors so hard that the plastic handles shattered under the pressure. The words he was hearing made no sense at all.

"Get to the office as fast as you fucking can!" he barked, incandescent with rage.

"Buster's gone and fucking robbed me!"

As the car cleared the traffic, Razor floored the accelerator and they sped the short distance along Upper Street to the pub. Billy could see a police car, a fire engine and a huddle of curious onlookers crowding around the entrance. They had their phones out and were filming away. It was a frenzy of posting, uploading and streaming. His place of safety, his sanctuary and home from home was swarming with unwelcome attention.

As he absorbed what his eyes were showing him and tried to make sense of what he'd just heard, he realised that his special day was well and truly, monumentally ruined. This Wednesday of Wednesdays, the day that he'd been waiting for months to enjoy, the one on which he'd launch his legacy and secure his safe future, had descended into an awful, unimaginable, incoherent farce.

Chapter 9

The train that Buster leapt aboard at Victoria Station offered little reassurance to a man intent on evading a lethal and fleet-footed pursuer. Not only was it a tediously slow, stopping service, but it was also litter-strewn and infused with the odour of stale fried chicken. To make matters worse, it was hot, packed and heading towards Eastbourne, the least likely getaway destination he could imagine.

He'd only got as far as the second carriage in his dash along the crowded platform before the conductor's whistle panicked him into leaping through the nearest set of doors.

Once on board, sweaty and breathless, he found himself surrounded by excited school children who'd evidently been to see a West End matinee performance. They were clutching programmes, eating takeaway, and for a man who needed to think clearly, making an obscene amount of noise. Every seat was occupied except for one, onto which the apparently unsupervised scholars had piled their bags and belongings. Since no one was going to offer that seat to an odd, bin bag-clutching adult, he was left to stand dejectedly in the door lobby, holding tight as best he could, as the train lurched and rattled out of the dark station.

The happy kids chatted, shouted and played on their phones. Everything about their cheery banter jarred with his mood. As the train clattered through the south London suburbs he was acutely aware of the slowness of the journey. This was not the fast getaway he needed.

It wasn't until Clapham Junction that his heart calmed to a manageable rate. As the train passed through the station, his head was a jumble of plans, escape routes, adrenaline and fear. He knew that whatever action he took in the next thirty minutes would affect the rest of his life. If he got it wrong, the time he had left could be short and very unpleasant indeed. As he looked out across the neat rows of south London's Victorian rooftops, he wished that he was cosily tucked away beneath one of them, watching banal TV, ordering pizza and living a safe but boring life.

In his pocket he had his passport and a business-class ticket to fly to sunny Barbados. The train was due to stop at the airport in twenty minutes. He also had plenty of cash and several sets of clothes in his binbag. These were all positive factors and the instinct to jump on a plane and get as far away as possible from the mess he'd just created was strong.

But on the downside, his now ex-boss would no doubt dispatch a car to intercept him there before he was due to take off in five hours' time. He also had far more cash than was practical to travel with, as well as the gun and boxes of ammunition. He knew the weapon would be an advantage if Billy ever got anywhere near to him, but as he'd never even handled one before, the initial comfort he'd derived from having it in his possession quickly started to wane.

He could always put the cash and gun into a luggage locker at the airport, he thought, leave them there for the time being and sneak back when things felt safer. He wondered if things would ever feel safe again. But how secure were left luggage places anyway? Did they actually exist at airports or had he just seen them in movies?

He considered buying a new ticket to a destination Billy wouldn't think of. He wasn't a well-travelled man and would never dream of a flit to India or Africa. Real criminals went to Spain, he'd reason. They bought villas, opened pubs and taunted the police with expensive lawyers.

But did he really want to end up in the back of nowhere and on the run forever? Would anywhere in the world ever be safe from a furious and embittered madman? As the train raced relentlessly towards the airport, he wracked his brain to recall if Billy had ever mentioned any contacts at Gatwick. He had people all over the place who'd spy, snoop, snitch and report back to him, either for money or because they'd done something stupid that he'd found out about or managed to film. He loved to catch people doing all sorts of things, when they ought to have known better. He had contacts in the police, council and even the nation's parliament who'd been pressured into looking out for his interests. Buster knew all the names as he'd been the one recording the bribes. But unfortunately, he didn't know any of the corresponding faces, so the information was of little practical use in the current predicament.

He concluded that the airport wouldn't be the least bit safe. There would be enough cops and customs officers roaming the place without having to dodge Billy's boys and all the other unknowns on his payroll, lurking in the shadows.

Switching trains at Haywards Heath and going straight to Brighton was another option. It was the place he'd grown up and knew best. His oldest friend Dexter Ward, one of the most unreliable people he'd ever met, was still there and might be able to help in a pinch. Dexter was also the only friend left who wasn't somehow linked to Billy's circle. It was also an obvious choice and another place his pursuers would be certain to look. As the world outside rushed by, he couldn't think of any more options.

Buster worked out that even with all the stops and changing of trains, he'd still get to Brighton before Billy or his boys possibly could by car. It was Wednesday evening and the roads south out of London would be clogged as usual. They'd have to drive out through Croydon and Coulsdon and that was going to be slow going.

But even if he did get to Brighton before his pursuers, there was a good chance they'd have called ahead and arranged a welcoming party of doormen and other associated thugs from the clubs and bars that Billy controlled down there. It was a risk, but one probably worth taking. He'd feel safer on his home turf and if he was going to be tracked down by a bunch of tooled-up meat heads wanting to do him harm, he'd rather have it happen in a place where he knew all the streets, rat runs and bolt holes.

As the train rumbled through Horley, he committed to the plan. It wasn't ideal, but it was the best he could think of. He was stressed, panicking and running out of time. He'd run the gauntlet of Brighton station and take his chances from there. He texted his old friend, hoping for a prompt reply. As he typed the words, he wished there was someone more sensible he could reach out to.

DEXTER MATE IT'S BUSTER. I NEED YOUR HELP. I'VE DONE SOMETHING STUPID AND YOU'RE THE ONLY ONE WHO CAN HELP. PICK ME UP ON TRAFALGAR STREET UNDER THE STATION AT 2120 TONIGHT. WE'LL NEED TO MAKE A QUICK GETAWAY BECAUSE PEOPLE WILL BE AFTER ME. I HOPE I CAN RELY ON YOU. PLEASE DON'T LET ME DOWN MATE. DON'T TELL ANYONE ELSE. THANKS.

The message that came back was garbled and confused. Just an emoji and a selection of random characters. Buster knew that he'd have to call and clarify matters as soon as he had a chance. If Dexter couldn't be made to comprehend the seriousness of the situation, then all hope was lost.

By the time the airport stop approached, the carriage had thinned out and he was able to find a seat for himself and an adjacent one for his bags. As the doors slid open and people dragged their suitcases away, happy and excited about their holiday flights, he pushed himself down into the upholstery. Feeling exposed and alone, he turned up his collar and scanned the platform for any signs of danger.

Stress, anxiety and paranoia clouded his mind. It dawned on him that this was how life would be from now on. The mild relief he felt as the train pulled out of the station was tempered by the knowledge that the countdown to his arrival in Brighton had already begun. He was now just one change of train and a few miles of line from the most dangerous moment of his life.

Chapter 10

The night that Buster texted him out of the blue, Dexter Ward had decided to visit the pub. It was his home from home and the place where he felt most comfortable. He did all his business there and spent most of his money over the bar.

The Unicorn was just one hundred and twenty-eight paces from the front door of his tatty apartment building. Adding together the sixty-three stairs, two landings, three fire lobbies and the time it took to cross St James's Street, the total journey time from his living room couch to favourite bar stool was around two and a half minutes. It could be longer if he was stoned and needed to buy fags and a bag of crisps on the way.

The Unicorn was appropriately named. It was a rare and almost mythical anomaly in a city full of trendy reimagined bars. The pub had not changed significantly in fifty years. It had been left alone and unmolested by the whims and fashions of the fickle hospitality trade.

Anyone who could pay their way and mind their own business was welcome to stay and drink. Gay, straight, black or white - no one cared, remembered or judged. The CCTV system hadn't been repaired after a drunk pulled a camera off the wall, and that situation suited everyone perfectly.

The long mahogany bar encouraged punters to sit and chat to the staff, most of whom had been there as long as anyone could remember. Secrets were told and life stories shared. Always busy and full of characters, the Unicorn was a Brighton institution almost as famous as the Palace Pier or Pavilion. Not quite as old, but with just as many tales to tell and secrets to keep.

Dexter arrived at 8 pm. Bursting through the doors with the unkempt look of a man who'd not long been awake, he was relieved to see that his favourite stool at the end of the bar was still free. He always sat there if he could. It offered the best view of everyone coming and going. It was close to the toilets, for when he wanted to hand over a bag of weed, but closer still to the fire escape in case he needed to dodge a creditor.

From his favourite seat he could keep an eye on all the other tables and booths. He had full command of the room and could see if anyone was taking any undue interest in his business activities. Dexter could spot a cop a mile off, with their clumsy earpieces and warrant cards stuffed in their back pockets. He could never understand how they allowed themselves to look so obvious and out of place.

But more importantly than business or anything else, sitting on his special stool made it easier for him to buy drinks for any single females who wandered in and caught his eye. He'd nod and wink as he had them sent over by an embarrassed member of staff, anxiously anticipating some sort of reciprocation. Dexter considered himself to be a lady's man, a smooth operating maverick, with his tattoos and long hair. He was the life and soul of the Unicorn, the pub jester who was always ready to charm and entertain. But others rarely saw him in the same light and, more often than not, his free drinks one-liners were rebuffed.

Perched at the bar was the best place to be if you were alone, he thought. Sitting at a table made it look as if you were waiting for friends to arrive to fill the spare chairs. Tables made you feel awkward and exposed if you were by yourself. Too much space for one person to occupy. The bar was his rightful place in the pub.

As he went to grab his special stool, a stern voice rang out.

"Dexter Ward, get out of my pub right now, you disgusting little sex pest."

The voice was that of the landlady, Martha Webb. Her words stopped him in his tracks and stunned the pub into silence.

"Stop right where you are, young fella. Now turn around and sling yer hook. We're not having a repeat of what you got up to last night, I'm afraid. Go and find another pub to drink in for a week and see if they'll put up with your filthy antics."

He felt the judgmental eyes of the entire room bearing down on his unsteady frame. What had he done? What did she mean? Martha Webb was considered to be one of the most formidable publicans in the city. A solid woman in her sixties, she'd been known to eject an entire gypsy wedding party on her own, using nothing more than sharp words and the force of her personality. She was not a woman to tangle with. She was also smart enough to refrain from banning her most lucrative customers for more than a week.

"I'm not quite with you, Martha. What have I done, exactly?" he answered with all the innocence he could muster, smiling thinly, fully aware that the rest of the pub also wanted the answer to that exact same question.

As the words passed his lips, he had a faint recollection of what he might have done, but the details were a little sketchy on account of all the alcohol he'd consumed less than twenty-four hours before. He could feel his face reddening in the spotlight.

"What have you done exactly? I'll tell you what you've done, you dirty little shit."

Certain details of the previous night's cavorting started to coalesce in Dexter's clouded memory. He thought that, on balance, Martha Webb probably did have moderate grounds to be annoyed. A few things were coming back to him that might indeed be considered poor behaviour, even in a place as broad-minded as the Unicorn. But a week-long ban... surely that was excessive?

"You went and got your cock out at the bar last night, that's what you've bloody gone and done, Dexter Ward. You spent all night buying that poor skinny girl shots and giving her coke. And don't think I didn't notice all those trips to the bog.

And then when you're both completely off your nuts, you obviously forgot you were in the pub, because you went and got your fucking cock out. And then you started to……"

"Martha, Martha. If that's indeed what I did, then I'm deeply, deeply, sorry," said Dexter, cutting her off before things got even more awful, hoping that she wouldn't insist on continuing with this public humiliation.

The whole pub stared in disbelief, stunned but eager to hear the rest of the story. The Unicorn was a place used to bad behaviour, but this titillating revelation was enough to shock even this jaded crowd into silence.

"Okay, okay, I'll leave right now and I won't darken your doors until I've repented and mended my ways," he conceded, trying to snatch the initiative and stop Martha from revealing any further details of his previous night's misbehaviour.

And with those words he bowed, blew a kiss to the rear of the pub and made his retreat. As the door closed behind him and he found himself on the cold pavement, his phone buzzed with a text.

He read the message three times. He hadn't seen or heard from Buster for over a year, so it was odd and confusing for him to be sending such an urgent and specific text out of the blue. The use of capitals made Dexter's head hurt and he wished he hadn't opened it. What the fuck had Buster done and why was he asking for help? He was also irritated that helping would mean having to move his campervan. He'd spent ages the previous day trying to find a parking space big enough to put it in. Being stoned hadn't helped with all the tricky parallel parking. A queue of traffic had built up in the road before he'd finally negotiated the old van into the gap on his eleventh attempt.

The space was streets away and he didn't fancy the trek back to find it in the dark. There would also be all the stress of trying to get the van started again. The VW was ancient and Dexter hadn't got around to getting it serviced in the last couple of years. His beloved old van still ran, but just not very well.

He was struggling now to even recall where he'd parked. He was sure it was nearby, but he couldn't visualise the precise location for the moment. It would come to him in a minute.

Maybe he could just ignore the message and make out he hadn't received it. Buster was moving with some heavy people nowadays, so perhaps it was best to stay out of his business. It made sense. He could just turn his phone off and say he'd been out of town. Buster would be none the wiser. Yes, that's what he'd do. That was the plan. Glancing at his phone, he noticed that he'd accidentally replied to his friend with an umbrella emoji and a string of random letters while he'd been dithering and worrying about the van.

Stopping to get a bag of crisps and a bag of tobacco on the way, Dexter returned to his flat and rolled a joint. The place was a mess. Even by his own standards it was in an appalling state. His living room floor was littered with the remnants of takeaway boxes, cans and clothes. Two cereal bowls overflowed with the detritus of smoking and the only clear space on the floor was an area he'd kicked clean whilst playing on his Xbox. Not to worry though, he thought. His mum was coming at the weekend to pick up his laundry. She was bound to feel sorry for him and have a little go at making the place look better. It was only superficial. Just a matter of filling a bin bag or two and running the vacuum around. That's what mums were for, right?

As he sat back and exhaled a long plume of aromatic smoke, his phone rang on the sofa cushion next to his right hand. Realising it was a mistake as he did it, but unable to stop himself quickly enough, he instinctively answered the call.

"Dexter, mate, is that you? It's Buster. Did you get my text? What was the umbrella thing all about?"

"Wow, man. Buster. How you doing, bruv?"

"Listen Dexter, I'm on a train. I'm going to be in Brighton in twenty minutes. I *really* need you to come and get me. Pick me up on Trafalgar Street please. Right at the top where it goes under the station. Make sure you keep the engine running. We'll need to make a quick getaway. That okay?"

Buster barked the words without a hint of the banter or humour that had always been the foundation of their friendship. This was a serious, anxious Buster, not the fun version he'd known for years.

"Dexter, mate, can you hear me?"

Buster sounded desperate and Dexter wished he could think of a clever way to end the conversation.

"Dexter, you there?"

"Don't stress man, I'll be there. It's cool. Brighton station. Tonight. Cool. I'll be there. No worries."

"Dexter, mate, I'm relying on you. This is serious. I've got some proper nasty people after me. You won't let me down, will you?"

"It's sweet man. I'll be there. So, this is tonight right?"

"Yes, Dexter! I need you there in twenty minutes, mate. You got that? If you're late I'll be a dead man. Actually, properly, not breathing dead. Do you understand what I'm telling you?"

"So, Buster, mate, chill. What you been up to anyway?"

"Dexter! I can't talk now. I really need you to concentrate on what I'm saying. Just listen. I need you to meet me at the main train station. Please, Dexter. For old time's sake. I'm finished if you don't, mate."

"Sweet, bruv. I'll do my best. Just gotta find my van first."

And with that final comment, he dropped the phone on the floor and lost the connection to his old pal Buster.

"Bollocks!" he shouted to no one in particular.

He realised that through his own stupidity in answering the call, he now had no choice other than to do what Buster wanted. He'd have to go and pick him up from the station. The tone in his friend's voice had been unnerving. It was way too serious for his liking. This wasn't going to be the least bit fun or enjoyable. All this hassle, on top of getting banned from his favourite pub, was very unwelcome indeed.

Starting to panic, he slipped on the trainers he'd just taken off, grabbed his coat from the floor and made for the stairs. He crashed down the landings, upsetting his already annoyed neighbours with the noise. The building's heavy front door slammed behind him as he careered out into the darkness. Running in the general direction of his van, he tried to recall any features that could help narrow down the search. A busy road with white terraced houses was all he could remember. Brighton was full of streets like that. Following his nose, he crossed his fingers and hoped for the best.

Five minutes, a quick smoke and four streets later, he had his first luck of the night. He stumbled across his van, wedged tightly between an Audi and a BMW. The back wheel was on the kerb and the driver's side window was open. 'An exemplary bit of parking,' he thought to himself as he readied the vehicle to drive away.

The engine started reluctantly on the third attempt. Its exhaust pipe kicked a plume of black smoke into the faces of a couple passing by, who coughed and banged angrily on the van's rusty rear panels. After some swearing and a few nudges of the car behind, Dexter freed the van from its confinement

He raced along Kemptown seafront and took the roundabout at the Palace Pier a little too quickly. The breeze from the open window had helped clear his head but he started to feel sick and cold as he neared the town centre. What if the people after Buster decided to get rough? What if they didn't get away? He really didn't want to get involved with any of this. He loved his routine of Xbox, sleep, weed and the pub. Why the hell had he answered the phone in the first place?

As he drove up West Street towards the Clock Tower, he wondered if it would be easier to just turn around and make out that he'd misunderstood Buster's instructions. Their whole exchange of words had taken less than a minute and, after all, he had been stoned. He could make out that he'd got the time or the place mixed up. It wouldn't be out of character and Buster would surely forgive him in time. And to be honest, it really didn't matter if he didn't forgive him. They never saw each other these days and Buster's family had hated him ever since the incident at school.

Despite his doubts, he continued to drive. They'd grown up together and a nagging loyalty to his friend kept his foot on the gas. Crossing North Street, he passed the Clock Tower and drove on towards the station.

Approaching the grand old terminal, the gateway to Brighton, the traffic became clogged with taxis and cars dropping passengers off. It was too late to turn back now. Buster might have already seen him. His last chance to slip away, smoke a spliff and think of a credible excuse to let his friend down had gone.

Lurching into a gap that had formed in the queue of traffic heading down from Seven Dials, Dexter turned right into the top section of Trafalgar Street that ran below the station forecourt. People and cars were everywhere. He felt paranoid and exposed. He hated crowds and busy places. Wondering if Buster would even turn up, he cursed himself for not bringing a joint to calm his nerves.

Stopping the van in the gloomy half-light of the tunnel, he reached down to pick up the remnants of a roll-up he'd dropped on the floor a week before. His trembling foot slipped off the clutch and the engine stalled. Sitting in the cold and realising that this night probably wasn't going to end very well, he fretted and stressed about how bad things were likely to get.

Chapter 11

Billy Murphy sat fuming in an office chair, staring grimly at the screen on his desk. He'd slipped in through a side entrance, keen to avoid the curious crowds and vaulted the stairs to the top floor with the agility of a man half his age, fuelled by adrenaline and rage. He was desperate to take control of whatever horror had just unfolded.

He poured a whiskey in a vain attempt to douse his anger. He downed a second glass when he caught sight of his precious safe, unlocked, open and empty. There was no money or gun. Just a gaping emptiness he'd not seen since its installation twenty years earlier.

The screen was split into eight sections, each corresponding to a camera on the outside of the building. Billy ground his teeth in disbelief as the unreal images flickered before his eyes.

Behind him stood his boys, Derek and Anthony, barely able to contain the shame of what they'd allowed to happen and rightly fearful of their boss's response. They knew what he was capable of. They assisted with the retribution he handed out on a daily basis. He reacted badly to a word out of place, so they struggled to comprehend how he'd respond to this cataclysm; one they'd allowed to happen at the heart of the operation.

However, for the moment they could only stand and wince as the cameras replayed every aspect of their recent misjudgements in crystal-clear, high-definition clarity. Their reactions at the time had seemed instinctive and professional, but now in the cold light of the digital playback, there was nowhere to hide and their mistakes were obvious and glaring. They were in the wrong and they'd been made to look foolish. They'd been tricked, hoodwinked and taken for mugs. The safe was empty and the boss had every reason to be in a murderous frame of mind. They both wished they could be anywhere in the world other than here in Billy's office watching the painful detail of how they'd been played by an odd man in a suit and the boy they'd taken to be one of their own.

To one side of Billy sat Razor, quiet and relieved that he'd not been implicated in this unparalleled disaster. Things were going to get vicious and he was secretly enjoying the tension. He used a mouse to control the CCTV playback, responding to the boss's grunts and finger stabbing at the screen, going backwards and forwards in time and from one camera to the next, trying to make sense of what had just occurred.

It was soon painfully apparent what had happened. A slim man in a suit had crossed from the other side of Upper Street carrying what appeared to be a scarecrow. It was the sort of creation that kids used to make in the run-up to Bonfire Night. A ragtag, scruffy, 'penny for the guy' assemblage, wearing a man's suit and stuffed with what looked like pillows and newspaper.

He stopped outside the pub and used a ball of string tossed over the cross member of a lamppost to hoist the effigy by its neck. He doused it in a clear liquid squirted from a plastic bottle. A lighter had then been used to send the whole thing up in flames, before something heavy had been thrown through the front window.

The man stood for a second, defiant and brazen, making a one-fingered gesture directly to the camera, a satisfied smile clearly visible on his recently injured face. He then made off down the road with a rucksack on his back.

Thirty seconds later, the boys could be seen leaving the building and pelting after him as quickly as their heavy frames would allow. But it was obvious from the playback that they never had a chance of catching up. What had seemed like a sprint to them at the time now looked like the hopeless scuttle of two fat rats leaving a sinking ship.

Three long minutes elapsed before Buster Brett, Billy Murphy's defacto son, could also be seen departing. He had a suitcase in one hand and a black bin liner in the other. The recording showed him glance awkwardly up at the camera as he turned in the opposite direction to the others, before dashing towards Highbury and Islington tube. Billy made Razor play this ten-second section over and over again. It was as if he wished that on the next viewing, things would be different, and his golden boy would not be stealing from the doting boss who'd treated him so well.

"Does anyone want to tell me what the fuck just happened here?" snarled Billy, slowly and quietly, spinning around in his chair to stare up menacingly at the two men behind him. They hated it when Billy talked this way. They'd seen his practised prelude to violence many times before and knew where it was heading.

"Cat got your fucking tongues, has it, gentlemen?"

They stayed silent for fear of saying the wrong thing and sending him into a rage any sooner than was necessary. Heads were bowed and Derek and Antony stared at the ground that they hoped would soon swallow them up.

"I'll tell you what's happened. I've been taken for a cunt, that's what. That wanker burning that fucking doll or whatever it was outside here was just a diversion to get you meatheads out of the office so that young Mr Brett could steal me fucking money, wasn't it?

And you two fell for it like a right couple of numpties. As if you were ever going to catch him anyway, you fat fucks. If you didn't spend your whole time stuffing your faces with pies and shit we wouldn't be sitting here, right now, having this fucking conversation, would we?"

Derek and Anthony stood shamefaced and continued to look at their laces, praying for divine intervention. They had no response to offer. Billy was right. They'd failed at their jobs and the empty safe and images on the screen were testament to their incompetence.

"You two had one fucking job to do - just protect this business and stop cunts like this lot from ripping me off. So, what do you do? You rush off down the fucking road like a couple of girl guides just because some cunt burns a fucking, whatever it was, outside. Some cunt you had no chance of catching, because you're a couple of fat twats who couldn't go half a round with Mary Poppins.

Am I wrong lads?

And you left Master fucking Brett here by himself, in me office, with the safe wide open and no one to keep an eye on the slippery cunt. And, as a result, he gets to leg it down the road like Linford fucking Christie with all me cash, while you two useless dough balls waddle off in the opposite direction.

Have I got this right boys?" growled Billy, reaching for another whiskey.

"Well, have I then?" he asked again coldly, staring at a frozen image of Buster Brett making his escape.

"Fucking answer me then, you useless couple of cunts!" he suddenly snapped.

"We'll catch 'em, boss, don't you worry about that," mumbled Antony unconvincingly, avoiding eye contact with his boss.

"We'll find out who the bloke in the suit is too. We'll get it sorted," added Derek, lamely.

"We'll get them if it's the last thing we ever do," continued Anthony, wishing immediately that he'd kept his mouth shut. It was clear to everyone in the room that it was likely to be the last thing they ever did, regardless of whether they caught Buster or not.

Billy stood up and turned to face the boys, his face crimson with rage.

"Shut the fuck up, you useless fat fucks. Just find Buster and all that stuff he's nicked. And the little git in the suit too. Get those tiny little brain cells of yours working for a change. Work out where Buster is and bring him back here so I can proper hurt the devious little shit.

But first off, make yourselves useful and arrange for someone to get the guns from me loft. I think we might be needing them when we find him. And don't you dare say a fucking word to Mrs Murphy while you're about it, whatever you do. Last thing I need is her fussing around, trying to stick her nose in."

The boys hesitated for a second longer than was good for them.

"Do you fucking understand?"

The boys winced, nodded and continued to stare at their shoes.

Billy sat back at his desk, calming momentarily.

"In the meantime, I need to work out exactly what he's taken and get changed out of this golfing clobber. So, which one of you dickheads picked me suit up from Eastwoods?" he asked, glancing at the boys.

The blank looks on their startled faces were enough to start the penny dropping.

"Please, please, tell me one of you useless fat fucks picked up me suit."

Derek and Antony remained silent and continued to stare at the floor, not sure how to answer their boss's odd questions. Why was he worrying about a suit when he'd just been betrayed and robbed by the person he trusted the most?

"For fuck's sake!" exploded Billy, realising exactly what had happened. He slammed his fists on the desk before punching the screen so hard that it was sent flying, smashed and useless, into the corner of the room.

"Get downstairs now. Bring up whatever's left of that thing that got burned and tell Eastwoods I want a copy of their CCTV up here within half an hour or I'll come down there meself and burn their fucking shop down."

The boys snapped into action. They had one last chance to put things right and save their skins. Calls were made, guns collected and a new screen was borrowed. Footage was scoured and Billy soon learned that his suit had been collected by the same man who'd then burned it in front of the pub. The exact same individual whose blood had caused it to be sent to the dry cleaners in the first place. A man who owed them money but who had no obvious links to Buster Brett, as far as they could make out. He learned that Buster had run down Upper Street like a man possessed before disappearing into the tube station, most probably on his way to Gatwick Airport.

And with the tenacity of a terrier shaking a twitching rabbit between its jaws, Billy Murphy started to work out how to find and punish the people who'd stolen from him and ruined what should have been his best Wednesday in years.

But most of all he wanted to destroy the boy who'd betrayed his trust. Buster Brett, the one he'd welcomed into his home and shared his table with. The favourite he'd groomed, protected and rewarded. The son from another world he'd allowed to get closer than any of his own kids had ever managed. The person who now had to be hunted down, held to account and made to pay with his life.

Billy was not a man inclined to analyse his feelings. Long ago he'd learned that it was best to keep them suppressed and buttoned up tight. He preferred to express himself through the simple media of anger and violence. But if he had allowed himself a greater understanding of his emotional workings, he'd have realised that his heart had been broken by the young boy from Brighton and, as a consequence, pure cold unadulterated hatred had now begun to coarse freely through his old veins.

Chapter 12

Ewalina Kowalska was waiting for her man. Standing discreetly beneath the awning of a busy snack bar, she studied the stream of passengers passing through the automated barriers and onto the bustling concourse of Brighton Station. To any casual observer, she looked like any well-heeled young woman waiting patiently for her date or friends to arrive. Alert, watchful and searching for a particular face in the evening crowd.

Of no interest to her were the tourists, with their trashy clothes, rucksacks and guidebooks. Their day return tickets were snatched away by the automated turnstile as they spilled off the platform and disappeared into the night.

Her attention was focused on the suit-clad male commuters who carefully swiped and retained their valuable season tickets, ready for the next trip to the London office. He'd be putting it safely away in his fat designer wallet, next to his cards and cash. She was sure he'd have plenty of money and the cards would be platinum or gold. Nothing less prestigious would do as she had standards to maintain and didn't want to waste her time on somebody who had to worry about what he owed. Her man used his credit cards to pay for expensive purchases, not juggle his debts.

She scanned the passengers' faces. Some were happy, others blank or tired. She was sure that her man would be exhausted. It was to be expected and her most common occupational hazard. After all, that lovely money didn't earn itself. He'd be tired out from his high-pressure job and might have had a quick beer on the train to help him relax. But he'd soon be pleased to meet her and, if he was reluctant, she'd step up her game. She had techniques and strategies for every outcome.

A noisy hen party of drunken plain girls, carrying between them an anatomically correct inflatable man doll, held up the flow at the barrier. With her view blocked, Ewalina began to panic at the prospect of missing her special date. All tattoos and hooped earrings, the girls had created their own microclimate of cigarette smoke, cheap perfume and foul language.

Get out of my way you stupid bitches. I've been standing in the cold for three hours, I'm freezing and now you're ruining it for me. She hated the local women with their fat ankles, bad skin and complete lack of manners.

Each of them wore a pink cowboy hat, matching feather boa and a cropped T-shirt printed with a bawdy slogan berating the bride-to-be's less than chaste reputation. As much as she loved her adoptive country, this was a tradition she'd never understood. Ewalina stared at them in disgust. The girls had clearly forgotten about the requirement to present their tickets at the barrier and in the confusion, they'd blocked the way for a throng of impatient travellers. A mass of bodies piled up in their wake, irritated by their drunken trashiness.

As they fumbled through handbags full of cigarettes, half-bottles of convenience-store vodka and bargain makeup, trying to find the right part of their Croydon to Brighton day returns, frustration began to build. Ewalina stepped forward to improve her view. It was dangerous to reveal herself to the station's CCTV, but it was a waste of time being there at all if she couldn't find her guy. The crowd, held up by the girls, pushed and complained. Voices were raised and insults began to fly.

Tired after a long day and not wanting any more problems, a uniformed member of station staff opened a side barrier and the hens stumbled gratefully out, screaming and laughing as they teetered away on their high heels, eager for the night ahead and oblivious to the cursing commuters in their wake. Good riddance to cheap nasty trash, thought Ewalina.

She could see from the arrivals board that another train was due at 21.23. It was only another three minutes to wait. What difference would that make after all the time she'd already invested?

Anticipating the rumble of an arriving train beneath her feet, she felt relieved that her long wait would soon be up. One way or another, she'd be out of the cold within minutes. Her last chance to make something of the evening would soon be pulling up at Platform 4.

Chapter 13

Detective Sergeant Samuel Edge's tea had gone cold. The promised biscuits and sugar had failed to arrive and now the mug of murky grey liquid sat defiantly on the desk, forcing him to concede that the evening had probably been a waste of time.

His earlier child-like enthusiasm for the zoom, tilt and pan controls of the railway control room's CCTV system had evaporated after an hour of trying to make sense of the sixteen wall-mounted screens. They covered every angle of the platforms, concourse, forecourt and retail areas, but the system was over-complicated and daunting. The five minutes of instruction he'd been given by the Station Manager, keen to leave at the end of his shift, had been rushed and inadequate. The guy had promised biscuits and pastries, but had immediately forgotten, leaving him to slowly deflate.

He'd briefly considered warming his tea in the microwave in the corner of the room, but even that now looked daunting at this late stage of the day.

The control room, high above the station concourse, would once have afforded its occupants a grandstand view of the comings and goings of railway life. The ebb and flow of passengers alighting and boarding could all have been seen clearly from up here, along with the goodbyes and greetings, loitering, waving and waiting. But the windows had long since become dirty and obscured as the desire to record, rewind and review with ever more complicated technology had made them obsolete. The room was now a tatty, cold and lonely place to be on a Wednesday night.

Samuel felt underwhelmed. He'd watched the screens for as long as he could but it reminded him of kicking at an ant's nest when he was a kid. Too many individuals to focus on and nothing specific to grab his attention. He desperately wanted to do a good job and catch what the local newspaper, The Argus, had dubbed the Bondage Stalker, but tiredness, frustration and now hunger were taking hold.

He decided to give it ten more minutes before calling it a day. He'd debrief his team in the pub and call his boss with the bad news once he'd had his first pint. Tonight had always been a long shot, but DI Weston was unlikely to be sympathetic and Samuel needed all the Dutch courage he could drink.

The Bondage Stalker wasn't an entirely accurate description of the person he was trying to catch, but there was a grain of truth in the headline and it had caused a ripple of panic amongst the local population. Eight men in nine weeks. All robbed in their own homes or the city centre hotel rooms they'd been persuaded to rent by a smartly dressed woman who'd befriended them in the close proximity of Brighton and a variety of other local railway stations. She'd been variously described as Dutch, German, Polish and even Welsh by her victims. The fact that she probably wasn't a local girl was one of the few facts his team could agree on.

On each occasion, they'd been chatted up and charmed before being spiked and rendered incapable. They'd then been stripped of their cash, cards, watches and anything else that was valuable and easy to carry away. Some had also been persuaded to transfer funds to a Polish bank account in their befuddled state. Several of the victims had woken up to find themselves tied to their own beds. Samuel Edge and his team were of the professional opinion that this was simply a precautionary step taken by the woman keen to keep herself safe whilst searching for anything further to steal. However, once the Argus had got hold of this tasty little morsel, they'd relished the opportunity to inject her actions with a sinister sexual motive and the Bondage Stalker had been born.

A week later, the nationals picked up on the story and the Brighton Bondage Stalker acquired an infamy that was making Samuel's life hell. His entire working life was now devoted to finding this woman who was getting more notorious and problematic by the day.

In reality, there were likely to be many more victims who hadn't dared to come forward. Their shame, embarrassment and the strong desire not to have their wives find out would have made them hold their tongues and nurse their bruised egos in private. And now, despite the best efforts of Sussex Police, the perpetrator was proving impossible to apprehend. No useful DNA had been recovered from the scenes and there were mixed and conflicting descriptions from witnesses whose accounts were clouded by alcohol, shame and regret.

But now, the bosses were getting impatient for a result. Memes had appeared on social media and the police were being mocked for their apparent inaction. Council chiefs were stressing about a hit to tourism and even the local MP had publicly demanded action. The Chief Constable had made a few stern calls and in turn the pressure had come to rest on the weary shoulders of DS Samuel Edge and his team of detectives.

As he wondered whether he needed to turn anything off or lock up before leaving the control room, his Nokia Airwave radio crackled to life and the screen lit up with the number of one of his two plain clothes colleagues on the concourse below. They'd been using a back-to-back channel specifically allocated for this evening's operation in order to free themselves from the busy and distracting chitchat of the regular divisional communications system.

"Sarge, you free to talk?"

"Go ahead, Richie, what's up?"

"How long you thinking about giving this tonight? I'm not moaning or anything but I'm freezing my nuts off down here and I could do with a brew. Plus, I've not seen anyone doing anything vaguely suspicious. Apart from some pissed bloke who asked me if I could sell him a bag of weed. Over."

Resisting the temptation to roll his eyes at the lackadaisical attitude of the young Special Constable, whose earlier enthusiasm in the warm briefing room had been more impressive, Samuel replied,

"I'm thinking another couple of minutes. There's a train due in at 21.23, but I think that'll be the last one for us. All stragglers and pissheads after that. Plus, all the reported incidents so far started before 21.00. Did you get that, Gary?"

"Yes, Skipper," replied DC Gary Evans, who was also freezing, but knew better than to mention it over the airwaves. It pleased him that the young Special often spoke before he'd had a chance to think. Saved him having to say anything. Out of the mouth of babes and all that.

Richie and Gary clearly thought they'd been dealt the rough end of the operation, thought Samuel. Ninety minutes of standing against the windows of the ticket office, coffee shop and then Marks and Spencer, rotating positions whilst looking out for anyone who might possibly resemble the Stalker, must have left them drained. It was bitterly cold and there was a cutting wind howling through the station.

"I've got eyes on another female who roughly fits the description," chipped in Gary, clearly energised by what he'd seen.

"She's under the awning of the snack bar, so you probably can't see her up there. I'm just moving a bit closer to get a proper look. I think she's checking out who's arriving. Could be her. Could be nothing. I've had about ten tonight just like her, all done up for their dates and pissed off that they've been made to wait in the freezing cold. She's just looked at her phone. Probably just her fella saying he'll be there in a bit."

"Let me know if she moves," replied Samuel, gauging from his colleagues' tone that he'd got about as much as he was going to get from the lads tonight.

Gary Evans was a twenty-five-year veteran and his opinion was always to be valued. A couple of divorces and a messy disciplinary file had meant that he'd never taken his sergeant's exams. He'd remained a constable for his entire career, despite being one of the sharpest officers on the force. If Gary thought that this could be their girl, then it was worth hanging around for a few more minutes.

"Sam, quick, look at your screens now. She's just moved out from under the awnings. There's been a kerfuffle at the barriers and it's unnerved her for some reason. I'm going to move in to get a better look."

Samuel spotted the girl immediately. On one monitor he could see the back of her head. Another showed a smaller image of her taken front-on by a camera on the far side of the concourse. Two others showed a bunch of rough-looking women in cowboy hats, carrying what appeared to be a blow-up doll.

The girl was about the right height and build. She was well dressed with hair that matched at least two of the witnesses' reports. But there was nothing distinctive to make her stand out from all the other similar girls who'd passed through the station that evening. She was clearly alert and waiting for someone, but unless that person was a potential victim and they were somehow lucky enough to catch her in the act, with the drugs she used to dope her victims, this was going to be a difficult case to crack.

"Keep your eyes on her Gary. There's another train's going to be here in a minute. Let's see if she goes for anyone getting off that. If not, we'll wrap it up and get somewhere warm. Richie, can you see who we're talking about down there?"

"Yes, Sarge. The classy-looking blond bird in the boots," replied Richie, using language that wasn't strictly training school approved.

"Looks like a proper syrup on her head."

The daft lad could be right thought Samuel, as he listened on his earpiece, trying to conceal a smile. He knew a wig when he saw one. The hair was just a little too shiny. It didn't hang quite as naturally as it should. The colour wasn't a precise match to her skin tone.

He could see Gary move through the crowd to within a few feet of the girl. It could be nothing, but his years of experience told him that they might be on to something. Tingling with anticipation, and his copper's nose fully attuned to the girl's every move and expression, Samuel watched her as she waited for the train to arrive at Platform 4.

Chapter 14

Sitting on the connecting service from Haywards Heath, Buster felt alone and desperately unprepared. He could have been flying away without a care in the world if he hadn't tipped his life on its head. He would have been on a beach within a few hours, with a drink in his hand, and nothing more taxing to trouble him than pulling a girl and tending his tan. Instead, he was about to arrive at Brighton with no certainty of escape and a high probability of receiving a beating.

The opportunity to wallow in regret was cut short by the sobering sight of Preston Park station as it slipped past the carriage window. There were no more stops now. He'd run out of time to think or worry. He'd be in Brighton in less than two minutes. If he could make it off the platform without running into Billy's welcoming party, then perhaps, he could start to put things right.

It felt like a long shot. He knew that he'd put too much faith in Dexter, but it was too late now to do anything about it. He wished there had been someone more sensible he could have called, but there wasn't. His friend's voice indicated that he was stoned, drunk, or both. The moment that conversation finished, he'd turned off the phone, removed the SIM, snapped it in two and pushed the pieces down the back of the seat. He was sure that Billy would have an expert on hand to track the signal if he kept it with him. He felt naked and alone without a working mobile, but better that than carrying a beacon for his pursuers to follow.

The train slowly entered the curve of Brighton station and his pulse began to race. He prayed that only his friend, and no one else, would be waiting. He thought about what to do if Billy's boys were there. He'd bolt out through one of the downhill exits. He'd try to lose them in the tight-knit streets of the North Laine area. He'd ditch the binbag and hope that the boys down here were as unfit as the ones he worked with in London.

As the train slid silently towards its final stopping point, the other passengers gathered their belongings and made their way to the doors. Buster tucked his tie into his shirt and checked his shoelaces. He re-tied them tightly with a double bow and wished he'd thought to change into his new trainers.

Once on the platform, he allowed the crowd to surge in front of him as he walked slowly towards the barrier. He held back as long as he could, trying to see if any of Billy's people were there for him, watching from the shadows and ready to pounce. He tried to scan every face waiting on the concourse, but there were too many to assess.

As the crowd melted away, he felt exposed and terrified. Standing out from the drunks, the elderly and the other stragglers he found himself walking with, Buster looked everywhere for danger. The relative comfort of the train had been replaced with a sense of absolute vulnerability on the cold and windy platform. As he approached the turnstile his heart was pounding. Clasping his ticket, time slowed, events blurred and adrenaline took over.

Chapter 15

Ewalina watched, alert and poised, as the passengers from the 21.23 flowed along the platform. Nobody caught her eye. Her senses bristled as she analysed the faces. There was absolutely nothing here for her. Sensing defeat, her confidence started to crumble.

The stragglers from the train reached the head of the platform. They were always the ones burdened with kids and the heaviest suitcases. The sick and the old, mixed up with the drunks who'd fallen asleep. None of these interested Ewalina. She watched in disgust as a man leant against the side of the locomotive and urinated.

She checked her watch and started to walk towards the exit. This wasn't her night and it was time to go home and get warm. Taking one final glance, she noticed a lone man on the platform. He was unusual. He was odd. He was walking slowly and staring at the concourse, as if reluctant to leave. He was wheeling a smart suitcase in one hand and carrying what looked like a black bin liner in the other. He looked unhappy and apprehensive. He was sweaty and pale. His tie was tucked into his shirt and he didn't look very well. Surely this couldn't be her man?

Taking a closer look, it was obvious that his shoes and suit were expensive. A good sign. His demeanour and the bin bag were bad signs. What kind of man took a refuse sack on a train? He certainly didn't look as if he was up for a good time. He met hardly any of the criteria she normally sought. However, it was late and she had bills to pay, so what the hell she thought, she'd give it a go.

As he checked through the turnstile, Ewalina became Eve and prepared to do what she did best. The automatic barrier swallowed his ticket, which was another bad sign, but by now she'd committed and there was no turning back.

Although she had no idea what his name was or anything else about him, the nervous-looking guy with the sweaty face was about to become Ewalina's latest man.

As he walked towards the exit, she slipped in behind him and dropped a crumpled £20 note on the ground, before quickly stooping to pick it up.

"Excuse me, excuse me, you dropped this," she said warmly with a practised smile, catching up with her mark and trying to pass him the cash.

#####

"Fuck off, will you! I'm not interested," shouted Buster wildly, as a woman he'd never seen before tried to push a note into his hand.

This was not the time for a random stranger to be making an approach. This was the last thing he needed. He was sure that he hadn't dropped any money, but glanced at his case, just to be sure.

Again, she tried to slip the money into his hand as they progressed awkwardly across the concourse.

"It's not my twenty, now just piss off, will you, and leave me alone."

He knew he was being rude, but he didn't care. He didn't have time for this. He just needed to get out of the station and meet Dexter without any unnecessary complications.

The woman looked startled by his words. Her expression was puzzled, as if she'd been expecting a different reaction. But he really did need her to leave him alone.

"I said fuck off," he snapped again, losing patience with the persistent stranger.

"What part of that don't you understand?"

She looked shocked, but still kept apace.

"Get away from me, you nutter," he yelled, picking up his stride.

"I was only trying to give you back the money you dropped!" she replied, full of indignation.

"What's the big deal?"

As he broke into a jog, so did she, seemingly unwilling to give up. Whoever this person was, he knew that he had to leave her behind. Instinctively, he started to run, unsure if this was part of some deadly trap that he'd not foreseen.

Chapter 16

Before Samuel could think any further, the excited voice of Richie filled his earpiece.

"The bloke who's just come through. I bloody know him. It's Buster Brett. We were at uni together. I'm sure that's him. I saw him on telly last night. He works for some massive criminal in London. I can't bloody believe it. He's a right bell-end."

On those words, Samuel leapt to his feet, his heart pounding. This was a major development. He'd also watched the news last night and cursed on hearing that slippery old Billy Murphy had avoided getting locked up. He'd followed the career of this unpleasant mobster for years, the man responsible for huge swathes of criminality across Brighton.

Although he didn't recognise the figure on the CCTV himself, if this really was the arrival of one of his closest lieutenants, right under their noses, it was a critical piece of intelligence. They needed to make the most of their good fortune.

"Ok, guys, stand down on the girl. If this is Murphy's bloke then we need to find out what he's up to and why he's here. And if we can think of any grounds for a stop, let's do it. Let's see what he's got in that bloody bag. We need to get this right though. He loves nothing better than getting his lawyers to tie us up in knots. Both of you follow him and I'll get the car. Don't let him know you're onto him, whatever you do."

And with that, Samuel bolted out of the station control room, leaving the lights ablaze and the door unlocked. He bounded down the external metal stairs three at a time and raced out onto the street to retrieve the unmarked car they'd left parked nearby.

Gary's voice rattled excitedly in his earpiece.

"Skip, you're not going to believe this, but I think Murphy's fella just got picked up by the Stalker. I can't be sure, but that's what it looks like to me. She's gone and chosen the wrong fucking mark there."

"Are you having a laugh?" Samuel responded, trying to manoeuvre the car out of a particularly tight space.

"That's what it looks like. They're just leaving the station now. He's started to run for some reason and she's sticking with him"

"OK, stay with them. I'm in the car now. Get on the divisional channel and let comms know we might need some backup."

Following Buster across the concourse, trying to keep up as he accelerated away, Richie made direct eye contact with his old college mate as he momentarily glanced back. Despite the distance between them and the baseball cap rammed tightly on his head, he knew instantly that he'd been rumbled.

"Stop! Police!" he shouted instinctively, to everyone's surprise and his colleagues' absolute horror.

Chapter 17

As Buster clattered down the ramp below the station forecourt, fighting with his luggage and making as much haste as he possibly could, he was relieved to spot Dexter's battered old van in the gloom. It was sitting half on the pavement and its lights were off. There was nothing coming from the exhaust to suggest that it was primed for a quick getaway. He could make out his friend's arm lolling out of the driver's side window, with what looked like a joint in his hand.

"Dexter! Start the engine! We need to go!" he screamed from a distance, to the alarm of several passers-by.

He glanced over his shoulder, but the crazy woman was still there, two paces behind, frantically trying to keep up. She looked focussed and hard. In the rush, her hair had slipped off her head. He still had no idea why she was there or who she could be.

In his panic, Buster misjudged the momentum of his suitcase and it slammed heavily into the corroded flank of the van, sending flakes of rust cascading onto the tarmac beneath.

"Let me in! Open the bloody thing will you!" he yelled, unable to get the front passenger door to open.

"The lock's bust, mate," mouthed Dexter, clearly startled by the look of fear on his old pal's face. Buster could see him turning the key in the ignition, but nothing was happening. The reassuring rattle of an air-cooled Volkswagen engine failed to fill his ears.

"Get in through the side," shouted Dexter, pointing frantically to the handle of the sliding rear door. He looked horrified at the sight of the agitated and dangerous-looking mad woman who'd just caught up with his friend.

Buster struggled to slide the door open. It took all his strength to shift it. The slope meant gravity was against him. He threw his bags inside and used his knee to block the crazy woman, who was inexplicably trying to clamber in too. He wondered if she was having a psychotic episode or had simply mistaken him for someone else. She was shouting at him in a foreign language and was turning out to be much stronger than her slender build would suggest.

Dexter watched the commotion in his rear-view mirror. He turned the ignition key again. The engine didn't respond and all he managed to do was illicit a series of clicks and whines from deep inside the old dashboard. Perhaps he shouldn't have left the lights on while he was waiting. The woman had now barged past his friend and was wedged on the backseat with a look of fierce determination on her face.

"Get out of this van, right now!" shouted Buster, foregoing any formal greeting or introductions. He tied to pull the woman's hand away from the internal handle she was gripping with all her strength. Her white knuckles contrasted sharply with her red manicured nails. Rather than cooperating, she kicked back sharply with her heel, narrowly missing his face.

"Dexter, please just drive, will you?!" wheezed Buster. He was out of shape and struggling for breath. The sprint to the van and his back seat scrap were clearly taking their toll.

"Get off me now!" screamed the woman, as she took another swipe.

"And you, hippy in the front, get a fucking move on! Don't just sit there!"

In his mirror, Dexter could see Buster locked in a stalemate with the girl. They pushed, pulled and wrestled each other, with neither of them managing to gain the upper hand. Both were red in the face and sweating profusely.

Dexter did as he was told. Pushing his foot on the clutch and releasing the handbrake, he allowed the van to start rolling down the hill in neutral. Slowly at first, the VW gradually picked up momentum.

Despite the struggle, Buster sensed the motion. The engine wasn't running. Dexter was trying to bump-start the van. The idiot was going to get them killed. He released his grip on the girl for a second and looked out through the front windscreen.

He knew that the brakes and steering wouldn't work properly until the engine kicked in. He watched a group of drunks on the left-hand pavement, willing them not to step into the path of the silent-running VW. When the van had acquired just enough speed, Dexter put the gear stick into second and lifted the clutch. It was a relief as the van lurched and engine spluttered and wheezed into life.

As it did, the girl in the back slapped Buster firmly in the face.

"How dare you try to kick me out of this van!" she yelled.

"How dare you get in it! Who the fuck are you anyway? Why are you still even here?"

"Don't you talk to *me* like that!" she screamed.

As the row rumbled on, Dexter navigated the old VW back to where it had been parked just half an hour before. He kept checking his mirror to make sure they hadn't been followed. By chance, the space he'd recently vacated was still free. The Audi had driven away making it easy to negotiate the van into the double-size gap.

Turning the engine off, he turned to face the two pugilists in the back. He gathered his thoughts and took a deep breath.

"Will you two just shut the fuck up for a second and tell me what the hell's going on?" he shouted, as loud as he could manage, immediately grabbing their attention.

For the first time since their short journey together had begun, there was a moment of stunned silence in the van.

"Dexter, mate, I've got absolutely no idea who this lunatic is," wheezed Buster, trying to catch his breath and nursing a cheek still reddened from when it had been slapped.

"I almost got caught by the old bill when I arrived at the station. They were waiting for me near the turnstiles. I vaguely recognised one of them. It's a long story, but I think my boss might have tipped them off. This nutter tried talking to me or something and when I went to run, so did she."

"And then, when I was trying to kick her out of the van, you started driving. I didn't even hear the engine start until we were half-way down the road."

Ewalina listened indignantly, before cutting Buster off in mid-flow.

"You almost got caught by the police? You think they were there for you do, you dumb fuck? They were there for me, obviously. That's why I ran. Why would the police be there for you, you idiot? And I wasn't running with you. I was running to get away. You just happened to be going the same way as me. What the fuck's wrong with you people?"

"So why did you try and get in my van?" added a bemused Dexter, all too aware that this exotic stranger could be dangerous within the close confines of the vehicle.

"Because it looked like the best way of getting away. You think I'm going to stop and order a fucking cab, do you, when I've got the cops running after me?"

"But there weren't any cops."

"How the fuck was I supposed to know that?! They were in the station, that's for sure. One of them was waving his badge around and shouting like a massive wanker."

"So, why would the cops be after you?" asked Buster, his wits beginning to return after the craziness of the last few minutes. He was beginning to see some sense in the madness at the station. His apprenticeship with Billy had taught him to recognise a hustler if nothing else.

"Was it something to do with that trick you tried to pull with the £20 note?"

Ewalina looked stumped for a split second. It was just enough for Buster to see the truth behind her eyes.

"It was, wasn't it?! I knew it! So, you think the cops were after you for pulling your cheap scam shit, don't you, darling? You really have no idea what you've got yourself mixed up with here sweet heart, you really don't. No idea whatsoever."

"I don't pull cheap tricks, you fat fuck. Do you read the papers? Have you watched the news? There's nothing cheap about what I do."

Before she could open the door and escape into the night, the blank, stoned face of Dexter Ward, started to smile. Somewhere deep inside his addled, stressed-out brain, some synapses snapped together and joined up the dots. The local news he'd watched the night before and the events of this evening came crashing together, causing his mouth to open and the following excited words to come tumbling from his lips.

"You're that fucking stalker, aren't you?! Buster, she's the Bondage Stalker. For fuck's sake, she's all over the bloody news."

Buster had no idea what Dexter was talking about. He hadn't had time to watch the news recently - unless it was related to Billy's latest antics. He was busy trying to work out if this crazy small-time con woman, who'd thrown his already shaky plan into disarray, had made his position better or worse. If there was any advantage to be taken from her continued presence in the van, then he needed to make the most of it.

Ewalina's shoulders slumped. She knew the game was up

For a moment the van became quiet. Buster was thinking and so was Ewalina. Dexter was just cold, confused and in desperate need of a smoke and a pint. He was also in awe of the pretty celebrity criminal he'd just become acquainted with.

"I've got to get off the street, Dexter," said Buster seriously, breaking the silence.

"I've done something really awful and I need to tell you about it."

"It's me they're after!" snapped Ewalina, still indignant that her version of reality wasn't being accepted.

Ignoring her, Buster continued to talk.

"Dexter, can we just go to your place for a bit and work out what to do? You can come too, I suppose," he added cautiously, still unsure what to make of the girl.

And for want of a better plan, that's exactly what they did. Walking quickly through the quiet residential streets of Kemptown, they followed Dexter back to his block. Glancing behind as he went, fearful that he'd be spotted, Buster couldn't wait to get out of view.

Frustratingly, Dexter insisted on stopping to buy some beers on the way, seemingly indifferent to the urgency of the situation. The wait for him to pay and make small talk with the shop owner was excruciating. Buster wanted to tear his hair out and strangle his friend as they endured this unwarranted delay. He only started to feel calmer as they climbed the stairs to the flat.

"By the way, mate, removing the number plates from your van was a nice touch," he commented, trying to look for positives in the chaos of the last half hour.

"It was the first thing I noticed when I was running down the slope to meet you. There was bound to be CCTV at the station, but without plates, the Old Bill will struggle to identify your van. Nice one, mate. Big respect. Your clever move's bought us some time."

Dexter smiled but hadn't got the faintest clue what his old friend was talking about. If the plates weren't attached to his van, then he had absolutely no idea where they could be.

"No worries, Buster. Anything to help a mate."

Chapter 18

All good police officers know that criminals get caught when persistence, hard graft and luck come together at exactly the right time. But, on this cold Wednesday evening Samuel Edge had all of these in the bag, apart from the one over which he had absolutely no control. His luck had deserted him the moment he bolted for the car.

All he could do now was review the damning CCTV footage ten minutes later, when it was all too late. Sitting with his officers in front of the bank of monitors, they hung their heads and watched a woman in a wig and heels run with a man across the station. Not necessarily running with him, but certainly next to him, her hairpiece had become dislodged by the exertion. It was unclear from the images whether they knew each other or had just been thrown together by their mutual desire to evade the police.

Samuel noted that if his officers hadn't been tripped and floored by a random drunk, then they might have caught their suspects. The man running with the suitcase had accidentally slammed it into the back of an inebriated man's already unsteady knees while he'd been gamely chatting up an entire hen party. He'd been sent spinning and reeling straight into the officers' path.

In the sprawl of bodies, boas, foul language and spilled vodka, the only two people of any interest that night were able to slip away. His team didn't make the stop, nor did they get to see what was in the bin bag and Samuel now felt the weight of the world on his tired shoulders.

They watched further grainy footage of the man and woman running down Trafalgar Street towards an old VW camper van parked beneath the forecourt. The van had no rear registration plate and the monochrome playback made it difficult to work out what colour it was. Maybe orange, but possibly green was their best guess. Brighton was a town full of old campers, thought Samuel.

The man jumped in and so did the woman a few seconds later. Perhaps they did know each other after all. The old van pulled away with a sluggishness that contrasted sharply with their suspect's sprint to reach it. It was driven by someone with long hair and skinny arms covered in tattoo ink.

"Lads, I think we can all agree that tonight's been an unmitigated fuck up," he said, trying to keep things professional and resisting the sarcasm he felt burning on the tip of his tongue.

The cold station control room made the failure of the night seem even more bleak and the playback only served to confirm the ineptness of their response. They each knew they'd played their parts in the evening's dismal conclusion.

"Richie, I think you let your nerves get the better of you just now. What on earth were you thinking by shouting out like that? We're going to have to review if you're really suitable for these sort of ops in the future."

"I'm sorry, Sarge, but I think I got carried away when I saw it was Buster Brett. When he recognised me, I suppose I just panicked. I didn't want him to get away. I'm so sorry. I didn't think the girl would run as well."

Samuel could see that Richie was close to tears, so he reigned in his desire to give him the biggest bollocking of his short career.

"You messed up. There's no way of sugar-coating it. You did something stupid and you blew our cover. I know we all do ridiculous things occasionally, but that was off the scale, mate."

Samuel could see the tears welling up in Richie's eyes.

"We let the Stalker, and I'm pretty sure it was her, get away. And to make things worse, we allowed one of Billy Murphy's top boys to slip through our fingers when that bloody bin bag gave us the perfect grounds for a stop. For all we know, it was stuffed with drugs.

On the other hand, we've some pretty clear images of the woman, so that's some consolation. Now we need to establish her connection to Brett, if there is one. So, Richie, you've got your work cut out if you want to make up for earlier."

The young Special nodded, pleased to hear he was still on the team for the time being.

As he continued his debrief, Samuel fretted over what to tell his boss. They'd missed a trick tonight and there was no easy way of hiding it. Intelligence was useful, but arrests were what the management demanded and that's what he'd be judged on. DI Weston was a stickler for detail and he'd want to know how two suspects, under close observation by three officers, had managed to get away. He'd have to justify his decision to get the car and explain how an inexperienced officer had been allowed to blow the operation.

He might even want to review the CCTV if the conversation went really badly. Samuel shuddered at the thought of having to watch the footage of his men sprawled on the floor in a tangle of hen party bawdiness, with his incredulous boss spitting feathers over his shoulder.

As soon as they'd copied the CCTV coverage onto memory sticks and driven back to the nick, he let the lads go. They were keen to have a pint and Samuel needed to find a quiet space alone to phone the DI. This wasn't going to be an easy call. He'd accentuate the positive and try to play down the lack of arrests. He took a minute to gather his thoughts, before dialling the number. He put his game face on and tried to sound as upbeat as he could when his boss answered the phone.

"We've had a really positive development this evening, sir. I think we've managed to identify the Stalker, which is great news," said Samuel professionally, trying to put the best possible spin on events.

"But you didn't make an arrest?" came the immediate irritable, dour reply, cutting straight to the chase.

"Not exactly, sir, but we were very close. It was all a bit odd because she interacted with one of Billy Murphy's people, a bloke called Buster Brett."

The DI's tone changed immediately.

"What? When exactly did this happen? Where was he? Was he on a train? Where are they now? I need you to find him… them… as quickly as possible."

Samuel was pleased by the Inspector's interest in Buster Brett. He'd been ready to take a lecturing for letting the Stalker get away, but somehow, he'd managed to dodge that bullet.

"Don't let this go cold, Samuel. I'm guessing they won't have got too far. Not in that vehicle. I want you and your team to work through the night if necessary. I'll authorise overtime of course. Get on ANPR and do whatever you need to do. But I do stress that we need to find this man, and the woman, of course. Call me if there's a development. Anytime. I'm relying on you. No more embarrassing mistakes, please."

The line went dead and Samuel felt relieved. He wasn't sure his team would be too impressed at the prospect of being paid time and a third, but at least the call had gone better than expected. Whilst that was welcome, the obvious downside was that they'd have to crack on with their inquiries well into the night. It made operational sense, so Samuel hadn't mentioned that he'd already let his colleagues slip away.

He called Gary in the pub and explained that they needed to drain their glasses and get back. They'd only had a pint each, so it wouldn't be a problem. They'd buy some mints on the way. Samuel softened the blow by telling him that the DI had authorised overtime, but he could tell from the flat response that he'd rather be sinking another beer. Despite his reluctance, he said he'd be back in fifteen minutes. Richie chimed in, saying that he wanted to come too, keen to make amends.

Samuel switched on his computer and waited for it to fire up. The DI was right. It was likely that the camper van would be parked up somewhere close by with a warm engine and a full set of clues as to the whereabouts of the people who'd just used it.

He plugged the memory stick holding the station's CCTV into the computer. The grainy images of the van in the underpass didn't offer much enlightenment at first sight. Just a rusty old van with no number plate. His copper's brain told him that there would be clues in these images that would only become apparent if he thought hard and interpreted the information in the right way.

In the ten minutes of peace he had to himself before the lads returned from the pub, he stared and thought. And as he looked, tiny grains of information sprang from the screen. As they coalesced into larger fragments, he could feel the fire reignite in his belly.

The suspects may have got away and made him look foolish, but they'd left clues. They'd probably be sitting pretty right now, thinking they were safe. But Samuel was on to them. They weren't as smart as they thought they were. With a bit of luck, he'd be knocking at their door very soon. And with a few clicks of his mouse and a tap or two on his keyboard, a virtual world opened up shining a thin shaft of light onto their fleeing footsteps.

Chapter 19

As soon as he finished talking to his sergeant, DI Simon Weston went to the kitchen and poured himself a large glass of wine from a bottle his wife had left in the fridge. He drank it in one go and then poured another. He needed to steady his nerves.

Standing quietly for a moment, he checked to make sure he could still hear his wife in the living room. She was laughing along loudly to a show on the television, seemingly unaware that he'd even left the sofa. His teenage son was upstairs, glued to his Xbox and unlikely to come down anytime soon.

Confident that he wouldn't be disturbed, he stood on a chair and slid open the small drawer in the unit above his double-stacked ovens. It was too high to be practical and had been filled with items the family rarely used. Pushing aside a gravy boat and a lemon juicer that had been a present from his mother, he took out an old sweet tin. Opening it, he retrieved a manila envelope from beneath a stack of unused charity Christmas cards. Inside was a cheap supermarket phone fitted with a pre-paid SIM card he'd purchased the week before.

Turning it on, he stepped out through his patio doors and into the cold garden. He called the one and only number stored on the device and waited for an answer.

"Billy, is that you?"

"Of course it's fucking me! Who else do you think it would be? Who's this?"

"It's Simon Weston here, in Brighton. I've got news for you."

"That was fucking quick! What you got for me, copper?"

"That person you asked me to look out for earlier. He's in Brighton. He got off a train at around half nine this evening. My sergeant and his team were going to stop him, but somehow, he got away. It's a positive ID though. One of the officers was at university with him, apparently."

"I'm impressed Simon, my boy. Bloody good work. You're not all as fucking useless as I give you credit for. Give yourself a pat on the fucking back, son.

But what I need you to do now is find out exactly where the thieving cunt's gone and let me know pronto. You got that? Understand, do you?"

"I can't keep doing this, Billy, I really can't. If I get caught, I'll lose everything."

"Well, my dear boy, that's not really my problem, is it? You should have thought about that before you started messing around behind lovely Mrs Weston's back, shouldn't you?" said Billy down the line, with a chuckle.

"I can't believe you've managed to keep your grubby little secret safe from her all this time. Not exactly been discreet, have you? Listen, son, stop worrying. You sort this for me and I guarantee those photos will disappear and be gone for ever. They'll vanish into a puff of smoke, never to be seen again. Can't say fairer than that, can I?"

"I'm a very reasonable man, after all," he added.

"But just to avoid any crossed wires, if I don't hear back from you, those prints will be on your Superintendent's desk by the end of the weekend. And plastered all over your Facetwat account, or whatever it's called. Am I making myself crystal fucking clear, old chap? We don't want any misunderstandings now, do we?"

Before Simon Weston could reply, the line went dead. He returned the phone to its hiding place and drained the rest of the wine. Wondering if this nightmare would ever end, he went to join his wife on the living room sofa.

As he watched the comedy show that was making her shriek with laughter, he couldn't think of a single reason to ever smile again.

Chapter 20

Samuel Edge often wondered how police officers managed before the internet came along. He was just about old enough to remember a time before social media and search engines, but he'd become so reliant on his computer that it was difficult to fathom how he'd ever coped without it. The big systems like HOLMES were great for major crimes and murders, but for day-to-day, street-level work, Officer Google was an integral part of the team.

Although the rear number plate was missing, the distinctive shape of the brake light cluster and chrome bumper assembly had enabled him to work out that it was probably a vehicle built between 1969 and 1974. He'd flicked through a series of classified ads on a VW heritage site before he found one that matched the footage and from that, he'd identified its age.

Trying to make out the colour of the van from the monochrome images was trickier. The light was poor in the underpass and the reflection of the multicoloured street lighting confused the picture even further. He was sure that he could rule out deep colours such as black, red and navy blue. It was most likely light green, beige or yellow, but the online forums had informed him that vans like this were regularly resprayed and customised, so he couldn't take too much information on the database for granted. As these were the wheels of choice of students, surfers and hippies he concluded that informing the DVLA about a new paint job would rarely be a priority.

The system indicated that there were 14 campers of this vintage registered at Brighton addresses, fitting the possible colour profile. But in a city with a huge student population, he appreciated that this particular van could be from almost anywhere in the country. Any sensible undergraduate would have their wheels registered at a parent's home, in some distant leafy safe location, where the insurance quote would be considerably lower than in edgy Brighton. Samuel decided not to worry about that for the time being. The van had a sticker on the rear bumper for a surf shop on Hove seafront called Ocean Sports and that was enough to support his hunch that this vehicle was local.

He only recognised the sticker because he had the same one plastered across the back window of his own battered hatchback. It had come free with a sweatshirt he'd bought a year ago when he'd tried to smarten himself up to impress a girl on a dinner date. He didn't like to be reminded that it was the last item of clothing he'd bought, as well as being the last meal he'd had out. The date hadn't gone well, they'd not met again and he'd shrunk it in the tumble drier a few days later.

He now had to coax his reluctant team into employing some good old-fashioned door-knocking in order to eliminate the vans on the list. Just twenty-five minutes after he first sat down at his desk, enough information had been extracted from the grainy images to produce a short list of addresses they needed to visit.

He'd take half with Richie the Special, who was desperate to make amends for his performance earlier, and Gary would take the rest. He knew that he'd prefer to work alone. They'd start with the nearest ones and work outwards. It was getting a little too late to be making house calls but the Inspector had stressed that he wanted them to work on into the night, so that's what he was going to get.

Samuel was intrigued by the connection between his two suspects. They didn't feel like a natural fit. Buster Brett was a big fish from a big pond. The girl was just a small-time hustler who'd happened to cause a media storm. She'd only become a problem after the Argus caused a citywide panic in order to sell more copies of their nasty little rag.

People like Buster and his boss normally operated under the public radar. The Stalker was on a much humbler level of the underworld hierarchy altogether. He needed to work out if they knew each other and why the accountant to the biggest criminal in the south of England had been collected by a scruffy camper van and not the normal top-end BMWs or Mercedes favoured by the upper echelons of the criminal fraternity. None of it made any sense.

Out in the car, Samuel got chatting with Richie as they made their way to the first address on the list. Despite the spectacle he'd made of himself earlier, he still had a soft spot for the young Special. He was enthusiastic and hadn't yet become jaded and world weary like many of his older colleagues. He was also funny and had a directness of speech that Samuel found refreshing.

"So, how exactly do you know this Buster character?" he asked, as they pulled away. Richie didn't need any further encouragement to tell his Sergeant everything he knew.

"Basically, we were at uni together. He was alright I suppose, to start with. Clever, but a bit up himself. One of those sheltered middle-class kids who turns up to college thinking they're better than everyone else. Things went right downhill when he got a weekend job working for some shady businessman.

His boss was a drug dealer or something, I think. We never really got to know for sure, but all sorts of rumours were flying around. He bought himself all this designer clobber and was flashing his cash around, thinking he was God's gift. He started looking down his nose at me and all the other regular students.

I asked him one day where all the dosh came from, but he just laughed in my face and asked me if I was jealous. I suppose I was a bit. I was doing twenty hours in Tesco each week back then, just to pay my rent. One day he turned up to uni in a brand-new Porsche. Asked me if I wanted a lift home and I said I'd rather get the bus than get in some drug dealer's motor. We didn't talk anymore after that and he dropped out of college altogether a few weeks later. And that was the last time I saw him, until tonight. Didn't miss him or give him a second thought until his sneaky little face popped up at the station earlier."

Samuel detected a distinct hint of bitterness in his young colleague's voice as they pulled into the first street on the list.

The first two addresses weren't helpful. Both owners were annoyed to have been disturbed. One pointed indignantly to his van on the street outside and told them that it had been parked up all night. The cold exhaust confirmed this fact. The second had been asleep and explained that he'd sold the van two weeks before. He'd very impolitely suggested that they should get their facts right before waking people up in the middle of the night.

With apologies all around, Samuel and Richie moved on to the next address, feeling deflated and tired. It was a few minutes' drive away on St James' Street, where a van was registered in the name of a Dexter John Ward.

Chapter 21

Thumping bass was coming from behind a door on the first floor as they climbed a stairway that stank of refuse and homemade curry. Dodging bikes chained to the bannisters, Buster wondered why his old friend still rented the same type of rotten student accommodation they'd shared years ago. In his bubble of money and luxury, he'd forgotten that people lived like this.

An overwhelming aroma of stale cannabis smoke filled the air when Dexter opened the front door and ushered his guests into his cramped living room. Buster momentarily wondered how he'd had the misfortune to end up in such a miserable place on a dark and cold Wednesday night. The flat was filthy, but at least it was warm, and for the moment, it felt secure.

It was good to be off the street. Buster felt safer now. Dexter's tiny flat felt anonymous and safe, high up on the third floor of an unloved Victorian block. Its corner position would have afforded a great view of the street outside if Dexter had ever bothered to clean the windows. Like everything else in the flat, they were dirty and smeared with an accumulation of grime.

Ewalina pushed a pizza box off the sofa using the edge of her mobile phone and sat down, trying to avoid anything sticky that might stain her expensive jeans. The sneer on her face made it quite clear that she thought the place was a shithole. Opening the can of beer that she'd reluctantly accepted from Dexter, she started to check her phone.

"Hey, mate, do you mind if I pop the kettle on?" said Buster, gesturing over her head for Dexter to come and join him in the kitchen. She appeared to be absorbed by her messages and took no notice as they left her alone.

In the tiny, cramped room, Buster did his best to ignore the rubbish piled in the corner and the putrid aroma that wafted from the fridge when he opened the door looking for milk. The idea of drinking, let alone eating anything prepared in this room was far beyond contemplation. He put the kettle on anyway, hoping that the noise would offer them some privacy.

"Thanks for picking me up, mate. I'm sorry about that fucking nutter in there. I hadn't bargained on her," he said, nodding towards the living room.

"What the fucking hell's going on Buster? Why are you here? What have you gone and done? Please don't tell me you've fallen out with that psycho you work for."

"Yes, mate, unfortunately, I have, after a fashion. Mr Murphy and I have gone our separate ways. We're no longer colleagues, you might say. My employer and I have parted company, is another way of putting it. He's not technically fired me, but as of this evening, I'm no longer on the payroll. A slight falling out has occurred, although that would be to underplay events to some extent. The reality is somewhat worse, if I'm honest. A lot worse."

Buster was speaking quietly and the words didn't fit with the stress that was etched across his face. He was finding it difficult to articulate the truth of what he'd done.

"So, you've resigned or something? Just tell me what's happened, will you?" said Dexter optimistically, hoping that everything that had happened so far could be resolved with a simple and plausible explanation.

Buster paused and stared at Dexter before the gravity of what he had to say caused the truth to spew from his mouth.

"Of course I haven't resigned, you donut. Do you think I'd be here right now if I'd left on good terms? It's way, way worse than that, I'm afraid, mate. I've done something unbelievably dangerous."

He paused for a second, trying to find the courage to express his thoughts.

"I've robbed Billy Murphy and done a runner. I've taken around a million in cash, plus all his records, a gun and even his poor wife's jewellery. I'm in the shit, Dexter, and I don't know what I'm going to do about it."

The words rushed out of his mouth as if a dam of vocabulary had been burst.

Buster paused, shocked by the sound of his own voice, and waited for Dexter to process the information. His actions sounded very much worse than he'd anticipated when spoken out aloud.

"And that's why I was running from the station like Usain Bolt."

Dexter smiled, hoping that by some slim chance, his friend might be joking.

But Buster was smiling now too, a little too manically for Dexter's liking.

"And do you know what? I feel absolutely terrified. I think I've done the right thing. I really hope I have, anyway. The problem now is that he's going to try and kill me."

Dexter nodded, unable to formulate a response to Buster's crushing confession. He didn't want to know anymore, but he couldn't stop listening.

"Imagine how that feels, mate, to know that someone who's perfectly capable of murder now wants you dead in the most painful way they can think of? It feels fucking shitty, I tell you. It's been building up for ages, but tonight, for the first time ever, I had a chance to steal a load of money. To actually do something good for a change. To start making things better. That's never happened before. And now I can't believe I actually did it. What the fuck was I thinking?"

Dexter stood and listened, unable to understand why his friend would do such a ridiculous thing.

"Fucking hell, Buster mate. Why the fuck have you gone and done this? Didn't you have everything you wanted working for that outfit? I thought you were well-sorted, man. Last time I saw you, you were driving a Porsche for God's sake. I thought you was happy."

The expression on Buster's face changed abruptly. He looked serious again and pained.

"Happy mate? Stuff doesn't make you happy, Dexter. Not when you know about all the misery that went into making the cash to pay for it. You can have as many flash cars as you like, but if you're dead inside then it's all just a fucking waste of time. But you are right, in a sense. I did have it all. The flat, the designer clothes...and so much money, mate, you wouldn't believe it. I couldn't even spend it all. But I was starting to die in here."

Buster touched his chest with his fist.

Dexter was stunned. He had no idea how that might feel. He'd never owned a vehicle that was less than twenty years old and the thought of having so much money that you couldn't spend it all didn't seem like a huge problem. He'd have been willing to give it a go any day of the week.

But for now, he just wanted Buster to stop talking. He only wanted to hear about when he'd be leaving and what his plans were for getting out of his life. He really wished Buster would go right now and take the crazy girl with him. He'd done his bit by helping but now he desperately needed things to return to normal. He just wanted to roll a joint and beg Martha to be allowed back into the Unicorn.

Not realising that he'd lost his old friend to his thoughts, Buster took the silence as his cue to continue.

"I didn't actually plan on doing this today. Yeah sure, I'd been unhappy for ages, but today was just a fluke. A sign maybe. Do you believe in fate, Dexter?"

He didn't wait for a reply.

"I was supposed to be going on holiday tonight. Can you believe that? I should have been in the Virgin Upper-Class cabin right now, drinking Moët, and chatting up the stewardesses. But instead, here I am, on my bloody birthday with you and that nutter in there. And all because I took a split-second decision to change my life for the better. And who's to say it will be any better? I'll probably end up dead in the next few hours. It's funny how quickly life can change, isn't it?"

Buster was on a roll now and the words were pouring out of his mouth unchecked. It was evident that he still had plenty to get off his chest.

"So, every Wednesday night we count the cash. Billy leaves it to me to supervise the boys because it's normally his day off. The money piles up in the safe all week and then we take it out and count it on the big table in the office. Billy normally turns up later on and I have a meeting with him about how we're going to clean it all.

This time, I did the twenties and fifties. Took ages because it's been a busy week and those meatheads can't count for shit. Anyway, Billy's got this CCTV screen on his desk so he can see what's happening outside the office and in all his other places.

We'd just finished the count and were putting the cash back in the safe when we spot this scruffy bloke outside setting fire to something. Then there's this smashing sound from downstairs. Looks like he's lobbed a brick or something through the pub window. Well, I've never seen those lumps shift so quickly. For fat lads they were down those stairs like a pair of whippets.

Zero chance of catching him though. They basically sit around all day eating pizza and drinking tea, followed by an hour in the gym where they stick steroids in their arses. Always weights and zero cardio, so they're not exactly what you'd call fit.

So, I'm standing there all by myself for the first time ever with the safe wide open. And I just did it. I filled my suitcase with his cash and left. I didn't even think too much. I just acted on how I was feeling inside and went.

I knew the boys wouldn't be long, so I legged it as quickly as I could in the opposite direction. I reckoned they'd soon realise they wouldn't catch matey boy and come wandering back with a sausage roll and a Snickers each.

I wish I'd been there to see their dozy little faces when they realised I'd cleaned the safe out. I bet they absolutely shat themselves. I actually feel a bit sorry for them. They had absolutely no reason to think I'd do what I did. None whatsoever. Billy will have gone ballistic. And the rest, as they say, is history. Here I am in your filthy fucking kitchen! Sorry mate, I didn't mean to be horrible," he added, sensing he'd gone too far.

"But I am completely fucked now, mate, however you look at it. I'm under no illusion about that. I'm a dead man if I don't come up with a plan. It's just a good job I've got you to look after me now, eh, Dexter boy," Buster joked, making a gun with his fingers and waving it at his friend's sad-looking face.

"You'll save me won't you, mate? Protect your old pal Buster from all those nasty big boys?" he added with a laugh, sticking his fingers in Dexter's ribs and taking the joke too far.

"Ah, come on. It's not all bad, is it? Why the sad face? A few years ago, we'd have never imagined that we'd be in your flat with a suitcase full of cash and some mystery foreign blond sitting on the sofa. Where's your sense of adventure gone, Dexter, me old mucker? It's you and me against the world again. Just like the old days. Butch and Sundance, out and about, ducking and diving. Getting ourselves in scrapes, but this time with a shed load of money to spend. What's not to love?"

Buster could see that he'd overdone the banter. Dexter looked totally miserable.

"Yeah, I know. You don't have to say anything. I'm fucked. I don't really expect you to get involved, either. I really appreciate what you've done so far. And I know I've not been the best mate over the last few years."

He was about to continue when Dexter suddenly snapped out of his silence. He'd heard enough for the time being.

"Not been the best mate? Are you fucking shitting me? You've been a really crap mate, Buster. You haven't wanted to know me since you got involved with that lot. When did you last call me? I can't remember, it's been so fucking long. We haven't had a drink or smoke together since I moved into this place, and that was over three years ago. Working for them's turned you into a proper arsehole, if I'm honest. Do you remember when we bumped into each other in the street last year? You couldn't wait to get away. You made me feel like a worthless bag of shit. And I'm not even sure why you've called me tonight! Am I the only mate you've got left?"

"Truth is, you're the only one I could trust not to call Billy," replied Buster, seriously.

"Everyone else I know nowadays either works for him or has some other connection. And he's bound to be offering a shedful of cash to anyone who can tell him where I am right now. But you and me, we go back. We're old school. We've got history and that's got to count for something in a scrape. Do you remember that first day at school, when you came over to me and gave me a tissue to wipe a snot bubble off my face? Or that time Janet Ellison stole your sandwiches and I put a worm in her lunch box the next day? I called you because I knew you wouldn't be straight on the blower to someone as soon as I asked for help. Well, at least I hoped you wouldn't," added Buster, quickly checking his friend's face for any flicker of guilt or emotion.

Dexter just looked weary. It hadn't even crossed his mind to double-cross his mate, but the idea of a big reward certainly had its merits, now that he started to think about it.

"Buster, what's going to happen now? How are you going to get out of this mess? We can't just spend this money. They'll be onto us in no time. Brighton's a small place. You know that."

Buster looked pained again. Although he'd acted on impulse this evening, he'd been fantasising for months about what to do if he ever had a chance to right the wrongs of the past five years. He'd imagined all sorts of scenarios in which he could undo some of the misery he'd had a hand in creating. And here he now was, in a position to actually start putting those plans into action.

Standing in Dexter's kitchen, Buster couldn't believe the gulf between where he'd been in life a few hours before and his current predicament. It was as if he'd been on autopilot. The chasm between the comfort of the morning and the terrifying liberty of the evening was almost too much to contemplate. It didn't yet feel real.

He was in a filthy flat with a potentially dangerous stranger and his stoner friend, with only the vaguest idea of what to do next. But for a second, he felt as if the younger, optimistic version of himself had come crashing back into his skull, dislodging the nastier version who'd been squatting there and pulling the levers for the past five years.

"So, Buster, seriously, what's the plan?" pleaded Dexter, hoping that his friend would take the lead and say something that would make a little sense and guide them out of this terrible predicament.

Just as he was about to answer that question, Buster watched his friend's face glaze over, his concentration slip away and his jaw hang slack.

"What the fuck's up with you, mate? You alright?"

"I just remembered something about last night," said Dexter, his voice trembling, as he raised his hand to cover his mouth.

"Something really important that I shouldn't have forgotten about. All this stress with you has really messed up my head."

Dexter looked upset and close to tears as more memories of the previous evening decided to pay him a visit.

"And I'm pretty sure it's just going to make things a whole lot worse."

Chapter 22

Ewalina listened as best she could to the idiots in the kitchen. Whatever they might think, the police had definitely been at the station for her. It was only a matter of luck that she hadn't been caught. She'd definitely have to move on now. It was no longer safe to stay in Brighton. She'd have to think about the best way to pack up her flat and leave. That had to be better than getting caught and sent to prison.

She'd warmed up slightly after her fruitless evening of standing in the cold. The cheap beer had helped take the edge off her nerves too. She'd wiped the rim of the can with her sleeve, wary of the germs that were sure to be lurking there. Despite the mess she found herself sitting in, things could have been much worse.

They must be really stupid to think that she couldn't hear. As well as being the filthiest place she'd ever been, the flat was also tiny and the men's voices were clearly audible over the burble of the boiling kettle. People were poor at home, but no one lived in their own dirt like this weird guy. Her family might have next to nothing, but they did have their pride. This dirty freak clearly had none.

Listening as discreetly as possible, she couldn't believe what her ears were telling her. The man from the train worked for Billy Murphy. Even she knew the significance of that name. She thought he said he'd stolen a million pounds and a gun. Her English was good after five years in the country, but when she was tired and people spoke quickly, she occasionally lost track. She must have got it wrong. She concentrated even more intently on what they were saying. Listening to every word, she pretended to be on her phone, oblivious, and in her own little world.

But now she needed the toilet. It was inconvenient and horrifying considering where she found herself. The beer, the cold and a long night on the station concourse had all taken their toll on her bladder. She'd put it off for as long as she could, but now she really had to go. The thought of what she would find in this odd man's bathroom had put her off moving for several minutes, but now she could hold it no longer.

Judging by the state of his living room and the glimpse she'd seen of the kitchen, the bathroom was going to be beyond dreadful. She rummaged in her bag and was relieved to find some tissues, confident there would be none in his bathroom. She'd try and get this over with as quickly as possible and then block the experience from her mind.

Since only the kitchen lay off the living room, the bathroom had to be accessed via the tiny internal corridor they passed through on entering the flat. She wouldn't disturb the idiots by asking if she could use the facilities.

They'd say yes anyway and she wanted to have as little interaction with them as she could get away with.

Getting up, she made her way to the grubby corridor. The men in the kitchen didn't notice. The train guy was doing most of the talking, droning on about something he'd taken and all the trouble he was going to be in. The other one was too stoned to string a sentence together by the look on his dumb face.

There were two doors off the dark passage, in addition to the one they'd come in through. The entrance door looked as if it had been recently damaged and repaired. She could see where the lock had been repositioned on more than one occasion. A second lock had been added in an attempt to beef up the security. This was a door that was accustomed to being kicked in. She deduced that the stoner probably owed people money or had a jealous girlfriend - one with a violent temper and a vicious kick. Whatever it was, there were people that he didn't want to let in who were prepared to do damage and make a lot of noise to get at him. Or maybe he was just a guy who lost his keys on a regular basis.

She begrudgingly admitted to herself that these two individuals were marginally more interesting than she'd given them credit for. She'd need to watch them carefully, particularly the one with the suitcase. Could it really be full of money? They'd be trickier to deal with than her normal train fodder, but nothing she couldn't handle. She was at the top of her game and they'd already underestimated her in the short time they'd been thrown together. Once she'd emptied her bladder she could focus on the task at hand… how to make the most of these oddballs.

Not wanting to get her hands dirty, she gently kicked open the first door, hoping to find the bathroom. The room was dark and smelled of unwashed clothes and mildew. She wondered how anyone could get used to this and not think to open a window or do their laundry. She reached into the dark opening, hoping to find a bathroom pull cord. Instead, her hand landed on a standard wall switch. Instinctively flicking it down, a dim bulb illumined the room.

As her eyes got used to the weak light, curiosity took hold. She ventured several cautious steps forward. It had to be the stoner's bedroom, or at least the place she assumed he slept. It certainly didn't look like any bedroom she'd ever seen before. Driven by a desire to understand the man whose flat she was using for refuge, she studied the chaos before her.

The floor was covered in detritus and rubbish. Underpants, stained T-shirts, tissues, cigarette butts and food waste covered it from wall to wall. There were no carpets or curtains, just bare boards and a grimy window with a grey sheet draped across it.

Along one side was a narrow mattress. Filthy and threadbare, with no sheet or duvet, it had a solitary thin pillow at one end. On the other side of the room were ripped bin liners from which more jumble spilled on to the floor.

As she was about to leave, certain that there was nothing to make her want to remain in this dirty room a second longer, she noticed a thin dirty duvet scrunched in the corner behind the door. She hadn't noticed it at first. The old bulb had taken a while to warm up and her eyes a few seconds to adjust to the gloom. It had been hidden by the door when she entered and had only become apparent as she turned to go.

Protruding from the top of the duvet was a mop of black hair and from the bottom, what looked like an emaciated human foot. Her heart raced as she realised that someone was under the cover, lying silent and still in the corner of the room.

Her immediate reaction was to get out as quickly as possible. Not just from the room, but away from the flat and the awful people who'd taken her there. The smell, the darkness and now this wretched body in the corner made her want to bolt through the door, throw herself down the stairwell and run out screaming into the cold night air. Taking her chances on the street with the police had to be better than staying a moment longer in this house of fools and horror.

But holding her nerve, she thought about the suitcase full of cash. It was too good an opportunity to miss, even if it did mean having to control herself and stay put. If what she'd heard was true, the guy who worked for Billy Murphy. That made him vulnerable and she was the master of using such a weakness to tip the odds in her favour. She wanted the cash and she had the skills to take it if she kept her wits about her. She'd spent years learning the tricks of her trade and here, right now in this awful place, there could be the perfect opportunity to use them. Despite her desire to run, she held her nerve and forced herself to stay.

Curious to know more about her grim discovery, Ewalina edged forward and lifted the edge of the stained duvet. An emaciated female body lay beneath. Eyes shut and naked except for a pair of briefs, she looked lifeless and cold. She touched the body's leg with her boot. It was tense and rigid and didn't flinch or move with the contact. 'The stoner has an actual dead girl behind his bedroom door,' she screamed silently in her head. He's either killed her, or she's died of God knows what, and he's too off his face to know what to do. Either way, she'd discovered a secret that could be used against him.

It occurred to her that perhaps this wasn't an opportunity at all. Perhaps she was in extreme danger. What if he was just an old-fashioned psychopath and she was in line to be his next victim? Panicking, she backed out of the bedroom.

Quickly using the facilities that were behind the other door off the hall, which were just as awful as she'd imagined, she flushed and returned to the living room. She needed to figure out how the body would fit into the plan that her poor racing mind was frantically patching together. She wanted to know if she could use it to her advantage, but more than anything, she needed to stay safe. She didn't have the luxury of time and she certainly didn't want to be stuck with these two strangers and their weird corpse for a second longer than necessary. Instinctively, she realised that drastic action was her only option.

Standing in the middle of the living room, she took a deep breath and screamed as loud and as hard as she could manage.

"You two idiots, get in here right now!

There's a dead body in the fucking bedroom!"

Chapter 23

Buster and Ewalina stood in the doorway, stunned into silence by the horror before them. Neither wanted to venture any further into the foul room. The smell, the mess and the darkness kept them rooted to the spot. They watched as Dexter knelt next to the dead girl. She lay awkwardly in the corner of the bedroom, surrounded by stale clothes and the detritus of his chaotic life. For a few seconds he felt her wrist before turning to the others with a look of abject shock on his pale white face.

"She's fucking dead, guys. There's no pulse and she's as cold as ice. I completely forgot she was in here. And I can't remember what her fucking name is either. I only met her last night. She was bloody lovely too. This is what I was just going to tell you about, mate."

Dexter sounded bemused, thoughts tripping from his mouth as quickly as his memory could drag them from the foggy swamp of last night's intoxication. He was clearly as surprised as the other two by the grisly discovery behind his own bedroom door.

"How can you forget you've got a fucking dead body in your bedroom, you idiot?!" shouted Buster, cutting him off.

He was rapidly losing patience with his old friend. He'd known that asking him for help was risky, but this was far worse than anything he could have anticipated. Dexter's stoned state had been faintly amusing up until this point, but now Buster was angry, aware that this morbid complication would make his own fragile position even more precarious.

"This is fucking serious, mate. Do you realise how much shit we're all in now because of this? What the fuck have you gone and done, Dexter?"

Dexter looked as though he was about to cry as he tried to explain what had happened.

"I was out with her at the Unicorn last night and we ended up coming back here when we got lobbed out. I think I did something daft and the landlady kicked us out. I think she said she was foreign. Eastern European surname or something. She was trying to get me to pronounce it, but I couldn't. She sounded like she was from Brighton to me though. We stayed up talking shit all night, until it got light.

We was smoking weed in the front room and playing on the Xbox. Then I think she said she was tired and wanted to sleep, so I said for her to go and have a kip on my bed. And that was the last time I saw her. I woke up on the sofa this afternoon and completely forgot she was here. I went to the pub and then you texted me and I went rushing off to find my van and didn't give her a second thought. And now she's fucking gone and died. What are we going to do,

Buster?" sobbed Dexter, tears running down his cheeks, as the awfulness of what had happened sank in.

"What are *we* going to do, Dexter? I don't know what *we're* going to do mate. You're going to have to sort this by yourself, I'm afraid. If you hadn't already noticed, I'm up to my ears in shit as it is and the last thing I need is to get involved with a fucking dead body."

Dexter looked forlorn.

"But, Buster, I came to help you as soon as you asked me. Can't you just try and help me out a little bit? What shall I do, mate? I'm not thinking as clearly as I ought to be right at the moment."

"That's a fucking understatement if I ever heard one, isn't it, Dexter," snapped Buster.

"You're completely away with the fairies, aren't you? Why do you still smoke all that shit anyway?"

Buster knew that he was being unkind, but in his anger and frustration he didn't care and couldn't stop himself twisting the knife a little further.

"How have you managed to get yourself in such a state, Dexter? Your flat's a shit hole, you're off your face and now you've gone and killed this poor sod. What are you doing with your life? You're a fucking disgrace. I appreciate you picking me up and everything, but I'd have never asked if I'd known what I was letting myself in for."

"Do you think we should call an ambulance?" mumbled Dexter, shocked at his friend's reaction.

"Say we can't wake her up, or something like that. I mean, it's not as if I've killed her, is it? We was only having a laugh and doing a bit of gear. I didn't think she'd end up dead or anything, did I? Do you think she's gone and overdosed?"

Buster final ounce of patience ran out as he cut off his old friend's ramblings.

"Are you out of your fucking mind, Dexter? Well, obviously you are but that's a different matter. Of course she's fucking overdosed. It's not Ebola, for Christ's sake, is it? So, you're suggesting we should call an ambulance for someone who's clearly been dead for hours, do you? Someone you've been feeding drugs to all night by the sounds of it. You think that's a good idea do you, Einstein? And who do you think would rock up here as well?"

Buster waited for what seemed like an age for a response that failed to materialise on Dexter's blank face.

"Yes, mastermind, I'll spell it out for you, shall I? The Old Bill, that's who. And how do you think that's going to pan out for me? Oh yes, officer, of course I can explain why I'm in this dump with a million pounds in a suitcase, a dead body in the bedroom, a paranoid stoner and some low-rent hustler you've been trying to catch for weeks.

And oh, I almost forgot to say, I've also got a gun in my bag that you'll no doubt link to a whole string of violent offences. But it's all perfectly innocent officer, honestly it is. We'd all get nicked. That's what would happen, you dozy numbskull."

Dexter looked completely defeated as he listened to his old friend tear into him.

"So, we're not going to call an ambulance, the fire brigade or the fucking Girl Guides," continued Buster.

"We're going to sit tight and try not to panic and work out *together* how to get out of this fucking shit storm. Are we all clear on this?"

Dexter nodded in agreement, relieved that Buster had just said *together*.

Ewalina, who'd been listening quietly, turned to leave the bedroom.

"Don't think you can keep me here," she said over her shoulder, as she made her way along the corridor.

"Whatever mess you two are in, I don't want anything more to do with it. Dead bodies aren't my thing, so I'm off," she added.

She put her hand on the front door handle, almost theatrically, as if she was waiting for a reaction.

"You're not going anywhere for the moment I'm afraid, sweetheart," chimed in Buster, putting his palm on the door just above hers, preventing her from opening it.

For a second, she looked pleased with herself.

"If you leave now, with cops all over the place, you could lead them back here if you got caught, and I can't let that happen," continued Buster, his voice cracking with stress.

"So, we're all going to be stuck together for a little bit longer, I'm afraid. I don't like the idea of being trapped in this crap hole any more than you do, but for the moment, it's our best bet."

"Best bet for you maybe," said Ewalina sarcastically, flouncing back to her spot on the living room sofa.

"I'm perfectly capable of looking after myself," she whispered with a smile, glancing at the suitcase that was still sitting on the filthy kitchen floor.

Dexter and Buster made their way back to the living room and sat down wherever the rubbish and pizza boxes would allow. Dexter sat next to Ewalina on the stained sofa and repeatedly caressed his Xbox controller, as if trying to seek comfort from a familiar object. Buster took the only chair in the room, from which he first removed a stack of old newspapers and porn magazines.

"What are we going to do now, guys?" asked Dexter to no one in particular, hoping that a simple solution to the body in the bedroom problem would drop helpfully from the heavens. The question was left hanging in the room, as each one of them searched for a way out of their particular aspect of the dilemma.

Buster was about to reply when he stopped suddenly and stared. His face froze in horror and the words he was about to say stalled on his lips. Over the heads of Ewalina and Dexter, he looked beyond the sofa to where an apparition had appeared in the doorway behind them. As time appeared to slow to a halt, all he could do was raise his arm and point, his jaw hanging wide open in terror.

As Dexter and Ewalina spun around to see what Buster was pointing at, they recoiled in panic and scrabbled across the floor to get away from the scene that confronted them. Ewalina screamed and Dexter visibly wet himself as he howled in fear at the sight of a ghostly figure.

"Whoa, guys! I didn't mean to freak you out," said a thin pale girl, who was standing by the entrance to the hallway.

The same dead girl with the shock of black hair, who'd been in the bedroom moments before, was now reanimated and talking as if she'd never been deceased. As well as coming back to life, she'd put on a T-shirt, skinny black jeans and a pair of grubby white trainers.

"Like, what time is it anyway?" she continued, glancing at the phone in her hand.

"Fuck me! I was supposed to meet my old man in the Unicorn an hour ago. He's come down from London, apparently. I've gotta run Dexter. Last night was fun. Your bed smells of piss though, man. I had to go and sleep on the floor.

Nice to meet you two guys. Sorry if I freaked you out. I'm Sophia by the way. Sorry I didn't wake up earlier and get to meet you all properly, but I sleep through absolutely anything when I've had a smoke. Anyway, laters guys. See you soon Dexter, hopefully."

And with that the girl turned, opened the front door and disappeared from the flat, leaving the three remaining occupants to gather their senses and regain their shattered dignity.

As Ewalina and Dexter got up from the floor, Buster managed to find his tongue once again and articulated what all three of them were thinking.

"What the actual fuck just happened there? Dexter, didn't you say she was dead? Didn't you check her pulse?"

Dexter dabbed his damp crotch with one of the newspapers that Buster had just removed from the living room chair. He looked sick with stress and was fully aware that his mistake had made him look foolish, not to mention the state of his soiled clothing.

"You guys saw her too. She looked dead to me, man. I mean, I tried to find a pulse, but I'm not a fucking doctor, am I?"

He gave up with the newspaper and made his way to the bedroom to change his clothes and to get away from the criticism he knew was coming his way.

"I'm glad I did fuck up though and she's not really dead.

I wouldn't want that on my conscience," he shouted from the bedroom, glad to get away from the others while they were mad with him.

"And at least I know what her name is now," he added under his breath, knowing that they wouldn't find this comment helpful.

Ewalina regained her composure and sat back down on the sofa. She turned to Buster with a look of total disdain on her face.

"So, Mr Control Freak, let me see if I've got this right. You're desperate to stop me leaving this shit hole, but you're happy to let that little tramp run off into the night and go to the pub to tell anyone who's interested all about the huge fright she's just given us lot up here?"

Buster was stumped. The hustler was correct. The dead girl could be telling the wrong people, right now, about the menagerie of oddballs she'd just run away from in the flat across the road. He needed to take control of a situation that was, yet again, veering dangerously out of control.

"You're right. I shouldn't have let her leave. I also shouldn't have believed my retarded friend when he said she was dead," he conceded, realising the necessity of keeping her on side for the time being.

He hadn't yet decided if she was useful or just another unpredictable liability who needed to be watched at all times. But he had noticed her sideways glances at his suitcase. If she'd happened to hear any of the earlier conversation with Dexter, then the information he'd rashly given away could make her dangerous. He needed to think on his feet and come up with a way of dealing with her before she became any bolder.

"Look, Dexter is an old friend, but I think it's obvious that he's not Brain of Britain. Neither of us should have taken any notice when he said the girl was dead. I should have checked myself, but that room was so disgusting, I guess I just took what he said at face value so I could avoid going in there. My mistake."

Ewalina looked up at him, unable to restrain her catty response.

"Your mistake was to steal Billy Murphy's money! Your mistake was to get the worst getaway driver on the planet to pick you up from the station! The police might have been onto me, but at least I'm not completely stupid like you. You're in so much shit it's unbelievable," she laughed, unsympathetically.

"So, you heard us talking in the kitchen, right?" he replied softly, sitting back down on the chair.

Ewalina nodded with a smile.

"Yes, of course you did. You're a smart cookie. And you know who Billy Murphy is, right?"

Ewalina nodded again.

"Of course I do! Every idiot knows who he is. And anyone with half a brain knows not to mess with him"

"OK, so you'll appreciate that I'm in a bit of a mess right now?"

Ewalina rolled her eyes, wondering where Buster was going with this.

"So, hear me out - how about you stick around and help me for a bit? I could do with someone clever and sharp, like you, on my side for a few days."

Buster calculated that flattery would sway her. He was certain now that he needed someone other than just Dexter in his corner if he was going to ride out this crisis.

"And obviously, I don't mean out of the goodness of your heart," he added, realising quite correctly, that Ewalina did very little in life without the prospect of a decent reward.

"I'll pay you well. I've got a few things that I need to do to get my life back on track. Will you help me? Probably no more than four days' work. How does five grand sound? Cash, obviously," he joked, the humour failing to elicit a response from the girl.

He'd judged that five thousand would be just enough to get her attention. If she really was a street hustler, then the most she'd be getting from each trick would be a few hundred pounds. If the police were onto her, then the thought of an easy lump sum would be even more enticing. He realised that he desperately needed her now. Dexter was in a far worse state than he could have anticipated. The dead girl drama confirmed that his friend's judgement was not to be trusted. He was amazed that he'd actually made it to the station in that death trap of a van. Looking around the flat, he concluded that his old mate wasn't a well man at all.

Ewalina thought for a few seconds.

"Ten thousand up front and you've got yourself a deal," she replied, coldly.

"Six," he countered.

Ewalina tried to look unconcerned as she came back with her final offer.

"Eight or you're on your own. Take it or leave it."

Buster was ready for her.

"Call it seven, with two upfront and the rest when we're finished."

Ewalina nodded.

"Done!" said Buster, a little too quickly. The look on the girl's face made it clear that she wished she'd held out for more.

She glared at him but Buster knew that he had her on the hook. He'd have readily paid her more if she'd pushed it.

He got up and went to the kitchen to retrieve the cash. He was relieved that he now had someone else to help him. She was an unknown quantity and obviously just in it for the money, but, at this particular moment, he couldn't be too fussy.

Ewalina's eyes followed him. He pushed a pile of dirty crockery to one side to make space for the suitcase on the cluttered worktop. She watched carefully as he opened it.

Even from the sofa, she could see the mass of tightly bundled notes. She stared as he took out two rolls and then struggled to close the catches again, fumbling around as he tried to prevent the precious cash from falling onto the filthy floor.

"Here you go," said Buster, calmly, casually passing Ewalina the money.

"So, the first thing we're going to do is go to that pub she mentioned and make sure she isn't telling tales that could get us into even more trouble. And then I'll tell you what my plan is and what I need you to do."

Ewalina shrugged her shoulders and stood up. Buster wondered if she was playing him. She was certainly showing less enthusiasm for her new role than he would have liked.

"Let's go then, Mr Boss Man," she said, trying to keep a straight face.

As Buster went to leave the flat, he felt as if he'd reclaimed a shred of control. He could start to make things better now. If he kept his wits about him, he could save his own skin and make up for the harm he'd had a hand in causing. He pictured the scene at the Chinese restaurant to remind himself of why he'd created this turmoil in the first place. He recalled the man's screams and the dreadful smell of his burning hair.

But at the exact moment he put his hand on the handle, intending to open the front door, an unexpected harsh knock came from the other side. A double rap, firm and brisk, followed by a voice just a few inches away. They both froze, aware that the slightest sound would be heard by whoever it was in the communal hall.

"Dexter Ward, it's the police!"

Whatever sense of calm Buster had just experienced evaporated in an instant, leaving him feeling sick and once again reliant on his stoned friend to come to the rescue.

"Can you open the door, please?" continued the voice on the other side.

"We need to speak to you about your campervan."

Dexter emerged from his bedroom wearing a long-sleeved t-shirt and a pair of black jogging bottoms that clearly hadn't been troubled by a washing machine for months. Buster felt a cold sweat pass across his face as he realised that his friend's reaction in the next few seconds could spell disaster for all of them.

#####

"Open up please, Dexter. We can hear you in there. This won't take long. We just need a little chat," said the voice, followed by a harder, more aggressive double knock.

Dexter gestured to Buster and Ewalina to move back into the kitchen. For all his faults, he was used to dealing with unwanted callers. The police, his weed supplier and his landlord were at the top of a long list of people who regularly wanted to get hold of him. If there was one thing he was good at, he thought, it was fobbing off uninvited visitors.

He'd found from past experience that the police were generally easier to deal with than other people who knocked on his door. They were less likely to be armed with hammers and knives. They generally preferred to chat first and were a lot less inclined to get punchy than the other non-official visitors who came to his flat.

Once he could see that the others were hidden from sight, he counted to five and opened the door. Two plain-clothed officers stood on the other side, waiting. They both took a step back, repelled by the smell of urine and weed coming from inside. As they tried to make sense of the scruffy character before them, Dexter broke the ice with his opening line.

"Officers, my sincerest apologies for the delay, but I just pissed myself and had to get changed. How exactly may I help you gentlemen this fine evening?"

Chapter 24

The man's voice was slurred and he was swaying from side to side as he spoke. It was difficult to imagine that he'd driven anywhere recently. Samuel looked beyond him into what he assumed to be a living room.

It was a typical junkie setup with rubbish strewn everywhere and a large television. Druggies always had big TVs. He saw places like this all the time. He often wondered at what point in people's downward spirals into drug abuse they stopped clearing up or looking after themselves. It was hard not to pity people who ended up living in their own filth.

"Are you Dexter Ward?" he asked, pretty sure what the answer would be.

"Yes sir, that is I. And can I please apologise for the herbal aroma? My neighbours like to party, if you get my drift. If you'd like to come in and look around, I can assure you that you'll find nothing in here that we shouldn't have on us."

Samuel doubted very much if that was true, but it wasn't the reason for the visit. If he spent his time searching every junkie for weed, pills or powder, no real criminals would ever get caught.

"That's not why we're here, Dexter. Do you mind if I call you Dexter?"

The stoner nodded.

"We're here to talk to you about your campervan. Are you still the owner of a yellow VW with a registration of BAC 236W?"

He nodded again.

"Can you tell me where the vehicle is at the moment? We're just trying to rule it out of an investigation we've got going on this evening."

The druggie stood silently, swaying from side to side.

"Did you hear me, Dexter? We need to know where your van is, please."

Samuel could see thoughts flitting across the man's addled face. The length of time it was taking him to answer was significant. As was the fact that he'd heard two voices in the flat just before he knocked. He anticipated that most of what he was about to be told would be lies.

"Sorry officer, but I haven't used that van for bloody ages. Took me a while to remember where I left it. It's parked a couple of roads away if my memory serves me correctly. It's a real bugger trying to park around here, as I'm sure you can appreciate."

There was another long pause as he continued to sway.

"Yes, that's it, I remember now. It's all coming back to me. I'm pretty sure I left it on Paston Place. Nearest spot I could find. Yes, that's definitely where it is, officer."

Samuel stared at the stoner. He was clearly lying but they'd need to check out what he was saying before they could do anything about it. He knew that they didn't have the grounds to enter the flat yet, let alone arrest this odd character.

"Are you sure that's where it is, Dexter? We're going to go and look for it right now, so if there's anything else you'd like to add, now's the time to do it."

The stoner didn't reply and continued to look unsteady on his feet.

"Dexter?"

"It's definitely, absolutely there, officer. Cross my heart."

The theatricality of his answer meant that the information was almost certainly garbage, but Samuel knew that he needed to actually see the van with his own eyes if he was going to escalate their encounter.

"Thanks Dexter. We'll go and have a look right now. Just to rule your van out of our investigations, of course. A couple of final questions before we go, if that's OK."

The filthy man nodded.

"Are you here by yourself at the moment?"

He looked panicked for a spit second.

"My girlfriend's here, but she's in the bathroom right now," he mumbled, pointing to a closed door behind him.

"She's not very well either, I'm afraid. Dodgy kebab earlier."

More lies thought Samuel, but until he'd checked out the van, he didn't have justification to spend any more time with this pathetic individual.

"OK, Dexter, one last thing. Have you been here all evening? Have you been out at all?"

"I've been here all day and all night, officer. I went to the pub last night and haven't been anywhere since then. I've been sleeping my hangover off, I'm ashamed to say."

"Thanks, Dexter. You've been very helpful. We'll quickly pop to check on your vehicle now, but if it's where you say it is and you haven't used it this evening, then you won't be hearing anything further from us. Thanks for your time, and I hope your partner feels better soon."

As he listened to the conversation, the cogs in Richie's memory slowly started to turn, pushing recollections of distant events into the foreground of his mind. As his Sergeant turned to leave, with the expectation that he would fall in behind, Richie stopped and directed a question straight at the startled hippy.

"What school did you go to, mate?"

Simple, direct and apparently completely irrelevant, Dexter answered naturally and honestly without a hint of hesitation.

"Varndean, bro. Why you asking?"

And without a further word being uttered, the officers left and Dexter closed the door, confused and not totally convinced that he'd handled the conversation in the best way possible.

If Samuel had been close enough to hear what was going on upstairs and hadn't been halfway down to the street, wondering why his young colleague had asked such a random final question, then he might have heard the following furious words bouncing around the walls of his potential suspect's third-floor flat.

"Fuck, fuck, fuck, Dexter. What the fuck did you just say to the feds, you fucking prick? The first thing they're going to do is go to Paston Place and see you're a massive fucking liar. We've got about two minutes to get out of here before they come back and kick the fucking door down, you absolute dick."

And if he'd been listening particularly carefully, he'd have heard poor old Dexter Ward sobbing to himself in a fit of self-pity as he realised that he'd just made this already awful night even worse.

Chapter 25

Buster knew that the police would soon be back. Dexter had made their position untenable with his hopeless story. Getting him involved had been a huge error. Now was the time to dump his old friend and get out of this trap of a flat.

Grabbing his suitcase from the kitchen and the bin bag from where he'd left it by the front door, he shouted to Ewalina,

"We've got about a minute before those coppers return. All they need to do is see that Dexter's van isn't where the cretin just said it was and they'll be back here, kicking the door off its hinges. Grab your coat and let's go. If we get stuck in this place, it's game over."

Without saying a word, Ewalina snatched her things from the sofa and rushed to the front door.

"Thanks for all your help, Dexter," shouted Buster, sarcastically.

"You've really helped me out here. Nice one! And it was great to see you again. We must do this again. It's been fun! I'll give you a call when all of this has settled down. That's if I'm not fucking dead, you muppet. When the Old Bill come back, just make out you made a mistake or that someone must have stolen your van, or whatever shit you feel like saying. It doesn't really matter now. You've not done anything wrong, other than give your mate a lift. Just say you were stoned or some other shit. It's not as if they won't believe you, is it?"

He opened the door and glanced over the bannisters, down into the stairwell. He wanted to make sure that it wasn't too late and the police were already on their way up. It was a relief to see it clear for now.

He started to make his way down, briskly taking two stairs at a time, the suitcase making a racket as it bounced wildly along behind him. Ewalina followed as quickly as she could in her heels, desperately trying to keep up. His panic was contagious and she almost fell several times in her haste to leave the building.

As Buster pulled open the heavy external door, the cold night breeze hit him. Taking a deep breath to calm his nerves, he realised just how foul the air had been upstairs. He held the door open, waiting impatiently for his new helper to catch up.

Seconds later he'd negotiated the rubbish-strewn entry steps and started his escape down St James's Street. The girl followed two steps behind. The pavements were busy with punters moving from bar to bar, but despite this cover, Buster felt exposed and vulnerable. With no specific destination in mind, getting far away from Dexter's awful flat was all that occupied his thoughts.

Chapter 26

Standing in his flat, seconds after Buster and the stalker departed, Dexter reasoned that if they were going to get caught anyway, which seemed the most likely outcome of the evening's events, then why shouldn't he, the loyal but not so loyal best friend, get something for his not inconsiderable trouble and inconvenience?

It would be fitting compensation for the stress and anxiety that Buster had wrought on his life by bringing an infamous criminal and the police to his otherwise peaceful home. These thoughts only entered Dexter's head for a short period of time, but in those fleeting seconds he found his phone amongst the rubbish on the floor, picked it up and started to dial.

In this brief episode of weakness, he rang his weed dealer, who called someone else, who, in turn, phoned Dexter back sounding very angry indeed.

"Right, you listen up, son," said the ice-cold voice on the other end of the line.

"I know everything there is to know about you, Dexter Ward. I've been told you're a delusional, paranoid druggy who got kicked out of school. I know you live in a shithole that hasn't been cleaned for years. I know what you had for dinner and precisely how much you owe your fucking dealer.

Oh, and I also know that you helped that little cunt Buster escape tonight. So, this telephone call is either going to turn out very well or very badly for you, son. There's going to be serious consequences, one way or the other, so, think very hard about what you're going to say to me. Do you understand?

And for starters, you're going to tell me, right now, this second, exactly where your little pal Buster's hiding out. And then I want to know where he's got me money. That all make sense, does it? Right, start talking, son, and hurry up. This is your one and only chance to get yourself out of this mess and earn a couple of quid for your trouble. But only if you're proper straight with me."

Dexter didn't know what to say. His fear of the person on the phone was matched by the realisation that he'd done something very stupid by trying to gain from Buster's misfortune. He froze in terror and his mind went blank.

"Son, I'm not going to ask you again."

In the second that Dexter hesitated, the voice on the other end of the line exploded with rage.

"You there, you cunt? Unless you want me to come to that doss house you live in and shove a blade between your ribs and twist it 'til you squeal like a little pig, then I suggest you start talking. Tell me everything, right now, or me boys are going to be digging you a cold little hole up on the Downs, you little prick. This is your final chance, I tell yer."

And with thoughts of knives and shallow graves flooding his mind, Dexter started to talk.

Times, places, specific addresses and the names of everyone involved tripped freely from his lips. And although no formal introductions were made, Dexter was pretty sure that the dreadful voice in his ear was that of the legendary man himself, Billy Murphy.

They only spoke for a minute, but in that short time Dexter managed to give away all the aces of information he held without negotiating a single thing in return for himself, least of all a cash reward or promise of immunity. The line went dead and Dexter was left stunned, realising that he'd betrayed his old friend for absolutely no reason other than to avenge a few harsh words that he was now struggling to even remember.

Coming to his senses and realising that his mistake had put Buster in mortal danger, he threw himself down the communal stairway and rushed out into the cold night air, panicking and desperate to make amends.

Chapter 27

Richie could contain his excitement no longer. As the officers got back into their car, he didn't wait to be asked before blurting out everything that was on his mind.

"Sarge, I'm pretty sure I remember that hippy from years ago. He wasn't so messed up back then, and didn't stink, but I'm sure it's the same geezer. I think he's an old school mate of Buster Brett's. He turned up once to a party with him and I remember thinking what a knob he was, even then. All he wanted to talk about was skateboards and weed.

That's why I asked him what school he went to just now. I remember Buster being a townie and talking about Varndean this and Varndean that all the time, as if any of us gave a shit. And that bloke's just said he went to the same place. It's got to be the same pal of his I met way back then."

Samuel listened carefully. It made sense. Dexter had obviously been lying about something and maybe it wasn't just to detract from the smell of the marijuana. What Richie was saying linked Buster Brett to the driver of a campervan and that was potentially the breakthrough they'd been looking for. On the other hand, lots of people had passed through Varndean School and Dexter didn't look like he'd been capable of driving anything in the last few hours. He needed to check out the story. If the van was cold and where he said he'd left it, then he probably wasn't the man they were looking for.

"One other thing Sarge; might be something, might be nothing. Just before we came out, I checked STORM at the nick and there was a serial that mentioned a Volkswagen. Some old dear on Essex Street phoned in to say that it bumped her car earlier and set the alarm off when it was trying to get out of a parking space. She thought it might be a VW but couldn't be sure.

And then she phoned again about a half hour later to say it was back in the same spot. I think she was expecting someone to rush over on blues to check out the damage. Was only a grade 3, but it caught my eye for obvious reasons. She didn't say it was a camper specifically, but who knows? Maybe worth taking a look? It's only a couple of streets away, so pretty close by."

Samuel was pleased that he'd kept faith in the young Special after his earlier catastrophic mistake. STORM was a real-time computerised log of every job called into the force across the county. From murders to complaints about noisy neighbours, it was all there in a queue, waiting to be dealt with.

Calls were graded from one to four, with the former getting blue-lights, sirens and officers rushing from every corner of the city. The grade fours would be lucky if they got a follow-up email days later. The log showed who'd been assigned to deal with the call and what action had been taken. It was a treasure trove of information for any police officer with the sense and patience to root out the gems amongst the hundreds of time wasters and irrelevancies.

Samuel encouraged his team to study STORM as often as they could. It was a sure way of getting a big-picture view of crime and police activity across the city. Patterns and trends could emerge, and sometimes, seemingly unimportant pieces of information would help transform a much bigger inquiry. He hoped very much that this was happening right now.

"Nice work, Richie. Let's swing past there first and have a quick look before we go check out that crap he told us about Paston Place. I think we both know his van won't be there, don't we? I'm actually disappointed he didn't bother to concoct a better story. It's disrespectful. He's actually taken us for a right couple of mugs.

I don't think he told us a single word of truth other than what school he went to, and he only did that because you caught him on the hop. We'd better be quick though. He'll realise we're onto him if he's got any sense left in that messed-up head of his. He wasn't exactly the sharpest tool in the box, was he?" added Samuel, with a chuckle, putting the car into gear.

Less than a minute later, they arrived at Essex Street. A few seconds after that they spotted a yellow VW campervan parked up in plain sight by the side of the road. Richie checked the exhaust. It was still warm. The rear registration plate was missing, but Samuel spotted it lying a few feet away against the front wheel of a black BMW with a scuffed bumper.

"It's almost as if that idiot's laid a trail of clues for us to find," said Samuel incredulously, as he tried the doors.

"I wish everyone we dealt with was so obliging," chipped in Richie, relieved that his hunch had turned out to be correct.

Based on the information on STORM, it was easy to visualise the plate becoming detached when the two vehicles had come into contact. It was no great surprise to Samuel that its digits matched the registration of the van belonging to the scruffy man they'd just spoken to. The bumper sticker was also identical to the one in his own back window. This was, without any doubt, the getaway vehicle they'd been looking for.

An elderly woman waved at them from the first-floor window of a flat on the opposite side of the road. Samuel smiled back and held up his warrant card to offer reassurance that her call had been promptly answered by Brighton's finest detectives, who'd apparently dropped everything to come and look at her damaged car. At least Sussex Police would have one happy customer that evening, he thought.

Dexter Ward couldn't have made this any easier for them if he'd tried. This was certainly no professional mastermind they were dealing with. There had been no attempt at concealing the vehicle, and the awful fob-off story, which they'd been able to rubbish within minutes, marked Dexter out as an amateur. Samuel was still unclear why a slippery con artist and a high-level criminal like Buster Brett would ever risk their liberty by getting into a vehicle owned by such a hopeless druggie.

He made a quick call to the DI.

"We've located the van, sir. We're just heading to the registered address to search for the occupants. I just wanted to run it by you in case we need to force entry."

"Yes, yes, but what about Buster Brett?" snapped back DI Weston, impatiently.

"He's the priority. Let me know if he's there. I want information the moment you have it. And by the way, the Regional Organised Crime Unit are looking at this now, so don't mess anything up. I don't want your team showing us up with any more cockups."

And he was right. In policing terms, the capture of a senior gangland figure trumped the Stalker. Despite this, snaring his nemesis remained Samuel's personal priority. He was convinced that she was the one he'd heard talking behind the door a few minutes earlier. He desperately hoped that she'd still be there. His confidence in actually arresting her was undermined by the fact that Dexter's cover story had been hopelessly inadequate. Anyone with half a brain left in that flat would have been sure to do a runner.

Richie radioed for divisional backup as they raced the short distance back to St James's Street. His voice was tense now and full of anger. Samuel knew this was becoming personal for his young colleague. It was clear that he'd been harbouring a grudge for years.

They screeched to a halt outside the block at the same time as two marked cars with blue lights flashing. The element of surprise had been lost, but Samuel still hoped they'd been quick enough to trap their suspects inside.

Samuel, Richie and two of the uniformed officers raced up the stairs and briefly knocked on Dexter's front door before Richie surprised everyone for the second time that night.

Without being asked, he rammed the door with his heavy frame, his shoulder making contact with the most recently repaired section. Unable to take anymore punishment, the lock gave way and the door sprang open, sending him flying across the internal corridor and onto the rubbish-strewn floor of Dexter Ward's filthy living room.

Chapter 28

A distant siren hastened Buster's pace. A blue flashing light on the street ahead sent a shot of adrenaline racing through his body. It couldn't end like this, not before he'd had a chance to put things right. He glanced over his shoulder to see another police vehicle approaching at speed.

Blue lights were everywhere now, reflected in the shop windows all around. People on the street stopped and stared. Buster kept walking, praying and waiting for the inevitable tug on his arm or the clatter of heavy police boots. Nothing came. Keep calm and carry on walking, he thought. It's not the end until they catch you. He wondered how the cold metal cuffs would feel. He hoped the police wouldn't be too rough. Take the next side street and get out of the light. Keep hold of the money. Act as normally as you can. Better the coppers catch you than Billy and his boys.

Just as he thought he might have made it, an arm slipped through his and pulled him violently to the left. Before he knew what was happening, he was off balance and out of control. Tumbling through a doorway, with a whiff of something stale and familiar in his nostrils, Buster found himself sprawled on the damp floor of a dim warm room.

Winded for an instant, he could smell stale beer and something much worse as he lay looking up at a brass chandelier fixed to a maroon ceiling. Regaining his senses, he became aware of Dexter's face just an inch from his own. The foul smell was that of his friend's rancid breath as they lay sprawled together on the sticky carpet of what looked to be an old dark pub.

As Buster got to his knees, he could see the eyes of at least twenty people staring at the motley selection of bodies who'd just tumbled in through their pub's front door. Ewalina had managed to retain most of her dignity by staying on her feet and was now trying her best to disassociate herself from the others. Dexter was lying on his back, laughing uncontrollably, tears of stress and relief running down his cheeks.

"Welcome to the Unicorn, Buster, mate," he said, finally controlling his hysteria.

"Looks like I just saved your skin again."

Chapter 29

As Buster struggled to get up, he was relieved to see his suitcase close by. Ewalina had stood it upright and was helpfully standing guard, with one hand resting on its plastic handle. As the pub punters turned away, nonchalant about another Unicorn drama and keen to get back to their conversations and drinks, Buster reached down to Dexter and helped him up from the floor.

"What are you doing here? I thought we'd left you back at your flat!"

"So, you actually meant to leave me there, did you?" he replied, sounding hurt.

"You left me to face the Old Bill all by myself."

"Dexter, mate, they're not interested in you. Honestly. It's me and this wrong 'un they're after," he said, with a sideways nod to Ewalina.

"They'd have had a quick scout around your place to see who was there and once they'd realised you were there on your tod, they'd have been on their way. And by the way, I'm sorry for the way I spoke to you back there. I lost my temper and I was out of order. You were right when you said I've been a crap friend. I'll make it up to you. You're my oldest mate and you didn't deserve any of that."

"Good job I did leave though, Buster," replied Dexter, looking at the floor as a pang of guilt flashed across his face.

"If I hadn't caught up with you and dragged you in here, you'd have both been in the back of a paddy wagon by now. The place is swarming with cops out there and you two don't exactly blend in. No offence or anything."

He had a point. Buster had felt as if the game was up when they'd been out on the pavement, exposed and in a panic. The pub felt dark and safe and he did feel a little grateful that Dexter had led them here, even if their entrance had been less discreet than he would have liked.

Dexter led them along the bar to an area at the far end, close to the toilets. He nodded at the barmaid, who slowly shook her head in response.

"You do know you're still barred, don't you, Dexter?" she said firmly, crossing her arms and scowling, as he sat down on a barstool.

"You're lucky Martha's gone home or she'd have slung you out again by now. But as it's late and you're already in, I'll let you have just the one, but then you'll have to go. We don't want a repeat of last night, do we? What were you thinking, Dexter? You'd better count your blessings the cameras don't work or you'd have been all over the internet by now."

"I'm so sorry about that, I really am," replied Dexter, straight-faced, trying very hard to sound as if he meant it.

"By the way, that girl you was chatting up last night, she's sat at the back," the barmaid continued, softening her tone and pointing to a booth at the rear of the pub.

"She turned up here about ten minutes ago looking like shit. Her dad's been sitting at the bar waiting for her for over an hour. I think they've had a bit of a barney about her time keeping. Probably best if you don't go over and say hello, considering the circumstances. I tried to make conversation as best I could, but he was pretty on edge for some reason. Looks like someone's given him a proper pasting. Probably wise not to ask too much, I thought."

Dexter's mood improved instantly on hearing the excellent news that his favourite dead, not-dead girl, was sitting in the pub.

Buster bought them a round of drinks and thought about what to do next. A hotel room was the obvious option at this time of night. However, as much as he wanted to sleep, it was risky. Billy was sure to have his network of spies briefed and on the lookout. He thought about asking the hustler if they could go back to hers, but she'd probably have a well-built boyfriend waiting in the bedroom with a baseball bat, primed and ready to take the cash.

For the moment, the pub seemed like the best place to be. He knew that it wasn't really safe as they were right under the noses of the police officers searching Dexter's flat. But in the darkness, cocooned by the comforting night-time crowd, hiding in plain sight seemed like the least bad option they had.

As Buster worried and fretted and kept an eye on the door, he was startled by a face in the crowd. A man made his way from a booth at the back of the pub, heading towards the toilets by the end of the bar. He was wearing a suit and had a face that was stitched and bruised. He was familiar, but Buster couldn't place him. The man stared back at him, before quickly passing by and entering the toilets.

Chapter 30

Dexter could just about see Sophia's head through the unruly throng of Unicorn customers. She was sitting in a booth with her back to him, with a glass of white wine in her hand. Her dad had just got up to make his way to the gents. Dexter didn't like the look of him at all. This would be the perfect moment to approach her, if only he could summon the courage. He realised that he had only a few seconds to make his move.

The dynamic with her old man held him back. Dexter didn't want him to return while he was chatting up his daughter. His beaten face made him look severe and unapproachable and Dexter felt intimidated by the hardness in his eyes. If father and daughter had rowed about her late arrival, she'd have probably blamed her new friend, the free-thinking cool guy who lived up the road. Dexter hoped she'd have said that anyway. And if he was right, it might not get him off to the best start with his potential future father-in-law. Dad's always wanted their daughters to meet responsible sensible guys, not rebels who wanted to smash the system.

He hesitated and decided to wait. Maybe she'd go to the toilet herself in a minute and he could gently grab her arm as she walked past and ask for a quick word alone. He'd think of something witty and endearing to say. He'd apologise for earlier and arrange to see her again. He could offer to take her for a ride in his van or go for a stroll on the beach. He hadn't been there in years, but it seemed like an appropriate place to go with someone special like Sophia. He'd seen other couples walking on the pebbles, hand in hand. That's what regular people did. He desperately wanted to do something to make up for his bed that she'd said smelled of piss.

And if she said yes, he could get his mum to wash his clothes and tidy the flat. He'd take a shower and buy some new socks, just in case. She was worth making an effort for, even if he had forgotten her name last night and left her for dead behind his bedroom door. It hadn't been the ideal first date, he had to admit, but perhaps now he had the perfect opportunity to arrange a second.

It wouldn't look good to appear too keen though. He'd only seen her fifteen minutes before. He might be a pothead, but he certainly wasn't a stalker. One of those in the pub was quite enough he thought, taking a furtive look at Ewalina.

Best to try and play it cool. But that wasn't going to be easy as he wasn't entirely convinced that Sophia had left the flat with the best impression of him. All that shrieking and the little accident with his wet trousers might have conspired to put her off. She had seemed happy enough when she walked out and she did say that she hoped to see him soon. But maybe she was just being polite and couldn't wait to get away from the person who'd ignored her all day. He desperately needed to speak to her and find out.

As Dexter dwelt on the awfulness of the evening so far, he wanted to kick himself violently in the head for forgetting that his beautiful Sophia had been alone in the bedroom for all that time. What a golden chance he'd squandered to hold her in his arms.

He was in no doubt now that it was all his old friend's fault. He was the one who'd initiated this wild goose chase. It was Buster who'd made him leave his safe cosy flat and put him at odds with the most dangerous criminal in town.

But it wasn't altogether one-sided. Dexter hadn't been entirely truthful with his friend. It was true that he'd pulled him in through the front door of the Unicorn to save his skin, but it wasn't to help Buster get away from the police, as he'd originally explained.

If he'd been inclined to tell his old pal the whole truth, he might have mentioned that he'd actually yanked him off the street to prevent him from being clocked by the occupants of a big black Bentley that had just pulled out of a side street right in front of them. And if he'd been particularly keen on rinsing every last honest ounce of truth out of the situation, he would have added that he was of the belief that the car most likely belonged to Billy Murphy, who was in that particular location at that specific moment because of a phone call he'd made less than two minutes before.

He hadn't wanted to make the phone call and regretted making it straight away, but there was no way of dodging the fact that he had actually made it. No amount of trying to justify his actions or block those seconds from his mind was going to alter the reality of the last quarter of an hour. He'd been angry at Buster for wanting to leave without him. He'd felt abandoned and used by his old friend. Buster had been sarcastic and those words had hurt.

And in that short spiteful moment, when they'd dashed out of his flat, he'd wanted to do something to get back at to his old mate; something that would even up the mix and make him feel better. His actions might also have been influenced by the substantial cash reward Buster had mentioned earlier, the one that would probably be on the table for information received by Billy Murphy. In truth, it was definitely and undeniably something to do with the reward, concluded Dexter, as he finished off his pint, full of remorse and keen to drown out the shame he was starting to feel in the pit of his stomach.

He was now trying very hard to forget the phone call he'd just made and the one he'd received in response. Other than those tiny little mistakes he could be very proud that he'd just saved his best friend from a whole world of pain. He'd risked his own personal safety to drag Buster and the Stalker into the Unicorn. He'd been their knight in shining armour, who'd ridden to the rescue with unflinching bravery, courage and selflessness.

He ran this idea through his head again and again until it started to gain some traction. The more he thought about this version of events, the firmer and more real it became. The harder he pushed the phone call into the recesses of his mind, the less significant it seemed. The faster he drank, the more plausible and agreeable this revision of the recent past felt.

Despite everything, Dexter was starting to feel warm again inside. His work on convincing himself that he'd done the right thing was beginning to pay off. The more shots he sank, the happier he became with his own behaviour. There had been a wobble or two, but things had turned out fine in the end. He'd been loyal to his friend when it really mattered and, in the end, those actions had saved Buster from capture. The grubby details of what he'd done immediately beforehand were now best forgotten. There was no point dwelling on the past. What really counted was the noble end result.

However, the satisfaction of a job well done was eroded each time he looked at his phone. He'd been aware of it vibrating in his pocket for several minutes. Each time he glanced down, the illuminated screen made his heart jump. Eight missed calls from the number that had called him back at the flat… the number belonging to the man with the voice from hell.

And although Dexter had given him all the information he'd asked for at the time, it was clear from all the impatient redialling that the cold-voiced caller was keen to chat some more. Not needing this on-going reminder of his moment of weakness, he went to the settings on his phone and blocked the number.

He then tried his best to do the same to the inconvenient memories of recent events by downing a further shot that Ewalina had just placed under his nose. He swallowed the bitter brown liquid, hoping it might block all thoughts of the maniac who wanted to stab him and bury him deep in the dark, cold countryside.

Chapter 31

As much as Billy appreciated his driver's lack of conversation, every other aspect of his technique put him on edge. For a man who could turn on the violence with a flick of the switch, Razor was an absolute stickler when it came to the rules of the road.

As they drove out through the south London suburbs, he stopped at amber traffic lights and let other drivers cut in front of the Bentley with a polite wave. He avoided bus lanes and cruised at one mile per hour below the indicated speed limit. And every time he did any of these things, Billy clenched his fists and snarled, the veins on his temple pulsing with frustration.

"Get a fucking move on, will you! Why the fuck are you letting that cunt out? Put your fucking foot down!"

But despite the shouting, swearing and abuse, Razor drove the car steadily and slowly out of the city, immune to the anger radiating from the back-seat driver. It was only when they reached the M23 and the first signpost for Brighton that he relented to his boss's demands and cranked the speedometer to eighty.

Behind them followed Billy's silver Range Rover, driven by Derek, with Anthony hunched in the passenger seat beside him. They drove in silence, fearful and apprehensive of what lay ahead. Every few minutes Billy called from the car in front, updating them over the hands-free.

They learned that Buster had been spotted at the train station. He'd escaped in an old campervan. He was with two unknown accomplices. The police were looking for them. It was obvious from Billy's increasingly testy tone that his mood wasn't improving as their little convoy travelled south.

It was a relief to Derek and Anthony to know that Buster was in Brighton. At least they'd have a chance of finding him there. If he'd fucked off on a plane, like they'd have done in his position, their task of catching him would have been impossible. Brighton was the worst place he could have gone, they reasoned. It was Billy's second home. They had a network there and it was clear from the information being relayed from the car ahead that someone inside the Old Bill was tipping them off. As the motorway ended and the affluent suburbs of Brighton began, they felt a little more confident about their chances of apprehending him and staying alive.

As their cavalcade of revenge headed purposely towards the seafront, Billy called with a further update. Buster was thought to have been in a flat on St James's Street. The police had just put the front door in, having found the getaway van parked nearby. There was a chance that they might be able to recover the cash, but only if they were quick. Billy barked at Razor to get them there as rapidly as he possibly could.

Alarmed by his boss's tone and realising that he'd pushed his luck, Razor ignored a red light, wrenched the heavy car into a bus lane and floored the accelerator. As a traffic camera flashed the rear plate over his left shoulder, he could hear his passenger talking to someone on the phone. He could make out snippets of names and places and even some manic laughter above the roar of the five-litre V12. Glancing in the rear-view mirror he was shocked by the rage and incredulity reflected from his boss's wild eyes.

Guided by the Bentley's sat-nav, Razor negotiated the car out of a narrow side street and on to the busy destination road a few minutes later. People were holding hands and laughing, drunks were stumbling into pub doorways and students were swarming all over the place. In every direction there were carefree, smiling, happy faces, all out having a good time. From the look on Billy's face, it was clear that he was repulsed by everything he saw.

It wasn't difficult to find the block where Buster and his crew had been holed up. There were police cars outside and a uniformed officer stood on the steps, checking everyone that came and went. Billy got Razor to pull up opposite, while the other boys held back in the side road. He cracked open the window and watched while he made another couple of calls. He then yelled at his driver to lead the way up to the house on Dyke Road Avenue. It was clear from his barely repressed fury that neither Buster nor the cash had been found.

As they made their way to what Billy considered to be the better side of town, he phoned yet again with an update on the latest developments.

"So, I just spoke to some little druggy cunt who helped our little boy Buster get away from the train station. Says he's got my money stuffed in a fucking suitcase and come foreign bird helping him out. Turns out he's prepared to fuck Buster over for a reward. I almost dropped the fucking phone when he asked for cash, I was laughing so hard.

Anyway, I've been texting the thick cunt back for the last twenty minutes but he's not answering me. My tame copper mate says they've done a runner, so there's no point in us driving around looking like a bunch of useless twats."

Billy talked without interruption. No one in the Range Rover dared open their mouth for fear of engaging with him. They'd heard this tone before. Cold attention to the task at hand and intense radiating anger were all things they associated with their boss at his worst. These conversations always led to violence. They let him talk himself out, not wanting to draw attention to themselves or add fuel to the flames.

"So, I've asked Inspector Dimwit to track this Dexter's phone so we can see where the little shit is. Chances are Master Brett's still be with him, I reckon. That'll teach Buster to treat me like a cunt by turning his fucking phone off.

He should have talked to me man to man about why he's done all of this. I'd have still killed the scheming shit, but I'd have respected him a whole lot more before I did. He thinks he's so fucking clever, but he's obviously not if he's holed up with a two-faced junkie weasel like this Dexter Ward geezer. If that's the best person he can find to crew up with, he's fucked."

Billy's phone vibrated whilst he was talking, putting him off his train of thought. He scanned a new text message from Fliss. She wanted to know where he was and what he was doing. She was moaning about dinner being ruined. He didn't have the patience to read it properly, never mind call her back and explain. He could manage without her opinion right now. She'd want him to stop, think, calm down and do all the other things that he had absolutely no intention of doing

He needed to hang on to his anger and let it ferment. He needed to draw as much energy from it as he could. Anger focused his mind and made him sharper. He needed to be dangerous at a time like this and he didn't need his stupid soft wife trying to take the edge off his carefully curated rage.

But alongside his anger, another emotion was jostling for attention. Disappointment was something that Billy was rarely accustomed to feeling. But now it was weighing him down and making him feel uncharacteristically reflective.

He was obviously upset at Buster for letting him down, but much more than that, he was disappointed with himself. He'd spent sixty years reading peoples' faces, working out how much they were good for, which way they'd jump and how far he could push them before they'd break. But this time, when it really mattered, he'd got it badly wrong.

He'd come across weak men and those that were harder than steel, but he'd never misjudged anyone as badly as he had this time. As far as Billy was concerned, Buster was the rightful heir to the firm. Up until a few hours before it had seemed like the unshakable truth. It was the gospel and written in stone, or so he'd thought. Buster was supposed to be the one taking brand Billy to new heights, while he kicked back and enjoyed a well-deserved retirement.

He'd often imagined Buster phoning him as he sat on a sun-drenched beach with a cocktail in his hand and a smile on his contented old face. He wasn't sure why he always pictured himself this way because he hated the sea and the thought of getting on a plane made him feel psychically sick. He was none too keen on cocktails or inclined to smile either.

In this happy, but now impossible future, Buster would fill him in on the details of their phenomenal growth, all the territories they'd taken over and who they'd canned to do it. They'd chat merrily away about the challenges ahead on the path to their glorious expansion. Profit margins and new opportunities would be discussed and Billy would guide his young protégé through the minefield of the criminal underworld. Buster would lap it all up and nod at the wisdom of his experienced and much-loved patriarch.

Of course, he'd known all along that he needed to toughen him up and get him out of his soft-as-shit middle-class ways, but there was supposed to be time for all of that. Billy wasn't finished with his education yet. They'd hardly got started on the meat and bones of his apprenticeship. He had no reason to think that such dark deeds were being plotted behind his back.

And although they never talked about much beyond the figures, opportunities and who owed what, Billy genuinely believed they were close. Closer than he was to any of his own fucking kids, that was for sure. Too close for Buster to have treated him like this. For fuck's sake, he'd even invited the little two-faced rat to the house.

Fliss had treated him better than one of their own, the silly old, deluded bitch. She'd gone too far though with the Christmas presents, the handmade birthday cards and the special crockery she only got out of the cupboard when little Prince Buster was coming to dine. The sad old lonely cow phoned him all the time too, which really got on his nerves. She'd want to talk and see how he was doing and check he was eating properly, as if it was any of her bloody business. They'd gossip away and catch up on all the news as if she were his doting mother.

He'd overheard them talking about books and holidays and all the other crap that years ago, she'd given up trying to discuss with him. Buster had got gullible old Fliss well and truly in his pocket, exactly where he wanted her. He'd indulged her and shown her attention and now it was crystal clear why. The little shit wasn't going to get away with any of this.

But the truth was, they'd both been taken in. The wolf in sheep's clothing with his posh accent, politeness and soft ways, he'd lulled them into believing that he was on their side. He'd fooled Billy good and proper and for that, perverse credit was due to the boy. He'd played a blinder in fact. Buster had taken off and cleaned him out and when people found out, he'd be a laughing stock. Billy Murphy, yesterday's man who'd got ripped off by his own number two and hadn't seen it coming. The lame old-timer whose power was on the wane. He might as well put a big fat target on his back right now and wait for someone to take a shot.

There was only one way now to re-establish the order that held Billy's world together and that wasn't going to work out very well for young Master Brett. Wherever he was and whatever he was planning on doing, he had to be caught and held to account.

In a rare moment of introspection, Billy wondered how he'd managed to miss the signs. There had always been grumblings from the others about Buster's place in the firm.

The boys bitched that he'd risen too quickly. He was distant and didn't join in their banter, they whined. He didn't work out with them at the gym or approve of the steroids they all shoved in their veins. But that was exactly what he'd wanted at the time. He'd seen it as a positive. Buster was his spy in the camp, his oil on troubled waters, keeping everyone on their toes and too afraid to rock the boat. Maybe he should have listened to those beefed-up simpletons before they'd become too scared to voice their opinions.

As Billy and the boys arrived at the house in Dyke Road Avenue, he thought about the first time he'd ever met the boy. He remembered all the whiskey he'd downed, the good stuff he kept for special occasions, all bright eyed and innocent, returning the cash he'd found on a garage forecourt. How impressed he'd been by the honest young stranger at his door.

But what had happened to the principles that made him stand out in the first place? How could he have stolen from someone who'd treated him so well? What had he done other than to take him in, pay him well and treat him like a son?

As the boys rifled through the freezer, looking for pizza, and drank beers from the fridge, Billy went to his study to pour himself a proper drink. He slumped into one of his armchairs and took a second to check his voicemails.

There were two, both from Fliss. She wanted to know why he hadn't called her back or replied to her text. She was wondering why she couldn't get hold of Buster. He punched the delete key before she got to the end of what she had to say, fuming that she understood so little.

The room was too quiet now. Memories of the night five years ago when he'd sat there with Buster filled his mind. There was so much anger to contain. He'd been mugged over for the first time in decades. He was a million pounds down with his reputation on the line. But worse than all of that, his precious work to build a legacy lay in tatters. The meticulous planning and his best-ever performance had been wasted. He felt drained and old. His future was less clear now, and although he'd never admit it, Billy was scared of what might lie ahead.

#####

Anthony and Derek were still trying to figure out how to use the oven and make sense of the cooking instructions on a frosted pepperoni box, when they suddenly stopped what they were doing. They shuddered as an animalistic howl resonated from the boss's study.

Wild, prolonged and chilling, they glanced at each other, realising in an instant how dangerous Billy had become. They knew that unless Buster was found soon, his hurt, rage and humiliation would inevitably be reflected on them. Death was coming one way or another, and there was nothing they could do to stop it.

Chapter 32

Buster snapped out of his introspection when Ewalina placed a shot glass down in front of him. She nudged his elbow with hers, coaxing him to pick it up. The glass was next to another that he hadn't yet touched. He watched wearily as Dexter and the hustler downed theirs and slammed the empty glasses down onto the bar.

Dexter was going to get them thrown out. The barmaid had said just the one but here they were acting as though they were on a big night out without a care in the world. He had hoped that Ewalina would have more sense than to draw attention in this way. There was more to her odd behaviour than he could currently fathom. He needed to watch her.

He'd come up with a plan of sorts. It wasn't a very good one, but it was all he could devise in his current stressed state. They'd get a taxi to Worthing. It was along the coast, quiet and out of the way. Billy didn't have any businesses there that he was aware of. They'd find a hotel for the night and pray that the cab dispatcher hadn't asked his drivers to look out for anyone fitting their description. He wondered if travelling with the other two would make things better or worse. The police would be tuned into their little ménagea-trois by now, but he wasn't sure if that information would have filtered its way back to Billy.

Buster's brain was hurting from evaluating all the possible outcomes. It was late, he was exhausted and here he was stuck in an awful pub with accomplices who seemed hell-bent on getting as drunk as possible.

He needed the toilet now. The stress of the evening had made him feel sick and the half pint of beer he'd already drunk had gone straight to his bladder. He got up from his stool and turned to make his way to the gents.

As he went to push open the door, someone coming in the opposite direction pulled it away from Buster's hand. He caught a whiff of toilet blocks and bleach as he found himself within inches of the man with the cut-up face he'd seen just a minute before. They stared at one another for an intense moment, each trying to work out how they knew the other.

The man with the stitches and the black-eye got there first. He slammed the toilet door hard against Buster's shoulder with one hand and threw a sharp punch with the other. Buster stumbled back, shocked and off balance, his face stinging with pain.

The man stepped over him and rushed back to where he'd been sitting, knocking over a table laden with drinks in his haste. Broken glass and liquid flew everywhere. A woman whose pint had been tipped into her lap screamed, as the rest of the pub became instantly absorbed by the violent drama unfolding before them.

Buster staggered to his feet, dazed and confused. He grabbed a beer towel from the bar to stem the flow of something wet and warm that was streaming from his nose. Through his bloodied peripheral vision, he could see Ewalina edging towards the fire exit, gripping the suitcase by its handle. She looked enlivened and focussed, and not the least bit concerned by his plight. Dexter was still on his phone, oblivious to everything that was happening.

The man who'd just thrown the punch grabbed a young girl by the hand and started to drag her roughly towards the exit, causing Dexter, inexplicably, to snap into action. 'Thanks for your help, mate,' thought Buster, 'Get your priorities right.'

"Don't you fucking dare!" yelled Dexter.

"I've got this, Soph!"

Buster watched his friend launch himself across the pub, hurtling towards his assailant. Maybe he had seen what had happened after all. Dexter caught up with the man just as he reached the Unicorn's front door. He threw his arms around his waist and allowed the momentum of his sprint to send them both crashing against the lobby wall.

"I've called the police!" shouted an angry voice from behind the bar, as Dexter's head cracked one of the door's etched glass panels.

"What the fuck are you doing, you absolute wanker?" shouted the girl.

"I was only trying to protect you, Soph. I didn't like the way he was pulling you around," replied Dexter, sounding shocked that his actions hadn't been better received.

Buster could see now that the girl was the dead Sophia. Through the fog of pain and confusion, he realised that the man who'd thrown the punch had to be the dad she'd rushed off to meet.

"Just get off him, Dexter, you idiot. We need to get out of here before those thugs in the corner get hold of him again."

She sounded angry and scared. Who were these thugs she was talking about? Buster spun around to see where they could be, fearful that Billy's boys had rumbled their location. He felt vulnerable and confused, unable to work out why he'd been attacked or what was coming next.

"Quickly Dexter, help me get him up. There was one of them in the toilet a minute ago. They work for Billy Murphy and they're out to get my dad. We need to leave right now."

As Dexter rolled off Sophia's dad, he belatedly spotted his friend's startled and bloodied face on the other side of the room. Buster's blood ran cold at the news that Billy Murphy's men were in the pub.

"Wait outside with your dad, Soph. Try to get a taxi. I've got to help my mate. Looks like they've attacked him too. I think he's in the same boat as your old man. Long story, but I think you lot might be able to help each other out."

When Dexter rushed belatedly to help his friend, Ewalina was already out on the pavement. The moment she saw Buster floored and the idiot hippy tearing across the pub, she seized the chance she'd been waiting for. Dragging the case, she slipped out through the fire escape unnoticed. Following an alley up the side of the pub, dodging refuse bins and stepping over a rough sleeper, she found herself back on St James's Street.

It was busy and coming up the road towards her was a turquoise and white Brighton taxi. Perfect timing, she thought. It was one of the traditional London cab models she always preferred to take. The screen between herself and the driver was ideal for reducing unwanted conversation and attention.

The car's orange light was illuminated, so she held up her arm to hail it. She was vaguely aware of some people trying to do the same thing behind her. There was no way they were getting this one. She'd fight them for it if she needed to. This precious taxi was hers. It was her way out of an awful situation and away from these fools. She had the money now and nothing was going to stand in her way of escaping with it.

The taxi indicated and started to slow down. The driver casually raised two fingers from the wheel to acknowledge her hail. She moved closer to the edge of the pavement, trying to estimate exactly where its wheels would stop.

The cab pulled up exactly where she'd anticipated it would. She went to open the back door.

"Adelaide Crescent, please," she said briskly through the open front window. Just saying the words made her feel safer and more connected with her home. A few short minutes and she'd be there. The driver nodded and flicked on the meter.

As she lifted the heavy case into the car, Ewalina's heart missed a beat as she heard an unwelcome but familiar voice just inches behind her.

"Nice one, Ewalina, mate. I thought you'd fucked off to the bogs, but you was actually doing something useful for a change."

Her blood ran cold. Absolutely no way. This could not be happening. What did she have to do to get away from this cretin?

"How did you even manage to get this cab so quickly? Well done for remembering Buster's suitcase though. I'd have completely forgotten about that if you wasn't here."

Glancing around, she could see Dexter grinning away like a fool, leading Buster towards the car. He looked a mess, dishevelled and broken. He had a beer towel over his nose and his shirt sleeve was covered in blood. For a second, Ewalina almost felt sorry for him. She could only stand, watch and hold open the door as they clambered into the back of her precious taxi.

"Oi! You two. Get in here!" shouted Dexter to the other couple who'd been trying to hail the cab.

It was the dead girl from the flat and an older man, who had to be the father she'd been late to meet. She had no idea why they were all getting in the car together. Moments ago, they'd been fighting and yet here they were stealing her ride and causing even more problems. She calculated that her escape plan had failed by about fifteen seconds.

More hangers-on and strays, she thought, as they slammed the door shut and the driver pulled away. But the desire to get home was now stronger than her urge to get away from this circus of oddballs, so she let the cab continue on towards her home. She had two spare beds and it was late. If she were ever going to get her hands on the cash, she'd have to be more patient than she'd ever been before. She'd almost got away with it tonight, but tomorrow, refreshed and energised, her chances would be better.

As the taxi made its way through the city, Ewalina watched Buster stare warily at the man who'd just punched him. Blood was still seeping from his damaged nose and he looked broken and scared. His attacker glared menacingly back from the opposite seat, his body tense and primed for further violence. An uneasy truce held in the back of the cab for the eight minutes it took to arrive at Adelaide Crescent, the most prestigious of Hove's stuccoed Georgian terraces.

Chapter 33

After a fitful night's sleep on Ewalina's sofa, Buster woke up to the sound of his host clattering noisily around her kitchen. She was making coffee with as much disruption to the early morning peace as she could muster. She banged the kettle down, rattled spoons and slammed her cupboard doors. Three eggs cracked in the fridge as she wrenched its door shut.

He glanced around the room, looking for the others.

"Your stinky mate's in the bathroom, in case you're wondering," said Ewalina coldly, handing him a mug.

"He's been in there for forty minutes now. He's flushed the toilet twice and run the tap. I've banged on the door, but I can't get him to come out. If he's made a mess, I'll kill him, the vile creature."

Buster had no doubt that she was being deadly serious.

"And your brand-new mate's still asleep. I heard you both droning on for ages last night. Blah, blah, blah. Thanks for keeping me awake. You two obviously had a lot to talk about.

So, I'm guessing you've forgiven him for smacking you, right? I wouldn't be so ready to kiss and make up if it was me he'd punched and dropped in the shit with all that suit-burning nonsense of his. Sorry for eavesdropping, boss, but you weren't exactly being quiet."

Buster smiled and ignored her. He had more on his mind to worry about than his sarcastic, moody, new assistant.

#####

On the other side of the bathroom door, Dexter was sitting on the toilet. He was wondering what to do with thirty-six text messages he'd received from his weed dealer on behalf of a clearly livid Billy Murphy.

The essence of the messages was that Mr Murphy was quite unhappy at having his number blocked and Dexter needed to get in touch immediately if he wanted any chance of continuing to remain alive. He desperately wanted to ignore them, but couldn't stop himself from looking either. Like a moth drawn to a flame, he read the messages over and over again, aghast at the situation he'd managed to make so much worse.

Aware that he'd been in the bathroom a while and conscious that regular people might want to use the facilities, he flushed the toilet again to mark his presence. He didn't want the others to think he'd passed out or drowned in the bath. As he pushed the chrome handle and the water spiralled away down the porcelain pan, he read the latest angry words and sank further into a pit of depression.

The texts had continued coming long after they'd got back to Ewalina's last night and only tailed off at 4 am. Dexter assumed that even the toughest of hard men needed to sleep at some point. But now they'd started again. Every few minutes the phone vibrated enthusiastically as another dark message polluted the screen. Some were friendly, offering cash and a pat on the back. The majority suggested violence and an unhappy end to their little caper. Like a rabbit transfixed by oncoming headlights, Dexter could only stare at the phone, desperate to make some sense of the words that were arriving on a regular basis.

He deleted the most aggressive ones as quickly as he could. They were too stressful to keep reading. The one that had just arrived was more interesting. It said that he'd be given ten grand if he were to simply give away Buster's current whereabouts. It was a lot of money and would clear his debts. He could get his van fixed and drive far away from all this madness. There would be plenty left over for buying weed and drinks for the ladies he'd meet along the way.

He flushed again for good measure and pulled up his grubby underpants. Still undecided as to what to do, he unlocked the door and plastered a smile across his face.

#####

Fifteen minutes later, everyone was up and assembled in the bright living room. With freshly made hot drinks clasped in their hands, it looked almost like a gathering of friends, chatting and reminiscing about all the fun they'd had in the pub last night.

But reality couldn't be further from this portrayal. Tension, awkwardness and fear dominated the atmosphere. Buster started to hyperventilate as he worked out how to articulate what came next. When the moment felt right he stood up, took a deep breath, and started to explain.

"So, as you all know, I did the craziest thing last night."

Ewalina ignored him and stared out of the window.

"I stole a whole load of Billy Murphy's cash when a one-in-a-million chance arose, courtesy of my new friend Zaid here. Apart from Billy himself, there's no one in the world who knows more about his business dealings than me. I've got a record of his every single transaction on a memory stick in my case. That's why he probably wants to kill me right now. That and the fact I nicked a ton of his precious cash."

Buster laughed nervously. The others stared at him stony-faced, willing him to cut the waffle and get to the bit that would give them some hope and a direction out of this crisis.

"So, about a week ago I watched Billy give a man a kicking. It was brutal. I'd never seen anyone get hurt like that or get as angry as Billy did that night. Well, that was when the penny finally dropped with me. Actually, it didn't just drop, it went into free fall. It dawned on me properly for the first time that every single line on one of my spreadsheets is a tale of human misery.

Every formula represents some poor bugger trying to keep his head above water, terrified about a knock on the door if he misses a payment. And I was a major part of the outfit that was dealing out the fear and causing all the pain. Obviously, that's something you've seen for yourself, Zaid."

Zaid nodded sadly, his face still bearing the scars of Billy Murphy's handiwork.

"It was at that precise moment that I woke up."

#####

Ewalina was growing impatient. She'd heard most of this sob story the night before when she'd had her ear to the door. The self-indulgent tale of a pathetic accountant boy who's grown a conscience like a regular human being.

She wasn't going to endanger her life just so that this pitiful idiot could do some penance in order to make himself feel warm and cosy inside. This was the real world. They had the police after them. Billy Murphy and his gang wouldn't be far behind. She didn't want to hear this grinning fool moan on about how rotten and unfair the world was. He'd better spit out what he had to say and stop wasting her valuable time.

"Can you just get to the point please, Mother Theresa?" she snapped.

"So what if some Chinese guy I don't know got hurt? There's nothing I can do about it. Please just explain what I have to do to earn the money you promised me, so I can do it, and then get as far away from you lot as I possibly can. Skip to the good bit, please, mister."

Buster ignored her and continued. He'd have a word with her in private about her attitude when the moment was right.

"So, what I'm proposing is that we act like modern-day Robin Hoods. I want to return the money in the case. It's around a million pounds, give or take. I want to literally send it all back in the post. I know the names and addresses of everyone Billy's ripped off. It's all on the memory stick. Every little detail of the ridiculous interest rates paid on loans and all the protection fees he's terrified restaurants into paying. I've got the lot.

All we need is a laptop, some envelopes and a trip to the Post Office. It's simple. And I want to send a message too. I need all those people to know that they're not alone. Billy and his crew amount to about eight people. Just eight unpleasant bullies versus the hundreds of people he's been ripping off.

But we don't have much time, I'm afraid. If I know anything about Billy, it's that he'll do anything to catch me. He's probably close by, right now, as we speak. So, are you guys up for this?"

At first, no one reacted, then Zaid cautiously raised a thumb. Soon there were nods all around. Ewalina was in disbelief that anyone would want to do something so stupid with a million pounds.

"Ewalina, can I borrow your computer and printer, please? I want to do this straight away before he finds a way to stop us."

Buster had already seen it on a table in the corner of the living room, but it was only polite to ask if he could use it. She glared at him before replying,

"For seven thousand pounds you can throw it out of the fucking window for all I care. Just make sure you save enough money to pay me. Don't go sending it all back to your silly little charity cases."

Buster ignored her again. He felt that he was actually on the brink of doing something good for a change. The envelopes could be in the post within a few hours. Lives would be altered and there was a chance that the curse of Billy Murphy could be lifted forever. No amount of negativity or sarcasm was going to undermine that.

"Great. Let's do this. Sophia, could you go out and buy some envelopes and pens, please? You're the only one who's safe on the streets for the time being. No one is looking for you, as far as we know. I think around four hundred will do the trick. Big strong ones, please. And grab some elastic bands while you're at it. And stamps too. First-class ones, obviously. Oh, and printer paper," added Buster, panicking that he'd forgotten something.

Sophia jumped up, keen to get involved.

"I'd love to. I'll go right now. Anything to help get back at that monster. No one gets away with treating my poor daddy like that."

As Sophia pulled on her dirty trainers and Buster handed her some cash, Dexter glanced at his phone. No more texts had been delivered in the past twenty minutes. Maybe they'd lost interest. He wanted to be part of his friend's plan now. Getting a reward didn't seem like such a great idea anymore. And if Sophia wanted to help out, then so did he. He'd impress her by demonstrating that he was on her dad's side.

The idea of an underdog turning the tables on a bully sounded good and noble. It was a cause worth joining. He tried to push the cold murderous voice of Billy Murphy out of his head and prayed that his dark nasty secret would remain hidden for a little while longer.

Chapter 34

Sitting in an unmarked car, sipping his first takeaway coffee of the morning, Samuel spotted Gary jogging slowly towards him along the seafront. He was twenty minutes late and clearly doing his best to make up time.

His hair was wet and he smelt of coconut shower gel as he jumped, puffing and wheezing, into the passenger seat. He offered his sergeant a pastry from a large paper bag by way of penance for his tardiness.

"Sorry, Skipper, I overslept. What we doing meeting here then?"

"We're here, Gary, because a phone belonging to that Dexter Ward character is somewhere close by."

Gary looked confused.

"Let me explain. So, the guv'nor called me at 3 am with a number he'd somehow acquired for Ward. I don't know where he got it. I don't know how he got it either. And before you say anything, I know I should have asked, but I didn't, because I was half asleep. Weird thing is, he didn't ask me to put the trace on, like he'd normally do. He said he'd do it himself, which was odd."

"That's very odd indeed," agreed Gary, biting into a pain au chocolate.

"Hang on, mate, that's not all. Listen to this. He phoned me back at 5 am sounding, how can I put this delicately? … he was *completely* pissed. Absolutely wrecked, in fact, Gary. Yep, that's the most accurate way of putting it.

So, after a lot of repetition and going around the houses, he eventually tells me that the phone's still switched on and the trace had been successful. They've run the checks and the handset's been tracked to Hove. On the downside, because Ward's got a crappy old phone that doesn't have GPS, they couldn't identify a specific address.

He said the techies could only come up with an approximate area based on mast triangulation. They gave a half-mile stretch of Hove seafront as the most likely location. And that, my friend, is why I asked you to meet me here. Apparently, he hasn't moved all night and no texts or calls have been made, but there's been a shit load of incoming messages. Oh, and he kept going on and on and on about this Buster Brett as well, and how we have to find him. He didn't mention the Stalker at all, not even once, which was strange."

"What's going on with him, Sam? Is he acting weird, or what? It's not like him to get drunk," mused Gary, flicking crumbs off his shirt.

"And I mean, if this Buster's such a big deal, then why didn't they just pick him up outside court the other day? Surely, if they needed to bring him in, he was fair game then. He's not going to do a runner in front of dozen TV cameras, is he?"

"I couldn't agree more, Gary. And do you know what? He's not wanted on PNC either. I ran him through the box just now and he's not got a single conviction. Not one. Not even an outstanding speeding ticket. There's something we're not being told about. But the boss did say the ROCU were involved, so maybe we're just being kept out of the loop for the time being.

The thing that really pisses me off is that the DI doesn't appear to give a shit about the Stalker now. He's been busting my balls for weeks to try and to find her, and now he can hardly bring himself to mention her name. I appreciate she's small fry compared to Murphy and his gang, but I'd still like to know what's going on. Whatever happened to professional courtesy?"

"Ours not to reason why, ours but to do or die," sighed Gary, wearily.

"Fuck that," replied Samuel, as they settled down to watch the passing traffic.

The area indicated by the phone company included some of the most famous regency terraces and squares in the city. Somewhere in one of the glorious flats or dingy bedsits of Brunswick town, it was likely that Dexter Ward and his associates were busy keeping their heads down.

As Samuel sipped his coffee and watched the rush hour traffic slip past along Kings Road, he considered how close he might be to the Stalker right now. She was likely to be very near, probably sipping her own brew and worrying about how much they had on her.

He wondered if it was her flat they'd run to or somewhere owned by Billy Murphy. Had Buster Brett had a falling out with his boss somehow? That would make sense. But how did that tally with the DI's sudden interest in him?

It was good to sit and watch for a while. There was a slim chance that one of the gang might break cover and go to the shops or do something equally as stupid. They wouldn't necessarily know that one of their phones had been traced. It was often the simple things like popping for milk and teabags that got people into trouble. They'd have covered all the big stuff, only to let themselves down with the details.

It was only a slight possibility, but it was better than sitting in the office, fretting about what to do next. Samuel had learned from his years on the job that small odds occasionally turning good could make all the difference to an investigation like this.

He started the car and drove them around the corner into Adelaide Crescent. He wanted to find a more discreet spot to eat his breakfast. He backed into a resident's bay facing the terraces and started on one of Gary's pastries.

"I don't get this at all," he mumbled with a mouth full of croissant, crumbs falling onto his lap.

"You've got a guy from one of the worst criminal organisations in the South of England getting in a crappy camper van with a dimwit like Dexter Ward and then going back to his shitty flat. And then he does a runner and disappears. And, on top of that, he takes the person we've been trying to catch for weeks with him. Well, at least we're pretty sure it's her.

And I'd put money on the fact that this Brett character and the Stalker don't actually know each other based on their body language at the station. He looked totally freaked out by her.

And if that's not enough drama for one night, our lord and master boss doesn't give a shit about us almost catching the person he's told us to move heaven and earth for and is only interested in this new bloke, for some weird reason that he hasn't bothered to share with the rest of us poor mortals. He's never even mentioned Buster Brett before last night as far as I'm aware. Something's not right Gary, it really isn't."

Gary sipped his coffee and digested what he was hearing. He had his own less than favourable opinions of DI Simon Weston, but he thought it best to leave them out of the conversation for the time being.

Suddenly, something on the road to their left caught his eye.

"Sorry to interrupt, Skipper, but look at that car. I think it's Billy Murphy's. In fact, it definitely fucking is."

"What on God's earth is he doing here?" replied Samuel, wiping croissant crumbs from his mouth and sitting up as adrenaline coursed through his veins.

As he said the words, a black Bentley slipped slowly past. It stopped a few meters away and started to back into a gap between the adjacent parked cars. The space was too narrow and the driver had obviously become rattled by all the shouting emanating from the back-seat passenger. Even from a distance and with their windows shut, the police officers could hear the commotion. He was screaming at the driver and talking to someone else at the same time. He was calling his driver a cunt and someone else a cunt. Every other word was an expletive.

"Wind down the window, Gary - we've got to have a proper listen to this."

As they listened, snippets of information fell into their burning ears.

They gathered that Billy Murphy was looking for someone who was a cunt, that he wanted to kill. His driver was a useless cunt who needed to learn to fucking drive. The people who he was talking to on the phone were fat cunts who'd be dead if they didn't stop eating and find the first cunt, who he also wanted to kill. They learned that no one took Billy Murphy for a cunt and if they did, something awful would happen to them, that the officers couldn't quite make out. They learned that some other cunt had told Billy that the first cunt he wanted to kill was in the Brunswick town area and that another cunt who wanted a reward hadn't answered his phone all night and was going to end up dead in a ditch for his troubles.

After three attempts to get into the space, the driver gave up and went to find somewhere easier to park. As the shouting subsided into the distance, the two officers looked at each other and burst into a fit of laughter.

"What the actual fuck did we just witness there?" said Samuel, struggling to regain his composure.

"I think we can safely assume that Brett and his little gang aren't holed up in any property belonging to Mr Billy Murphy. And that at least one of them has done something pretty bad to upset him so much. My money's on Brett. He's the only one we know who's properly close to Billy."

Gary looked puzzled.

"What I want to know though, Sam, is why he's around this area searching for them. We only found out a couple of hours ago, so how the fuck would he know where to look? And don't you think it's a bit odd that the guv'nor phones you in the middle of the night with Dexter Ward's phone number out of the blue and next thing we know we're looking in the same place for our little gang of wrong'uns as Billy Murphy's mob? And how did he even get hold of Ward's number anyway? It's all a bit weird if you ask me."

Gary was right. It did feel very odd indeed. But the other part of the overheard conversation about a reward did sound an awful lot as though one of the gang had been trying to strike a deal on the side. Someone was either keen to make a fast buck or was just trying to save their own skin. Maybe there had been a falling out and Dexter Ward, the Stalker or someone else with them was trying to make their own happy ending by providing Billy with information, which, no doubt, would have included the location of their current hideaway.

But if that was true, why hadn't Billy got his driver to park right outside the address he'd been given before booting the door in? From what they'd heard, it didn't sound as if he was sure where to look or what to do. In that respect, they were all in the same boat. It was all very confusing and, for the next few minutes, the officers sat in silence with the radio playing cool jazz in the background, as they ruminated on the facts and sipped their coffees.

Samuel was the first to break the silence.

"The guv'nor's on the take, isn't he, Gary?"

"Certainly looks that way, Sam, it certainly does," came the measured, serious reply.

Chapter 35

Simon Weston was still drunk at nine o'clock in the morning. But rather than being a happy inebriation, it was the miserable, paranoid, 'when will this nightmare ever end' variety. The calls and texts from Billy Murphy had been unrelenting. His anxiety and stress levels had never been higher.

Last night, he'd polished off what was left of his wife's chilled wine before drinking a further two lukewarm bottles he'd prised from a case in the spare room. She was saving them for Christmas, but that didn't matter anymore. He couldn't even focus on the day ahead. He'd been awake all night, wracked by shame and indecision and now he could feel the first signs of a momentous hangover starting to kick in.

He pretended to his wife and the kids that he was sick. It was easy to carry off because it was close to the truth. They'd left him alone, confused by his uncharacteristic behaviour. Once they departed for their day of normality at the shopping centre or swimming pool or whatever place they said they were going, he poured another glass and let the sadness wash over him. Holding his head in his hands, he wiped away the tears as they ran down his cheeks.

He needed to sober up. He needed to wash. He had to deal with the crushing hangover that was on its way. But more than anything else, he needed to find a way out of the crisis that was on the brink of shattering his life.

The previous night, he'd removed his secret phone from the kitchen drawer and put it in his pocket. Billy had been demanding information every half hour, so there was little point in keeping it hidden away anymore. First, he'd had to call him back with an update on the flat on St James's Street. Then he'd let him know about the scuffle at the Unicorn. Next, Billy insisted on an urgent mobile number trace. He'd continued texting every few minutes until he got the information he was after.

Simon Weston couldn't believe that he'd let himself get into the impossible position of being controlled like this. He'd let himself down. He'd let his family down. And if Sussex Police ever found out that he'd let them down, he'd be straight off to jail with his reputation in the gutter. He'd really messed things up and there was no obvious way out.

Despite the alcohol he'd consumed and his desperation, he'd managed to do a few of the basics required to maintain the illusion that he was still an upstanding and honest police inspector. He could just about remember phoning his sergeant during the night. Perhaps he'd called twice, but his recollection was too hazy to be sure. He cringed as he thought about his crude attempts to disguise the signs of his inebriation. No one at all would have been fooled.

At 9 am, his sergeant called him back and he took the call from his bed.

"Sir, we've just had the most bizarre encounter. We were parked up in Adelaide Crescent trying to get a handle on the phone triangulation info you gave us, when guess who rocked up?"

Without giving him time to respond, Samuel Edge cracked on with the story.

"Yeah, Billy Murphy himself, would you believe it, in an absolute bastard of a mood. He was effing and jeffing away on the phone and I think it was this Buster Brett character he was going on about. Thing is, what was he doing there? Someone's obviously tipped him off."

He could think of nothing to say in return. The situation was becoming intolerable. His officers and blackmailer had been within feet of each other. What if they'd heard something more specific while eavesdropping on Billy's conversation? What if his name had been mentioned? He wasn't sure how this nightmare was ever going to end. As he lay sweating on his bed, he struggled to even remember what lies he'd already told.

By 10 am, he'd managed to get up and dress himself. He brushed his teeth twice to remove the aftertaste of his wife's festive Chardonnay. His hangover was now crushing. His head was throbbing and all he wanted to do was lie down and sleep it off. It was tempting, but that wouldn't help him regain the upper hand. He needed to get into the nick and claw back some of the credibility he'd no doubt lost with his officers.

There was only one instant way to disguise a hangover like this. It had worked before and it would work again. He'd swing by the club for a sauna on his way into work. A quick half hour of sweating out the alcohol and he might just be able to trick his colleagues into believing that he hadn't been up all night drinking. It would also give him time to think and compose himself before he had to face his sceptical team.

He was worried that he'd already stretched his credibility too far. They'd think his behaviour was odd. Suspicions would have been raised already. It was a clumsy lie he'd told them about the ROCU being involved. A couple of well-placed phone calls could easily expose that deception.

Downing a pint of water and swallowing four painkillers, he searched for a way out of this mire. He needed a miracle that would result in Billy off his back and the Stalker in custody. Maybe it was wishful thinking after everything he'd done, but he couldn't allow himself to end up in prison. Awful things happened to coppers inside.

As he walked to the sauna, he felt uneasy. The club was where he'd got himself in trouble. It had only been a week ago, but so much had changed since then. Just one fateful night had started a chain of events that now saw his entire life spinning out of control. He'd not been honest with his wife and for a long time he'd not been true to himself. He should have come out years ago, but what with the kids and his precious career, he'd never found the courage. He'd been living a double life and now that truth was going to cost him dear.

Sussex police was a different place when he'd started out twenty years before. Less accommodating and more judgmental. Things were different now, but he'd missed the boat, kept quiet and got saddled with the 'solid family man' label, despite his inner turmoil.

But what had he really done wrong apart from letting himself get caught on camera by Billy Murphy? What he'd done was foolish, but it didn't make him a bad man. He'd been naive, stupid and gullible, but did he really deserve to lose his job and family just because he hadn't had the courage to open up about the person he really was?

The club wasn't busy at 11 am. The boy on reception was talking on the phone as Simon Weston leant wearily against the counter, sweating and trying to catch his eye. His head was pounding and his whole body ached. He hadn't been organised when he left the house and needed to hire a towel. It sounded as if the boy was trying to report a crime, the irony of which was not lost on the profoundly hungover DI.

"Yep, that's right, dear, it's an iPhone 14. Sort of silver grey. No, love, I don't know the serial number off the top of my head, I'm afraid, but I can probably dig it out though, if you give me a couple of minutes. It was on the counter at work and I must have turned my back for a second and it was gone. I reckon one of the customers must have swiped it. They're a lovely bunch on the whole, apart from the little sod who nicked my bloody phone, obviously.

CCTV system? Well, we do have one, but it's not working at the moment. It needs a new hard drive or something technical like that. It's an old system, so the bits need to be ordered from Japan. Not something they keep in stock, apparently. I think that's what the repair man said anyway. That's right, it's not been working for about three weeks now. Yes, the cameras all work, but the hard drive thingy that records everything is buggered, if you'll excuse my French. I'd have sorted the little wanker out myself if I'd known who did it, love, don't you worry."

Realising the significance of the conversation, Simon Weston forgot about his hangover in an instant. There was a sliver of hope in the words he'd just overheard. He waited anxiously until the boy stopped talking before striking up a conversation. He tried to keep his voice as calm and measured as he could. He knew that his fate, life and family all depended on the accuracy of the information he'd just received.

"Sorry, mate, but I couldn't help listening. Sounds bloody awful about your phone. Getting it stolen is bad enough, but the CCTV being broken at the same time, well, that's a right kick in the teeth. I really feel for you."

The boy seemed delighted that someone was taking an interest in his loss.

"Tell me about it! I'm absolutely gutted. I'd only had the bloody thing for two weeks. I've got my suspicions mind, but without the cameras working, I can't prove a thing. My boss, Mr Murphy, he doesn't take kindly to punters stealing from his staff, I'll tell you that for nothing."

"So why didn't he just get it fixed a bit quicker?" added the DI, cutting to the chase. He was desperate to extract the vital elements of information he needed as quickly as possible.

"Good point. He's a lovely man, don't get me wrong and I wouldn't say a bad word about him, but how can I put this?"

The boy beckoned Simon Weston to come closer.

"The problem is," he continued, in a hushed tone, "he's as tight as arseholes, he really is. He'd rather get the old system fixed which takes for ever because it's twenty years old and you can't get the bits, rather than just fit a new modern one that doesn't break down all the time. Anyway, what do I know? I'm just a sauna receptionist on minimum wage and he's a millionaire who drives around in a Bentley. All I know is that it's been broken for three weeks now and some chancer's got my bloody brand-new phone."

Before the boy could finish his piece, Simon Weston dashed for the exit. He felt physically sick. He'd been taken for a fool. Billy Murphy had called his bluff and, as a result, he'd almost lost everything. There were no photos or CCTV. There was nothing that Billy Murphy could post or email to the Superintendent. Billy Murphy's hold over him had been based on a lie.

On the street outside, he stamped on the supermarket phone. He picked up the pieces and put them in the nearest bin, making sure that the SIM card was snapped cleanly in half. He started to walk, but as he thought about how he'd been duped, his pace began to quicken. What an idiot he'd been to allow this to happen. Anger surged though his body as he broke into a jog. How could he have let his judgment get so clouded? Within moments he was sprinting as fast as his hangover would allow through the narrow streets of Brighton in the direction of the police station on John Street.

To save his skin he'd have to turn the tables on his blackmailer and the best way to do that was to get to Buster Brett before Billy had the chance to kill him. Whatever falling out the two of them had had, it held the key to putting the old man away for good. He knew that he was far from being in the clear, but his instincts told him that he'd been presented with an opportunity… a slim but real chance to pull his career, family and reputation back from the abyss they'd been on the brink of tumbling into.

Four minutes later, he arrived at the police station, puffing and dishevelled. He threw himself up three flights of stairs and burst into the CID office, wheezing and sweating, to the complete surprise of everyone working there. As soon as he was able to catch his breath, he clapped his hands together to get his officers' attention.

"Listen up everyone! We need to find Buster Brett. We really do. And I'm relying on you lovely bunch to do this for me. I mean for us, you know, Sussex Police."

He could hear his own voice sounding choked and tight. He steadied himself by reaching for a chair. He felt drunk again, sick and tired. His whole team were staring, wondering what had happened. His mind went blank. He had to continue talking, but could think of nothing further to say. His blood pressure dropped and a cold sweat engulfed his body.

"You're all fantastic, guys. I know I don't say it very often, but I love you lot. I really do."

There were uncomfortable looks all around. He wondered what had possessed him to use such inappropriate words. He realised that he was starting to talk rubbish but couldn't think of a way to stop himself from continuing.

"So, we need to find Buster Brett. And the Stalker of course. But mainly Buster. You're all bloody amazing, you really are. And why do we need to find him so urgently, I can sense you all wondering. Well, the answer is clear…"

His voice tailed off as his stewed brain failed to come up with a convincing continuation. The answer was neither clear to him nor anyone else in the room.

"I've been such an idiot," he whispered abstractly, momentarily overwhelmed by his problems.

"Sorry, where was I? Yes, Buster Brett, he's got to be found. Or else. And if we can get him in, I might be alright. What I mean is, we... we might be able to bring Billy Murphy down. And by that, I mean get him nicked at last. Yes, team effort and all that. Oh, and the Stalker too. Yes, the Stalker's good, don't me wrong, but if we can find this Buster Brett first, then so much the better. And if we can get him in alive, then that would be fantastic. Not that anyone's trying to kill him. Well, I assume they're not. But even if they were..."

He lost his train of thought again.

"You lot, you really are the best. I absolutely love working with you lot. And I can't stress how much I'm relying on you to find him for me, or us, by which I mean, well, you know..."

He rambled on incoherently for a further five minutes about Buster Brett falling out with Billy Murphy before abruptly dashing to the gents to be violently sick, leaving his startled team to wonder what had become of their normally sober, reserved and professional leader.

Chapter 36

Billy Murphy was unhappy. The morning hadn't gone well and he was starting to feel twitchy. Two frustrating hours in the back of the Bentley had pushed his attention span to its limit. The information about the phone triangulation had turned out to be useless and they'd wasted precious time as a result. To make matters worse, his tame copper had stopped replying to his texts. He realised that he'd pushed his luck with that one. The bluff had been good while it worked, but instinct told him that something had gone badly wrong.

The Inspector going silent meant there was now a chance the police might get to Buster before he could. That would be the worst possible outcome. The thought of the authorities getting their teeth into the boy with some sort of plea bargain panicked Billy. They'd offer him protection and immunity for all the juicy beans he could spill. Adrenaline pumped sharply through his system as he snatched the phone from the seat next to him.

"Right, you lot! Listen up!" he growled into the handset for the benefit of the boys sitting in the Range Rover on the opposite side of the road.

He suspected they were asleep or eating. He was instantly furious with them again for allowing this situation to happen in the first place.

"I've had enough of all this dicking around. If I see another queer picking up dog shit, or a hippy on a skateboard, I'm going to get out of this motor and snap the fucking thing in two. We're wasting our time here. They could be in any one of these shitty flats watching us right now, having a right laugh and waiting for us to get bored and fuck off. I'm not prepared to sit here any longer while a bunch of clowns takes me for a fucking cunt.

We've got Buster who's turned his fucking phone off and this Dexter geezer who's not answering his. And now that bell-end copper's decided he doesn't have to bother picking up either. They're all piss-taking cunts and I've had enough. We've been two steps behind the little shit since last night, thanks to that copper's useless information, so now we're going to get ahead of the game.

We're going to drive back up to the house and do some research. Use our fucking brains for a change. You got that, boys? We're going to get the phone books out, go on that fucking internet and do what we should have done in the first place. Do any of you thick cunts actually have the faintest idea what I'm talking about?"

Razor wanted to say that people didn't use phone books these days but knew better than to open his mouth.

Billy paused, waiting for some response from the boys in the other vehicle. He was annoyed that they were just sitting there mute and contributing nothing. He pictured their blank, startled, ignorant faces. They probably had their mouths stuffed with pies or crisps. They'd caused this problem by leaving Buster alone. This mess was their doing. He couldn't understand how they could remain so quiet, leaving him to do the thinking and take all the stress. He waited, willing them to fill the silence with at least a semblance of intelligence. Just one coherent comment was all he wanted.

Four seconds... five seconds. The boys in the Range Rover started to panic. What did Billy want them to say? Had his phone run out of battery? Why wasn't he saying anything? Six seconds... seven seconds. They stared at each other, desperately trying to think of a reply that would calm their boss down and prevent his anger from spiking any further. Eight seconds... nine seconds...

Billy could stand it no longer. His anger boiled over as he barked into the phone.

"Have you bunch of fat useless cunts got nothing to say? Why is it me who always has to do the thinking? You lot caused this fucking problem, so the very least you can do is answer me. Am I making meself crystal clear?"

One second... two seconds... three seconds...

"Sorry, boss. What do you want us to do?" said Antony lamely, just to fill the awful void.

"What are we supposed to be doing? We're not quite with you, Billy. Sorry. What do you want us to look up on the internet?"

Billy sighed, appalled at the one-sided nature of the conversation. Where was the spark with these boys? Could they really be so devoid of initiative and ideas? Were they so scared of him that they thought it was acceptable to contribute so little?

For a second, he felt deflated and unsure of himself. Although they had no inkling, he was willing one of them to speak up and offer a little reassurance and help lift some of the weight from his tired old shoulders.

It was at troubled times like this that he felt alone. Buster had been the intellect that he'd bounced off for the past five years, but now that foil was gone. And although he wanted to kill him in the most painful way he could envisage, the young man from Hove had left a gaping, painful hole.

But it wasn't a problem because he was the notorious Billy Murphy, he told himself, rallying his strength. He just needed to remind himself of what he'd achieved and how far he'd come. 'The Most Dangerous Man In London' is what it had said in the newspaper. He had the houses, the cars and more money stashed in a hundred different hiding places than he could ever spend.

He wasn't done just yet.

He still had the strength to deal with anything thrown at him. People just needed to be reminded that he was a living legend. Just focus the rage and turn it to your advantage, he told himself. Channel the anger to get the outcome you well and truly deserve. It's not too late to save the situation if you put the experience of sixty years to good use.

Plus, he was cleverer than Buster Brett, the police or any of the other chancers trying so hard to bring him down. He'd been in worse scrapes before and come up smelling of roses. He just needed to show the world what happened to anyone who crossed him. Believe in yourself, Billy boy. Hold steady, remember who you are and where you've come from.

"I'll spell it out to you brain-dead idiots in the simplest way I can, shall I? Buster's tried to take from me the things I care about very much indeed. He's tried to ruin me reputation, me credibility and me legacy.

I don't give a fuck about the money. I can earn that back in no time, but making me look weak is something I can't have. Not after I took Buster in and made him what he is today. Not after all the work I did in court this week to secure me future. No fucking way. So, think about it, what's the worst thing I could do to get back at a nice boy like our Buster?"

One second… two seconds… three seconds… Billy rolled his eyes and continued.

"I'll give you donuts a little clue, shall I? We're going after the one thing he values above anything else in the whole fucking world. And what do you think that could be, lads?"

The silence from the other car was deafening.

"His car! Are we going to burn his car, boss?" said Anthony, enthusiastically clutching at straws on behalf of the others.

Billy sighed and allowed a momentary flush of anger to pass before replying.

"No, you dummy, we're not going to burn his fucking car. As it's registered in me company's name, that course of action would be extremely counter-productive, wouldn't it? Any other bright ideas, before I put you lot out of your misery?"

One second... two seconds... three seconds... Billy clenched his fists and took a deep breath. Do the thinking for them, he thought. That's why you're the boss. That's why you've got a Bentley and the big house. Don't punish them for what they're not bright enough to understand.

"What we're going to do is go after his mum and dad. Yep, you heard right. We're going to get our mitts on his fucking parents."

The boys were confused. It was an unwritten rule of the criminal fraternity that families were left out of squabbles and fights. No sensible business would ever get done if parents and kids ended up as collateral damage when disputes broke out between rival parties. Billy was breaking a fundamental taboo with this idea.

"Don't you lot fucking dare go quiet on me again! That cunt's crossed a line, so the gloves are off. He's told me before that his folks live in Brighton, so that's how we'll get to him and if you muppets have got a problem with that, then you'd better say so right now."

Billy paused to allow anyone to speak up, knowing full well that they wouldn't dare.

"They won't be too hard to find. A mock-Tudor semi somewhere nice and quiet, I reckon. Probably got a Jag on the drive and a lovely little garden out the back. I'll wager he's still got a room there with posters on the walls and his cuddly bunny up on a shelf. Proper nice set-up.

We'll go and pay them a visit and invite them to join us up at Dyke Road Avenue. Then we'll call their dutiful son with the good news. He'll come trotting straight up to beg for clemency, bringing me money with him. Just like the first time we ever met. We'll all have a cosy little chat and get this whole nasty business put to bed in no time. Job's a good'un. So, what exactly do you gentleman think of that idea?"

One second… two seconds… three seconds… then Anthony chipped in again as if an idea had drifted into his head from the ether.

"Do you think his mum and dad will want to come up to the house, boss? I mean, it's not as if we know them or anything is it?"

This time, Billy didn't wait for the anger to clear before replying.

"I don't care what they want or don't fucking want. They're coming whether they like it or not. This isn't an invitation to a fucking cocktail party. You'll be knocking on their door with a gun in one hand and a roll of gaffer tape in the other. Do you get me? You'll ask them nicely just the once and if that doesn't work, then you know what to do. You do know what to do, don't you, boys?"

Billy was about to explode when the unanimous response that he so dearly needed to hear, burst across the airwaves.

"Yes, boss. We know what to do!"

And with those reassuring words ringing in his ears, Billy ordered Razor to start the car and lead the way back up to the house.

As he sat back, hoping to get a few minutes' rest before they arrived, his phone started to ring. It was Fliss. Yet again. Why couldn't she just let him have a little peace to deal with matters? What was it with all these constant calls and messages? He pressed the red button, settled back, and put her completely out of his mind.

He preferred to think about Buster's parents. Whatever peace Mr and Mrs Brett were currently enjoying, Billy was determined to make sure that it would soon be shattered by a ring, chime or knock at their door. As he imagined them baking cakes and sipping Earl Grey tea in front of a warm log fire, he smiled at the prospect of the chaos that would soon be wrought on their perfect little lives, courtesy of the son they clearly knew so little about.

Chapter 37

For a few minutes Buster struggled with the dated computer in the corner of the room. It didn't want to communicate with the memory stick he'd taken from the safe. He started to sweat as his plan hit yet another obstacle. But after a little help from Zaid, who was more technologically literate than his rough looks would suggest, three detailed spreadsheets of Billy's operation had been printed out.

He laid them out on the table and pondered the consequences of what he was about to do. Within the crowded lines of black and white print lay the power to change lives.

The first was a list of the 428 protection clients Billy tapped up for cash on a weekly basis. Mainly Chinese and Thai restaurants, with a few curry houses thrown in for good measure, 153 were in Brighton with the remainder in London.

Columns showed the monthly sum demanded, the total paid in the year to date and any arrears accrued. As he glanced down the list, he spotted a snag that he hadn't anticipated. He'd looked at these sheets a thousand times before at work, but it was only now when it mattered, that he noticed a flaw. All the addresses were recorded in a format that suited Billy's specific needs.

The Golden Dragon, 98 Upper Street
Pagoda Grill, Florence Road
Hins, Preston Street, Brighton

There were no postcodes and some didn't even have street numbers. Billy wasn't in the habit of writing to his 'clients' and as the boys knew exactly where all the businesses were located, the niceties of the full postal address had been overlooked. This was going to slow things down.

Since Buster intended to mail each of the victims a refund of what they'd paid in the last twelve months, they'd have to use the internet to find the missing details before hitting the post. That would take time, but if the work was divided between them, it was manageable. Buster looked at Dexter and thought better of asking him for help. He was staring at Sophie with a stupid grin on his face, lost in his own little world of stoned dreams.

The second spreadsheet detailed the loans to the 297 individuals whose chaotic lives revolved around their payments to Billy's debt collection team. People who feared what pain the knock on the door would mean if they hadn't scraped together that week's cash. Buster knew that he preyed on the poorest souls he could find, those whose kids went hungry and cold before they'd dare refuse the vultures at the door. It would be fitting for Zaid to work on this, as his name filled one of the cells.

Buster estimated that there would be just enough cash in the suitcase to refund each victim for the last twelve months, with a little left over for expenses and what he'd rashly promised Ewalina.

The final spreadsheet was his insurance policy. It was a damning document detailing Billy's entire drug operation. A comprehensive list of all the middlemen to whom Billy offered his wholesale services. Names, telephone numbers, territories covered and who owed what. Incendiary information if it were ever to get into the hands of the authorities.

The first two could be argued away in court as the workings of a semi-legitimate business service offered by a fine and upstanding entrepreneur, one who'd suffered the most appalling breach of confidentiality at the hands of a scheming and disloyal former employee. Any decent barrister could dress them up and neutralise the threat.

But not the third one. It was clearly about drugs. There were no codes or euphemisms. It mentioned grams and kilos. There were columns for cannabis, cocaine, crack and heroin. Many of the phone numbers could be linked to known drug dealers, who'd squeal like trapped rabbits rather than go to prison. If this was to ever find its way in front of a judge or jury, Billy would be going down for the rest of his life.

He'd often wondered why his boss allowed all this data to be gathered together so neatly, in one convenient and absolutely incriminating place. When he first joined the firm, Billy was still using note books covered in codes and scribbles that were designed to be pushed down drains or set alight if there was ever a whiff of getting arrested. This was the time-honoured and well-proven method of destroying evidence and staying out of prison. But once the new boy started to revolutionise the operation, Billy got a taste for organisation and technology.

He got addicted to knowing day by day, hour by hour, how much money he was making. He loved to be able to run his finger down the computer screen with Buster at his side, asking about this blip or that, before sending the boys out to deal with the problem. He'd put his faith in the new ways, without fully appreciating the trail they could leave. The desire to see his success laid out in neat rows and columns had outweighed his natural caution.

Buster could remember telling Billy about the flaws in the digital system, but the lure of the new had been too much for his old-school boss to resist. But now that cavalier approach could be the old man's undoing. He needed to work out how to use this information to his maximum advantage. He'd think about that while they worked.

Buster sat Zaid and Sophia at the computer table in the corner of the room, with half the envelopes, a couple of pens, the second spreadsheet and £100 000 he'd just counted out of the suitcase under Ewalina's attentive gaze.

The notes were all twenties and bundled up into thousands. That would be enough to get them started and they could ask for more as they worked through the pile. He told them to look at the column headed 'year to date' and round that figure up to the nearest twenty.

They were then to count out the correct number of notes and put them in an envelope along with a note that Buster had hastily composed and printed out four-up on an A4 sheet, using most of Ewalina's paper. He'd used the edge of the table to tear up the sheets until there was a note for every envelope.

To finish off, they had to write out the name and address of the recipient and tape up the edges of the envelope to make sure that there weren't any tears or giveaway spills of cash in the sorting office. They'd use the computer to search up any missing postal details and then they'd be done.

Buster printed out a duplicate of the protection money spreadsheet and gave it to Ewalina. He gave her the task of doing the same as the others with the first half of the entries, which he'd marked out with a fluorescent marker pen. He then sat on the sofa and started on the other half. She sat at her dining table and after some initial gripes about how long it would take, why was it necessary and how would it benefit her, she succumbed to the rhythm of the work. With her pen scratching away at the cheap brown envelopes, she looked almost happy to be at work.

Although Buster found the process of returning the cash deeply satisfying, it was soon clear that it was going to take much longer than he would have liked. He started to worry that the post office would be closed by the time they finished. No aspect of the work could be done quickly. Counting out the correct number of notes took a few minutes and had to be done accurately. Securing the envelopes with tape so that they wouldn't disintegrate in the post took a couple more. Writing out the addresses clearly and legibly added even more time, especially when information was missing.

Buster asked Dexter to sit next to him on the sofa and explained how he could use his phone to search up postcodes. But despite being shown how to do this five times, he was only able to offer up the required information at a pitifully slow rate. Eventually, frustration got the better of Buster. He gave up on his old friend and snatched the phone off him to do it himself. Dexter didn't complain or react as he settled back into the cushions to stare at Sophia as she worked.

When Buster occasionally looked up, he was heartened by all the counting, stuffing, sticking, writing and internet searching happening around the room. Slowly and steadily, the task progressed all day. A little bit of banter was thrown around and Sophia made up a lame song about them being a gang of modern-day Robin Hoods. She incorporated their names into the lyrics and tried to make them sing along. Robbing from Billy to give to the poor was the chorus.

Ewalina smiled but refused to join in the fun. Bit by bit, the weary production line neared its conclusion by late afternoon.

Buster's original thinking had been to walk the envelopes to a post office and send them recorded delivery. That would be the safest way to ensure the packages ended up in the right hands. However, it was Dexter, in a moment of rare lucidity, who pointed out that it would take hours to deal with such a vast number of items at any local post office. For once he was right. So, after a little weighing of the packages on Ewalina's kitchen scales and a review of the Royal Mail's tariff website, they decided that four simple first-class stamps slapped on the front of each envelope would be the most practical way forward. It was quick and simple and most of them would get safely to where they needed to be by the following morning.

Sophia had been asked to pop out for more envelopes, tape and twelve hundred first-class stamps at around 2 pm. This was followed by a further trip for coffee and sandwiches for the hungry workers at 3 pm. By 4 pm, every entry on the first two spreadsheets had been translated into a correctly addressed letter, stuffed with a corresponding sum of cash and a small note to its recipient added by way of explanation.

Please find enclosed all the money you've paid to Billy Murphy in the past year. His days as a bully are numbered. Be strong. Talk to your family, friends and community. Talk to the media, the police and everyone you know. Let them know that you won't tolerate being abused by Billy Murphy ever again. Stand together and he won't be able to touch you. You are the many and he is just an old man with only a few people to help spread his misery. You no longer need to be afraid. Be strong and be free. Spread the word!

It wasn't the best thing Buster had ever written, but it captured the essence of what he needed to say. He redrafted it several times after Sophia pointed out that it read like one of the inspirational memes she liked to share on social media.

Buster was just pleased that his goal was within sight after the chaos and darkness of the night before. Before him on the living room floor sat six supermarket carrier bags stuffed with the packages they'd been working on all day. A modest sight to most people, but it filled his heart with hope. He knew that he was now within grasping distance of the goal that had precipitated this perilous adventure in the first place.

"Guys, thanks so much for helping with this. I know it's not been the most riveting thing to spend all day doing, but the impact we're going to have on so many people's lives is massive. When these envelopes drop through their letter boxes, they'll feel they're not alone anymore. Well, that's what I'm hoping for anyway. But before that can happen, we need to get them posted. I'm thinking we should spread them across several boxes rather than just the one. We don't want to put all our eggs in one basket, or post box, if you know what I mean."

The others smiled sympathetically at Buster's weak joke but Ewalina's stern face showed that she wasn't happy again. She was impatient and had heard enough of Buster's waffling valedictory speech. She cut him off as he spoke.

"Sorry to interrupt, but can I make a suggestion please, Mary Poppins? I appreciate that you won't trust me to go and do the job by myself, so how about I go with the dead girl and we can make the post together before the last collection at 5 pm? I can think of at least five letter boxes within a couple of minutes of here. It's easy. She can keep an eye on me for you and I can make sure she doesn't get distracted by some loser trying to drag her into the nearest pub."

Dexter didn't react to the insult that went straight over his head. He was still staring at Sophia, oblivious to everything being said.

"I can wear one of my other work outfits and no one will recognise me. Absolutely no one. Not even you lot! I'm very good you know."

Buster thought for a moment. It was a risk. She was much more streetwise than Sophia and it wouldn't be beyond the bounds of comprehension for her to give the younger girl the slip and make off with the money. But that didn't seem very likely. They were holed up in her flat and there was only a slim chance she'd abandon everything she owned, as well as her beautiful home, to go on the run in just her wig and heels. He'd take the risk. Plus, the remaining cash he'd promised was another reason for her to return. Hopefully, she was just trying to justify the fee, which, in the cold light of day seemed ridiculously high for her muted contribution to the day's effort. He'd cross that bridge when he needed to.

"Okay, Ewalina, that seems like a great idea. Go with Sophia as quickly as you can. The sooner these envelopes are safely in the care of Her Majesty's postal system, the happier I'll be. Let's just get this done and then I'll treat everyone to a takeaway and a few drinks this evening."

There were appreciative nods all around, except from Ewalina, who sensed that events were leading towards another awful night with this feral bunch residing in her beautiful home.

An hour later, Sophia reported back that they'd put the envelopes into six different post boxes without incident. Ewalina hadn't tried to do a runner and they'd not been followed. Sophia added that Ewalina had actually been really helpful and completely unlike the rude and offish person they'd come to know over the past twenty-four hours. They'd posted the letters before the last collection time stated on each box and had even remembered to pick up the shopping list of wine and beer that they'd been asked to buy on their way back.

Buster ordered food from a particular restaurant in Preston Street that he knew was on Billy's spreadsheet. He felt a tingle of excitement as he spoke to the voice on the other end of the phone. As he ordered chow mien, sweet and sour and everything else he'd scribbled down so he wouldn't forget, he anticipated how they'd feel in the morning when the postman delivered his surprise package.

As the drinks flowed and food filled the nervous emptiness in his stomach, Buster thought that he might be sick. He knew that something good had been done today, but he'd not made himself any safer. He'd only done the easy, feel-good part of his plan. Tomorrow he'd have to tackle the tougher challenge of trying to stay alive. It was obvious that Billy would be enraged when he found out about the mail drop and the group's conversation skirted around that subject. No one wanted to face that reality or undermine their sense of achievement.

While Ewalina cleared away the plates and poured another round of drinks, Buster fretted about what to do with the third spreadsheet. The first two would help to put things right, but it was this final one that would keep him alive. He considered contacting the police in the morning to make a deal. He'd need them to act quickly before Billy got hold of him. He wondered if he should just walk into the police station's front office or call 999 and ask them to pick him up.

Seeing the memory stick still sticking out of Ewalina's laptop, he unplugged it and shoved it deep into his jean's front pocket. It was unsettling to think that without this tiny package of plastic and silicone for protection, he might soon be dead.

Chapter 38

Derek parked the Ranger Rover across the road from the house they'd been looking for. As he turned off the engine and glanced at Anthony, the silence in the car was momentarily comforting. Nice and carefully does it, he thought. Better safe than sorry.

He needed to check the facts before they made another move. Billy had made it quite clear that no more mistakes would be tolerated. One more minute in the warm car wasn't going to make a difference, one way or the other.

He was hesitant and not even sure if they were in the right place. Razor had found the address on the internet last night and Billy had written it on the back of a pizza box he'd taken from the kitchen bin. His writing was big and bold. There was an aggression in the pen strokes that made Derek feel the gravity of the task ahead. Billy was expecting results. There would be dire consequences if they fucked up again.

He was scared of making another error. He didn't want them to leave the warmth and security of the car before they absolutely needed to, but on the other hand, this was their one and final chance to make amends with Billy, so the sooner they got on with it, the better. He pictured the boss, hovering by the phone, waiting for news, desperate to hear that they'd done things exactly as he'd asked, with no awkward complications. There would be no more chances if the next ten minutes went badly. He figured that a few more seconds in the cosy car couldn't hurt.

He longed for his boss's forgiveness and to go back to the normal door-knocking routine in places that felt familiar. Neighbourhoods where people knew him and did what they were told just because he was one of Billy Murphy's boys. But this wasn't their turf. Nobody knew them here or appreciated the respect they ought to be given. He felt out of place and exposed. He could already feel the watchful eyes behind a hundred twitching curtains, noting their number plate and debating whether to call the police or alert the neighbourhood watch. One raised voice or scuffle and they'd be in real trouble.

Stay nice and calm, he told himself. Stick to the plan. Do things just like Billy said and it will all turn out fine. He can't blame us if we do things exactly how he said. 'These people are civilians; they don't understand our world,' Billy had explained. 'They're not used to our rules, so listen to what I say and do it my way.' And that was exactly what he intended to do. He just needed to follow Billy's instructions and get back to Dyke Road Avenue with the minimum of fuss. The boss could then take it from there. All he had to do was reach for the door handles, swing his legs out of the car and start events rolling. But a nagging doubt held him back. A few more seconds in the warmth and he'd commit to the plan.

The road was quiet and wide. Grass verges between the pavement and the tarmac were interrupted only by mature trees and cross-overs to herringboned brick driveways. Late plate Mercedes and BMWs sat outside most of the houses, mainly black or grey with the odd one in white. Probably for the wives, he thought. It was just as Billy said it would be.

He'd asked Anthony to do the navigating. The houses all had names rather than numbers and that had caused them their first problem. They were looking for number 56, but there were no numbers they could see from the car, just a Tanglewood, Glenside, Forest Lodge and other such bucolic names.

Back on their home turf, only the estates and tower blocks had names, not individual homes. It had taken a while to search out a house with a number on its door and then count back from there to find the one they wanted. Even that had caused a headache. Was it odds and evens on either side of the road, or did the numbers go up one side and down the other? They'd figured it out after a few minutes of peering and gawping and looking, to everyone who saw them, like a car full of kerb-crawling bouncers who'd strayed too far from a town centre nightclub.

The house was the same mock-Tudor style as Billy's, not as big or flashy but from the same period of safe and reassuring domestic architecture. Reliable and respectable, but dull and conventional at the same time. It had none of the railings and gates that Billy was so fond of and, luckily for them, there wasn't a CCTV camera to be seen, just a neat front garden with a bed of red and yellow roses and parking for two cars in front of a single-storey garage. Today there was just one car on the drive - a silver Passat. It was neither new nor old. Exactly the sort of sensible car a retired surveyor would drive to the tennis club.

Both he and Anthony now knew everything they needed to know about Buster's mum and dad. When they had got back to the house yesterday, they'd set to work on the internet. They discovered from the local newspaper's archive that Buster's dad had retired two years earlier from his post in the council's buildings regulations department. He'd put in thirty years of loyal service. He'd been presented with a set of golf clubs for his troubles and stated in a dull interview that he wanted to work on reducing his handicap. The boys had no idea what that meant.

Buster's mum was an award-winning gardener whose roses were admired from far and wide. She wrote a blog, whatever that was. He was teetotal and she liked to play tennis. She baked cakes for charity and he'd recently done a sponsored swim. They'd also raised the person who'd caused Billy so much harm. And as a consequence, they'd now have to take their share of responsibility for what had happened.

Derek watched the house. He'd volunteered to come up last night. It had felt like the right time to leave. He'd wanted to get away from the simmering anger that Billy was exuding, so acting while the iron was still hot had seemed like the perfect excuse to leave. But the boss had said no. The idea was a bad one and no further discussion was permitted.

House calls on an evening weren't a good idea, he'd explained. Normal dull people like these two could be out watching a movie or eating an average meal in a reasonably priced local restaurant. Or perhaps, they'd have invited an equally tedious couple over to eat fondue and talk about house prices and celebrities or any of the other things Billy imagined that people in suburbia troubled themselves with. These folks were just like the neighbours he hated in Chigwell, except they were poorer and had a kid who'd tried to ruin and humiliate him. And that made them quite different to anyone Billy had ever invited to his house before.

Billy made them wait until 7 am before allowing them to go in search of the unsuspecting Bretts. They'd look less incongruous then, he'd explained. People weren't on their guard in the morning. Catch them in their pants, with a warm cup of tea in hand and a nice slice of toast on the table. No one suspected a knock at the door first thing. They'd run to open it, thinking it was the postman or the paperboy. Who'd expect a gun in their face and an invitation to see the Most Dangerous Man in London at that time of the day?

Just as Derek was about to finally open the door, a man appeared in the front garden. He'd slipped out from the garage and was holding a watering can. He was younger and stockier than expected, but other than that he was certainly the man they'd seen on the computer last night. He ran a tap on the side of the house and proceeded to drench the roses. Derek had never seen anyone use a watering can before, let alone tend award-winning flowers.

For a moment, he was fascinated by this glimpse into a life he neither understood nor appreciated. A grown adult caring for something delicate and ephemeral was not something he'd encountered before. He watched as the man filled and emptied the can four more times, before returning to the garage and shutting the door behind him. There was no sign of the mother. She'd be making tea, or jam or arranging flowers, he thought. She'd jump when they rang the doorbell. The dad would probably be sent to answer, and that's when the fun would start.

Closing the car's heavy doors as quietly as they could, Derek walked with Anthony towards the house, still not feeling as confident as he would have liked. There was no one about and all was quiet except for the whine of a mower in a neighbour's back garden. He patted the handgun he'd slipped into his waistband. He checked that his jacket was hanging properly to cover the bulge. He didn't normally work with guns, but Billy had insisted they bring it. Fists and threats were all they usually needed.

The gun made him feel uncomfortable and off balance. He could feel it pinching his skin as he walked. He patted it again for reassurance. He hoped that he wouldn't need to reach for it, but if he had to, he wouldn't hesitate.

Anthony opened the latch of the low garden gate and held it as Derek walked through. He wanted this to be over with as quickly as possible now. They'd be back with Billy in twenty minutes if things went to plan and then all would be forgiven. Billy could do what he needed to do and, with any luck, Buster would return the things he'd taken. In a few days, they'd be out again doing what they did best - banging on doors they were familiar with. Doors that would be opened by people who knew why they were there and what the routine was. Doors that didn't require guns in order to be knocked on.

As Derek pushed the little brass button, he could hear a faint chime in the hallway on the other side of the door. As he glanced up, he noticed a momentary flicker from one of the bedroom curtains. A few seconds later, he rang the bell again.

Just as he was about to ring a third time, he heard a voice behind him.

"Gentlemen, how may I help you?"

And that was when the fun really started.

Chapter 39

Samuel showered and slipped out of his flat at 7.30 am. He bought a coffee and an almond croissant on his way in to the police station and was looking forward to making some sense of the past forty-eight hours. The office would be empty and he could enjoy a little peace and quiet while he tried to figure things out.

He made a mental note to buy some fruit next time he needed a snack. His taught waistline was a nagging reminder that he was getting fat. The pressure at his midriff became more apparent as he leant over to switch on his computer. He'd never meet anyone new if he got out of shape, no matter how many fancy new sweatshirts he bought. Dating was difficult enough as a slim police officer and he was acutely aware that piling on the pounds would make his chances of romance even more remote.

It was partly Gary's fault for turning up with a bag of something tasty every time they worked together. In the mornings it was croissants or a Danish. Later in the day, a pie or pasty. Pizza or kebabs were the norm if they were working late. His colleague meant well but Samuel didn't have the will power to resist. Gary's food offerings always took priority over the apple or banana he knew he ought to be eating. Quite how Gary managed to stay slim on a diet of beer, curry and assorted takeaways was a mystery. He didn't jog, cycle or do anything a regular person would do to stay fit.

Shattering the peace, the desk phone started to ring, demanding his immediate attention. Picking up and saying hello, his heart sank as he heard a familiar voice on the other end of the line.

"Oh, good morning Sergeant Edge, I was hoping you'd answer. This is the newsroom at the Argus. How are you doing today? Would you like to comment on reports that a Robin Hood character is operating in the city?

We've had several calls this morning about large sums of money being returned to local businesses. Apparently, they've all been paying a criminal gang for protection and illegal loans? Could you comment on a potential link to a Mr Billy Murphy?

Would you say that Brighton is a city controlled by organised crime groups? What measures are Sussex Police taking to curb these protection rackets? Hello? Sergeant Edge? Hello? Would you like to comment, please?"

Samuel slammed the phone down without saying a further word. He couldn't deal with this right now. He'd taken the flak when the Argus had blown the Bondage Stalker story out of all proportion, so he had no intention of talking to them about this latest twist, especially when it was something that he knew absolutely nothing about. They'd have to get their information from another source for the time being.

He called Gary and asked him to make some enquiries, irritated that The Argus had caught him on the hop. Minutes later, a very excited Gary called back. He couldn't get his words out quickly enough.

"You're never going to believe this Skipper; you couldn't make this fucking stuff up. It's absolutely bonkers."

Samuel listened patiently, waiting for him to calm down and get to the point. Gary always radiated nervous energy, but today, he was virtually on fire. Maybe that's how he managed to stay so slim.

"Well, I've got this bloke I know who runs a Chinese on Preston Street. Hins, it's called; you probably know it. Lovely gaff. I've been going there for years now. Anyway, he tells me what's going on the street, off the record like, and always chucks in a couple of starters for free. Nice geezer, very friendly. Lovely sweet and sour too.

So, I called him about the Argus story. Turns out *he's* received a bundle of cash in the post today too. Over nine hundred quid, he reckons. Completely out of the blue. Straight through his letter box. Bosh! Delivered by the regular postie it was, correct postcode, stamps and everything. Even says Mr Hin on the envelope, which is a nickname, not his real name. Totally random and unexpected. And it came with a note. Says the money is a refund on what he's been paying to Billy Murphy. Except, it's not actually from Murphy, obviously.

I mean, I didn't even know he was paying protection money or I'd have told him not to bother, but that's not the point is it. So, he's asking me what to do and whether it's legit or not when two other places run by his cousins call him to say they've had the same thing happen to them. So, I asked him to do a bit of digging and turns out these envelopes have been dropping through letter boxes left, right and centre. All Chinese restaurants. A couple of them got two lots because they'd been repaying loans as well as stumping up for protection."

Samuel was trying hard to digest the information that was rushing at him from the phone. He interrupted his colleague, who'd momentarily run out of breath.

"Hold on Gary, hold on. Where the fuck's all this money coming from?"

Samuel didn't expect an answer as he was thinking out loud.

"Seems a bit of a coincidence if you ask me. We've got Brett, who's potentially done a runner from Billy Murphy and then these envelopes start landing on people's doorsteps. You don't think he's grown a conscience, do you? Why would he even do that? It doesn't make any sense."

It was a question that neither of them could answer, but Gary gave it a go anyway.

"I've no idea Skipper, but it's got to be him because who else would know who owed what and where to send it? I mean, that's Brett's job with Murphy isn't it as far as we know? His dirty little accountant. Maybe he's had a moment of reckoning and decided to change his ways. Not fucking likely, I know, but who else would do this?

Whoever it was, Murphy's going to be absolutely livid when he finds out. The note says not to pay him anymore and that he's finished. They've gone and stuck the knife right in and given it a proper old twist. He's going to go batshit ballistic with whoever's done this to him. And if it was that Buster Brett, then he's a dead man. That's if we don't get to him first, Sam."

Samuel thought for a moment. Gary was right, it had to be Buster Brett. It was the only explanation. No one else would have the money, information or inclination to make a play like this. Whatever his reasons might be, he'd turned on his boss in a targeted and vicious assault. He'd hit Billy exactly where he knew it would cause the most damage.

Internal feuds weren't unheard of in the criminal fraternity, but this one was unique in its boldness. For an employee to humiliate a boss in such a public fashion was unprecedented. People would soon be talking and that would include Billy Murphy's rivals and enemies. This wasn't just about the money, thought Samuel, it had to be about wrecking the operation and ruining the old man's reputation. Maybe he was trying to topple his boss and take over, acting on some unseen opportunity. Perhaps it was something else altogether. Whatever it was, Buster Brett had thought it sufficiently important to take a chance and put his life on the line.

It still didn't make complete sense though. The execution had been too sloppy. Who'd rely on a stoner in a campervan to help with the getaway? Why give away money like this? And how did the person Samuel suspected to be the Stalker end up getting involved? Once again there were more questions than answers and the only people who could throw some light on the situation were a gangland leader and the boy he was trying to kill.

"Gary, go and see your mate right now and ask him for the note and the envelope it came in. And don't forget to bag them up properly as evidence. There might be forensics we can use. Let's see exactly what it says and where it was sent from.

Call the Royal Mail too. See if they can give us the heads-up on where they were posted. Try to get hold of any of the other envelopes too. Maybe we can use them to figure out how to find Brett before Murphy does. If he's got access to the sort of information that I think he has, then this could be our route to bringing the old man down for good. I shudder to think what he's got planned for the lad if he gets hold of him before we do."

"Will do, Skipper. I'll come straight to you via Preston Street. I'll pick up some fried rice and spring rolls while I'm there. That's what they eat for breakfast in China apparently. I'm fucking starving. See you in half an hour. I might have to get a sweet and sour too while I'm there. Oh, and prawn crackers."

Trying to think of reasons to justify eating Chinese food for breakfast number two, Samuel resigned himself to being fat and single for the rest of his life. He loosened one notch of his belt and undid the top button of his jeans. He stopped breathing in, relaxed his gut and waited for Gary to arrive.

Chapter 40

Anthony and Derek spun around, taken aback by the soft voice behind them. It was the man they'd seen watering the roses… the one they'd researched on the internet. The meek engineer who loved to play golf. Except he wasn't where they expected him to be. He'd taken them by surprise.

As they turned, the man stepped in quickly towards Derek. In a flash he grabbed the collar of his leather jacket and pivoted his bulky frame over an outstretched leg and hip. Derek, unable to react in time or control his momentum, crashed to the ground. As he fell, the man reached into his waistband and relieved him of the handgun. Derek's nose started to bleed from the impact with the concrete garden path. He let out a hapless moan as he lay winded and dazed, staring at the woodlice his fall had disturbed.

"What the fuck?" cried a startled Anthony, as he witnessed his colleague writhing on the ground, pinned down by the knee of the man who'd now raised the gun to face him.

"One move and you're dead, big lad. Now get down on the floor."

The man's voice was calm, his face blank. He wasn't afraid or intimidated like he ought to be. He'd slipped the safety off the gun too.

Anthony looked stunned, unable to understand what was happening. But rather than comply with the request, he raised his fists and prepared to deal with this civilian, who was daring to spoil Billy's plan, in the best way he knew how.

"Are you having a fucking laugh, mate? Do you know who we work for?"

As Anthony took a step forward, intending to punch the man and relieve the pressure on his friend's neck, a searing pain shot through his foot. At the same time, he became disorientated by the crack of a gunshot. The man had put a bullet through his foot. The gun was back pointing at his face before he had a chance to think any further.

"The next one will be in your chest, fat boy. Now get down on the floor and do as you're told, before I kill you. I'm not going to ask you again."

Antony did as he was told this time. The pain in his foot was excruciating and he could feel the warm blood oozing between his toes. He went down on one knee, put his hands out in front of him and lowered himself down next to Derek, trying to keep his weight off the injured foot. The pain in it burned more intensely with every passing second. The boys stared at each other across the rough surface of the path, unable to work out where they'd gone wrong. Billy was going to be livid.

Antony felt the man wrap something around his wrist. Quickly and expertly, he pushed and manipulated his thick limbs into the positions he needed them to take. The ratchet sound as they tightened together suggested cable ties. One for each wrist and two to bind them together. The makeshift handcuffs were tight and impossible to rip apart. As the man moved quickly from Antony to Derek, applying pressure with his knees and the gun, they felt helpless and exposed. Billy wasn't going to understand any of this. This wasn't what the internet had led them to expect. How had a retired engineer managed to get them on the ground and trussed up like turkeys?

The man wasn't finished yet. As soon as his wrists were bound behind his back, Antony felt a thin cold line being slipped around his neck. The man tied knots and used a small blade to cut away the excess length. In their peripheral vision they could see him working quickly and expertly. He's done this before, thought Derek. In a few seconds the ligatures were tight enough to feel, but not yet tight enough to restrict their breathing. Not for the time being anyway.

"Right, you two lumps, we're going to stand you up now. One at a time, nice and slowly. Bear in mind that you've each got a Kabul Choker around your necks. And if you don't know what that is, then my advice is to not pull or struggle."

The man judged that the two fat men on the ground didn't have a clue what he was talking about.

"Listen to me, you goons. It's a special ligature we developed for use on Taliban prisoners. The knot can only get tighter. It's a one-way thing. If you decide to dick around, I'll yank on the free ends and you'll be out cold within seconds as the blood supply to your brains gets cut. Got it?

And before you get any ideas, there's no way to release it without digging around in your neck flesh with a blade. Simple and effective, but also deadly. I've seen too many men die from these things, so please don't try anything. It's not a good way to go, I assure you, gentlemen.

Those ragheads thought Allah had their backs, but I doubt if you two lumps believe in any of that crap, do you? Right, so let's go for a little drive in that car of yours before the cops get here. That gunshot's bound to have got the curtains twitching around here.

They'll be here within five minutes, I reckon. It'll be a firearms unit first, so unless we're really unlucky and they're just around the corner, they're going to have some ground to cover before they get here."

The man helped each of the boys in turn to roll onto their sides before pulling up a knee and twisting them into a sitting position. From there, they struggled to their feet. Once up, they started walking to the car as directed by their captor. The man walked behind them with the gun against Anthony's back as he limped and complained towards the Range Rover, leaving spots of blood on the tarmac in his wake.

In his other hand, the man held the lines that ran from the ligatures. Just enough tension was maintained for the boys to realise that their lives, every movement and fate lay far beyond their own control for the time being.

"You two get in the front. Hop-along, you get in the passenger seat and let your mate drive."

The man sliced through the cable ties holding Derek's wrists together and used the gun to guide and prod him into the driving seat. He produced two fresh ties and secured his wrists to the wheel. Then he fed the leads from each ligature through the front seat head rests and fished the keys out of Derek's pocket. Putting them in the ignition, he turned the engine over and got in behind the boys.

"Right, now drive nice and safe. Any heavy braking and I'll make sure you garrotte yourselves. And make sure you look in your mirrors too, because we won't be using the indicators today."

He leant forward and put the car into drive.

"Now, tell me exactly why you're at my sister's house at this time in the morning and why you're carrying a gun. Every little juicy detail please, gentlemen. And if you ever do anything like this again can I suggest you check your weapon *before* you clear the car? That was the real giveaway.

And maybe don't spend ten minutes sitting outside picking your noses trying to decide if you've got the right place. I knew everything I needed to know about you two dickheads before you even opened the garden gate. I even had enough time to water the roses and get a few handy items out of the garage."

"So, you're not Buster's dad then?" said Anthony, as it finally dawned on him that this wasn't the man they'd seen on the computer last night."

"No, I'm not Buster's fucking dad, Sherlock," he sighed, rolling his eyes.

"So, who are you then?" added Derek, hopefully.

"All you need to know about me is that I'm your worst fucking nightmare," came the angry reply, as the man tightened the lines around their necks.

"Now drive, before the police get here. And start telling me exactly what's been going on."

Realising that things couldn't get much worse, the boys decided to talk, and once they'd got started, they couldn't stop. Whether it was the pain in Anthony's foot or the concussion from Derek's head hitting the ground, or just the lack of oxygen caused by the ligatures, they let it all out. Billy, Buster, the trip to Brighton and everything else spilled from their lips as the man in the back listened, horrified at what he was being told.

When they got to within a mile of Billy's house, the boys pulled over as instructed and listened as the man started to talk again.

"Listen up, you two, this is what we're going to do. You're as good as dead right now, so you might as well hear what I've got to say. Your boss will no doubt kill you when he realises you've failed in the simple task he set you. He doesn't sound like the forgiving type to me."

The boys knew that this was very true. They'd used up their last chance with Billy and unless they could now overpower an armed lunatic who'd shot one of them and placed nooses around their necks, they were in serious trouble.

"If you do exactly as I say, you'll have a chance of living. I promise not to kill you if you follow my instructions. You have my word on that."

The boys didn't feel very reassured by the man's cold words.

As he talked, Derek grappled with the conundrum that had presented itself. He could go along with this plan and save his own skin or he could resist and potentially end up dead for his trouble, either at the hands of this stranger or Billy himself, there was a good chance that his life might end today.

As the car turned into Dyke Road Avenue, Derek and Anthony glanced at each other. They each knew what the other was thinking. Only divine intervention was going to stop things from turning very ugly once they got to Billy's.

He would be waiting, expecting them to deliver Buster's parents. He'd be furious that they'd not answered their phones, which they'd felt ringing and vibrating in their inaccessible pockets. They didn't want to think what he'd do when they showed up with a dangerous psycho instead.

As the car pulled up to Billy's gates and they slowly started to open, it dawned on the terrified boys that they might just have minutes to live.

Chapter 41

The moment Samuel returned the handset to its base, it started to ring again. These people were persistent, he thought, his face flushing with irritation. Couldn't they just let him have a little peace?

The Argus had given him nothing but misery for the past two months. Now they wanted his instant cooperation and didn't want to take no for an answer. It was tempting to let it ring out, but he also felt like telling them exactly what he thought of them. His emotions got the better of him and he reached over to pick up.

"*Please*, can you stop calling this number? A press release will be issued at the appropriate time. Your constant calls are distracting the busy officers trying to work here this morning."

The office was empty, but they weren't to know that. He already felt better for being assertive.

He waited for a reply but there was no response from the caller. Maybe he'd been too aggressive. After a few seconds the silence was broken as a familiar voice chimed from the speaker.

"Sam, is that you? It's me again, Gary. You there? Hello, mate?"

Samuel hoped that his colleague hadn't taken too much notice of his rant. He needed to control his nerves better from now on. As his cheeks momentarily reddened, he composed himself and replied as calmly as he could.

"Sorry, Gary, I thought it was the bloody Argus calling again. They've been pestering me for a statement and they've pissed me right off."

"Forget that, Sam, have you got your Airwave on? There's been a shooting. Charlie Golf 99's taken charge and they want us over there pronto."

Samuel's blood ran cold. There was never such a thing as a good shooting. Even in a city as busy as Brighton, this was a rare event and a whole protocol of police actions would have been triggered into effect. Charlie Golf 99 was code for the response duty inspector who'd be responsible for dealing with the immediate aftermath at the scene. She'd have looked to see who was working in CID and called Gary, presumably having tried Samuel first without luck.

"Fill me in, mate, I've not turned it on yet. I was having a quiet ten minutes."

Gary couldn't get his words out fast enough. The urgency of his delivery kicked a surge of adrenaline through Samuel's body.

"A single shot's been reported on Holmbush Crescent over in Southwick, about ten minutes ago. Number 56. There's two firearms units making their way on the hurry up from Lewes. Gold command's involved too. Local officers and ambulance have been told to stand off until TFU get there in about four minutes.

Thing is, Sam, I've put the address through PNC and NICHE and it comes back to a Mr and Mrs Brett. When I found that out, I called Richie and he's sure it's Buster's parents' gaff. He's absolutely certain about it. There's a note on the CAD saying a neighbour's reported seeing two big guys leading a smaller man away, before they all drove off in a dark-coloured Range Rover."

Samuel jumped in, cutting Gary off.

"So, Brett's been hiding out at his parents place by the looks of it and Murphy's boys have caught up with him there. And a firearm's been discharged in the process."

"That's what I was thinking too, Skipper. Looks like they've got to him before we could, unfortunately. And if he hasn't been shot already, it won't be long before he's dead, once Murphy gets his hand on him."

"Let's RV there in twenty, Gary. Let's see if anyone's got any decent CCTV they can show us."

"Will do, boss. I've already grabbed us a couple of coffees and a pastry, so see you shortly."

Only Gary would think to grab a bite before heading out to a Grade 1 thought Samuel, putting the phone down. As he gathered together his jacket, keys and an investigator's notebook, he felt disappointed with Buster Brett. He'd never actually met the lad, but he felt let down, nevertheless.

He ought to have been smarter than this. Letting himself get caught somewhere as obvious as his parents' place was a dreadful mistake to have made. Hiding in plain sight was one thing, but a close family residence would have been the first place his boss would think to look. Buster should have known this and taken measures to protect himself.

Samuel desperately wanted to find Buster and negotiate a mutually beneficial way to bring Billy Murphy down. And if he could have got the Stalker too, then so much the better. But it looked now as if that opportunity had been snatched away.

Switching on the grill and windscreen blues of his covert Ford Focus, he buckled up, floored the accelerator and raced towards the Old Shoreham Road, the quickest route west to Southwick.

Chapter 42

Billy glanced at his watch. It was the eleventh time in the past ten minutes that he'd looked at the heavy vintage Rolex. He'd taken it from the wrist of Danny Delaney just before the liquid concrete poured over his dead body several decades before. Scratched and scuffed from all the scrapes it had accompanied him on, its sweeping hands served as a constant reminder that time was marching on.

He'd sent the boys out at just after seven. The drive to Southwick should have taken them twenty minutes, perhaps a little more if the morning traffic had been heavy. The local council had recently installed cycle lanes on the main road west, for reasons that Billy couldn't comprehend. Two lanes now squeezed into one, just so an occasional hippy on a bike could get to her yoga class a little bit quicker.

Maybe they'd stopped for a bite. He wouldn't put it past them. The lazy fat fuckers had eaten him out of bread and bacon without so much as a half-arsed promise to pop to the shops to get some more. They were probably hungry again as soon as they left the house.

If they'd stopped for breakfast, that would have added a quarter of an hour. They'd have got themselves lost too. They didn't know Brighton very well, let alone the sleepy suburbs to the west. He'd give them a further ten minutes to find the right house. That was an extra twenty-five minutes he'd allow them in total.

Billy tried to remember if the Range Rover needed fuel. It had a thirst on it, that was for sure, but as he never drove the thing, he couldn't be certain. He was just the mug they handed the receipts to when they needed to claim their expenses.

He'd factor in another ten minutes for a garage stop. That was being very generous, he thought. He wondered why the fuckers hadn't phoned him yet. They could have easily called to say they'd found the place.

He didn't want to phone them though. That was another of his golden rules. You never called someone when they were out on a job like this. They might be just about to put their fat fingers around some fuckers neck. A ringer going off at the wrong moment could give the game away.

He made a quick calculation in his head. Taking into account all the various factors he could think of, they should have been knocking on Buster's parents' door by 8.15 am at the latest. That was allowing for every hippy, lazy, greedy permutation of events that might have had a bearing on their time keeping.

Once they'd actually knocked, things should have moved along nicely. They ought to have been in and out in no time. It wasn't a complicated job. They'd have introduced themselves politely to start with. The parents would have been naturally suspicious. Who wouldn't be at the sight of a couple of meatheads making a house call at this time of day? They'd have been taken aback by the unusual invitation from someone they didn't know to go somewhere they'd never been.

If there was any hesitation, the boys would have pressed Buster's folks more firmly to accompany them. The parents would then panic. Out would come the gun and the gaffer tape, and they'd have been bundled up, and on their way back to Dyke Road Avenue in no time at all, with the minimum of fuss.

Billy continued with his calculations. Allowing for the conversation, a manageable scuffle and the awkward return journey, the boys should be back by 8.45 am. He'd give them until 9.00 am, just to be on the safe side. It would have been a thoughtful touch if they could have phoned on their way back though. A professional courtesy to a concerned boss, that they really ought to have remembered. He'd educate them on this matter when he saw them.

It was now 8.55 am and Billy was starting to feel nervous. Even when the boys did arrive with Buster's trussed-up parents, there was still more that needed to be done. Having his mum and dad as reluctant house guests didn't help a jot unless Buster actually knew where they were.

The next step would be to relay a message to Master Brett himself, one that was sufficiently forceful to invoke an immediate response from the boy. He would need to feel compelled to drop whatever he was doing and trot up to the house with everything he'd taken, before throwing himself prone and grovelling at his old boss's feet. He could then beg for mercy in exchange for the release of his disappointed and terrified parents.

But Billy was stuck on how to let Buster know about the morning's developments. The boy had turned his phone off and two-faced Dexter had blocked his number. He thought about calling the man who'd burned his suit outside the office and initiated this chain of chaos. He didn't know if there was a connection between the two of them, but his gut reaction told him that there had to be. He growled as he realised that Buster was the only person who knew how to pull the phone number off the computer.

To make matters worse, Fliss had started calling again. Three times she phoned in quick succession. On each occasion, he hit the red button before she had a chance to leave a message. 'Just get off the fucking blower you silly old cow,' he fumed, fretting that he'd miss a call from the boys. 'There is nothing that you need to say to me right now that can't wait until tomorrow.'

Then the landline started to ring. Losing control, he wrenched the cable out of the socket and slammed the handset against the wall, smashing it to pieces. She was the only person who ever called that number.

Billy started to pace. The wait was killing him. It didn't help that he had no one to shout at. Razor was downstairs, sensibly staying out of his way. He didn't say much at the best of times and had quite rightly realised that this wasn't the time to change that habit. He made sure he was just within earshot in case he was needed.

At 9.10 am, there was still no returning Range Rover to be seen. What were the useless fuckers playing at? Billy raged to himself, as he ran up to his first-floor landing. It offered a marginally better view of Dyke Road Avenue, but there was still no sign of the boys. His phone remained silent in his hand. He caved in and started to call them, but they didn't pick up. They were taking liberties now. They'd better have a good explanation for fuelling his stress in this manner. He started to pace again, unable to bear standing still.

"Razor, get up here now and bring your fucking phone, will yer? I want to try something."

Within seconds, Razor was up the stairs, knowing that any delay could send his boss into a further meltdown. He'd managed to avoid becoming the focus of his boss's anger since they'd left London and he didn't want to do anything now that would alter that fragile dynamic.

"Right, quick, dial this number."

"Who we calling, boss?

"We're calling Buster, you dickhead. Remember him, do you? Does it matter who we're calling? Stop asking questions and just do as you're fucking told. And put it on speaker too, so I can hear what's going on."

Razor didn't say anything other than to repeat the number that Billy was reading from his phone. The call went straight to voicemail.

"Hi, this is Buster! I'm sorry I can't take your call right now, but if you'd like to leave me a message, I'll get back to you as soon as I can. Have a great day and thanks for calling!"

Billy hadn't expected to hear Buster's voice. He certainly hadn't anticipated that he'd sound so happy, upbeat and unrepentant.

"That little cunt!" shouted Billy as he picked up one of his wife's favourite china vases and sent it crashing against the entrance lobby door below.

Momentarily calming himself, he looked at his phone again.

"Right, try this one next. It's that druggy Dexter cunt. The little fucker who wanted to help, then blocked me number. You try him. He won't have blocked you."

Again, Razor repeated the number out loud as he pressed the corresponding buttons on his phone.

This time there was a ringing tone. Five rings… six, … no voicemail kicked in. Both men stared at the phone in Razor's hand, willing someone to pick up.

Ten rings… eleven… still no answer.

'This isn't working,' thought Billy, wondering what to do next. His options were rapidly running out.

Fourteen rings… fifteen rings…

He wished he knew where the boys had got to. Not that it mattered if he couldn't get hold of Buster. He desperately needed a break.

Sixteen rings… Still no answer.

What the fuck was he going to do if he couldn't get hold of Buster?

Billy started to panic. His police contact had gone quiet, he couldn't find Buster and now the boys had gone missing. He started to realise that after all his years in the game, his luck might have finally run out.

Then, as the phone continued to ring and he was just about to punch the wall, a familiar car pulled up outside the gates. His face cracked into a grin. He knew then that at least some of his prayers had been answered. At long last, the boys were back.

Chapter 43

For the second morning in a row, sunlight flooded Ewalina's grand living room. But this time, the brightness taunted Buster as he tried to wake up. It illuminated and laid bare the foolishness of yesterday's undertaking. The hornet's nest had been well and truly poked, unleashing a silent fury that was too painful to contemplate.

As he tried to gather his thoughts, he felt sick and conflicted. At last he'd actually done some good. Hundreds of people were going to have a better day as the result of something he'd made happen. But on the other hand, only the easy part of his plan had been realised. Anyone could hide away and post a few envelopes from the shadows. Surviving Billy Murphy's rage in the longer term was an altogether more challenging prospect.

Ewalina was the only other person awake. She'd been good company last night. Having had more to drink than was good for her, she'd ended up dancing around the flat with Sophia and Dexter until a neighbour knocked on the door to complain about the noise. She looked hungover and pained as she prepared the coffee.

"Ewalina, what time do you reckon they'll get the letters we sent?"

Buster was trying to work out the exact moment the happiness he'd engineered would start to ripple through the city. He wished he could call every single person they'd written to and ask them how they felt. He wanted to gorge on the goodwill his magical packages would create. He needed another fix of positivity to counter the dread of what Billy would be doing, right now, to find and kill him.

"I've got no idea. They deliver to this block at around 11 am, but I guess with businesses maybe it'll be earlier. 8 am perhaps? Some of those takeaway places might have already had their post. Like I said, no idea. What does it matter anyway?"

She put a mug down in front of Buster.

He started to help her clear up. From the look of disgust on her face, last night's mess was clearly bothering her. The domesticity steadied his mind for a moment. There were bottles everywhere. Zaid had been on the craft beer. Sophia preferred cider. Dexter had shared a case with her before passing out. His tobacco and phone were on the table along with the food cartons they'd had delivered. What was left over didn't look so appealing in the cold morning light.

As Ewalina held open a bin bag, Buster carefully placed the rubbish inside. He wondered how five people could generate so much waste. If everyone did the same, there was no hope for the planet. He counted eleven plastic containers that they'd used for an hour and which would now spend the rest of eternity in landfill. Maybe he could do something to help the environment once he'd found a solution to the current predicament.

Buster lifted Dexter's phone so that Ewalina could run a damp cloth across the table. It was sticky from beer, wine and hoisin sauce. There were a couple of ring marks from where wet glasses had been placed on the wooden surface. He hoped they'd been there for a while. He didn't want to upset his house-proud host any further. He checked her face for a reaction, but she didn't appear to be overly concerned.

When the phone was six inches above the table, held delicately between Buster's thumb and forefinger, it started to ring. There was no name on the screen, just a mobile number. The noise and vibration startled him. The outside world was trying to intrude on the serenity of the flat. He put the phone down and stood briskly away.

It was probably just his dealer. He'd mentioned that he was being chased for money. Maybe it was another mate, but Buster couldn't imagine any friend of Dexter's being awake at this time of day. The persistent phone kept on ringing, demanding attention.

As Buster watched the illuminated screen he couldn't help feel that there was something familiar about the number. The ringing continued, tugging at his memory.

Eleven rings… Twelve… Who was calling Dexter?

There was something about the last three digits that struck a chord. Lots of people must have that combination at the end, he thought. Surely there were thousands of numbers that were almost the same, except for one or two characters. The phone didn't let up.

Fifteen… sixteen rings, …there was no indication that it was ever going to stop.

But then he realised where he knew the number from. He couldn't work out why this person would be calling Dexter. The peace that he'd felt just minutes before evaporated in an instant. There was only one way to establish the extent of the threat.

He reached down, took a deep breath and answered the phone.

"Hello, this is Dexter's phone. Can I take a message?"

At first, there was no answer, just enough cracks and snippets of background noise to indicate that the caller had the phone in loudspeaker mode.

"But that's not Dexter speaking, is it, Buster?" came the icy response, at last.

"It's your old pal Billy here, as you can probably gather. How you doing, son? You alright, are you? How you been keeping? Anything you want to talk to me about, is there?"

Buster's jaw fell open and he felt sick. He was lost for words. A cold flush ran across his face as his blood pressure dropped. He didn't have a clue how to reply. He knew that he'd have to deal with Billy sooner or later, but now wasn't the time, the place or the method he'd envisioned. He put

Dexter's phone on loudspeaker and placed it back on the damp table, not wanting to be any closer to the source of Billy's voice than was absolutely necessary.

"Billy, I'm sorry about what's happened. It's nothing personal, but I couldn't work for you anymore. You're a really bad man; that's the truth of it. And I don't think I am. Well, not anymore. I needed to do the right thing. And that meant getting far away from you.

I'm not going to talk to you now, Billy, because there's nothing I can say that will make things right between us. And I also know you've probably got some way of tracking this phone, so I'm just going to hang up now."

There was a short silence. Buster pictured Billy seething on the other end of the line, spitting profanities under his breath. He was desperate to end the call, but somehow, he couldn't force himself to push the red button.

"How's your mum and dad, son?"

Billy didn't sound as angry as Buster had expected. His voice was calm and measured. Something was terribly wrong.

"They keeping well, are they?"

Buster's heart began to race. It began to dawn on him that his worst nightmare was about to come true.

"Thing is, I sent the boys round to invite your folks up to the house for a little chat. And do you know what?"

Buster's heart sank as he anticipated where this conversation was headed.

"They've just arrived here! As we speak I can see your charming parents in the back of the car with Derek and Anthony. They're just about to get out, if I'm not very much mistaken. I'm sure they're all getting on like a house on fire. And in a second, when we've finished having this little chat, I'm going to go downstairs and welcome them into me house. Then I'm going to tell them what a sneaky little cunt you've been, over a nice cup of tea.

And you see, Buster, there's only one way that they're ever going to leave here alive and that's if you get yourself up here, right now, with me money and me gun and all the rest of the fucking stuff you nicked and explain to us all why you decided to treat me like a twat. You listening, Buster? You got that? All makes sense, does it?"

Buster was certainly listening, but he didn't know what to say. He'd heard Billy use this pattern of language before. The false calmness and veiled threats. The gradual build-up to some awful and violent crescendo.

"Yes, Billy, I'm listening."

"So, pack your stuff, son. Do your goodbyes, call a taxi and say your prayers. I want you here within the hour. Not an hour and a half. Not two hours. Sixty minutes, Buster. You got all that in your clever little head, have you? And I promise to play nicely until then. Be on me best behaviour. I'll even open a packet of biscuits. I think there's some Jaffa cakes in the cupboard, if I'm not mistaken. Can't say fairer than that, can I, considering?

But mark my words. If you take a longer, just one second, I won't be held responsible for the consequences. And I think you know me well enough by now to know what that means. So, bye-bye Buster boy. Toodle pip. See you shortly and bon voyage. I'll say hello to your lovely parents from you in the meantime and let them know you're on your way up to see them."

And with that final comment festering in Buster's ear, the line went dead.

As his host continued to clear the detritus of the night before, Buster felt crushed by the words he'd just heard. He slumped back into the sofa as tears welled up in his eyes. He'd allowed his family to fall into the hands of the person most motivated to do them harm. He thought about all the calls and messages from his mum he'd ignored. He hadn't given them a second thought. They were supposed to be on holiday and far away from any threat Billy could pose. He should have called her back and told them to stay away. But in his haste and spontaneity, he'd let them get caught in a deadly trap.

The game was up. There was no denying it now. He'd done a little good, but the time had come to fold. He dreaded to think what Billy would do when he found out about all the money he'd given away. Maybe he already knew. His liberation had been fleeting and ephemeral. In retrospect, all his plans and aspirations had been foolish and hopelessly optimistic. All he could do now was pray that the pain he was about to suffer at Billy's hand would be as equally short-lived.

"I think you've really fucked up, mate," said Ewalina unhelpfully, stating the obvious, as she cleared away the rest of the previous night's mess.

"And I don't think there's much any of us can do to help you now. Do you want me to call you a cab?" she smirked.

Chapter 44

This really had been the journey from hell. The air-conditioning packed up at Orleans and a speed camera flashed them as they approached Calais. To make things worse, they were almost out of fuel and Buster's dad was desperate for the loo.

Earlier, they'd booked the tunnel, cancelled the ferry and thrown their things into the car. Buster's dad thought the traffic would be lighter at night, so they left after dinner, driving swiftly though the darkness. But when he was wrong and they got caught up in a snarl on the Paris périphérique, they'd lost an hour. Moving from one lane to the next, Buster's mum commented that they always seemed to be in the one moving the slowest. A metaphor for their lives, thought Buster's dad, wishing he was tucked up in bed.

He also got them lost. He thought he knew the route and was too proud to ask for help. His wife was asleep and for a while going the wrong way seemed a better option than waking her up. They'd driven down an unfamiliar road for almost an hour before he nudged her and admitted his mistake. She'd asked him how it was possible to take the wrong turn on a journey they'd made fifty times before. He fumed and she nagged until they were both exhausted.

Once, he almost fell asleep and she had to grab the wheel, as they swerved into the path of an oncoming Renault. But now here they were, late, anxious and racing for the train. At the terminal, they chose the wrong queue for customs. The other one was moving much faster, sniped Buster's mum. He couldn't work the bloody ticket machine. It was impossible to know which lane to be in. The café was closed and the state of the toilets left a lot to be desired.

Theirs was the last car on the train for the 09.30 departure. Buster's dad joked that they'd arrive before they set off due to the clocks being an hour behind at home. His wife, with a stern face, replied that it wasn't funny. She tried calling her brother but he didn't answer. Hopefully he was out with the roses. Her instructions had been quite precise. Better blooms need rigid regimes, she'd told him. It was all written down so he wouldn't forget and taped to the fridge door.

She called Buster too, but his phone was still off. It was always off these days. She'd been calling him all week. That was something else to add to the list of things she needed to get off her chest. It was getting longer and angrier by the hour.

As much as they loved France, they'd never been too keen on the French. Lots of rules that they didn't understand. Too much bureaucracy and not enough people who spoke English. They wanted a radio station they could listen to, supermarkets that didn't close for lunch, and for their steering wheel to be on the correct side of the car. It was a blessed relief as the carriage slipped below ground. Buster's exhausted parents needed to get home. They longed for familiar things around them. They also wanted to stop having to worry about their son. But for now, they closed their eyes and enjoyed twenty minutes of peace, deep below the waves above.

All would be well just as soon as they got back home to safe and solid Southwick. Holmbush Crescent, where dramas never happened, was where they wanted to be. Dreaming of roses and tennis, cleanliness and order, the gentle motion of the train lulled them into a deep, restorative sleep.

Chapter 45

Buster was hyperventilating and starting to panic. All he could think was that he needed to leave right now in order to save his parents.

He hadn't expected to hear Billy's dark voice on Dexter's phone. The news of his parents' involvement sickened him to the core. He'd never allowed his work and family to have even the slightest overlap, and yet here they were, crashing together like ancient dying stars.

"And yes, I do want you to call me a cab," he snapped back at Ewalina, only just realising what she'd said.

"But don't think you've earned your money just yet. We only got around to doing the easy bit. I appreciate the use of your flat and everything, but writing a few envelopes and putting us up for a couple of nights doesn't warrant your bloody fee."

"By the way, can I use your landline please?" he added, toning down his attitude, frustrated that even now, he still needed her help.

Ewalina walked off to the kitchen with a smile across her face, pretending she hadn't heard, while Buster grabbed the handset anyway, ignoring her. Eight times he stabbed his mum's number into the keypad and each time she failed to answer.

His head flooded with questions. How did Billy get hold of Dexter's number? What could he do to protect his parents? Would Billy hurt them?

The more he thought, the more agitated he became. It was obvious that the only practical solution was to go immediately and face Billy in person. If he did nothing, his parents would die. Likewise, if he asked the police for help, then Billy would no doubt act in a fit of fury and do something unimaginably awful. There was no likely scenario in which things were going to end well.

He considered taking the gun and shooting whoever opened Billy's front door directly in the face. Perhaps he could force his way into the house and effect a rescue. He could picture this chain of actions in his mind, but the images didn't appear realistic or firm. In reality, he anticipated a painful family annihilation if he went down that route. He'd never even handled a gun before, let alone fired one. He was soft and unskilled in these physical, tough guy matters and Billy would instinctively take advantage of this weakness.

He cringed at the situation he'd brought to bear upon his family. His parents hadn't brought him up just for all of them to be wiped out in a gun battle with gangsters. That wouldn't have cropped up in their top one hundred worst things that could befall them. Buster wondered who'd dispatch the coup-de-gras. Billy would undoubtedly save that particular pleasure for himself.

He hated that these morbid thoughts were all he could come up with. Where were his wile and cunning? Had he learned nothing from his old boss? He kicked himself that he had not anticipated what Billy might do. It was blindingly obvious in hindsight.

All he'd managed to organise was a temporary fix to make himself feel better. He'd sent a few envelopes in the post and put a few smiles on some Chinese faces. It would all be forgotten in a week or so when Billy would inevitably force them to hand back the cash. Despite all the fine intentions, nothing good or long-term had been achieved.

Worse than that, he'd failed to protect his precious family from the hands of an enraged and dangerous madman. He'd given no regard to the long term. He'd concentrated solely on short-term gratification. Holding his head in his hands, he felt overwhelmed by the depths of his predicament. The levity and optimism of the previous night's celebrations now seemed hopelessly misjudged.

But before he could wallow too long in his deep pool of pity, he became aware of an arm around his neck and an acrid smell in his nostrils. Dexter had got up, sauntered into the living room and decided to show his old friend some love by sitting down and giving him a hug. It was all too apparent that he'd not washed for days.

"What's up, Buster, me old cocker? I thought you'd be all smiles this morning, spreading happiness all around the gaff yesterday, like Father Christmas. What a cool thing to do, man. You ought to be proud of yourself, mate."

"I'm fucked, Dexter," replied Buster softly, his voice charged with emotion.

"Billy's kidnapped my folks and now he's going to kill them unless I get my arse up there within the hour. I need to leave right now or they're dead."

As Buster spoke, Ewalina poked her head around the kitchen door from where she'd been listening and chipped in, trying to keep a straight face.

"The thing is Dexter, Billy Murphy made the call to your phone, which is a bit odd, don't you think? I didn't even realise he knew you? Weird, isn't it? I wonder how he got your number?"

Her tone suggested that she was very much enjoying the drama.

"Shit, man, that's fucking awful, bruv. What you going to do, mate?" replied Dexter awkwardly, ignoring Ewalina, as he backed away from his friend.

"I'll …I'll go and see if the others are awake, shall I? Ask them if they've got any bright ideas, or something. Many hands make light work and all that malarkey."

Buster was too consumed by his own misery to give any thought to Dexter's erratic behaviour.

Moments later, the peace was interrupted by a sudden crash, as the flat's heavy front door slammed shut. No one had heard it open, but they all heard it close. The bang was followed by the faint patter of feet running swiftly down the stairwell. A second softer thud was audible as the outer door closed heavily against the wind.

When Zaid and Sophia entered the living room moments later, dazed, hungover and half asleep, there was no trace of Dexter to be found in the flat…apart from his battered old Nokia which was still sitting on the damp table.

"I think your so-called mate has somewhere else he needs to be in a hurry," said Ewalina brightly, clearly enjoying Buster's discomfort.

"You do know he was glued to that thing last night, right?" she continued, pointing to the phone.

"It might even hold a few answers, if you want to be a mister nosey parker. You might as well get the whole picture before you dash off to meet your fate, surely? The taxi's going to be here soon, so you better be quick. Forewarned is forearmed is something you say here, right?"

Buster reluctantly picked up the phone, unwilling to accept that Dexter's departure might indicate a betrayal.

"It's locked and I don't know the code. He's probably just popped out for some fresh air, or something. He'll be back soon, I'm sure. Let's not worry about it."

Even as the words passed his lips, he knew that they were unlikely to be true. But on top of the conversation he'd just had with Billy, the thought of another crushing problem to add to the list was too much to contemplate.

"Your friend's an idiot," continued Ewalina, unsympathetically.

"The code will be 1234 or his birthday. He wouldn't be able to remember anything more complicated than that. I'm very good at working out people's PIN numbers. Trust me. I'm an expert, it's what I do for a living. Give it to me. I'll do it," she said, snatching the phone from Buster's hand.

Seconds later, the phone was unlocked.

"Like I said, 1234. The guy's an absolute cretin."

They gathered around and read the texts that Dexter had been receiving. Buster realised with a sinking heart that they'd had a traitor in their midst. Ewalina's flat no longer felt like the safe haven it had been just half an hour before. Billy Murphy, the arch manipulator, had skilfully turned the tables on their little gang of modern-day Robin Hoods.

While he waited for the taxi to arrive, he tried calling his mother's number again from Dexter's phone. It was answered by a generic woman's voice telling him that the person he wanted to speak to was unavailable at this time. He should call back or send a text. The words mocked him as he pictured the danger he'd put her in. He knew what unavailable meant. It meant that his poor mum was at the mercy of a homicidal maniac. Calling back or sending a text weren't options that were going to make a blind bit of difference.

Aware that he needed to face his destiny, Buster stopped calling his parents and pulled himself together. A plan of sorts was coalescing in his mind. In the five years he'd known Billy, only one significant weakness had ever become apparent. This was the moment to exploit that nugget of knowledge with as much cunning and attitude as he could muster. The survival of the entire Brett clan was now dependent on him successfully pulling it off.

Chapter 46

Billy watched the Range Rover drive in and stop directly in front of the house. It parked next to the Bentley with its headlights shining through the glazed panels to either side of the front door, illuminating the hallway below.

Things weren't right. The car just sat there. No one got out and the engine continued running. Plumes of vapour poured from the twin tail pipes as the hot exhaust gases mixed with the cold morning air.

This wasn't where the boys were supposed to leave the car. Only the Bentley was allowed to occupy this prime position. The Range Rover's allocated spot was to one side, next to the garage and by the hose. They were trained to wash and polish it when they had nothing else to do. He'd drilled them a hundred times on the routine and they'd learned long ago how he liked things.

Billy snapped his fingers at Razor, who appeared to be transfixed by the odd behaviour on the forecourt below. He shrugged back. From their position on the landing they could see the roof of the car and the torsos of the boys through the windscreen. They weren't moving. One of them had his hands on the wheel and the other seemed to be sitting on his. The pleasure derived from the conversation with Buster quickly evaporated as Billy realised that something was seriously amiss.

"Get down there right now and find out what those fat fucks are playing at," he snarled.

Razor ran down the stairs and went to open the front door as his boss followed, two steps behind. In the second they were between floors, the back door of the Range Rover opened and a dark figure slipped away into the shrubbery.

Blinded by the headlights, they could just make out Derek and Anthony sitting in the car's front seats. They were shaking their heads from side to side and making no effort to get out. Above the purr of the idling engine, Billy and Razor could hear the muffled sound of shouting coming from inside; desperate yelling that was making the boys go red in the face.

"What the fuck's going on here then?" said Billy, unable to identify the problem or establish any reason for their odd behaviour. Every instinct in his body told him that he was walking into a trap. He'd been right to worry about them taking so long. He checked that the front door remained open behind him, ready to make a hasty retreat.

"I think there's a problem, boss," replied Razor, stating the obvious and earning himself a withering rebuke.

"Of course there's a fucking problem, you dickhead. Let's get them out of the motor and inside. We're sitting ducks out here."

As they stepped forward, the boys in the car started to scream and shake their heads even more violently. Billy knew he was being set up but couldn't work out how. Maybe the Albanians had decided to take advantage of the situation, or perhaps it was the crazy Russians he'd had brushes with in the past.

Billy feared that word of his recent problems had spread. His enemies would sense his fragility. This could be their move. He felt vulnerable and alone outside. He needed to get the boys indoors so they could tool up and face the threat together, whatever it might be.

As Razor opened the passenger door and Billy simultaneously reached for the other, the screaming from inside the car stopped. Both doors seemed stiff. Something was preventing them from opening. Each opened a few inches before snagging. Through the gap, Razor could see what looked like fishing line tied around the interior handle, leading up via the headrest to a loop around Anthony's neck. The tension resulting from the door's movement had caused, whatever it was, to tighten around his colleague's throat.

Anthony was silent now, except for an unnatural gurgling that accompanied the foam bubbling from his lips. His eyes were open and bulging and his tongue protruded grotesquely from his mouth. Across the handbrake and gearshift, Razor could see that Derek was in a similar condition, except that his hands were bound to the steering wheel and his face had turned purple.

Instinctively reaching into his breast pocket, he brought out the knife that had earned him his nickname. It had served him well in street fights, but this was the first time he'd ever used it to save a life. Cutting the line from the door handle and leaning Anthony's head forward, he pushed the flat of the blade under the noose at the back of his neck. Less collateral damage at the rear he calculated, away from the windpipe and arteries, forgetting all about the spinal cord.

Once he was sure that the knife was under the ligature, he twisted it so the lethal tension was brought to bear against the sharp edge. The other side cut deep into Anthony's flesh as the fishing line pinged free. He gasped for air as Razor passed the knife over to Billy, who freed Derek's neck and hands with a great deal less care or finesse.

Derek and Anthony laboured for breath as blood from their injuries soaked into the pristine leather seats of the Range Rover. The boys were unresponsive as Billy slapped their cheeks and pinched their ears, hoping for a quick fix to what was clearly a serious problem.

"Wake up, you fat useless twats. We need to get inside!" he shouted, optimistically.

"I'll call an ambulance, boss, shall I?" asked Razor, realising they weren't going to recover without immediate medical help, however inconvenient this might be.

"You're not fucking calling anyone," snapped Billy, looking around wildly, waiting for the shot that would take him out. All he wanted to do was get back into the house and feel the weight of a gun in his hand.

"Do that and the Old Bill will be up here in minutes."

"But boss, they need help. I wouldn't be surprised if they've had their wind pipes crushed. What kind of animal would do this to them?" continued Razor, without irony, considering the violence he'd inflicted on so many others in the past.

Billy wondered this too, but now wasn't the time to think. It flashed across his mind that Buster could be the architect of this new mischief. All he wanted was to get back indoors. He needed to put a lock and a thick brick wall between himself and the headshot he was convinced was going to be fired at any moment.

"If you're so bothered about them, then you take them to the fucking hospital. Just dump them on the forecourt and leave. You've got fifteen minutes to go and get back here. And put your fucking foot down for once ...no driving at thirty."

Razor struggled to put Derek onto the back seat of the Range Rover and then took off with a squeal of tyres. His exit was frustrated as he waited for the gates to open sufficiently wide for the car to pass through. He grimaced as he felt Derek's still warm bodily fluids soak into his trousers where they had pooled in the base of the driver's seat.

By the time he was clear and accelerating away down Dyke Road Avenue, Billy was already back in his study, gun in hand, studying his array of CCTV monitors, watching for anyone who might approach the exterior of the house.

He felt safer now. The house was a fortress. He'd anticipated this eventuality and every window was fitted with bulletproof glass and locks that a sledgehammer would struggle to shatter. Whoever had ambushed the boys had no chance of getting inside. Fuck the Albanians, fuck the Russians and fuck Buster. If they wanted a fight, they'd get one.

Chapter 47

Buster and Zaid sat nervously in the back of the taxi as it pulled away from Adelaide Crescent. The driver tried his best to engage them with pleasantries and chitchat but soon gave up when he caught the anguish in their eyes. Turning up the radio, he concentrated on the road ahead and wondered what business this odd-looking pair had on salubrious Dyke Road Avenue.

After Ewalina made it clear that they'd all outstayed their welcome, she'd reluctantly offered to 'hold the fort'. She refused to engage in any further discussion about her role in the morning's activities. She thought it was best if Buster just went by himself and did what he needed to do. He was the one that Billy wanted to see and it was his poor parents who'd been taken hostage. There was no point in any of the rest of them getting hurt, she'd explained matter-of-factly, as she dried her coffee cups and put them back in the cupboard.

Zaid thought differently, much to Buster's relief. He sent his daughter home and offered to come along. He was still simmering from his beating and wanted to face the man who'd caused him so much hurt.

As the taxi made its way up to Dyke Road Avenue, by the slowest route possible, getting caught at all the lights and rarely getting out of second gear, Buster thought he saw Billy's Range Rover speeding past in the other direction. It looked like Razor at the wheel with Anthony slumped in the passenger seat next to him. He couldn't fathom where they'd be going in such a hurry. Perhaps to get reinforcements. Maybe to get more guns. None of the possibilities offered much comfort.

If his eyes hadn't deceived him, it meant that Billy would be lacking muscle for the time being. He'd only have Derek to help guard his parents and watch out for their arrival. Two against two didn't sound so bad, he thought, trying to convince himself there was still hope, as the taxi neared its destination. His stomach rumbled from the stress of the situation and he wished he'd gone to the toilet before they'd left.

Buster asked the cabbie to stop just short of Billy's house, in a spot he was sure the cameras couldn't see. Passing him a twenty and making sure he was busy rooting around in his bag for change, Buster slipped the gun and a box of ammunition to Zaid. He'd used one before and was an excellent shot, he'd told everyone last night, exaggerating greatly after too many few drinks.

The driver glanced momentarily in his mirror. He looked away just as quickly, horrified at what he'd just seen.

The second his passengers were out on the pavement, he grabbed his phone and started to dial the police.

Approaching the gates, Zaid slipped the weapon into the back of his trousers.

"Are you ready for this?" said Buster, keen to clarify their hastily made plan.

"Don't worry. We're going to make this work," came Zaid's measured, reassuring reply.

"Billy will want to talk to me first. I'm the one who's done him harm," continued Buster, his heart racing as the gritty reality of what was about to happen sank in. He was painfully aware that his off-the-cuff plan was reliant on a huge bluff and the help of a man who'd punched him on the nose just hours before.

"I'm going to tell Billy that I've left the memory stick with someone for safe keeping and if we're not back in an hour, that person is instructed to go straight to the police. He'll absolutely hate that. He knows there's enough information on it to put him away for life.

The problem is, I also know what Billy's temper's like. I'm not sure he'll be able to control it when he sees us on his doorstep, no matter what I say. So, if he does go for me, and I'd say it's fifty-fifty he will, bring out the gun and threaten him with it, and we'll go from there. We've only got one chance with this, mate, so let's not fuck it up. I just need to get my folks out of that place. Let's only use the gun if there's no other choice. We're better than him. Remember that."

"How could I ever forget?" said Zaid quietly, as he smiled and ran his tongue along the jagged remains of his broken teeth.

Buster entered the gate entry code. He'd used this number a hundred times before, but today, knowing that Billy would be watching and planning his painful demise, he forgot the order of the digits. On the third attempt he got it right. As the gates neared their wide-open position, he ducked into the garden border and lifted a heavy rock from the shrubbery. As he crouched down, he took the memory stick from his pocket and pushed it into the soft ground for safekeeping. He then placed the rock in the spot where the gates would close together, guaranteeing an escape route. He prayed that they'd be lucky enough to need it.

"One question," said Zaid, as they started to walk down the drive.

"Why didn't you just give the memory stick to Ewalina and ask her to go the police if you didn't come back? I mean, you're paying her enough, aren't you?"

Buster was shocked that he'd even asked the question.

"Would you trust that girl with the one thing you've got left that might save your life or keep you out of prison?"

The look on Zaid's face did the talking for him.

"No, I didn't think you would, and neither would I."

Walking towards the stone lions that guarded Billy's front door, Buster felt as if he was about to be ripped apart by real wild animals. His instinct to save his parents was only slightly stronger than his urge to flee. But as they approached the door, he started to feel stronger. He had nothing to lose now. He'd already factored in the pain and violence he was about to face. The only things that mattered now were getting his folks out of danger and proving to them that he was capable of changing his ways.

This was his time to shine and face the demon head-on.

Chapter 48

Unfortunately for Billy, the person he really needed to worry about had already slipped in through the front door while he'd been distracted with the inconvenient task of trying to save Derek's life.

As he studied his screens, poured a drink and started to feel a little safer, a man studied him carefully from a shadowy corner of the room. Hidden behind long dark curtains, he observed and smiled. He was enjoying himself for the first time in years.

He noticed that Billy was right-handed and had a stiffness in his left leg. He estimated his weight and age. He judged his strength and likely response speed, based on his musculature and gait. He'd already analysed the rest of the room. Billy's boxing posters, the medication on the desk and the gun taped beneath, had all been noted, assessed and taken into account.

As Billy got up to go to the toilet, the man slithered behind on all fours, silently tracking his prey through the house. He could have taken him then, when he was vulnerable, with his pants around his ankles, but, as he was having fun, he decided to hold off, wait, and make the most of the hunt.

When Billy returned to his office and started to relax, sprawling in his chair, the man crept up behind him. He reached silently into his pocket for what was left of the fishing line he'd used earlier. Wrapping the ends tightly around each hand, he pulled the length between them taut. He smiled to himself and waited for the perfect moment to strike

He was just about to attack when the doorbell chimed. It was unexpected, inconvenient and shattered the tranquillity of the house. The man stepped back into the shadows, irritated that his moment of gratification had been postponed.

Glancing at his screens, Billy started to grin and clenched his fists.

"Like lambs to the fucking slaughter," he muttered, reaching under his desk for the sawn-off he kept there for occasions such as this. Pleased that his plan was working, despite not actually having Buster's parents on the premises, he made his way to the front door.

His uninvited guest crept quickly and quietly behind him, ready to adapt to any threats or opportunities that this new development might afford.

Two figures waited under the exterior camera - Buster, and the man Billy suspected of burning his favourite suit.

"Two for the price of one," he snarled to himself, as he checked that both barrels had cartridges in place.

Undoing three locks, two bolts and a heavy steel chain, Billy opened the reinforced door and raised the gun to his callers.

"Buster, you little fucker, give me one good reason not to shoot you in the face right now."

Chapter 49

With the shotgun barrels just inches from his face, Buster tried to force out the carefully constructed sentences he'd been rehearsing in his head. But the words wouldn't come. Instead, his leg started to tremble and he that thought he might faint, right there and then, at Billy's feet. Being a tough guy was harder than he'd ever imagined it would be

"You've got five seconds, son, or you're dead."

The speech that he'd hastily prepared about his epiphany and the memory stick got stuck in his throat. He literally had no words. The rage radiating from Billy had sucked the ability to speak from his mouth.

"Come on, Buster, you're a clever boy, you can do better than this," snarled Billy, relishing the horror on his ex-employee's face.

"Five… four… three…I'm not joking, you little cunt. Haven't you got something you want to tell me before I blow your fucking brains out?"

Buster rallied his energy and pushed out the things he'd been meaning to say. His mouth was dry and his tongue felt heavy and dead as he forced out the specific set of words he knew could save his life. If there was one thing Billy respected, it was technology.

"Billy, I've got a memory stick with all your business dealings on it. I've uploaded the data to a digital hub that will automatically live stream the information to the Sussex Police WhatsApp drop-box in exactly one hour from now. It's a randomised crypto-server, with level-four binary security and the quad HD mobile processor. It's got the 32-bit transfer rate with the 12 mega-byte cache."

He'd memorised the last bit from an advert he'd seen on the headrest of the taxi they'd just got out of.

"The only way to get a stop message to the host is for me to enter the psychometric token I've got encrypted on my laptop. So basically, if you shoot me now, there's no way in the world of stopping all your secrets from falling straight into the hands of the police."

Billy hesitated and softened his grip on the trigger. He lowered the gun by an inch and glared at Buster. He had no idea what his ex-employee was talking about, but understood instinctively that the words were dangerous.

"You fucking kidding me, son?"

Buster could see the cogs ticking in Billy's brain, trying to work out if he was telling the truth and what the ramifications would be if he were. He'd deliberately used language that would impress and rattle his old boss. He hoped that he hadn't over done it.

"I want to make a deal, Billy. Let my parents go and forget about me, and I'll make sure the memory card data is permanently deleted. I'll disappear and you can tell people you killed me or whatever you want to say, to save face. And then you can carry on just like normal. I'll even leave you the codes for the office computers and all that other stuff that only I know about."

Buster was relieved when the words were out. They'd sounded convincing and reasonable. He'd delivered them with all the sincerity he intended. He watched carefully for any flicker of reaction on the old man's face.

Billy stared down the gun barrel, conflicted, trying to process the mix of anger, hatred and hurt he was feeling. He wanted to kill the boy, but he didn't want to go to prison. He didn't want the police to know anything about his operation, but he really wanted to see Buster dead on his hall floor.

"You're having a right fucking laugh, aren't you, son? Are you a piss-taking cunt, or what?"

Buster could see the red mist starting to rise in his boss's face. It was the same look he'd witnessed at the Chinese restaurant. He realised that the bluff might not be strong enough to overcome Billy's instinct for extreme violence.

Billy's finger twitched on the trigger as he lifted the gun again. His fury began to outweigh the logical downside of the words he'd just heard. He levelled the barrels at Buster's nose. Fuck the police and fuck Buster.

Behind Billy's back, Buster spotted a figure appear from the gloom of the hallway. It wasn't big enough to be Derek, but the face was oddly familiar. The person closed in silently on Billy as he spoke.

He then recognised the uncle he'd not seen for years. Uncle Bob, his mother's brother, was inexplicably in Billy's house. The impossible was happening right in front of his eyes. The black sheep of the family, who'd spent years in jail for killing his prisoners in Afghanistan, had appeared like an angel in this moment of crisis. Assuming that he must have been shot and was in the process of ascending to heaven, a smile spread across Buster's face.

"I don't know what you're so fucking happy about, son," snarled Billy.

Ghostly Uncle Bob raised his arm in the air as he took his final step towards the old man. He had a gun in his hand and the look of the devil on his face. There was an unmistakable glint in his eye as his hand started to swing towards its target.

"Sorry, son, but you fucking asked for this," said Billy, as he prepared to shoot, completely unaware as a gunstock slammed firmly into the side of his head.

Bang.

Billy crashed backwards onto his hall floor, blood rushing from a gash on his temple.

"Buster, my boy," said Uncle Bob calmly, as he stepped over his inert victim and kicked the shotgun away.

"What on earth have you got yourself involved with here then?"

Buster was too shocked to answer.

"I'm pretty sure this nasty character isn't someone your poor old parents would want you to be associating with, is he now? Am I right?"

Buster wasn't sure if the question was rhetorical or not. Clearly, Billy Murphy wasn't someone that any mother would want their son to know. Despite his surprise at seeing his uncle under such strange circumstances, Buster fought to find an answer.

As he waited for Buster to speak, Uncle Bob rolled Billy roughly onto his side, placed his hands behind his back and secured them with a selection of cable ties he'd slipped from his pocket. Zaid watched in awe at the speed and confidence with which this new ally handled the heavy limp body of their mutual foe.

"You're absolutely right, Uncle Bob," said Buster. He was just about to explain things fully when the absurdity of the situation caught up with him.

"By the way, what the actual fuck are you doing here? Billy led me to believe that he had mum and dad up here, not you."

Uncle Bob smiled.

"Unfortunately for this piece of shit," he said, kicking Billy, who'd started to moan and writhe on the floor, "his idiot scouting party got me instead. They turned up under-prepared, misjudged their mission and didn't prepare for contingencies."

The men talked more as they dragged Billy back into his office and lifted him roughly into an armchair. Buster explained about his plan to put things right as Uncle Bob listened and nodded, not quite understanding how his nephew could have taken such deadly risks with so little forethought. As he dressed the wound on Billy's head, he couldn't figure out if his nephew was an idiot, a simpleton or had simply lost his mind.

Chapter 50

As the men talked, Billy secretly listened. He'd been out cold for a minute, but now he was just playing dead. He'd also been quietly twisting and tugging away at the cable ties holding his wrists together, looking for a weakness or flaw in the material keeping him restrained. He couldn't believe what he was hearing.

As Buster explained how he'd given away most of the stolen money, his blood began to boil. When the boy told his uncle about the note sent in the envelopes, he could hold his peace no longer and exploded.

"Buster, you fucking piece of shit!" he screamed, writhing in the chair, taking everyone by surprise.

"You just wait 'til I get me hands on you, you sneaky little cunt."

Before he could add anything further, Uncle Bob calmly took a sheet of paper from the desk, crumpled it up and pushed it straight into Billy's open mouth.

"I see someone's woken up with a sore head," he said softly, sitting down on a chair opposite Billy and staring him directly in the face.

Billy glared back, seething with hatred for this unknown adversary. The casual coldness in this man's eyes was disturbing. As he stared back and studied his captor, he thought he could detect a hint of pleasure in the man's narrow eyes. He was being toyed with. This man was in no hurry to get out of the house. For the first time in years, he realised that he was in very serious trouble.

Chapter 51

"So, what exactly are we going to do with you, Mr Murphy?" said Uncle Bob, enjoying the rage expressed in Billy's darting eyes.

"In my experience, characters like you seldom forgive or forget. The problem is, if I let you live this morning, then I predict you'll pursue my young nephew here until you manage to kill him under a more favourable set of circumstances.

And as I can't always be here to protect him, the unavoidable conclusion is that if you live, he dies. Maybe not tomorrow, or next week, but probably within a year and when he's least expecting it. Am I right, Billy? Yes, I think I am."

Billy went red in the face as he tried to reply.

"Let's just agree to disagree, shall we?" continued Uncle Bob, relishing his discomfort.

"The one thing I think we *can* agree on, is that he's not the toughest weapon in the arsenal. But to be fair to the boy, he's probably a bit smarter than both of us in other ways. I understand he's actually helped you make quite a lot of cash over the years. Wouldn't you agree, Billy?

No great surprise then, that he wants to do something good for a change. Can't blame the boy for that, but his mother would *definitely* blame me if I had the opportunity to terminate his would-be killer and didn't take it. Do you get my drift?"

Billy couldn't disagree with anything his cold-eyed adversary was saying, but he didn't like the direction the monologue was taking. He tried to speak, but the paper choked his words and all he achieved was to increase the flow of saliva down his chin.

"So, my proposal, Billy, is that I shoot you cleanly in the head. You don't need me to tell you that it'll be quick and painless. I doubt you'd have given the boy the same consideration if things had turned out differently, so count yourself lucky."

Uncle Bob glanced around the room, assessing its layout and contents.

"Yes, it's probably best if we do it just where you are, sitting in the chair. No point in over complicating matters. If it's OK with you, I'll use one of these lovely cushions to mute the sound. We don't want your nosy neighbours hearing and calling the police now, do we?"

He spoke with all the coolness and indifference of a man chatting about the arrangements for the local harvest festival.

"And then I'll squeeze you into the boot of that Bentley I saw outside. Beautiful car by the way; great British marque. Have you got the keys handy, by any chance? I might have to get one of the others to help me with that. You're a chunky specimen, aren't you? What are you? Seventeen, eighteen stone I'd say, give or take. No offence, Billy, but I'm just looking at the practicalities. Someone has to, don't they? After all, you won't be around to help, will you?

I reckon it's just about big enough. How tall are you? Five nine, five ten? It might be a little tight, but I'm sure we'll be able to fit you in with a little pushing and bending.

Once you're all loaded up, I'll drive out to the middle of nowhere and torch it. A dignified cremation for you and the police will assume it's just some sordid turf war and that'll be that. All done and dusted. No one gets hurt."

Uncle Bob soaked up the anger in Billy's eyes. He was really on a roll now.

"Well, apart from you of course!" he continued, laughing out loud.

#####

Buster was horrified. The whole purpose of his flight from London had been to right some wrongs and find a way to turn his life around. Although he'd never worked out how to deal with Billy, shooting him in the head with a cushion over his face was not a scenario he'd envisioned.

How could he continue down the road to redemption with a murder on his conscience? His uncle was making it all sound so reasonable and justified, but he knew that despite the measured, logical words, the end result would still be a charred corpse in a burnt-out car, in a desolate spot in the back of beyond.

He'd be no better than Billy if he allowed this to happen, but he couldn't think of a better way out. As he listened to his uncle playing with Billy, he wondered if he should just follow the grisly plan. He'd subdued his conscience for the past five years, so perhaps he could do it for a little bit longer if the trade-off was that they'd all get to survive.

But coming to his senses, he decided that the idea was ridiculous and would undermine everything he'd set out to achieve. He hadn't come this far just for his crazy-arsed uncle to reverse his search for salvation.

Despite the fact that Billy had just been on the brink of shooting him, Buster needed to think on his feet and find a way to save him before it was too late.

#####

"So, Billy, shall we just get on with it?" said Uncle Bob, matter-of-factly.

"No point in delaying the inevitable and I'd rather just crack before anyone else turns up here to spoil things. Any last words?" he asked, tugging the paper out of Billy's mouth, being careful to avoid presenting the condemned man with a last chance to bite.

Billy's face was purple with rage. The thought that this rabble would end his days in his own armchair had driven him into a fury the likes of which he'd never experienced before.

"Shoot me, you cunts, and you'll fucking rot in hell for ever. And my boys will track you down and..."

Uncle Bob shoved the paper back into Billy's mouth.

"Not exactly the eloquent final words I was hoping for, but suit yourself. Nobody wants to hear any more from that potty mouth, I'm afraid."

Billy's face was crimson as Uncle Bob reached behind his back for one of the cushions he'd been leaning against.

"This one'll do the trick nicely. You'll have to let me know where you got them. They're beautifully soft."

He held the cushion over Billy's face and lifted the gun to his forehead.

Billy knew right then that it was the end of the road. This was his 'Delaney Brothers' moment. He wondered in that instant what would become of his Rolex.

But in the second before the trigger was pulled or Buster could act, fate intervened and the office door slammed open. They all turned to look, shocked and startled, as a new voice rang out.

"Drop the fucking gun, or the hippy gets it!"

To everyone's surprise and Billy's obvious relief, Razor was framed in the doorway. He had a pistol in one hand, and, with the other arm he held Dexter in a neck lock. The gun was held to his temple and it was clear that not for the first time recently, he'd lost control of his bladder.

"Sorry, Buster, mate, I think I messed up again," whined Dexter pathetically, as everyone else in the room frantically calculated what their next move should be.

Chapter 52

Buster's parents' normally tranquil home was swarming with emergency services. White and blue police tape looped around trees, bushes and fence posts to prevent inquisitive neighbours from getting too close.

This was the most exciting thing any of them had seen for years. Not since a bonfire got out of hand three years earlier and a whole row of Leylandii lit the night sky had the curtain twitchers of Holmbush Crescent been so fully occupied.

Four police cars, two vans, an ambulance and at least four officers with black helmets and machine guns crowded the street. The houses were bathed in the rhythmic flashing of multiple blue lights. Cameras snapped away as gossip was created and spread. False concern dotted every conversation. Poor souls they said, such nice people. A lovely couple who kept themselves to themselves, they unanimously agreed. Shame about the son, they whispered. He'd got in with the mafia by all accounts. Heads were shaken and people assumed the worst. They didn't deserve to go this way. Blood, guts and bullets all over the place, apparently.

Two plain clothes officers could be seen entering the cordon. Probably detectives, thought the people in the house opposite. They'd just finished coffees from takeaway cups and stuffed their faces with what looked like croissants. Perhaps they should have had their breakfasts before they came on duty, thought old Mrs Perkins at number 54. This wasn't how detectives behaved on television she concluded, prickling with indignant disappointment.

"So, the house is empty. It was all locked up when foxtrot lads got here and they had to put a side window in to gain access," explained Gary.

"But the kettle's still warm and the dishwasher's on, so someone's been here recently. We've got blood on the pathway right here and just the one shell casing that we've located so far," he continued, pointing to a dark patch on the ground.

"The neighbour opposite says he saw a black Range Rover drive off with three people in it. Couldn't be sure though. He's a bit sketchy on the details, but thinks it was two big blokes in the front of the motor. Bouncer types, he said."

Samuel stared at the ground. A theory was brewing in his mind.

"I don't think we can necessarily assume it was Brett Junior they were after. Could be that Murphy decided to go for the parents instead. Makes sense. Easy pickings in soft suburbia. It would be a great way for him to put pressure on Brett if they've had this big falling out the gaffer was banging on about."

Gary nodded. His sergeant's theory made sense, but there was no evidence yet to back it up.

"I think you might be right. Way more likely than him sitting over here like a lemon waiting for them to turn up and catch him. He wouldn't be that stupid, surely? If he gets the folks, then the son will come running along soon enough. That'll be Murphy's thinking. But on the other hand, the witness said he saw three people leaving the scene. So, what happened to the other parent?"

Samuel knelt down and examined the bloodstains on the path.

"I'm picturing some sort of scuffle when his lads knock on the door. Someone's panicked or decided to be brave. A firearm's been discharged and either the mum or dad or someone else has been hit."

"That's what it looks like," concurred Gary.

"I've tried calling all the numbers I can find for the parents to try and rule them out, but no joy yet. Apparently, she's the only one with a mobile and the bloody thing's turned off. Sam, the other thing I'm struggling with are these items here on the ground."

Gary pointed at two white cable ties and some short lengths of fishing wire that were lying next to the blood-stained section of pathway.

"Murphy's lads probably used the ties to secure Brett's parents' hands, if we're going with that theory, but I've no idea about the line."

"Maybe they just fancied a spot of fishing," quipped Samuel as he wondered what to do next. He already had officers actively checking for useful CCTV and a team of PCSOs going house to house. The CSI team had just taken photographs, swabbed for blood, bagged the shell case and set a tent up to protect the scene.

That was the basics covered. But experience told him that the decisions he'd need to make in the next few minutes were more important. They would determine whether Buster Brett's poor parents died or survived. He was well aware that he couldn't afford to make a mistake or take a turn down a blind alley.

As he tried to think, his mobile phone rang in his hand. He took the call and digested what he was being told, realizing immediately that everything he'd taken for granted about the scene would need to be revised. Events, yet again, had caught him on the hop.

"Listen, Gary, there's news. Two badly injured men have just been dumped outside the RSCH in Brighton. And I mean literally dumped on the A and E forecourt. They've both got some sort of damage to their necks and one's been shot in the foot. They're now in intensive care and fighting for their lives by all accounts. Big lads too, apparently.

One of our officers was up there dealing with a constant-watch and saw them get pushed out of a Range Rover. It sped straight off and clipped an ambulance on the access ramp. Luckily for us, the smart lad caught the VRM and ran it through PNC. Comes back to a company registered in the Cayman Islands."

"So, you're thinking that's related to this, then?" asked Gary, pointing to the ground and wishing straight away that he hadn't said anything.

"Doh. What do you think? Of course, it's related. A gunshot here and a man in hospital who's been shot. A Range Rover up there and one here too. Billy Murphy's behind all of it. And he's exactly the sort of character who'd funnel his assets through an offshore company.

I've got no idea whatsoever where the neck injuries come into the picture, but we've definitely made some wrong assumptions about Brett's parents. All we know is that some poor bugger's been shot and someone else has probably been kidnapped. Either Brett himself or more likely his parents. And everything points to Murphy.

We need to pay him a visit right now. Get TFU to meet us up there in twenty minutes and let's knock on that old fucker's door. We've got the grounds now. Plenty of grounds. Tell them to RV on Woodruff Avenue so he doesn't get wind."

As the officers rushed to their car, Samuel called the DI to get his authorisation for the armed raid. On the second go, he answered his phone. Today he was sober and sheepish. They skirted around the question of his bizarre behaviour the day before. That awkward conversation would have to wait for another time. After a short factual exchange of words, DI Weston agreed to meet them there and the line went dead.

While Samuel talked, Gary digested the chatter on the divisional radio talk group.

"You're not going to believe this, Sam. Some taxi driver has just called up to say he's dropped some blokes outside Murphy's gaff. He says they had a gun and a box of bullets on them. You couldn't make this stuff up, Skipper."

Gary turned on the blues and two tones and accelerated away from Southwick, while Samuel held on tight and wondered if these new developments had any link to the elusive Stalker. He decided to put all thoughts of her on the back burner for the time being. The faster the car went, the more vividly he could sense his professional career disappearing into a bottomless rabbit hole, one from which the only possible escape was to find Buster Brett alive and get him to cooperate.

He felt sick as the croissants and pint of coffee he'd just consumed gyrated uncomfortably around his stomach. At every corner, he struggled to suppress his urge to vomit. Despite the nausea, Samuel suspected that all the answers he needed lay somewhere inside Billy Murphy's infamous mansion.

In minutes, they'd be outside and ringing his bell. Either they'd be invited in or something altogether more violent would unfold. He consoled himself with the thought that whichever way events turned out, he'd soon have the chance to see for himself what murky secrets lay hidden behind that dark and ominous front door.

Chapter 53

Razor waited but no one moved. The reaction he desperately wanted failed to happen. The crazy guy didn't flinch, and if anything, he held his gun tighter to Billy's head. He could see the veins throbbing in his boss's temple. A mumbled gargling emanated from his mouth as he struggled to expel something lodged there.

Buster, the traitor, and the man they'd watched on the Islington CCTV just stood together, startled by the rapid change of dynamic in the room. At least they feared him and looked concerned for their friend's life. An awful smell filled his nostrils and he could feel something wet and pathetic trembling against his leg. He needed to move things along. He tried again, more forcefully, hoping for a better outcome.

"I said drop the fucking gun or your mate gets it in the head. I'm serious! Drop the gun right now or I'll shoot him."

No one moved. The gun remained stubbornly close to the boss's face. It dawned on Razor that he might actually have to shoot the dirty little man he was holding. He'd only just caught him outside the house, but if the mad guy didn't release the boss soon, then he'd have no choice but to carry through with the threat and deal with the bloody consequences. He wished he was back in London where threats worked, guns were respected and people did as they were told.

"I'm not going to drop anything I'm afraid, whoever you are," said the man slowly, with a poker face that showed not a flicker of emotion.

"I really don't know why you think I'd be bothered by that specimen. Crack on. Do whatever you want. Your boss is going to die one way or the other."

The man then spoke directly to Billy, sounding almost concerned.

"Shall we get this over with? Sorry about the delay. It must be very frustrating having to listen to all this nonsense when you're preparing to die."

Billy started to writhe and moan in the chair, his eyes demanding that Razor take immediate action to rectify the situation.

But Razor didn't know what to do. The man's voice was cold and calm and he could detect a ruthlessness in his tone that made him fear for Billy's life. He also feared for his own. There was something about the way the man was holding the weapon that suggested he knew exactly how to use it. He could see the sinews in his forearm drawn tight, poised and ready to recoil.

This couldn't be allowed to continue, but what choices did he have? The wet foul man was his hostage, but one that no one seemed to care about. Once he was dead, things would degenerate into a straight shoot out and Razor didn't fancy his chances. Driving the car and keeping his mouth shut was what he'd been hired to do, not fighting lunatics.

As Razor stared at the man, hesitant to make the next move, his heart started to race. He calculated that he had only seconds left before he lost control of the situation.

Chapter 54

Buster could sense from Razor's hesitation that his former colleague was out of his depth. He'd managed to stop his boss from getting shot in the head, but seemed stuck on what to do next. The challenge now was to make sure that his poorly executed rescue plan didn't go any further in getting the old man off the hook.

Uncle Bob's voice in the background was calm and reassuring. It was clear from his unflustered tone that he had the situation, and Billy, firmly under control.

Buster thought about what he could say to talk Razor down without anyone getting hurt. He was brighter than the others and would be able to see with his own eyes that this was the end of the road. They could offer him a way out with his dignity intact. That had to be better than somebody getting shot.

Glancing over at Dexter, he could see his head held firmly by his hostage-taker's well-developed forearm. With his other hand, Razor held the pistol. He was gripping it awkwardly as if he were unsure where to point it.

The moment Dexter caught his eye, his face became wildly animated. For a second, Buster thought that he might be suffocating or sick. He was rolling his eyes up and down and blinking manically. It was obvious that he was trying to communicate something, but it wasn't clear what that could be. But then Dexter used his left hand to point at the arm around his neck and it was obvious what he intended to do.

Before Buster could decide if it was a good idea or not, let alone signal back, Dexter took the initiative. Turning his head sharply, he bit down hard on the muscular arm restraining him. He clenched his jaw with as much ferocity as he could muster. His teeth tore into his captor's tattooed flesh and he tasted his warm blood. At the same time, he lifted his feet off the ground and used both hands to pull down on Razor's wrist with all his modest weight.

Off balance and staggering to one side, a shocked Razor howled in pain. As his other hand instinctively clenched the Glock 18, a fat finger slipped accidentally across the trigger. A flash burst from the muzzle and a bullet was sent flying towards the ground. Buster instinctively flinched from the crack. The lead round hit the parquet, bounced back up and hit Uncle Bob in the shoulder, instantly knocking him down.

As Buster rushed over to help his uncle, Dexter looked up from the floor. He gazed in quizzical disbelief at the consequences of his actions.

"You fucking idiot, Dexter! You just got my uncle shot!"

In the confusion, Billy seized the chance he'd been waiting for. With the gunshot ringing in his ears, he struggled out of the armchair and kicked his injured would-be assassin sharply in the head, followed by further blows to his groin and stomach.

For the last few minutes, he'd been twisting the cable tie binding his hands back and forth. He'd been bending, stretching and rubbing it on an upholstery spring he'd discovered down the back of the chair. Substantially weakened, it gave way as he tensioned every sinew in his wiry old torso. The moment his hands were free, he punched the man on the ground for good measure, grabbed his gun and jabbed it in the direction of Buster and Zaid.

To Buster's absolute horror, Billy was back in charge.

Chapter 55

"Thank fuck for that," the old man said to no one in particular.

"So, Buster, I bet you thought you had me beat there for a minute, didn't you?"

Buster was absolutely convinced that he'd had his old boss beat.

"I actually thought the same for a bit," Billy continued, telling the truth.

"That bloke's good. I'll give you credit for that. Sort of geezer I'd like to have on the team. The cunt had me worried for a minute or two, I must say."

Buster watched his uncle lying inert and face down on the floor. A pool of blood was rapidly spreading beneath his left shoulder. He was furious at himself for not preventing Dexter's misguided attempt to help.

"But luckily, things haven't quite gone your way, have they, son? Your so-called mate over there provided a very welcome distraction, I must say. I think he was trying to help you, but he's actually fucked you right over, hasn't he? Lovely friend he is. One in a fucking million. Wish I had a mate like that."

Billy started to grin again as he took in the odd sight of Dexter trembling and sobbing on the floor with Razor's blood all around his mouth.

"Which means I have to decide what to do with you now, don't I, Buster. Um, let me think… Yep, that's a tricky one, for sure."

Billy pretended to be thinking with his hand on his chin and a fake quizzical expression on his face.

Buster knew exactly where this was going, and then he started to laugh. A dark false laugh that he forced out for effect.

"Sorry, Buster, I'm playing with you, mate. Can't help meself, can I? I know exactly what I'm going to do with you, you little cunt. And I think you know too. For starters, I'm going to shoot you in each of yer fucking knee-caps. Nice and painful it'll be too."

Buster winced as he visualised the scene. But the fear that he would have previously felt, was rapidly turning to anger. The cruelty that Billy had just dealt out to Uncle Bob had stimulated a rising fury, the strength of which was beginning to make him feel reckless.

Billy continued, enlivened by the prospect of violence.

"Then I'm going to watch you roll around in agony for a bit. The pain will be excruciating, of course, and you'll wish you'd never been born. I'm going to enjoy every last moment of your misery I'm afraid, son. It's the very least I fucking deserve after everything you've put me through. It's only fair.

You're probably going to tell me how sorry you are and beg for your life and all sorts of shit like that. But it won't make any difference, will it? You know that already, don't you, Buster? You know what I'm like, don't you, son? That's all assuming you can even get your words out. Then I'll kick you in the head a couple of times just for good measure. Probably in your fucking bollocks too, if I don't think you're sorry enough."

Buster knew that Billy was capable of all of these things. But right now, he no longer cared. All that occupied his mind was the hurt that had befallen his uncle. He watched as his breathing became shallower and his life energy gradually ebbed away.

It was obvious from the look on Billy's face that he was deriving a huge amount of enjoyment from explaining what he intended to do.

"Then, when I get bored of all your grizzling and pleading and sobbing, I'm going to shoot you in the fucking head and that'll be that. Game over. About bloody time. Buster's dead and the rest of us can move on with our fucking lives at last. Thank fuck for that and praise the Lord."

There's was a second's silence and Buster could sense the cogs ticking in the old man's brain.

"Boom!" shouted Billy abruptly, lunging forward, pretending to shoot and making everyone flinch. A satisfied grin spread across his face as he soaked up the fear in their eyes.

Buster stared at his old boss and loathed him. He wasn't scared any more. He just wished he'd allowed his uncle shoot him when they'd had the chance.

In his peripheral vision, he became aware of Dexter trying to make eye contact. He ignored him and kept his eyes firmly on Billy, not wanting to inflame the situation any further. He hated hearing the narrative of his own murder, but the longer Billy kept talking, the more time he had left alive.

"Psst, Buster mate, I'm sorry," whispered Dexter, loud enough for everyone to hear, causing Billy to stop what he was saying and stare in disbelief at the person who'd dared to interrupt him.

"I was wrong to let you down, Buster. I'm so sorry, bruv. Don't know what I was thinking. I only came up here to see if I could help. Thought you might need me. The gates were propped open and I could see the cars on the drive, so I slipped in. But then this gorilla jumped me by the door."

Razor's hand slapped the side of his head, shutting him up.

"Sorry to interrupt you, young man, but I think *I* was speaking, wasn't I?" said Billy indignantly, turning to give Dexter his undivided attention.

"No fucking manners," he tutted, assessing the unusual figure before him.

"So, I take it you're that pathetic little druggie cunt who tried to make a few quid out of poor old Buster here. Wasn't it you who contacted me to rat on him? Told me the whole story, didn't you, when you thought you might get a few quid. What a piece of shit you are."

Dexter sobbed as he held his head in his hands. Buster felt sorry for his old friend. He might be useless and he'd certainly double-crossed him, but he had also tried to atone by coming to the house. He wasn't all bad, like Billy.

"Yes, I think you definitely did, you two-faced little weasel. You ought to know the truth Buster. Don't want to go to your grave with questions unanswered, do you? Not that you'll be getting a grave, if I'm honest. Depends on your definition really. Does a hole in the fucking ground count? Probably not.

Anyway, we can't stand here all day gossiping like a bunch of cunts, can we? Some of us have got business to attend to. I'll work out what to do with you, son, once I've dealt with your mate Buster here. Let's just get this over with, shall we, and then I can clear up the mess. Time is money and all that fucking bollocks. I've got a lot of catching up to do after all the trouble you lot have caused me."

As Billy continued to speak, distracted by his conversation with Dexter, Buster's eye was drawn to the CCTV monitor on the desk. In one panel he could see a vehicle pulling up outside. It looked like a taxi. Someone got out and the driver handed them a bag from the boot. Another captured the image of a small figure tapping away at the security pad. A camera by the front door showed a person walking slowly down the drive towards the house.

Buster's heart raced as he made out the faintest rattle of a key in the front door lock. Then a muted thump and click as it closed. Delicate footsteps in the hallway followed. Heels on polished parquet. A subtle hint of a familiar perfume entered his nostrils. An aroma he knew well. It took him back to a place where he was valued and loved. It reminded him of the person he wanted to become. He was unsure whether to panic or be elated by what his senses were telling him.

To his alarm, Billy stepped closer. He looked serious now. He'd had his fun and was done with the banter and theatrics.

"Let's just get this done, son, shall we?"

But as he lifted the gun, Billy too detected the faint scent. It was one that he'd come to hate over the years. Flowery and fresh, he associated it with all the domesticity he did his best to avoid. He screwed up his face in disgust. This could not be happening. Not here, not now. Couldn't he just get a moment's peace to do what he needed to do? The last thing he needed was a load of fuss and interference. His fears were confirmed by a soft voice from the hallway. He lowered the gun, hesitant and unsure how to react.

"Hello! Anyone in? Billy, are you here? Billy? What on earth has happened to my vase!?"

All Buster could hear was the voice of an angel.

Seconds later, Fliss Murphy entered the office. The smile on her face evaporated instantly. She looked horrified and perplexed by the scene before her. Razor stepped away from Dexter and put the gun behind his back, trying his best to look the picture of innocence.

"What the hell is going on here?" she said sternly, gazing at the odd selection of familiar and new faces before her.

Noticing the weapon in her husband's hand, she narrowed her eyes and stepped towards him.

"What do you think you're doing, Billy? You can put that thing down for a start! Right this second, please, or you'll have me to deal with. And I mean now, right now! And who's that fella bleeding on my floor? And for goodness' sake, what have you done to your head?"

Buster realised that her voice was the only one in the world that could have made Billy stop doing what he was about to do. It was a voice that he hadn't expected to hear. With the wind well and truly out of his sails, Billy joined the others in staring at the diminutive figure who'd just stepped into the room.

"Fliss, what the fuck are you doing here?" he suddenly snarled, pulling himself together, furious that he'd been interrupted mid-murder.

Buster knew that she'd never actually caught him in the act of doing anything like this before. He glared at his wife and she matched his stare. Lines were blurred and Billy wasn't sure whether to backtrack or continue.

"I'm here, Billy, because you've disappeared for days, that's why. You sent for the guns in the attic, the ones that you don't think I know anything about, and then I hear on the grapevine that Buster here's taken off.

Plus, you've not answered your phone once or bothered to call me back. I tried ringing you three times from the train station just now, thinking you might send a car to pick me up. I even tried the landline, for goodness' sake. No answer, of course, so I had to get a bleedin' taxi."

She looked around the room again, shaking her head, trying to make some sense of the chaos.

"And now I know why, don't I?! I don't need to be Einstein to work out you're up to no good, do I? Did you really think I'd just sit at home watching telly and wait to be told that Buster's dead?

No, Billy. I might be old, but I'm not completely useless. Not yet, anyway. And it's a bloody good job I did decide to get the train down here, isn't it? Because the moment I walk in I find you about to put a bullet in the head of someone I care about very much. Someone *we* care about very much.

For fuck's sake, he's family, Billy! How could you even think about doing something like this? Whatever he's done, there's got to be a good reason for it. You and I both know he's a good boy, so I'm not going to let you hurt him, I'm afraid."

Buster was relieved to hear the conversation's direction of travel. Perhaps if it carried on this way, she might even call an ambulance for his uncle.

"There's got to be a better way, Billy, there really has. You've forced our own kids away, so I'm damned if I'm going to let you take Buster away from me as well. He's the only one I've got left now."

Buster watched as the mention of his name prompted a fresh wave of rage to flash across Billy's face.

"You stay out of this, Fliss Murphy. This has got nothing to do with you. This is business. He's taken us both for a couple of cunts. Especially you, you dozy old cow. He's had you wrapped around his little finger, he has, waiting for an opportunity to rip us off. And now I'm going to shoot the little cunt in the face, whatever you say, because that's the least he fucking deserves.

Nothing, absolutely nothing, is going to change that, so just get the fuck over it will you, and back off. Go and put the fucking kettle on or something, and leave this to me. Let me deal with things the way I see fit and then we can carry on just like normal."

Billy raised the gun to Buster's chest and looked him straight in the eye. Buster stared back at him and felt nothing but pure hatred. If this was to be his time, then he wanted Billy to know that his spirit had not been broken.

In a moment of clarity, Felicity Murphy realised that things could never be normal ever again. She could see the man she'd married for what he really was now. She'd couldn't change the past, but now was her chance to make amends. No more excuses or kidding herself, she thought. No more turning a blind eye. There was no longer any point in pretending or wishing that things were different.

"Billy, I said no and I meant it. I've only got a few weeks left and I don't want to spend that time grieving for Buster. If you've ever loved me, you'll put that gun down right now."

There was a slight pause.

"Billy?"

Billy was too wrapped up in his anger and the task of killing to comprehend her words. But Buster knew instantly what she meant. All their recent conversations now made perfect sense. The introspection, reflection and tying up of loose ends, which had made him feel uneasy at the time, all aligned perfectly as she spoke her final words.

Before Billy could squeeze the trigger or the gun muzzle flashed, Fliss had already started to step in front of Buster. Her last act on earth was a deliberate move to protect her adopted son. Her eyes met with her husband's as he realised, just too late, what her intentions were. The bullet that Billy had intended for the boy caught his wife fairly in the chest.

He watched in horror as it entered the body of the woman he'd shared his life with. The opportunity for things to be normal ever again had just gone. As the round ricocheted around her chest cavity and her knees began to gently buckle, Billy observed stunned, momentarily disabled by the atrocity he'd just committed.

Zaid seized the opportunity to reach for the gun in his waistband. He pointed the weapon at Billy and pulled the trigger.

But nothing happened. The mechanism didn't work. The gun appeared to have jammed. He began to tremble as Billy's wits rapidly returned and he levelled his weapon to fire a second shot.

Instinctively understanding what had happened and sensing that he only had one chance left, Buster leapt across and wrenched the gun from Zaid's faltering grip. This was his moment. His life would be defined by the next few seconds. As Billy aimed, Buster slipped the safety catch off and pulled the trigger three times in quick succession.

Bang. Bang. Bang.

The first two shots hit the wall, but the last one struck Billy in the chest. For a few seconds he stood immobilized, a thin trickle of blood running down the front of his crisp white shirt. His face was a picture of indignation, fury and surprise as he looked down at where the bullet had entered his body.

"You little fucking cunt!" were his last words, as he started to rock on his heels.

The venom on Billy's face did not waver as he fell back with a crash. As he lay motionless, the life drained from his open eyes. The terror and energy that had been the notorious Billy Murphy transformed into the dead corpse of an old fat man wearing a twenty year-old suit and a drawer full of gold jewellery.

Buster stood stunned and silent as Fliss and Billy lay together in death. His ears were ringing from the gunshots and the smell of cordite filled his nostrils. He couldn't believe what had just happened. Sadness and shock dominated his thoughts. He felt sick and relieved, acutely aware of the sacrifice that Fliss had just made to save him.

Razor put his gun on the floor, wanting no more involvement in this nightmare. He didn't want to die. He'd done as much as he could for the boss, but now it was all over and the spell was broken. He raised his hands and hoped that he'd be able to leave the house alive.

"I think we need to get out of here," said Buster quietly, articulating what the others were starting to think.

"No, I mean we *really* do. Right now!" he shouted, pointing to the CCTV monitor.

The screens showed at least five police vehicles outside the house. Officers in black body armour and helmets could be seen getting out of a van with machine guns held across their chests. They were placing ladders against the railings and getting ready to make an assault.

"We're fucked," said Dexter, unable to control the tears that had started to cascade down his cheeks.

Buster had never imagined that Fliss would end up getting shot as a result of his actions. He'd not had a chance to explain to her why he'd run and now he never would. She'd trusted him right until the end and was now lying dead for her troubles.

But then, in the mix of sadness and anger that was swirling around his mind, he sensed an opportunity, as a memory of a conversation from long ago surfaced in his consciousness.

"Maybe we're not fucked," he said cautiously, looking directly at Razor.

"You told me once that Billy has escape routes out of all his places. You know, because he's so paranoid about getting caught. Over the roof in Islington …through the cellar in Chigwell. Well, what I want to know is, did the old bastard have the same thing here?"

Razor looked around the room. As they'd been adversaries until moments before, he wasn't sure if Buster now wanted to kill him or accept his help. He judged that it was safe to speak.

"He owns the big house that backs onto this one. He rents it out but keeps the garage for himself. There's a car inside, one of those shit people carrier things. It's fuelled up, charged and ready to go with the key in the glove box. If we can get to it without being seen, then we might just be able to get away."

"And how exactly will we get to the garage without the cops knowing?" asked Buster, looking for the flaws in what Razor was saying, desperately hoping that he wouldn't find any.

"You know that big evergreen hedge down the side of the garden? Well, it's been hollowed out down the back to create a sort of covered passage. He gets the gardener to keep it nice and clear and just wide enough for us lads to squeeze through. It leads down to the fence with next door.

And we cut a panel out of that so we could kick it through, if we ever needed to leave in a hurry. The feds are bound to have a drone up, but the hedge will give us some protection from prying eyes. And with any luck, they won't clock us in next door's garden. They'll be too busy working out what's going on in here, especially now they've heard shots. But we need to go right now."

Buster listened to what Razor was saying. He was desperate to get out, but other concerns were holding him back.

"What about my uncle? He's badly hurt."

"Sounds harsh, but the best thing is to leave him here," continued Razor, keen to hurry matters along.

"The Old Bill will be through the front door in minutes. They don't do firearms ops without medics on standby. They'll get help to him much sooner than we could if we tried to take him with us."

It wasn't ideal. Buster didn't want to leave his uncle. Losing one person he cared about was bad enough. But for want of a better plan he conceded that there wasn't a better alternative.

Still fired up on adrenaline, he led them out through the back door. The others followed, dazed and horrified by what they'd just witnessed.

#####

Razor was the last one out of the office. He momentarily ducked back to place the gun that Buster had just fired in poor Mrs Murphy's palm. He put his own gun in Billy's free hand.

He hesitated for a second, wondering if it was wrong to portray her as the one who'd just shot her own husband in the chest. She was the only person he'd ever known to stand up to Billy. She'd been braver than any of them today and had paid dearly with her life. Wrapping her warm dead fingers around the gunstock, he decided that the practicalities of staying free trumped any moral considerations.

He'd wiped both guns for prints but his blood was everywhere, thanks to that idiot Dexter. There just wasn't enough time to make a better job of sanitising the scene. He resigned himself to the fact that nothing in life was perfect, as he grabbed the hard drive from the security system. Not making life easy for the police was a lesson he'd learned from Billy long ago. He caught up with the others as they squeezed into the damp passage behind the hedge. Brushing away spider's webs and dreading what lay beneath their feet, they made their way quietly and quickly along the garden border.

Razor was still worrying about the consequences of their actions as the motley selection of survivors from the Murphy residence reached the fence. Hopefully the cops would conclude that Billy had shot Fliss and Buster's crazy uncle before she fired back in self-defence, falling to the floor mortally wounded. It wouldn't make a whole load of sense, but it would at least deflect attention from who'd actually fired the fatal rounds.

Zaid booted the loose panel away and they sprinted across the neighbour's garden, before diving in through the back door of the garage.

Razor then got down to doing what he did best. Without a screech of tires or revving of the engine, he drove the car slowly out and away down the road. With all the haste of a man popping to the local shop to buy a pint of milk, he made their getaway. Nothing to see here officers, just a man out for a casual relaxed drive in his nondescript beige family vehicle. The plates were cloned from an identical people carrier owned by an unsuspecting grandmother in Worthing, should any cameras have recorded their modest escape. Everyone was thankful that Billy had planned the emergency departure routine with such meticulous care and attention to detail.

In his wing mirror, Razor could see a police van at the end of the road and a drone in the sky above the garden. As he turned left into Tongdean Lane, everyone in the back held their breath, scarcely able to believe that they'd made it this far. They were alive and Billy was dead. Two of his boys were in hospital and the other one was doing a fine job of leading them to safety.

As the car got further away from Dyke Road Avenue, a huge weight began to lift from Razor's shoulders. The quiet loyal driver and follower of all traffic regulations, felt strangely liberated. He'd grown tired of the constant criticism, back-seat seething and the cloud of anger he'd had to convey from one place to the next. He felt light-hearted for the first time in years, despite the pain in his arm and his odd travelling companions.

In his humble opinion, the world was already a better place without Billy Murphy.

Chapter 56

"Dexter, mate," said Buster, when the car reached the end of the road.

"What time does that pub of yours open?"

"In about half an hour, I think," replied Dexter, his eyes lighting up at the mention of his favourite happy place.

"So, does anyone else fancy a drink to steady their nerves, or is it just me?" continued Buster.

"I know I need one. I'm shaking like a bloody leaf. This has been the worst day of my entire life. I've actually killed a man, for fuck's sake, and a person I care about very much is dead. And on top of that, my poor uncle's fighting for his life because of me, and I can't do a single thing to help him. I really do need a stiff drink, right now, to steady my nerves.

I didn't think in a million years that Mrs Murphy would end up getting shot. I wouldn't have done any of this if I'd known. I'd have found a better way. She was my absolute rock. I absolutely loved that woman. She could always see the good in me, even when I couldn't see it for myself. And today, she actually took a bullet for me. What an absolute legend.

And I can't believe that I've just left my uncle lying there, I really can't. My bloody parents are going to hate me for ever now. I feel like getting absolutely shitfaced if I'm honest. So, come on then, are any of you lot going to join me?"

The unanimous opinion of everyone in the car was that they all absolutely wanted to join Buster in an early morning drink. There was a lot to discuss. There was much to understand and digest. And there were plenty of plans to be made for the future.

Ten minutes later, they were parked up outside the Unicorn and counting down the seconds until opening time. A rattle of bolts and the turning of keys preceded the opening of the pub's heavy double doors.

Martha Webb was too shocked by the sight of her first four dishevelled, stained and malodorous customers to remember to say anything to Dexter about his ban. She wisely decided that this wasn't the time to ask questions or enquire about the events that had led to their arrival at her hostelry in this state. Whatever they'd been up to, it was way too serious for small talk or pleasantries.

She simply did what any good landlady would do. She poured four drinks, turned up the music to cover their conversation, and set about minding her own bloody business.

Chapter 57

"What do you think's happened here, Skipper?" asked Gary, scrutinising the room.

For once, he wasn't holding a coffee or eating a snack, which was a good thing, as even his cast iron stomach would have been turned by the chaos and gore before them. Scattered everywhere were bloody dressings, transfusion bags and all the other detritus of modern emergency medicine.

"Difficult to tell until forensics have done their stuff."

Gary tried to ignore the fact that his boss was stating the obvious.

"Yes, but what's really gone on, Sam? I mean, the CCTV recorder's been taken and Billy's holding two guns. Looks staged to me. And what about these cable ties on the floor? Same ones we saw in Southwick."

"Gary, I've got no idea at the moment, but I guarantee Buster Brett was in this room when those two died and there's a link to those goons who got dumped at the hospital."

Gary let his mouth run ahead of his brain. The notion that the two recently deceased bodies had shot each other was just too convenient. His mistrustful copper's mind wanted to look beyond the obvious. He tried to evaluate every possibility that could have culminated in the hellish scenario before them.

"But if Buster was here, then how did he get out?" he mused.

"We were already on scene when those gunshots were heard, and the front door was put in less than two minutes later. We just got in here a little bit too late, didn't we? That fucker's been running rings around us for days now, hasn't he?"

Samuel gave his colleague a sharp look to shut him up. Highlighting their failings was not something he wanted to hear right now.

Before they could examine the evidence or discuss things any further, they became aware of a third person entering the room. DI Weston had arrived wearing a white forensic suit and matching overshoes.

He walked over to where Billy Murphy lay stiff and pale and stared at the body.

Although he couldn't be sure, Samuel was convinced that he heard the Inspector mutter the words 'fucking excellent' under his breath, before turning back to face them.

"I don't know if you two are aware who this deceased woman is, but I recognise her from my intelligence briefing pages. It's almost certainly Murphy's wife, Felicity.

So, do you gentlemen think this is some sort of domestic? Or a murder-suicide pact? The word is that she's had an aggressive form of pancreatic cancer for a while and only had a limited life expectancy.

The pathologist will be able to tell us more. Perhaps the old man decided to put her out of her misery and then turned the gun on himself. A mercy killing if you like. They'd been together for over fifty years, apparently, so maybe the old rogue didn't want to go on without her. It's a long time to be married, so that's the most likely explanation, in my opinion.

I don't know who the injured male is, but my hunch is that he's one of Murphy's employees. Maybe he tried to intervene for some reason and got shot for his trouble. I think those are the lines of investigation you should follow initially. It's all terribly tragic, of course, but I don't suppose too many people will shed a tear for Mr Murphy here. Let's just try to get this put to bed as soon as possible, please, gentlemen. We need to focus our resources and move on with our divisional priorities."

Samuel stood mute, stunned and unable to comprehend the rubbish that was flowing from the boss's mouth. But more than the meaning of his words, he couldn't understand the expression on his face. He looked gleeful, ecstatic and positively thrilled with the situation. His facial muscles had contorted into a picture of happiness that jarred with the grisly tableau behind.

"Anyway, keep me in the loop. And when you've got a moment, I want a full update on the Stalker. I'm aware that you've not made any real progress on that matter yet.

I'm actually rather disappointed, considering the amount of overtime we've thrown at it. I've still got the Chief breathing down my neck, so crack on please chaps. I'm expecting some results! And no more bloody cock ups like the one at Brighton Station. I can only cover for your team for so long."

On those final words and with both of his subordinates wanting to slap the ridiculous smile clean off his face, the DI turned on his heels and left.

Samuel counted to ten in his head, not wanting to say anything that he'd later regret. Nothing his boss had just said fitted with the information they knew about the crime. The lines of enquiry he'd just suggested appeared to been plucked randomly from fresh air. Double murder investigations were never wrapped up quickly, as the DI had implied.

However, of more concern was his demeanour. Nobody should be that happy at the sight of a double slaying. Whether it be common decency or simple police professionalism, the presence of two recently deceased corpses should preclude the broad grins and smirks that they'd just seen plastered across his face.

"What the fuck's going on with him?" asked Gary, as bemused and angry as his sergeant.

"One day, he's pissed out of his head, the next, he's puking in the office. And here he is, looking like he's dropped an ecstasy at a fucking double murder scene."

Samuel couldn't have put it better himself. He felt insulted and degraded by his superior officer's behaviour. He'd shown them no support or appreciation. He'd spoken to them as if they were fresh-faced rookies on their first day out of Police College.

Not for the first time in the past few hours, Samuel suspected that the upstanding DI Simon Weston was somehow involved. He didn't know how or why, but he was sure that his instincts were right. With that conviction in mind, he decided to ignore everything he'd just been told to do and to investigate the matter with as much rigour and determination as his twenty years of experience would allow. Whatever it took and however many feathers needed to be ruffled, they would get to the truth that lay behind the odd events of the past few days.

"You thinking what I'm thinking?" he said to Gary.

"Pretty much," replied his friend, without a second's hesitation.

"Shall we just get this thing properly investigated, Skipper, and bring that stuck-up bastard down a peg or two?"

Once again, Samuel thought that he couldn't have put it better himself.

Chapter 58

Buster tried his best to join in with the conversation, but as the others drank and swapped accounts of the morning's drama, embellishing and exaggerating with every word, his mood slumped even further.

He had lots to be happy about, not least the fact that he was alive and Billy was on his way to the mortuary in the back of a coroner's van. In addition, a quick phone call to the hospital established that Uncle Bob was in a stable condition and conscious.

But as hard as he tried to look on the bright side, his thoughts were with Fliss. He'd never dreamed that she'd come to Brighton and put herself in harm's way to protect him.

He couldn't accept that the quick conversation they'd grabbed the week before was the last they'd ever have. He should have listened more carefully to what she'd had to say. The hints and signs of her illness had all been there, but he'd been too self-absorbed to notice. The brutality of her death dominated his thoughts.

He owed it to her to make the most of the opportunity she'd gifted him. Fliss had given up what remained of her future so that he could have one. As he sipped his pint and watched Zaid dress Razor's arm with the contents of the pub's first aid box, he had no idea what to do next. Staying safe from Billy had seemed like such an improbable challenge that it hadn't crossed his mind what would happen next if he actually succeeded.

Certain things he knew had to be done immediately. Speaking to his parents was top of the list. He was dreading that conversation, but he owed them an explanation. Thanking his uncle was also a priority. He tried to put the thought of him lying in a hospital bed, high on medicinal drugs, out of his mind. He'd probably have a couple of bored coppers sitting in his cubicle, waiting for him to shed some light on events.

Buster knew that he'd have been slaughtered if Uncle Bob hadn't intervened. Worse still, his parents could have been tortured and killed. He cringed as he thought about the stress and trauma he'd placed on a man who'd tried so hard to rehabilitate himself.

There were other things that Buster just wanted to do for himself. He had to find a new job that made a positive contribution to the world. Sending the money back was a start, but it was only a drop in the deep ocean of misery that Billy had inflicted over the decades.

But what job could he do and who would employ him? He'd dropped out of university without finishing his degree and his CV had a five-year chasm in it that would be tricky to explain away. The concept of an interview where he'd have to discuss his skills and career to date seemed alien and improbable. He thought about joining the police and helping them fight organised crime with his expertise and experience. He'd be a good poacher turned gamekeeper. Buster snapped out of that fantasy as Martha Webb placed a fresh tray of drinks on the table.

"I assumed you lot would want another round, so I took the liberty of bringing

them over. Dexter, you can settle up in a minute. That looks nasty, love. Looks like someone's bit you," she said, peering at Razor's wound with a look of curious revulsion on her face.

"Got to be careful with those. Probably got all sorts of infections in there. The human mouth's got more germs in it than a pub urinal, apparently," she added, before heading back to the bar as Razor's attentive eyes followed her.

Buster raised his glass with the others and they drank to the memory of Felicity Murphy. He couldn't let her down now. There had to be a fitting way to honour her sacrifice. He thought about becoming a teacher or setting up a charity. Perhaps he could train to be a doctor or a scientist or some other job that reduced the toll of unhappiness in the world. Nothing he could think of fired his imagination. Nothing was realistic or achievable. None of the options seemed to fit the skill set of a reformed young gangster who wanted to go straight and make the world a better place.

"You know what, don't you?" asked Razor, demanding Buster's attention and dragging his wandering mind back into the moment.

"Billy was always worried someone would fuck him over. He was paranoid in fact. The gun in the safe... the cameras covering everything... his escape routes... the way he wanted me to drive like a lunatic. It was all about staying ahead of trouble. He spent every waking minute thinking some cunt was going to take him out. And they did in the end, didn't they?"

Buster looked confused.

"You mate. You fucked him over, and he's dead as a result."

Everyone looked at Buster. It was true. He had taken on the legendary Billy Murphy and shot him in the chest. It hadn't been pretty and the outcome owed a huge amount to luck and the intervention of others, but the end result was just the same.

"I don't think he ever thought it would be you though, that's why he let you get so close," continued Razor, not waiting for Buster to react.

"He thought it would be some tough fucker off the streets, not someone like you. That's probably why he took it so bad when you nicked his stuff. No offence, mate, but the final score's still the same. He's heading to the churchyard and you're the geezer who's knocked him off his perch.

So, it's all yours now for the taking. I'm sure me and the other lads would rather have you as the new gaffer than some other cunt we don't know. I know we didn't always take you that seriously, but at the end of the day, you're the clever dick who's challenged Billy and come up stinking of roses. No other fucker even got close to that, so respect where it's due and all that."

Buster couldn't believe what he was hearing. The thought of having anything more to do with the operation turned his stomach. The misery and heartache generated by the business needed to be stopped forever. The idea of perpetuating what Billy had created undermined everything he'd sought to achieve.

"I don't think so, mate," he replied, not wanting to offend Razor.

"I'm not the man for the job. Plus, it's not what I want to do."

"Why the fuck not?" replied Razor bluntly, unable to understand why anyone would go to the lengths Buster had gone to without wanting to reap the rewards.

"You know the business. You're clever. You've learned from the best and you know us lot. You've got a level head on your shoulders and everyone'll be fucking terrified of messing with you since you killed Billy. But more than any of that, you've earned it."

Razor beckoned them to gather closer and started to whisper, as if he were about to divulge a state secret.

"But mark my words, there's going to be one hell of a battle if you don't. Things'll get proper nasty, that's for sure. You'll unleash the biggest turf war that London's seen for decades. Once the Albanians and the south London crews get a sniff that there's no one in charge, there's going to be all sorts of carnage to see who's the next top dog."

Razor drained his pint and wandered off to the bar. He ordered another round and did his best to flirt with Martha. He'd taken a shine to her as they'd rummaged through the sparse selection of bandages, ointments and plaster's that passed for the Unicorn's first aid kit. She smelled good, owned her own pub and knew how to dress a wound. What more could a man ask for in woman, he'd concluded.

Buster thought about what he'd just heard. He wanted to stand on a table and shout out that he'd not intended for anyone to get killed. Not even Billy. He'd have been quite happy for the old man to remain alive and well, if only he could have agreed to leave him alone. Running away and doing some good were the only things on his mind. There was no hidden agenda or secret ambition to wrestle power for himself. He simply wanted to make things better.

But what if Razor was right? If the victor in a turf war turned out to be worse than the Murphy gang, then things could get a whole lot tougher for the people he'd been trying to help. How simplistic and naive he'd been. In his desire to make his own life happier, he'd only offered Billy's victims a sticking plaster in the post, whilst allowing a whole new pack of wolves to circle the door.

The people he'd sent a year's worth of refunds to would be safe for a week or even a month, but before too long, they'd get a visit from someone new, the replacement Billy, who'd insist on starting the cycle of pain all over again.

In an instant, Buster saw that he had a responsibility. What he'd achieved so far amounted to no more than an egotistical stunt. He'd only been thinking about himself. His obsession with envelopes landing on doormats was all about salving his conscience. He'd massaged his own ego and given no thought as to what would happen to everyone else involved.

He knew now what he had to do. In order to mend things properly, he needed the police to act on the information he'd got saved on the memory stick. And in order for them to understand it properly, he couldn't just hand it over. He needed to sit down with officers and explain everything in minute detail, line by line, name by name, until it was all out in the open. And if he incriminated himself in the process, then so be it; he'd have to live with the consequences.

He had a duty to shine a bright light on every dark corner of Billy's operation. There was enough information for them to bring down the whole pack of wolves who fed off Billy's scraps; dozens of middlemen, hundreds of dealers, a complete who's who of life-ruining criminality. There was only one true path now, and that was the one he'd already started to walk. He needed to get back to the house as soon as the police had left and retrieve the memory stick hidden in the garden.

He was about to put his thoughts into words when Dexter chipped in.

"By the way, that girl you left all your stuff with. I don't trust her one little bit. Isn't all the money you've got left still in her flat? Might be a good idea to go and get it, mate."

Buster sat bolt upright. How could he have overlooked something so important? The anxiety of the last two hours had made him forgetful. The alcohol in the Unicorn had numbed his senses. Dexter was right again. Ewalina, for all her hospitality and stylish living, was not someone to be trusted.

Three minutes later, they'd drained their glasses and were strapped into the beige car, on their way back to Hove.

#####

Razor drove particularly slowly as he calculated whether the three pints that he'd just consumed would be enough to push him over the drink-drive limit. Normally, the prospect of being in violation of a road traffic law would have chilled him to the core, but not today.

He wasn't too concerned because he was happy for the first time in years. He had Martha's phone number in his pocket and a temporary boss who didn't keep screaming in his ear every time he stopped at a red light or flashed to let a bus out.

Chapter 59

What a wonderful morning it was. From her balcony, Ewalina could see the Palace Pier to the east and the saucer-like capsule of the i360 tower slowly making its ascent. The view to the west was less spectacular, but despite this, her attention was focused in that direction.

It was cold and her thin dressing gown offered little comfort against the stiff sea breeze. The third coffee of the day warmed her hands, but the remainder of her body was telling her to get inside. Despite the increasing discomfort, she stayed where she was, not wanting to miss anything happening on the street below.

Ewalina had been much happier since her guests left. She'd cleaned everything twice and thrown away all the bedding Dexter had soiled. She'd happily never see that strange man ever again.

Buster and Zaid had left three bags for safe keeping when they jumped in the taxi to meet their fate with Billy Murphy. She wondered how that had turned out for them, fully anticipating that they'd never be seen alive. Nevertheless, she had promised to look after their belongings, so that's what she'd do. At least until she was sure they'd disappeared for good.

But it wasn't just the flat she tidied. Buster's bags had also been calling out for a proper examination. She'd tried her best to resist the temptation, but curiosity got the better of her after only ten minutes alone.

First, she'd opened his suitcase. It now contained a paltry £23,460. She counted the cash onto her table before putting it all back with the notes ordered by denomination and bundled together with paperclips she'd found in her drawer.

Compared to the fortune it had previously held, the remaining money looked overwhelmed by the empty space around it. Ewalina thought she'd do Buster a favour by putting his clothes back into the case. Having a bin liner in the hall also offended her sense of style, so now that there was plenty of room to spare, it seemed like the obvious and helpful thing to do.

She'd emptied the clothes onto the floor before carefully folding them up again. His stuff was nice. He had good taste. All the designer labels she admired were represented. If they'd met under different circumstances, then perhaps she might have been attracted to him in these expensive threads.

When the suitcase was full again, she hesitated before removing the £5,000 she was still owed. She was sure he couldn't object. A deal was a deal, after all. In reality, she didn't really care what he thought. She'd delivered on her part of the agreement and helping herself would just save the embarrassment of having to ask for it, if, by some miracle, he ever came back.

The balcony was freezing now. Her coffee was cold and it had started to drizzle. But she still didn't want to move. She watched in horror as a dog walker on the lawns opposite picked up the mess his pet had deposited on the grass. He put the warm plastic bag in his pocket and threw a ball for the animal to chase. Ewalina could think of nothing worse than owning a dog. The thought of pet hair on the floor and having to be at the beck and call of a yapping bundle of irritation filled her with revulsion.

On the corner of Adelaide Crescent, a postman appeared pushing a big red trolley. It had bicycle brakes and two large hoppers holding all the items he had to deliver. He disappeared down some basement steps, leaving it to get wet on the pavement above.

Ewalina stepped inside and closed her balcony doors against the elements. She slid on her slippers and grabbed a large black holdall from the bottom of her wardrobe. She took off her dressing gown and put it on a coat hook in the hall. Wrapping the tie handles of a garbage bag around one hand, she put the door on the latch with the other. She'd not been able to find her keys and didn't want to lock herself out.

Counting out time in her head, she trotted down the communal stairs to the lobby, wearing just a skimpy t-shirt and shorts. She was ice cold, but that suited her plan perfectly.

Leaving the holdall on the floor, she went to open the external door. It blew sharply inwards as the wind caught hold. Ewalina took just one step out before running into the startled postman. Her timing had been perfect.

"Oh God, I'm so sorry. I was just trying to put this rubbish out. I had no idea the weather was so bad! Anything for me this morning?"

Ewalina's words were just as natural and causal as she'd practised in her head. The postman didn't know where to look, but managed to have good peek at her cleavage before his manners got the better of him.

"Which flat are you, love?" he replied, flustered.

"I'm in number 2," said Ewalina, pulling her t-shirt down and crossing her arms in a display of fake modesty that only served to focus the postie's attention.

"Must be your birthday or something, darlin'. Half my load's for you today. You run a business from home or something, do you love?"

"It's nothing exciting, I'm afraid," explained Ewalina, running out the stock answer she'd prepared earlier.

"These are just returns from my customers, unfortunately. I run a make-up business and they get to send the things back they don't want in the envelopes I provide."

The postman made four trips from his trolley to the front door with all the mail he had for Ewalina, while she squeezed it all into the holdall she'd just carried down.

Her plan had revealed itself the previous day. Buster had given her a list of people to send money to and she'd sat down with every intention of carrying out his instructions as honestly as possible. She'd started off well, writing out the Chinese and Indian names of people who'd been stupid enough to pay protection money to Billy Murphy.

She'd counted out the correct number of notes for each and put them in the envelopes provided, with a copy of Buster's pathetic little letter. She'd finished off the job by writing the addresses and putting stamps in the corners as per his patronising instructions.

After the first three or four, she'd started to wonder what these sad individuals had done to deserve such an unexpected windfall. So far as she could fathom, they'd just been weak. Checking that Buster was busy on the sofa and everyone else was absorbed with their own work, she wrote one envelope out to herself and put it under the ones she'd already completed. No one noticed. No one even looked up.

That first letter led to ten more and those had led to the rest. Several hours later she had piles of envelopes in front of her, neatly bundled up with elastic bands and ready for the post. Each had a couple of correctly addressed specimens on the top to disguise the deception beneath.

When Sophia had been nominated to deliver the letters to a post box, Ewalina had spotted a weakness in her plan, which she'd quickly mitigated by offering to assist. Buster had fallen for her ruse without a moment's hesitation. And since then it had just been a matter of waiting, playing the perfect host and trying to get everyone to leave.

The best thing about her plan was that no one would ever find out. Even if Buster wasn't dead, how would he know if all the entries on his list had received a letter in the post or not? The chances of him checking up were negligible. Enough of them would have got what he ridiculously thought they deserved, for the plan to feel like it had worked.

Back in the flat she counted the 124 letters she'd written out yesterday. Each had her name and address on the envelope and was stuffed with the cash the Buster had intended for some random little takeaway or restaurant.

Ripping open the packages, she counted out her freshly delivered cash - £116,940 to add to the fee she'd already been given. Despite her initial reluctance to get involved, this had been the most spectacularly profitable episode of her life. No more hanging around at Brighton station trying to meet drunk stupid men from now on. No more danger for a modest reward. Her life as the Stalker was over and good luck to any police officer who tried to find her now.

Pulling on her warmest clothes and hiding the cash under her bed, Ewalina pushed a thousand pounds deep into her coat pocket. She slipped on a beanie hat and checked out a pair of sunglasses in the hallway mirror. She looked anonymous and felt safe. Satisfied that there was nothing about the way she was dressed to attract attention, she searched in her bag for her keys and phone. As her keys weren't there, she took a spare set from a pot on the sideboard.

Leaving the flat for the second time that day, she went to find the most expensive bedding the city's shops had to offer. She'd buy new mugs too and throw away the ones her guests had used. She couldn't bear the thought of drinking from the one that Dexter's lips had touched and since they'd all got mixed up in the sink, the whole lot would have to go.

Facing the wind and rain, she tried to put the last two days' ordeal out of her mind. She was almost rich now, but this was just the beginning. She'd invest the money wisely and become a player. She aspired to the respect that Billy Murphy commanded.

Maybe she'd even go and pay him a visit. She could tell him how she'd tricked Buster and even return some of the cash if that would help her to gain his trust. He might need someone to help him out, now that he'd most probably killed Buster and Zaid. She imagined what words she'd use and where they could take her. She'd convince him that she'd be more loyal than his last assistant.

Her head was filled with endless possibilities and optimism as she crossed the main seafront road. The little league was behind her now and she was well on her way to the top. Stepping onto the promenade with a distinct sense of purpose and a spring in her stride, she started her march into town.

Chapter 60

All the conviction and swagger of earlier drained away as Ewalina pushed open her front door. She dumped her haul of designer shopping bags on to the hall floor, sensing immediately that something was terribly wrong. She'd only been out for two hours, but in that time, her world had been turned upside down.

The flat was a mess. Drawers were pulled out and doors that had been closed, stood ajar. The contents of her kitchen bin lay tossed across the living room carpet. Tea bags and toast crusts lay everywhere. She felt physically sick, painfully aware that her deception had been exposed.

There was a note on the table that explained everything. Written in a bold hand that she recognised straight away, the words mocked everything she'd recently achieved. Reading the scribbled lines, she pictured, quite accurately, the events that had recently unfolded in her precious home.

She cursed every assumption she'd made in the past few hours.

If she'd not underestimated Buster Brett and discounted his departure as the last journey of a condemned man, then perhaps things would have turned out differently.

She might have noticed him slip her keys into his pocket as he rushed for his cab. If she hadn't been so rude and sarcastic, then perhaps, he might have been more inclined to trust her. He wouldn't have thought it necessary to make sure he had the means to get back in to her flat.

But most significantly of all, if she hadn't been greedy and helped herself to five thousand pounds from his suitcase, then a deeply disappointed Buster might have resisted the temptation to have a good root around her home before departing with his bags. That way, he'd have remained unaware of the mass of ripped envelopes in her kitchen bin or what lay hidden beneath her bed.

But by the time he did leave the flat, ten minutes after arriving, all her darkest secrets had been exposed. As he struggled down the steps with his suitcase, Zaid's rucksack and a heavy black holdall that he'd never seen before, Ewalina's lost keys were back on the table waiting for her and her shopping to get home.

Under the keys was a welcome home note that Buster had quickly scribbled on the back of an unused envelope.

```
HEY, CLEVER GIRL. SORRY TO SPOIL YOUR FUN
BUT I CAUGHT YOU OUT. MAYBE YOU'RE NOT AS
SMART AS YOU THINK YOU ARE. IF YOU WANT TO DO
SOMETHING GOOD FOR A CHANGE THEN GIVE ME A
CALL. YOU WOULDN'T BELIEVE HOW GREAT IT FEELS.

BUSTER xx
```

With special thanks to:

Graham Bartlett
Eve Seymour
Scott @ Manicminotaur
Sadie Graham
Polly Sutton
Pauline Webb
Sam Harrington-Lowe
Lesley Brett
Mandy Suhr
Mischa Eligoloff
Natascha Lampert
Jonathan Warren
Andrew Kay
David Camici
Simon Darcy Abbott
Coco Franklin-Webb

And of course, the *real* Buster Brett.

Printed in Great Britain
by Amazon